I0831265

The Battle Wasn't Hers

A Novel

J.M. HARRIS

P.O. Box 36634
Grosse Pointe Farms, MI 48236
USA
(313) 466-3994

ISBN: 978-1-7340303-03 (sc)
ISBN: 978-1-7340303-2-7 (hc)
ISBN: 978-1-7340303-3-4 (e)

Library of Congress Control Number: 2020923871

Lulu Publishing Services rev. date: 12/15/2020

This Book is Dedicated to:

El Elyon who taught me tough lessons on healing, forgiving,
grace, & mercy, because of You father many shine lights
in a world of darkness & I am forever grateful.

To my Family

Who in our brokenness allows God to always guide our paths…
and in our togetherness love beyond our own imaginations.
John D. Harris, my husband and grandma, Dorothy Richardson.
Four sons: John Allen, Sean Anthony (Donna),
John Wesley (Janelle), & Jacob Mekhi
& grandchildren Nathan & Katelynn

Chloe

A woman is who I am, but a fierce warrior embedded with a magnanimous spirit reaps from my soul. Building of character took place from fighting to stay sane and the guarding of my heart until I showed up face to face with my own enemy. It was then my true self emerged. In search of peace which only the Supreme one gives, worry set in, but prepared for the struggle ahead. I stood firm on the battleground of life, ready to fight, but on shaky grounds, feelings of taking on the world like a storm. A soldier once told me the best ways to fight, full of pride as she stood tall; I looked up to her kind until one day she became humbled. The attack had me staggering from scales that adorned my eyes, finding my path amidst the world without a speck of light. The attacks were violent, temptations were incessant, the balls of hell ensued my heels, as he appeared only to kill and destroy. Evil demises dripped from his chin as he licked his lips of pure, unrelenting desires. I sought to be strong, brave, and encouraged until I found the war was coming from within. The accusatory voices of failure, being unloved, undeserving, fear, you're not enough, and so much more rang louder than the faith I had once known. He twisted words, and searched my weakness, the lies echoed my brain to be the truth. I realized I had lost when it appeared, I'd won as the forceful rain of blows shot down from his dagger, striking my weary, wondering soul—A harsh impact. The blood shed had me reaching for answers from all the wrong places, leading me right into the palm of his nasty hands. The battle without amour offered me no confidence, sustaining only by holding onto to my last hope. Seeking guidance, instead they scoffed, realizing they were part of the enemy's evil plans. He laughed, yelling I'm stronger than any mere man. Fought with courage and grace but struck by his final impact and failed without renewed strength from His graceful words. Therefore stumbled, and broke, not in one sense, but many—please help me, I cried. My shattered pieces went down into the palms of redemption. I cast in my filthy sins, but—God. Whispered He, have no worry, I am here. Scales slithered off, and I was anew, as the revelation unfolded; the battle was never mines—but the Lords. Staggered and groaned as I laid in despair, refusing to give into woes of his deadly sneer. He reached out his hands and caught each tear. It was then He rescued me… Strongholds fell and cast to the sea, so thankful He freed me. He bestowed the entire body of amour on my renewed body. Praise God who trained my hands, my mind, and nourished my soul. The gift of the Messiah is an honor in which only He can provide, the almighty and powerful sword—His word. Sealed with a kiss and adorned with passion, as I stepped into each piece well suited just for me. Settling on the rock, knowing who's I was with an enlightened sense of love. My body arose filled with the truth of the Almighty… I became magnificent, victorious, and a warrior, therefore I am finally free.

Standing in my office reading an assignment submitted by one of my students, I love it, noting I had become distracted from searching for my paperwork. The thirst for war prevails as she revealed her powerful emotions through her words. Her article made me feel powerful. I studied it for a moment, forcing me to think of the many battles I've encountered in this old lady's life, because of the Lord I'm still here alive and well. Preparing for a new battle seems evident, but this submission has given me some much-needed courage. Looks like I found it just in time. I am a woman whom she speaks of and proud of it. There I said it as I flumped in my office chair with ill posture, noting how inelegant I must look. Ugh, I love my life as it is living high in the mountains; I figured life would bore me; however, it has been the opposite seeing the many wonders of the world right at my fingertip. The gorgeous mountain views, the city views below, and the various creatures that flicker through my landscape have been exciting and scary at the same time. It's home. 'The Valley of the Sun' high altitude living has been a blast over the last twenty years, minus a fallen cake here and there. Hours spent viewing striated mountain slopes, with mixes of faint green and scattered cacti, drifting animals' speckle in and out of the many burrowed holes. Which reminds me, I must give my neighbors a call.

I'd been looking at life through broken glass lately, been doing that since the window in my study shattered. Mr. Waipa, who recently moved here from Michigan with his wife following her job as a reporter for a local news station, delighted to see they were from my neck of the woods until I got a taste of his attitude. Learning to play golf in his miniature golf course, he struck his ball right into my window for the second time within a week. Such a frail prude of a guy who refused to believe his aging values meant nothing to us as he condescendingly spoke of his intent to repair our office window. If he played the game correctly, we wouldn't have this problem; however, his interest seems fixated on how we got our home and our race. The nerve of him, I realized the old me was flaring up, and that's not the relationship I wanted with my new neighbor. You'd think in today's time we wouldn't have racism; here we are, right in the smack of it. I could have gone there, but I've changed, not my job to alter anyone, nor stoop to his level. Instead, I killed him with candor kindness. It worked, as he trudged off the porch looking like a man twice his age because of his hatred, with his wife dragging him by the arm, scolding and loving on him at the same time. Our conversation ended with him getting estimates on our window. Arms folded standing on the front porch, leaning on the pillar, I released an astonishing jubilant smile that I shifted as I watched them off, mingling in occasional waves as he turned back, taking a break from his tantrum. Missing our old neighbors, who played golf for the last ten years, never saw a ball of any sort. Now we have this character. Hosea walked up behind me, redirecting my attention.

"You scared me plumb out of my shoes," I hollered.

"What are you looking at?"

"Are you smoking in the house?"

"Naw, I was coming to get you and just tried it out on my way. Couldn't resist, it's the cigar I got from my boy… The King of Denmark one. You know, the one that only elite folks smoke wrapped in crystals and gold. Even got his name on it, it's sweet I tell ya."

Hosea removed the cigar from his lips, relinquishing it in a nearby plant. The smoke singed my eyes but placing that nasty smelling thing in my plant is unacceptable. I pointed straight to it. "My palm tree does not smoke buddy and if one leave curl because of it… your head will roll right onto a dinner platter and it will be the end of you."

"Promises, and more promises. It isn't in your plant, just resting on the plate on the side. I'll be out of your little special room as soon as I see what's going on. Let me look at the window, will ya?" He shoved me to the side, peering it over.

"We need to hurry and get that window fixed, woman; it's been a while. Why are we waiting?"

"It's only been two days. I am waiting on the estimates. Well, I was also looking for a meaning in it. What do you think?"

"Please elaborate my fine Cognac and cigar are waiting for me? I haven't thought that far. Don't want anybody getting hurt, is what's important right now. These windows are costly, stained glass and lead trim… you should have had Mr. Waipa fix it right away."

"It will be fine; he said he'd replace it, just need patching until it's repaired. Notice how the narrow stained-glass window which ran from the ceiling to the floor, however, shattered in two places. I love how strong the glass appears along with the bracing of lead holding it together. Seems as if it would not have easily broken."

"Well, he did, not once but twice."

Hosea leaned closer to the window, looking through one of the clear pieces, "Look at him out there practicing golf at this moment."

He slipped, forcing glass to rain to the floor as if it had shattered again. "Ouch! I think glass got in my hand." Rising his finger right for his mouth.

"Stop, you may have glass in it."

Piercing at his injury without looking up, "What's your thoughts on it?" he asked.

"Hm, I've been thinking..."

Looking out again. "I figure it's like problems in my life. Mystifying when I would stand back and try to see the big picture, it's all distorted, but clearer when I took a single piece of the broken glass to focus on the target; I could see the entire city. Including our wacky golfer."

Squinting as I looked around window once more, bouncing around the cracks.

"Oh yeah? Let me see," he said as he looked through the window.

"I see what you are talking about. What about it, though?"

"It could be a sign to focus on the minor problems which would prevent us from facing bigger problems? It could be God broke the window just right to teach us this lesson. He's taught me many lessons in life; you think this may be another?"

"I guess—you got all that from peeking through the broken window?" Rumbling around looking at the glass fragments on the floor.

"Yes, been so busy lately jumping to fix the enormous problems in my life; I failed to realize I've been doing too much. Found that if I focused on the small things in my life, maybe everything else would not be so overwhelming."

What a lesson to learn at sixty-something, all due to the mishap of my neighbor playing golf and missing his target. Looking at Hosea, I noticed he hadn't paid me any attention, still focusing on his darn finger. His savored finger was only a minor cut. The moans that echoed stated likewise. He insisted it needed no bandages at the moment. I dismissed him but kept glancing over his shoulder at his cut, assuring he was ok. I don't know why I even bother telling him my thoughts; he seldom listens.

"I've made it worst almost falling through it, I will tape it tonight," he said.

Searching the room for the broom, I brisk past as he continued to focus on the fragmented glass that shattered across the floor. Feeling a small tug at my hand, I stopped and glared at him. He pulled me into his arms and kissed me on the back of my neck. He whispered in my ear, "The sun has gone down… I noticed the sparkles glistening along the cracks of the colored glass and I wanted to share that with you. I think it just beautiful, just like you."

Relaxing in his arms, trying to calm down the nerves that were responding to his delicate touches. Deepening breaths to smell his lingering drink and the cigar on his breath, along with the sweet scent of his body wash, which smelled incredible, drove me deeper into his chest.

"Thank you, I think the starry sky resembled scattered crystals as if someone poured them out in a special arraignment. The stain glass looks like it placed a rainbow around it."

The sight weakened me and believed he was too. We both were speechless for a moment. Enjoying this beauty of a night, I'd forgotten about cleaning up this mess.

"Look at heaven LP. It's beautiful."

He rarely calls me LP anymore. Never forget that he said I was his love potion and shortened it. Nothing makes me laugh more than his crazy thoughts of me—a smile of ecstasy laid on my face.

"Never imagined feeling like heaven and looking at it."

"Man, I love you."

"I love you too." Giving me a tight squeeze.

"Back to reality, my dear. We'll let him do the estimates, but if it takes too long, we'll fix it ourselves and send him the bill. I'll get back to you about my thoughts on the window." Becoming fixated on his finger again. He relieved my plant of his cigar.

"Come on out babe, I want to spend some time with you while I smoke my famous cigar."

The morning sun gave the brokenness of the colored glass a whole new light, then the night glitter shown. Stain glass always embarks the feel of being in church, early morning fresh breeze was a bonus creating the perfect fondness of old memories. I imagined sitting in a pew listening to the pastor with the warmth of the rays seeping in and pointing to the floor as I Cleaned up the broken glass; with fragments of our preacher shouting words that filled his heart to help save us. Bless his heart.

Almost felt like I should have been looking for some clothes pins to hang my sheets. Been years since I've hung anything. Sweet smell of freshly hung clothes never goes out of season, but I've become lazy, throwing the stuff right in the dryer. Besides, in these days my neighbors would straight have a fight, seeing clothes dancing around the yard. The warm rays seeped in and pointed to the floor as I swept the pieces into a pile resembling a sea of glass. The sparkles given off seem to shimmer brightly, not to mention the rainbow effect that resonated around the room like a mystical diagram.

Our date night turned out nicely. Long night of chatting, with him enjoying his special cigar. Each puff absorbed relaxed him until he got too tired to take another puff. I wish he'd stop for health reasons; however, I secretly enjoy watching him. The phone rang. I froze. I had a strong sense of fear come over me, such an unfamiliar feeling. It's rare for me to react this way. Attempting to gather myself, I grabbed a paper bag off my desk and began breathing; these panic attacks were becoming annoying and happening more often. Not knowing what caused my horrid pain put me in an unfamiliar state of mind these days. I have been so hard on myself; fear sank dead into my soul as I've been waiting for my test results. Things just didn't seem right. Trying to use the dustpan, my hands trembled like I had been drinking pots of coffee, noting my body was not cooperating with my desire to just get my darn work finished. Hunched shoulders I cupped my chest relieving the tightness before it went into a full-blown panic attack. I hate them. Why hadn't I jumped to answer the phone to put my mind at ease? Hosea noticed I was having an episode. He rushed in, giving my shoulders a firm massage, which ended with him talking me into calmness. I could breathe normally again.

"Whew."

"Woman, you're tense as a cement wall—you ok?"

"Yes, I am. Thank you."

I sighed, "I'm fine, I've been such a nervous wreck for the past week. Today I had no hope, courage, or positivity in me, not sure what was so different, I wish the answer wasn't scary, I wouldn't be too frightened to answer."

His stocky figure stood over me, with his hands still working over my shoulders.

"Oh, oh, oh please be gentle babe, I'm really sore."

"Do you want me to call her back?"

"No, I'll pull myself together. I appreciate you, though, my shoulders feel much better. Thank you, sir," weakly smiling at him.

"Alrighty now don't say I didn't help ya," he said.

Embracing me in a tight bear hug, caused pain that would have woke up a dead person. Today was terrible for me, my feet felt like I was walking on raw bloody bones, not to mention my tender joints.

"Dang it, I can barely breathe as it is, and it hurts, I muttered, struggling to break loose. You know I hate tight hugs like that, it drives me crazy, personally I think your trying to kill me off."

"Be nice young lady, just wanted to help you laugh."

"It never fails… just not feeling myself today. Maybe I'll take a nap to calm my nerves or refresh my mind with a hot bath."

"I agree, both will be good for you."

I groaned, knowing he was right; both would do me good. The phone rang again, and yet I hesitated. Being real with myself, I already knew the answer. I just couldn't face hearing it, making it concrete. The phone stopped ringing rather quickly this time; it relieved me. Candace stormed in, informing us it wasn't the doctor's office but a young lady.

"Please take a message, thank you."

"Yes, ma'am," she stated as she glanced the most beautiful smile. I didn't overlook Candace' preppy steps while she walked away. Her greying hair sparkled like she had small diamonds tacked on the strands. She's always so happy and calm, but today she was extra. I enjoy having her around. I considered few of our housekeepers a friend, but none did such detailed work. Others came to do their job and—well, that's it, nothing more or less. I laughed to myself because that's what they get paid to do. Friendship has never been part of the deal, so I have never counted it as a requirement. I trudged into the bedroom to prepare for my bath. It weighed my entire being with many thoughts of this cancer monster, I had allowed myself to become overwhelmed and seemed to have lost any positive outlook I had. Entering the room, I gasped at the excellent job Candace did cleaning our bedroom. She even left a small snack basket at the end of the bed. These subtle details were priceless. The stuff we liked too, dark chocolate and salted caramels, hot chips, and chocolate-covered pretzels. Everything shined brilliantly like a high-end hotel. This lady cleaned every nook and cranny, leaving not a spot. Look at the fine details in her cleaning. This woman has brightened my spirits. What an excellent choice we made in hiring her. She's only worked here for a few months, and she never ceases to amaze neither of us. I must think of something special to do for her, like a surprise—yes, we must do it soon. Revived from the blah mood I was in, with bed covers neatly pulled back, ending with a crisp point. The invitation to jump was overwhelming to get to pampering myself, I couldn't wait. She also cleaned the adjoining bathroom to my liking, with my robe and bed shoes laid out.

I decided on the sauna, removing my clothes, glimpsing myself in the mirror. My arabesque mirror fine details are always a treasure to stand before. The hand-carved wooden frame shown its age. As I gazed at the intricate curves produced along the crowning edges, ending with flower clusters over-laid with vibrant, bold colors. Its engraving says: Her prayers have moved mountains-Here stands a warrior. I treated myself to this mirror because it's unique and shows my true self, finding as beautiful as the day I purchased it. Today was no different. I am taking special note of my breast, along with the scars left from the biopsy. Nothing major, yet another battle scar. Unexplained pain all over my body should not mean the end of the world; I have overcome so much in life. I am sure I can surmount this too… have your little faith, lady, when you can do all things through Christ? Flashed across my mind, it took my breath away—perfect timing.

My body is nothing like it used to be, nothing could prepare me for the fine lines that graced my body. I missed my youthful curves; instead wrinkles sat in the most interesting places nowadays, and my battle scars seemed to be most prominent, where I had the worst fights. Children, surgeries, injuries are just a few things my body handled well. So why am I terrified? First, I need to love my aging body, Hosea still says I'm sexy—I love this dear man, which proves him a definite keeper. Once I feared aging, but it had arrived. All at once, being 'sixty and fabulous' was not enough. I was having a terrible life crisis because I hadn't lived my life the way I wanted, leaving me with doubts and ideas of failure. My mind was not in the right place, was I too caught up in titles, and seeing what others were doing, which left me questioning the paths I'd chosen or perhaps I'd missed my true purpose in life. Could I have done more or lived differently? Still, I was growing hysterical thinking of all the things I hadn't done yet, trying hard to figure things out before—before what? The question hit me like a stun gun charged with a million volts. I asked myself; as the slow whisper seeped from my soft, thinning lips. Before old age sets in and I cannot do the things with this crippling pain that has taken over my body over the past two years. It has left me on the couch stripping me of all my dreams.

Looking dismayed and withered, dragging a long hard soul-draining breath out of my exhausted body. Why? I questioned myself because of–LIFE. I'm tired. The times just seemed to flash, like darting stars, with me half-crazy trying to ride these strong winds till the end. Tears flooded my face, claret-red dusted cheeks that once loved puffing up with gorgeous smiles were instead hanging down like weights hung heavy on them. I struggled to lean over towards the mirror while piercing deep into the woman's eyes. Who knows what happened to that schoolgirl who had powerful dreams? What happened to the woman who wanted to impact the world? One who overcame many obstacles and barriers? The one who battled and refused to let this world move her? Is she even here? She is me?

Somewhere I lost her. Reaching for my bible off of the table and gripped it with all my might, bending the cover along with the fragile pages. I prayed, I asked for answers while waiting. All I heard was—silence. It scared me! *God, where are you?*

Enough of the pity party, lady, pull yourself together, I told myself, throwing my hair back. Get some strength and dignity about yourself. My shaky hands smeared the tears from my face, I composed myself and marched off to the sauna. On my way, my knobby fingers twitched fast texting Hosea, 'meet me in the sauna.' It didn't take him long for him to appear wrapped in a white towel and his slap-slurp sounding flip flops, ready to jump right in. Before making it to the bench, he grabbed the bamboo ladle, spooning water over the pebbled rocks, creating more steam. The comforting feeling of steam wrapped around our bodies like a double layer of skin. The temperature was steamy hot, taking no time before the soothing scents to invade the entire room, drawing in a subtle sniff of the drifting fruity smell. Before I could identify it, he added a few sprinkles of essential oils.

"Hm, you selected lavender?" I savored the scent, forgetting the original one.

"Yes, hoping it encourages you loosen up a bit."

He made his way over, seating himself one step below me, wiggling around until he became comfortable and positioned himself to play with my feet, he kissed my toes, pressing me to relax even more.

"The sauna always makes us feel so good. If nothing else works, sweating your concerns away may be the answer."

"Or my man kissing and massaging my feet may prove to work."

He smiled.

"Anything for you, Babe. I assume you're nervous about the test results. What can I do to support you? I don't mind."

I sat listening to him.

"Well, I—"

"I appreciate you asking. It's something I have to deal with but surely as I get answers, I will need you."

"Bay I may not understand but remember that we are a team." With his wide brown colored eyes glaring at me.

"We have 30 years between us, babe, how can I forget?" Imposing a perplexed glare his way.

He ignored me, chattering on, rambled himself into a different subject.

"Ya—I got some ideas about the damaged glass we talked about yesterday."

"What did you come up with?" Crammed with excitement, it's rare he returns with thoughts on earlier subjects. I was eager to learn.

"I figure it's like our marriage: two broken people… who mend their relationship, with God's grace. In return, he shatters our old broken ways—encouraging us to return to him the shattered pieces, he heals us. I think of the replacement glass as a fresh way of life or a double chance," he explained.

"Enlighten me, so you are saying it only works in marriages?"

"No, I'd imagine it can represent any relation, such as our family," hunching his shoulders.

"Hm… good perception of the topic. I like your answer better than mines. I hear you… it is a valid point, in particular all marriages and families. Our situation was a stormy mess at one time. Thank God he saved it."

"Uh hm, what about your issue with pain, you are broken. Prayers of healing mends your broken pieces, making you whole again... pain free."

"Another good idea. Really it stimulates deep thought on the subject."

Hosea sipped some water to cool off.

"Babe, can you turn the temp down?"

"You got it," he said.

Quietness filled the room. My focus went from the conversation to the knobby wood arrangements on the walls, seizing my mind away from any and everything, especially damaged relationships. I needed to give my overworked brain a rest. Hosea was chilled, back propped against the wall with his head resting on the empty bar, as he dangled his fingers between my sweaty toes. I was fighting to clear mind. It wasn't easy grabbing his hand with a firm hold without a double thought.

"Ugh, so much to think about... a few weeks ago, I was fine; now, I'm a mess."

"Well, until you are ready to share your feelings with me, I'll be patient. Do you know this affects me too?"

He got up to leave. I tugged on his hand, refusing to release my grip.

"You feel I have been selfish about this?" looking perplexed.

"Yeah, you have… maybe it's normal, I—don't know for sure, but I am and will be an important part of this. I wonder when you will figure that out?" He firmly stated.

His statement hit me like a speeding train. I had to admit to myself silently I had been. At the moment, I wasn't ready to respond to his statement; I wanted to think about things before I replied. I needed the right words to say and now wasn't the best time.

"Will you still love me if they find nothing wrong?" Stated timidly.

"Babe, come on now, you know I will." Pulling his hand from my grip, he grabbed his towel, wrapping up to leave.

I yelled, "I knew your answer already. I just needed to hear it."

"It's the truth; I love you—crazy lady. Let me know when your next appointment," he yelled back.

I released a deep sigh. Re-entering the bedroom, I glanced at the clock, noting it was 3:33 p.m. I speculated a reasonable nap would do me well; I set my alarm clock. The clock glare caught my attention again, noting the 3:33 timeframe. I've seen those numbers a few times. Not sure what it meant. Here I am sitting around as if I nothing to do, resembling a lifeless sack of potatoes. Pulled the drapes closed, blotting out the stinging rays of the sun that danced around my room. I wanted to give in to the invitation to join in on the dance, but I knew I was too tired to move another muscle. I love the sun, so much energy. Hosea was right in his thinking; I have been selfish, just like he says. He knows me well. I couldn't ignore his statement, but I couldn't dwell on it either.

Hosea awakened me by sitting on the side of the bed, soothing my hair in place. He appeared calm.

"Hey babe," he murmured as I struggled to focus on things around the room.

He smiled, ripping the curtains back open, allowing the sun's rays to dance around the floors once again. I moaned as I planted my soles on the floor. Hosea chuckled, making fun of my small feet as usual. He has such a foot fetish; he chatters on a women's feet; but mines get called nubby or pegs. Not one thing sounds cute about either of those names. I'm happy when they can walk, He enjoys picking my polish colors and raves about their softness.

"You need to wake up, or you won't sleep well tonight. Oh wee, look at your little nubs," he stated.

"Stop it, slapping his hands away. You're right. Let me get dressed; I'll join you in a few."

The pain ran through my body; assured the nap would have calmed the horrid nerves that ran over most of my body. These old soles felt as if I was walking on raw bloody bones. Fifty men didn't beat me up, so why did it feel like it? The extreme tiredness was debilitating, feeling like I drug a dead body across the room. The sad part I was very much alive. Hosea nodded and shuffled away.

He pivoted, "Oh, before I forget, Candace has left for the day. She says a young lady called a few times today for you, refusing to leave a message."

"Thanks for letting me know," with a slight shrug.

I gained the most dreadful headache, searching my drawer for something to relieve it.

"Did you speak to her?" I asked.

"No, she has been asking for you, not me, Candace tried to take messages with no luck."

"Okay, maybe it's a student from the university checking on her grades."

"I have no idea, I'll see you in a few, right?" he said.

"Yes, you will."

Sitting on the side of the bed, an array of birds flew around my window caught my eye. Anxiously, I took short, but hastened steps to the window, groaning the entire way. Collapsing my limp body into the seat as if someone dropped me there, I tried locating the painful spots, which existed over my entire body. Leaving me unrefreshed from my nap; I was feeling worst, had too much going on in the brain. Propping my tanned legs on the bench, feeling as if I could drift back off to sleep. Then I saw visions of Hosea acting cranky over ruining the rest of the evening. Bless his heart, he knows I will sleep my life away. The birds outside my window displayed peace, with not a care in the world. I need to take notes from them, or should I be listening to that small voice in my heart telling me the same loving father who takes care of them—takes care of me too. He's been doing a superb job keeping me well attuned to a good life, so I should be encouraged more than the birds, at peace, carefree, and trusting. Please Lord, hear my prayers… I need answers.

I'd made it to my appointment to get my test results, Friday had come quicker than an exploding firecracker. The doctor knocked on the door. Noting she was wearing a summer dress. Never had I seen Dr. Michelson so spruced up. Thinking to myself. She's been my doctor now for 15 years — she's changed things up on me, naturally glowing. After asking her secret, her reply was getting older and was trying some new things to revive herself. Stepping around with her brightly colored floral print dress, about knee-length. Her mid-heel shoes looked comfortable and matched the dress well, along with her new updo. Her lab coat was crisp, as if it were new. As usual, her presence pleasantly filled the room.

"Good Morning, Mrs. and Mr. Gomar," rendering her gracious, warm smile.

"How are you two doing today?" Taking her seat at the computer, releasing a deep breath.

"We're fine, thank you. How are you today, doc?"

"I am doing good myself, thank you for asking. Now the topic at hand," Dr. Michelson sighed.

Feeling nervous, starting to fidget with my hands—I knew the answer by her greeting. She turned the computer to go over my chart in greater detail. Well, you know we've been doing extensive testing concerning your complaints.

Her face appeared weakened, "we're back at square one..."

"I'd figured it. What we can do now?" Hastily stopping her.

"Honey, calm down," as if he studied her for answers.

"Well, the good news shows its nothing serious, compared to cancer, Lyme disease, psoriatic arthritis or lupus and no joint damage, which would force you to take a ton of harsh medications."

I faintly smiled, "good news, right?"

"Yes, good news, but the rheumatologist suggest you have fibromyalgia."

"All those imaging machines, testing, and poking and prodding, this is the results. So really nobody knows what the actual issue is?"

She shared his notes to the last detail; stating I tested positive on all the pressure points, which determined my diagnosis.

I have a diagnosis after years of unbearable pain; which has just about forced me into early retirement and it turns out to be nothing major to them? Piercing over her awards and pictures, I noted how her family radiated happiness.

"What's the treatment plan?"

"Mrs. Gomar, there is no treatment plan. He suggested that you make an appointment with a psychiatrist and therapist as soon as possible."

"That's it? What will they do?" I quivered.

"That appears to be it, I'm not for sure what the treatment will be." as she wandered over her notes.

"How can they help my fatigue, memory issues, pain in my back, joints, and feet pain, frozen shoulder and pelvic bone, loss of my hearing, constant ringing in my ears? Doc, I feel like I am dying."

"Well, well, you have been really stressed," he added.

"You are darn right I have. Nobody knows the burden of suffering I have been going through. Who cares how distressed I am and how my body has diminished into nothing, awaiting answers? And now, it sounds like you are suggesting it's all in my skull and I'm insane?"

"No, Mrs. Gomar, that is not what we're suggesting, but please understand they mandate this approach for everyone who has this condition."

"Is there any medication that can help me?"

"Yes, we have a few options."

"Now that's a blessing. I am thankful for even that," squeezing Hosea's hand.

"Looking at your test results, overall you're in good health."

"Test wise, yes. But, in reality I am sick… any diagnosis could have been better than this, cancer or any of the arthritis that you mentioned!"

"Babe, who wants any of those issues you named?"

"Me. At least someone would care about helping me. This fake illness doctors throw around means nothing to nobody, and they have the nerve to say I'm just sick in the mind. It seems as if you are saying go home and die, because that's how I take it."

"I understand Mrs. Gomar, but that is what we have at the moment. The rheumatologist suggested running additional testing… to rule out a few other things."

"Will I be seeing you for this?"

"No… I'm afraid I don't treat fibro patients."

"Really—why?"

"That's not my area of expertise… I am sorry. But I still will see you for your regular check-ups."

"Fine, I'm looking forward to that—Not," placing my head in my hands to relieve the headache that came on after hearing this mess.

Sitting in the doctor's office waiting to schedule more appointments, I noted Hosea looking as if he was a masterpiece sitting on her burnt orange crushed velvet sofa with a lovely burnished wooden trim. It was a precious color for him as it made his deep brown chocolate skin glow. Doc reappeared after speaking to the receptionist concerning the upcoming appointments. Humph, more proof of the fake illness, jumping straight into an attitude. A million thoughts raced through my mind, noting my heart sprinted just as fast. I had to calm down, as I felt a panic attack brewing. Please, not now. I talked myself out of the raving beast that wanted to take over just like dealing with my neighbor. I was tense. Hosea was a gem; he took care of the rest of the meeting, making sense of everything. His demeanor was unhurried, he got straight to the point. I enjoyed listening to him. It didn't change the fact I still had more tests and was a nervous wreck, but I listened to her advice to reduce stress. She clarified her opinion, saying things could become worse if I didn't. To drive the point home, Hosea joined in on the notorious lecture on 'stress'. By now, I had had enough; this babbling was becoming stressful. All this talk about stress itself was stressful. I listened, noting full well I would be bedbound for the next four or more days if I didn't. The tension set in my body left me looking as tense as a board, with a fickle interest in the topic. Before I know it, I was working on controlling my stress at this very moment. A small whisper — "I will bring health and healing to it; I will heal my people and will let them enjoy abundant peace and security… Jeremiah 33:6, NIV."

❧

Doc suggested a pain journal, I changed it up making it on gratitude one instead and incorporated a must do this summer list. I am deciding to live, even if I have to tiptoe around this world. Sitting in my office on the sofa, I thought of what I can do to fill myself with splendor? You know to feel whole again? It's been a long time since I asked myself that question. It has to be something grand, because I'm already living a good life. However, I could always find room to do some amazing things. I'll just have to rest and try not to do too much. I love nature; God's creations always fascinate me. Holding my pencil to my nose, bumping it with the eraser, then pushing a crease just above my pointy tip. Laughing to myself because it's the same thing my grandma used to do when she was in deep thought. I smiled at her too, when she did it. You know what they say; you become those who raised you, even if you don't think it will happen. The repairman came to fix my window, interrupting my thoughts. He was loud in his pursuit, bumping, clacking, and dragging his materials across the floor. Searching the floor for scratches but found none. He was noisy.

"Mind if I stay?"

"No problem, ma'am."

"Please let me know if you mind my presence; I'll leave if you do."

"No, ma'am, you're fine, let me know if you have questions. Shouldn't take me long."

Watching him work, I could tell he takes great pride in what he does. Something caught my attention, though.

"Excuse me, are you using copper instead of lead?" I asked.

"Yes, ma'am," wiping his hands on his grungy towel. "It's how we fix lead glass nowadays—are you concerned about it not matching?"

"Please call me Matea," prudishly looking over his work, "Yes, that's my concern; I prefer the window back to its original state."

He stood next to me, piercing the window from every angle. I looked at him as if he grew two heads and was insane. Stepping back, he laughed, scratching his balding head.

"Are you scrutinizing my work?" he questioned.

I stood silent for a moment, shifting my eyes from the window back to him.

Abruptly I responded, "I am."

His head dropped, glanced away for a moment and licked his lips. Giving in to a faint chuckle revealing his yellow and brown marbled teeth rendering a toothy smile, he appeared irritated.

"Excuse me, may I?"

"May you what?"

"Finish my job. I am on the clock. They paid me to do the window just like this, I promise you won't be disappointed."

"Fine," stepping away.

"Wait, wait… hear this; nothing broken has ever been the same. This window will be in much better condition than when I started."

"Sure, it was broken."

"Have you ever heard of kintsugi?" he exclaimed.

"No, I'm afraid not."

He faintly chucked, "The Japanese take broken glass pieces, such as bowls, plates, and cups. Mending them together with various materials. Once mended they add a gold overlay. Similar to what I'm using," he picked up a piece of metal wire, showing me the details of it.

"Ok."

"They take the broken pieces and put them back together again with this copper or gold foil. The flaws mended, making it more beautiful and stronger than before it was broken—making it useable again."

With my pointing finger placed over my mouth, I studied his message, grabbing my phone to see some examples. "Beautiful, oh my, and so detailed. As you stated, more appealing to the eye than the original."

"After a while, the copper I'm placing on this window will tarnish, encouraging it to blend over time."

"Interesting, it's gorgeous… learned something new today."

"Matea, there is beauty in our flaws. If we glance back on traumatic incidents in our lives and concentrate on the positives. We find growth occurs from learning and advancing through these experiences, what one would expect to damage us, instead enhances our genuine beauty."

"Your definition is the best idea I've heard pertaining to broken glass yet. Did you come up with that yourself?"

"Na, I am not that resourceful. I've done some reading on it."

"Thanks for sharing, you have enlightened me. It looks like you have everything in control, sadly I must leave," shaking his hand, "it was a pleasure meeting and learning from you."

Reaching the kitchen, Candace fluttered her fingers, catching my attention.

"A young lady has been trying to contact you for a few days now."

"Did she leave any messages?" I asked.

"No, she won't; she just hangs up after I tell her you're busy."

"Hm, you think it's a student?"

"Don't know."

"Well, I don't have a clue either," shrugging my shoulders.

I didn't contemplate it for long, with no desire to talk to anybody until I took care of myself first, with no apologies. A moment of concern struck me. It may be a student, but I will call back when they leave behind a number. Memo to self: Stop giving your home number out to students. Drew in a savoring sip of coffee, it was delightful reaping of the sweet smell of brown sugar caramel, just perfect. Breaking my indulgence, Candace came back with the phone, putting it on the dinner table besides me.

"I'm picking up a few groceries, need anything?"

"A few boxes of peppermint tea will be great, thank you."

"Oh, Matea, I left the phone just in case you get that special phone call from the doctor or that young lady."

"Young lady?"

"Yes, the one that keeps calling, you don't recall—"

"Oh yeah—her," rolling my eyes.

I did a few tasks to escape my mind since I was home alone. I moseyed into the living room; suddenly thought I'd left behind the phone on the counter. I didn't feel up to going back, so I let it be. I noted the maroon plush sofa inviting. Classical music cascaded into the air, supplying my mind with soothing tones. As great as the concert reflected, I couldn't shake the funk. Realized what I lacked, some spiritual food, I turned to gospel music, giving into releasing my lungs into the air, I'm a terrible singer, similar to blowing like a northern elephant seal, according to Hosea. Right after he said it, I looked them up to see what they sound like, finding that females keep the males away with their sounds. Wailing out loud; he may have struck the nail on the head with that one. Yet, I needed something more to pick up my spirits; this was a sure path of accomplishing it, leaving me snorkeling and grunting all over the living room; at least he was already gone. Singing with my pretend mic, enjoying myself until one song took me back to singing in the choir as a teenager, 'He Changed My Name'. My belching to the tunes turned into hums, reducing to rocking myself to hymns relinquishing back to some old remembrances. I curled deeply into the sofa. Going to church with my granny, she showed me the way to God.

The phone rang, and I heard it. Rarely do I hear the phone ring in other rooms. Being hearing impaired for over 20 years should have put me in the right mind to go back for the phone; now, laziness has settled in, and I hated to move. Struggled to get off the sofa; the plushness pulled me back into my seat. One suitable hoist to my feet took all my energy. By now, it had stopped ringing. It only took me forever to get my rear end moving. I drug myself across the house to retrieve it. Looking at the caller ID, I noticed it was a Michigan number. Michigan? Hm, I haven't talked to anyone from Michigan in a while, more like years. Who could it be? I redialed the number, and a young lady answered.

"Hello, I am returning a phone call," the phone went dead.

Did she hang up on me? I called again.

"Someone just call from this number?" call disconnected.

Who in the heck would call me again and hang up? Call them back. They hung up again. Things were becoming creepier by the minute. A few hours elapsed as we enjoyed dinner, again started working on our puzzle. Hosea had just arranged about three pieces raising his score by nine points.

"Who in the heck would call me again and hang up."

"Call them back, they hung up again."

Things are becoming creepier by the minute. A few hours elapsed as we enjoyed dinner, again commenced working on our puzzle. Hosea had just arranged about three pieces raising his score by nine points and won. He jumped up and started swinging his arms in a wave. The bottom half of his body was shaking as if he was blowing himself with forceful air. Then the pumping of the muscles started, first the left side, then the right. His puffy arms hung muscles that had aged. However, he is a master of making them stand erect and pump up and down. The revealing his pearly whites resembled Chester the Cheese off those crazy commercials. Eyes big as two golf balls with failure to blink glared at me. Sickening. Sitting unmoved but enjoyed every second.

"Stop all that mess cheater," I said.

"No, I'm not. Sore loser."

"No, I'm not."

"You just can't stand losing."

"That's not true."

"I can't stand all that foolishness."

Hosea is so comical that he makes losing worthwhile. Never does he have the same response when he loses, nor do I when I win. Either way, I respond quietly and reserved. After scoring his points, he set the clock for my round, still pumping his broken muscles and smiling. Candace announced I had a call.

With a look of concern on my face, I whispered, "who is it?"

"That young lady," she stated.

I slammed the timer, forcing it to a halt. A look of disgust twirled upon my face. Already livid with the childish game of phone tag. After this call, I'll have future calls blocked, muttering as I stubbornly took the call.

"Hello?"

The line went dead. I was furious. It rang again.

Hosea answered the phone this time, relinquishing the phone my way, "It is for you."

Even he was ruffled over the frequent calls. I reframed the desire to yank the phone from his hand, but it was close.

"HELLO?" I snapped, leaving no time to catch the voice on the other end.

"Good evening, Mrs. Gomar—"

Immediately I knew who it was and was ashamed of my behavior, posture dropping as if my body limped out on me. She cleared her throat, speaking again.

"Hello, Mrs. Gomar?"

"Yes."

"Oh, good. Her voice recovered to its cheerful state. This is Dr. Michelson. Is everything okay?"

"Yes, yes, everything is fine," clearing my throat, "I thought you were someone else. Sorry about that."

"No problem. Look, I have your results and would like to go over them with you. What day is good for you?"

"Can we talk over the phone?"

"Sure."

"The additional testing came back, and the diagnosis is final. Fibromyalgia it is."

Smiling wearily at him before releasing tears that dogmatically flew across my face. His body proved he was clueless as to his next question or movement to console me. He released his stance, just hugging and rubbing my aching back.

"It will be okay, honey."

"Augh, I feel like I am dying, and nobody cares," I welled.

"It's okay, babe, you are better than this, right? What did the doc say about stress?"

"I know, I know," swiping the tears from my face with my palms until he passed me a tissue.

"Honey, stop. Let's not give up hope, there are always other opinions, I am sure we can find a doctor who knows about this. Carrying on like this only steal and destroy the moment we have right here in front of us."

Okay."

"Let's not talk about it, that way we can enjoy the rest of our evening. Let's go swimming."

❧

Reaching the pool before Hosea. Taking a moment to gaze over the porcelain tiled swimming pool and glistening waters as the lights sparkled, reflecting the beautiful array of colors below. I sat on the edge, not wanting to disturb the beauty of it. I dove in, stroking to the negative edge, breathing in the fresh smell of chlorinated water. Hugging the border, I peered over the city, wondering how everyone was handling this fiery heat. The sky was beautiful. As I wade my legs against the forces of the water — I heard a quiet voice from inside. Have I ever let you down? It was so peaceful that I had to believe it was—God himself. He had never let me down, and I had to believe that this was no different.

Minutes later, childishly I splashed globs of water across the pool at Hosea. Enjoying the evening with this crazy man was always comforting. Not to mention that message eliminated all fear.

As I dried off, the phone rang. Abruptly answering, a soft voice quivered.

"May I speak with Matea — Gomar?"

"Who is this?" I sneered.

"Is this Matea?"

"Maybe, who wants to know?"

Silence filled the phone; I could tell she was still there, but heard nothing but someone breathing.

Forcefully I stated, "No answer... I will hang up, and when I do, do not call back, you hear?"

"Grandma?"

"Who — you have the wrong number."

"Grandma, this is Chloe."

"Chloe—?"

"Your granddaughter, Chloe Reinhart."

My body dropped clear across the chaise in disbelief.

"Chloe… Jezreel's daughter?"

She chuckled faintly, "Yes, I'm Jez's daughter."

"Oh, my goodness, I haven't seen you since you were born."

"That's what my parents tell me."

"Uh, I don't know what to say. Is everybody okay?"

"Yes, everyone is fine," silence took over.

I didn't know what to say. My thoughts just hung in the air, floating around as I tried my best to put them together like a puzzle. I couldn't connect them to make a complete statement. Breaking the silence, I spoke.

"Assuming you are about twenty-five now?" Praying I was correct.

"You remember how old I am? Wow, that's cool."

"I sure do, like it was yesterday."

My goal became to control my feelings of discomfort and instant pain; it was hard.

"You know, I'm just going, to be honest… I don't fathom what to say — You sound so beautiful. What got you thinking about me, honey?"

Hesitantly she fumbled her words, "Grandma, I don't know what to say either."

Releasing a shaky laugh, "It was hard for me to call. I let my nerves get the best of me and kept hanging up; I apologize for that."

"Who gave you my number?"

"My parents—I — I was cleaning the attic and found a beautiful peacock colored greenish blue sparkly crocheted jacket. It appears someone made it. I love it, never seen one like it, does it belong to you?"

"Oh my, yes, it does. I never knew what happened to it. That coat is ancient. I bought it; it wasn't handmade made, dear. Everyone loved that coat. It has a silk lining, right?"

"Yes, nicely made. My mom told me it might be yours. I wanted to wear it but figured I should ask you first. Thought it would only be right."

"Sure, you can wear it, if it's still any good—that coat is old, over 25 years. Honey, you didn't have to ask me; I would be more than happy if you did."

"Well, I also found something in the pocket," she hesitated.

"It's a-a key, with a tag, and I was wondering what it was for, is it's yours?"

"Your parents had you call me?"

"Yes," flatly stated.

"Interesting."

"You didn't want me to?"

"Oh no, I'm thrilled to hear from you, honey I am just wrapping my mind around this whole thing. That's all."

"Grandma, the key had a tag on it that said to give it to Hosea. What is it to, it's such an intriguing key?"

"The key belongs to my private journal. I'd been looking for it for years."

The chaise held my lifeless body as one would keep someone who had been shot and was lifeless. No way did I want to tell her about my key. Frankly, I wasn't for sure she was who she claimed to be. My brain flickered like a twirling Rolodex, thinking who I could call to prove this was my granddaughter.

"Grandma?"

"I'm here."

"Honey — are your parents around?"

"No, not at the moment, I am at home."

"Well, the key belongs to my journal."

"You still have it?"

"Yes, I do."

"Can I read it one day?"

"Chloe… let me think about it. I'll let you know."

"Okay… I also wanted to ask you one last favor," pausing.

"I - I have to do my final graduate studies in Arizona this summer so I can graduate. I figured I would ask if I could stay with you all for the summer?"

My mouth fell right onto the ground, filling the line with silence. Is this real? Did I hear this, correctly?

"Hello?" she echoed.

"Yes, yes, I am here," closing my eyes with many questions swirling in my head.

"When? How long?"

"In two weeks, I will be there. I checked the distance to my school from your house; it is only ten minutes away. Not sure if you and granddad still work, but I can help with anything you may need doing."

"Whew, okay. In two weeks, aye?"

"Don't worry, if it's a problem. I can make other arrangements—I always wanted to get to know you both; this would be perfect if I can."

"Yes, it will be fine."

We talked for an hour before I became too tired to hold my eyes open. They drooped with long pauses between each blink. I just knew one extra sec would render me to la-la land. Today much happened. I needed rest.

"Let's speak soon to make the final arrangements—Okay?"

"Yes, that will be great, grandma!"

"I am so happy you called — can't wait to see you. Goodbye."

"Goodbye."

The Meeting

One who has mastered the ability to listen, hasten his words and is unwilling to give into anger has accomplished much and bonded many relationships. She had arrived in the fabulous Arizona. Candace scheduled the driver to collect Chloe. She arrived an hour later than expected.

"Is there something I can do, while we await your guest?" Candace asked.

"You can carry this woman out back and beat the frizzled nerves out of her," Hosea joked.

"You realize Hosea, you're a humorist and a hot mess. Anything else I can do for you?"

"No, that will be all, thanks," I said.

After she disappeared, Hosea eyed me, his eyebrow sculptured with profound concern.

"Don't stare at me, you're the one that's a hot mess."

"What did Chloe say when she called the second time? How are you certain she is who she claims to be? You know, she could be an intruder playing you, woman."

"Hosea, you do this every time. Repeating myself drives me insane."

"I know. I want to make sure things in order when she arrives."

"I spoke to Jez last week… he affirmed that this was Chloe's decision. It's been over twenty years since I spoke to Jez. I missed his voice. Can't imagine I'd forgotten it."

Rubbing my hands in a continuous circle, it's my usual response of my nerves getting the best of me. Noting the dryness of them today.

"When did you talk to Jez last?"

Hosea was observing me with concern, "bout the same."

I stared off into the distance, recalling the phone call. He shared nothing emotional, just the facts—explaining Chloe's excitement in visiting.

"Jez said everybody was doing okay, that was it." Looking at Hosea, my throat tightened from wrecked nerves.

"I told him I loved him before getting off the phone; he even dismissed that."

"Honey, are you okay?"

"I am… just edgy," Hosea moved closer, rubbing my stiffened shoulders.

"Relax, it's what you always wanted… right? If it's too much, we can cancel."

"I will not; she's here now. Don't you dare think I can't handle it! I can. You think anyone told her about everything that happened? What if she hates us? We waited twenty-five years for this day and could've died waiting."

He chuckled, trying to lighten the mood, "But we didn't; we both got our right senses, and we're blessed to see this day. I feared, too, that we would never have her in our lives. Let's be grateful honey and enjoy the moment."

"But we don't know her — what do we say when we see her?"

"Hello, for starters, then ask for identification," he laughed.

I gave him a wicked stare and rolled my eyes, "Eh, you do understand the issues you have?"

"You will be fine, continue."

He propped himself in his recliner like he was listening to the nightly news, legs crossed and an unlit cigar in his mouth.

"The young lady coming today is our granddaughter, who we haven't seen since she was born," I told him in an irritated tone.

He nodded as he flicked his fingers for me to continue. Suddenly, the room swayed, forcing me to have a seat. It hit me hard when I mentioned I hadn't seen this child since she was born. I was in shock again. Hosea noticed my demeanor and changed the subject.

"Where's the notebook that goes with the key, babe?"

"It's a journal, not a notebook."

"Okay, where is the journal?" I stood again, moving restlessly, trying to avoid his questions reluctantly answered, "It's here."

"I don't understand… what's so important about this dat blame journal and key? Why can't I see it?"

I shrugged, "It's just my accounts of my life, but I'm not sure I want to share it with our granddaughter, whom we only seen once in her life."

I was feeling on edge now, "We've received no letters, pictures, or phone calls—nothing. Now that Chloe found my key and coat, now she wants grandparents?"

Hosea grabbed me and pulled my tensed body close to his, whispering in my ear, "Calm down, things will work out."

I shielded myself as best I could before I ended up in one of those bear hugs I detested. Instead, he kissed me on the forehead, saying, "You got to be cool, babe; it will be okay. You will look back at this day and laugh," he pulled back, playfully eyeing me.

"I don't reckon I know much about a journal or key; I don't see the frustration about sharing it… must got some real juicy secrets in it."

"If you don't want to share it, why didn't you just say that to her?"

As he acted out, he placed his hands on his hips, and pranced around as if he was me.

"Honey," he smacked his lips and mocked me. "I guess you mean well, but you can't have my journal—the end. And she'll say girl fine."

"You are a real fool. I can't with you."

He laughed, wanting my undivided attention. Ignoring him, I stared out the window at the elevations. They brought much peace, reminding me of all the mountains God had moved for us. I prayed phasing Hosea the entertainer out. Knowing things will work towards the best, yet I was still a mess, Lord help me. No matter what, I was ready to face her.

"While we wait, you can go check on that good-smelling cake that you're baking," Hosea suggested.

The house reaped the sweet aromas.

"Oh yeah, the cake," I hustled off to the kitchen.

"What kind are you making, again?" Hosea asked, scurrying behind me.

"I'm making—"

Wait, don't answer… blueberry-lemon, with a cream cheese limone' glaze.

"She should enjoy it, right?"

"We shall soon find out."

Propped against the counter, enjoying the vibrant sweet smells of plumping blueberries that exploded as they baked, Hosea focused on the new lights over the island.

"How long is she staying again?" he asked.

"You ask a bunch of questions," as I removed the cake from the oven.

Quickly smacked his hand with the towel, "We are expecting a guest, buddy."

My heart pounding fast, as if it would pound right out of my chest. I needed to pull myself together, fast.

"She'll be here for the summer."

"What's she going to school for?"

"A biomedical scientist."

"Wow, a smarty, just like her dad."

"We talked awhile; about traveling this summer in-between her classes. I told her I've planned a few things for us to do and would chat more once she got here."

Before Hosea could reply, the doorbell rang—she was here!

❧

She looked radiant. Standing taller than I thought she would; she seemed about five-foot-six. I'm about five-foot-one, and thought, no way she got that height from our side of the family! I'm sure it came from her mother's side. She had a bright face that lit up the doorway along with her cheerful disposition. Her hair was long and full, with streaks of golden blonde offsetting her slim stature.

"Well, Hello, Chloe. It is so good seeing you — finally! It's blazing hot out here; child come on in."

"Hi," rendering a nervous wave.

"You are gorgeous young lady."

"Thanks."

I could still see the baby I had once seen in her, except back then she was plump and bald. Now look at her. For a moment, I froze with sheer happiness.

I finally got my baby here, snapping quickly from my stance.

I was holding back my composure, wanting to do and say all kinds of things out of pure excitement. Closing the big metal laced door behind her, I straight away looked her over once more, like mothers do when they first see their newborns. I couldn't keep the grin from my face.

She stood before me in the foyer, blushing profusely.

"I can't believe I have finally met you, grandma Gomar."

My heart just melted as I pulled her to me. We hugged for a few minutes, which felt like forever. "Girl call me grandma; that's good enough," I told her before Hosea's big mouth came roaring across the room, breaking our long comforting embrace.

"Come on in, have, have a seat," I said.

As we turned to him, I had a smile glued to my face, accompanying my million-dollar feeling. You could tell Hosea had fallen in love with her immediately. He looked as though she had hypnotized him.

"Well, well! She looks like your twin when you were young Matea," my smile grew wider.

"I noticed that as well, babe."

"Hello, granddaughter. Mi casa es tu casa."

He walked over, giving her a big bear hug, like those he was always giving me.

"Augh, let loose the girl! Gonna choke the air out of her lungs," smacking him broadside.

"The girl will have lung problems when you get finished with her."

Chloe chuckled, "You know Spanish, grandpa?"

"Girl, you just heard his whole Spanish vocabulary," Hosea stood back, making goofy faces and hand gestures.

Chloe walked into the living room and looked around.

"This house is so beautiful and huge—I love it. Did they build this house into the mountain?"

"They did. The view from the back of the house shows the mountains up close, you'll see it."

Walking further, she noticed the view from the windows.

"Oh, my gosh, look at the mountain views. I've seen nothing like this, ever," she turned her gaze to the pictures we displayed over the fireplace.

"Look at you and grandpa, is this your wedding picture?"

"Our vow renewal," I stated with pride.

"Wow, beautiful," she said.

"Thank you," I smiled at her warmly, taking her hand.

"I'll take you and show you around soon. Might as well get you familiarized with everything since you'll be here for a few months. We'll introduce you to the staff as well; you can let Candace know some of your favorite foods and snacks so she can stock the cabinets."

We just kept gazing at each other, stealing glances of how much we looked alike. I laughed at one point, telling Chloe how I couldn't wait to share my younger pictures with her. You will swear we were twins, leaving me smiling and renewed at having someone look like me.

They seemed to have done an excellent job raising her; she was so graceful and had impeccable manners. Hosea was in the kitchen, doing only who knows what, so I was used to the moment to enjoy this one-on-one time with her.

"How was your trip here? Have you been to Arizona before?" I asked.

"Yes, it's been a long time, though. My trip was amazing; I had no problems," Appearing timid, she tucked her hair behind her ear.

"It was my first time flying alone, though. I was nervous, but I handled it."

So many years had passed. She felt like a stranger sitting in front of me. I could only imagine how she felt, finding all of that disappeared as we chattered within minutes.

"Let's get cake, shall we?" I excitedly exclaimed.

"Cake?"

"Yes — from scratch… blueberry with cream cheese drizzle. I pray you like blueberries?"

"I do," she smiled.

❧

Walking down the vestibule to the kitchen, we went on about her parents. She exclaimed they were doing fine; old memories filled my mind, I pushed them out of the way. I shook it off, concentrating on the blessing of having her here now. Why would I want to bring up old crap ruining this gift? I'm grateful for this opportunity; wanting to savor every minute. Gripping her arm, encouraging her to take in the view from the foyer. I call this the hall of visions. The entire wall appeared transparent, giving way to panoramic windows that displayed the most exquisite views I'd ever seen, making each day unique in its way.

Today, the clouds were fluffy and arranged strategically around the sun. The clouds appeared to have golden rays embracing their edges, as though it illuminated them from behind. Together, the sky was perfect—only God. As beautiful as it appeared, it was smothering on the other side of the glass. I guessed it was about 110 degrees of dense, dry heat. It was too hot to go out and enjoy its beauty on the other side, but these windows always did the trick to bring us closer to nature on these blistering days. Not to mention, the view of the mountains that hugged the clear blue sky was also amazing. Chloe was in awe over the views, rambling on as we continued to the kitchen. This hallway just had a way of doing that to everyone as I watched her bright face as she spoke with such passion. She was full of life and appeared happy as can be.

Filled with excitement, she announced, "I can't wait for you to show me around the entire house!" Smiling, I patted her shoulder.

"We sure will, but first let's have cake."

"Sure, Dad told me you love to bake."

"Oh, he remembered?"

She nodded, laughing joyously with her big marble eyes—twinkling like stars. "Dad advised me all about how you lit up the kitchen when you baked, you're in your private world."

"He says that because I often pretended that I am on the cooking channel, with an audience, chatting away in my head jokes and announcing the ingredients. I looked like a fool, but it keeps me entertained."

"That's funny, yeah, I'm sure that's why."

"She is funny when she does it, making up accents and everything. I actually enjoy it. Never a dull moment with her."

"Why didn't you become a baker instead of a scientist?"

"Well, I didn't start baking until I finished school. Besides, I think I like science a tad more than baking."

"I'm excited to try some of your cooking, grandma."

Hosea joined us, chiming in, "I can cook too, lady — don't underestimate this old man!"

We burst out laughing as we lingered to the kitchen.

"Like you said, your grandma cakes… ooh wee. The best.com," licking his fingers, was a sure sign he had already been playing around with my cake.

"Yes, granddad, he told me you cook too. I think he said — you love the bad foods, and grandma loves the nutritious foods."

"Now stand by for one-minute, what's bad food? You mean fried chicken, pork chops, salmon patties, barbequed ribs that fall off the bones, smoked meats, fried shrimp, and mashed potatoes—the homemade kind, none of that box stuff, don't even mention my Mac n-cheese, eight different gooey cheeses, and fresh cream. Oh, wee, making me hungry."

"He mentioned you love butter," she smiled.

"I do. Your dad ain't told you nothing wrong so far!" Hosea said, rubbing his pudgy belly.

"Didn't get this here pouch from eating just salad."

Chloe shot back, "Whew, all this talk of food is making me hungry, as we speak."

"Girl, if you don't watch it—you'll leave here with a belly yourself," hollering in laughter.

"Since we moved here, grandpa and Asher got a food truck, and they travel all over, catering events and doing challenges. They won a few trophies for their truck, smoked meats and barbeque—I'll show you everything later."

Chloe raised her eyebrows, licking her lips.

"Well — I don't love cooking. I've learned to tolerate it. I enjoy eating fresh fruits and vegetables. You know, healthy eating," I exclaimed.

"Sho'll be tasting so good for someone who doesn't like to cook. Um hm," Hosea joked while dancing around the table.

I mocked him for including the fact he could cook, but never willing when I ask him. He made faces back at me, being a big-time jokester, never a dull moment with Mr. Hosea.

"Get a load of this Chloe, if I start that woman will have me cooking every day, ya feel me."

"Eh—, your granddad takes advantage of my cooking skills. Just to let you know this old man ain't slick, and I got my eye on you."

"The evil one or the good one?" he said.

"Before I leave, I will judge who cooks the best. To let you know, it will be tough, so you better be as good as you say."

Candace sliced cake as she introduced herself to Chloe. The aroma from those fresh blueberries filled the room, an invitation to dig in. For moments, we didn't say a thing, just moaning sounds.

"Grandma, humph. This is so dang on yummy, with these fresh blueberries popping as you take each bite."

"Thank you. The blueberries were huge this time of the year, just perfect for this recipe."

"Is the recipe passed down from your mom or your grandma?"

"No, but it is an old recipe that I started using over thirty years ago—hey, I may pass it down to you! Start a tradition. What do you think about that?"

Chewing for her became forced until she stopped. Her eyes reddened and filled with tears.

She composed herself. "Yes, I would love that, grandma," as she took a hard swallow of the last bite.

I was scurrying around, finding tasks to keep me busy. I started polishing silverware; it was a quaky attempt at pretending not to see Chloe's emotions were overwhelming, trying not to become a hot mess myself.

"Do you cook?" I muttered, trying to ease the tension of the moment.

"Well, um, uh… Well, I do, but I don't," searching for words.

As she wiped the crumbs from her mouth, "I cook because I have to eat, but nothing fancy. I don't when I can get out of it," forcing a smile.

"I made coffee to go with our cake if you would like some?"

"Yes, please."

Coffee and cake were sinfully good together. I shall not lie, left me rolling my eyes in mere circles.

"Girl, you better learn how to cook. Your about to get married in a few months—right? Has anyone ever told you that a way to keep that man's heart is good ole home cooking?"

She groaned, "I know grandma. He met me without knowing how."

"I know that's why I said to keep him, my dear. He doesn't even know what's right for him, but I tell ya it's a fact."

"Since I am here for the summer, I can take a few lessons from you guys. Right?"

"You sure will, missy."

"So, grandma, do you still teach at the university?"

"I do, but only the semesters I'm interested in—you get old, you can't do those kinds of things. I just taught a chemistry and biology course last semester. It was overwhelming; I might only do one next semester or some tutoring."

"That's cool."

I shrugged, "Let's see, so much going on."

"Grandma, how do you stay looking so young at sixty-eight years old? What's your secret?"

"Thank you, my dear… the secret is prayer."

"You too, granddad; both of you look so good for your age."

"My beauty secrets… use soap and water — every day. That's all missy."

Chloe looked at him forcing a chuckle, "I see I have so much to look forward to, youth and humor run in my family."

"Yes, Lord. You stop laughing and enjoying life might as well die. Life is serious enough on its own."

"You're beautiful yourself, young lady, and ambitious… you must tell us about all the things you have been doing," Hosea said.

I nodded in agreement, "We have a lot to catching up to do—25 years' worth. We'll have plenty of time… girl the entire summer."

"Please, treat yourself to all you need while you are here, make yourself at home… our home is yours like your granddad said earlier."

"Whew," I for sure I felt the rigidity of my bones as I showed her around the kitchen.

"Are you ok?"

"Yes, I'm fine. I'll show you to the casita where you'll be staying."

"Well, alright—the casita it is. First the restroom?" As I pointed the way.

Hosea grabbed my attention, "I don't know," glancing around shifty-eyed, he whispered.

"Sounds like that journal may open up too many old memories for you. Are you ready for that, Matea? I'm just saying, can you handle going over some things you put away? I see how disturbed you are by it. I'm just concerned, that's all."

"I agree with you babe and I'm thinking about it."

He wished to convey more instead he backed off.

"Okay — Okay," he stopped talking as Chloe reappeared.

We were thrilled about everything: however, I should take notice. He's right; I shouldn't let anything overwhelm me right now. I understood his feelings, as I remembered all the things he worked out for me when I was at my lowest. Really, I do appreciate him not wanting me to suffer like that again. Snickering to myself. Dealing with my old man is an adventure. He hadn't changed a bit since I met him; always looking after me, every step of the way. Man, I love him; I didn't need to put him through it either.

"Are you ready to go to your room to freshen up and unpack? Candace had your bags taken to your place."

"Yes, grandma, that's cool. Thank you."

"I'll have Hosea take you, is that okay?"

"I'm good with that," she collected her belongings, "I'm ready."

The thought crossed my mind. "*Children's children are a crown to the aged, and parents are the pride of their children, Proverbs 17:6 NIV.*"

❧

It's been years since I've seen or talked to my family, now I have our grown granddaughter here with us. As great as it sounds, it scatters my emotions. I refused to let past hurt stop me from enjoying the blessing of having her here with us. Focusing on old problems only steals the joy of today as a thief — with my permission. If I were smart, I'd be thankful for this moment and move forward. As an adult, we can enjoy her because it was purely her choice. I'm still reserved about sharing my journal, though. It holds my life within its pages; which has protected some of my worst memories behind that small lock. Like Hosea asked, am I ready to share it? Thinking back to a conversation with my best friend Shiloh, who passed two years back. Her words opened my eyes once more than I reminisced on one of her most comforting pieces of advice. I could hear her voice in my mind clear as day, "Girl, you can change nobody, and you sure can't force anybody to love you or treat you right. Chasing and begging folks only makes it worse for both of you. Either you accept the behavior or let it go. Best to pray and release them like a captive butterfly set free. He will flutter away to encounter the world, and if it's meant to be, one day he'll be knocking at your door, or the situation will change."

Sadly, I had to admit that she'd been right. It had been painful to hear her words, yet deep down she was right. May her soul continue to rest easy—I miss her. Well, my buddy, it has happened. She knocked at our door.

Lost Time

The tears he wiped as my former life passed away—I found comfort. Sashaying into my prayer room with my journal in hand, stumbling on the end of a tattered rug—the journal fell. Picking it up, I felt the strain in my back. The music I hummed and moved to had me feeling outstanding, not paying attention when it happened. I eased down on the leopard print chaise, pushing my back into the cranberry-colored Mongolian pillow. I tossed the journal into the bin along with other disarrayed papers. Stored for many years, it now sat amidst clutter. The white pages had turned yellow, but still, each one held tight my memories of such a difficult life of the person once I once was. The pages infused with multicolored handwritten accounts. Poor penmanship from nerve damage and surgeries rested on each page but were legible enough for me to recall the accounts. Details of my existence which ranged from my early years to my latter. The regularity of my accounts had not been consistent, because I wasn't afforded a stable life for lengthy periods. It was unfortunate because I am a living example of how we can lose the grip on life and spiral until we find one finds their true self, but my struggles have molded me into who I am at this very moment. I should have shredded these memories long ago. They are the past and that's where they should stay. Somehow my idea was to share them at one point and time, with whom I hadn't decided or with anyone ever. I didn't understand what self-love was. A lost child, hating myself so early in life, haunted by past secrets and stress from years from crazy decisions. One of misfortune before I lived. Do I want her to know this about me? Am I ashamed?

As I retrieved the journal, a photo slipped out, twirled to the floor.

Without notion, I just stared at it for a moment's time. My body made cries like pork cracklings bending over to retrieve it. Me in my younger days, looking just like Chloe. Why did I feel so harsh about sharing my past with her? Look how far I've come from living a life of pain in the hood in absolute disarray to a large home in the mountains beaming in peace and happiness. Happiness is not something you find—nor found in things, but a journey that never ends. With closed eyes, I could hear my granny's favorite motto… 'nothing stays the same, everything changes' and it happens whether you want them too. When we resist change do our hearts harden? I perceived at one time mines had, with life being so unpredictable, the heavy load of stress, life let downs and turn rounds… went on like a severe storm waiting to happen until it did and I just about lost it all.

Prayer time. It's quiet today. I just needed to spend time with God. My soul was thirsty. For sure my thoughts have been all over the place lately. Realizing I haven't allowed him to lead since I've received this call and without him, I am feeling stressed. No power exists in me without His presence. Why am reminded of this? I believe he sent the person he wanted me to share it with, came. I needed the key to open the journal—she's the missing piece that found it. I'd left the journal in my safe deposit box for twenty-five years, with no wish to retrieve it until yesterday. With her leaped of faith to visit, I can open my heart to give her what she asks for — me.

❧

Engrossed in my little world, Hosea came in, showing Chloe the house.

"There you go in deep contemplation, my dear, you got that perfect image of overthinking. Is it ok if we come inside?"

"Sure, come on in. What look are you talking about?"

"The look, woman… too much on your mind."

I was mimicking him behind his back before clearing my throat.

"What the heck granddad has on… grandma?" She wailed, ending with a snort.

"Girl, didn't he look like Moses, as if he was auditioning for a movie? He draped this shawl around himself and tied it around his waist. The towel over this head gives him a finished look. Helped soak up the sweat keeping him cool."

"Your roman sandals granddad and your ashy feet," she yelled out.

"Wait one minute, he doesn't have ashy feet. He may be ashy anywhere else, but no baby, not on his feet. I can vouch for that."

"Too much information."

We almost died from laughing, leaving us turning colors with churning stomach cramps.

"Grandma, please don't tell me you visited Egypt?" Her eyes rendered to such bigness.

"We sure did, spent two weeks out there… my most favorite part — the pyramids."

"Look at ya'll in front of them. Oh, my…"

Bouncing with excitement.

"It's beautiful there. We had a wonderful tour guide. That's us on a cruise of the Red Sea—it was nice. So full of culture — detailed information on lost civilizations, Pharaohs and kings, and the Nile River. We were in awe the entire time," I stated with excitement.

"Girl!" Taking a deep breath, regaining my composure.

"You must see Luxor and Karnak Temples, Valley of the Kings, and burial grounds of the great Pharaohs. Oh, honey… you will love it. Go in December when it's coldest."

"We were going to be like you'll one day, traveling the world," as she brought her attention to the end of the pictures.

I took a swift twirling to keep up with her, to carry on the conversation. Meantime, looking around, Hosea slipped away.

"I hope so, I would love for you both, heck do better than us. We haven't been around the world, yet."

"This book…," retrieving it from the messy container.

"It looks mysterious; what is it? This lock ain't no joke, either."

Looking over the detailed embossed leather, the uniqueness, and the thickness of the cover. It intrigued her.

"That my dear is the journal."

Her eyes widened, giving a sneered smile, "Thee journal?

"Yes."

"This is well-made grandma leather?" Taking a good whiff, smelling the delights of the sturdy covering.

"It is. Don't sniff too hard, child might flare up your allergies. That book is old as an ancient mummy," smiling at her.

"I haven't even read the book; heck didn't even know nothing about it till now. Guess I ain't special enough, or is it a girl thing?" Hosea exclaimed, quickly reappearing, startling us.

"Neither, I just never thought about it, is important enough to share it. We can read the journal together if you would like."

Hosea's eyes grew, returning to the original state — body drops, scanning the book.

"Naw haven't read it in all this time, I'm good… I came to inform everybody; Candace said dinner would be ready soon," Hosea scurried out, absent-mindedly running into the door.

"Awe man that hurt," he yelled out while rubbing his arm and leg.

Chloe ran up to catch him, making sure he was ok. Stopping mid-step before returning the journal, she smiled.

"Thanks, love."

Consuming the book close to my chest — I must prepare myself to share.

"I can't wait to read it, grandma. See you at dinner," I nodded.

❧

Entering the bedroom, eyeing Hosea as he was preparing for dinner. He rattled on concerning the tour with Chloe.

"She wants you to help decorate their new house."

"That will be fun, you know I can do it, I can't wait."

"Yeah, I agree. That's what you love to do, will decorate anybody's house, won't ya?"

"Sure will, I'm so happy to see Chloe and learn about her, it's exciting, don't you think?"

"Eh—yes, very exciting, but we have to be careful, babe, we don't know her well. Besides, we aren't any spring chickens no more; folks do many things nowadays. Heard from Jez at all?"

"No, I haven't."

"Well, be careful, babe, keep an eye out and see how things go—remember slow and steady," running his hands across the air to reinforce his opinion.

"I need to check the casita."

Wondering if it is clean enough. Been a long time since anyone stayed there, I'm glad it's getting used. "Time sure is moving fast today. Must be the excitement of having Chloe here?"

Looking at Hosea, I passed him, while he continued waving his arms around… repeating "slow and steady."

Piercing him with a slight smirk, I slide past him. Forcing him to seep the words out of his lips instead.

"I hear ya," I stated.

Scurrying to meet Chloe before dinner at the casita, found the temperature cooled down. You could breathe and enjoy the sunshine now. Palm trees lined the yard as I noted the faux grass curling on one edge. Cutting the corner, noting a jackrabbit darted across my feet, stopping to nibble on some leaves. Amid distraction, she jumped from the side of the house with a loud roaring scream, startling me halfway to an early burial.

"Girl, you know I am too old for that kind of foolishness."

Instantly, her smile faded, standing erect like a soldier. She apologized.

"No, it's ok, holding my heart. Girl, you almost finished me," we both laughed.

"Is that water I hear?" Searching around to see the direction in which it came.

Chloe cleared her throat, "Grandma, it's me, I'm about to take a rain-shower outback… forgot my towel, never had a shower outdoors before."

"Awe, yes, towels in the linen box on the outside of the shower. After dinner, enjoy a swim, I will join you."

"Yes. I was planning on dipping into the pool this evening after supper. I'm looking forward to it. Grandma, I have the key."

Cheerfully dangling it in mid-air, until slipping from her fingers plunging back into the muddy gutter spout. Without delay, our eyes fell as if we could catch it — Our bodies froze as we just stared at the hole.

"Disgusting," she moaned with disappointment.

We both shared the sense of disgust peering at the dark waters, which contain a concoction of leaves and other debris. Rambling in the compost bin, she retrieved a wicked-looking stick, breaking it in half before digging in the hole. It measured deep about three to four inches, with much trouble moving it around because of the amount of garbage mangled within. I drew in a deep breath, plunging my hand in the water, reminded me of a swamp as I moved the mush from side-to-side piercing for evidence of the key.

"I got it."

Something prevented it from coming up—the stick snapped. The key resettled.

Kneeling with the shorter end of the stick, began digging, removing what debris she could—no key. Moving things over to see better. she plunged her hand right in the sea of garbage. The smell of compost lingered the wretched rot filling the air, which yielded us to mere gagging.

"I got it. But — I…"

Wiggling it from various angles, seems stuck on something, as if we'd given into a game of tug of war.

"While you have it, Chloe, let me get the broken stick to help secure it."

While she held the key, I began helping by working whatever it was stuck on to loosen it.

"I think I — I have it."

Something snapped, releasing the key, quickly pulling it out. We both showed signs of frustration. What a way to blow off time. My thoughts were all over the place merely ending with making sure I had someone fix this preposterous hole. Our hands were disgusting. We didn't think about gloves until now, as we disposed of the debris.

"Whew, that was close, thought I'd lost it," Chloe exclaimed, wiping the sweat off her forehead.

"It ain't no joke out here, it's hot."

"Like a furnace, girl, not to mention it cooled down. Do you have a key ring for it?"

"Yes, I'll do that right away," thanks, grandma.

Chloe disappeared inside the casita to retrieve her towel, I followed. I moseyed around, assuring everything appeared tidy for her. I yelled out to her, letting her know my intentions. Making sure beds had clean sheets.

It comforted me as the house gleamed with the spotless work of Candace. The freshness of crisp apples filled the air, carpet lint-free, and dusted furniture. I was pleased. It's been a while since I'd been in here, forgetting how cozy the décor appeared. The black sofa sucked you into the most comfortable position, rendering it difficult for you to get up. My art from the former house fit the place well.

Checking my watch, I informed Chloe dinner was about ready.

"Chloe, hurry and shower before dinner," I yelled.

She reappeared with a steady pace of walking back and forth. She paused in mid-step, abruptly twisting, "Hey grandma, would it upset you if I don't stay but a few days?"

Holding her head high, she appeared to struggle for words.

"No, dear, but we hate to see you go. Do you mind me asking why? It's only been one day?

"Well, I can't believe all the years you and granddad never reached out to me. I feel if it wasn't for me calling you, the key, and school…"

She ceased talking as fast as she began looking away, eye moistened with her eyes fluttering to prevent tears from falling.

Giving in, she forced words through her tears, "WHY GRANDMA, I'm twenty-five — about to be married. Twenty-five years, both of you have missed my entire life," waving her finger in my face.

"Chloe… don't do that. It is rude and will not be tolerated. Please—," I pushed her hand away. She shoved her hands in her in her shirt pockets and marched right to my Anatolian wood and crystal-clear epoxy marbled sofa table. As she clenched her fist and slammed her fist dead into it. She shook with anger. My eyes widened with fear as she stayed in place as tears rolled down her cheeks, smearing the wetness down her face with her sleeve. Stunned, I dropped dead weight onto my amber colored shelled back armchair — I listened. I knew this would happen; I just didn't think this soon. She pulled herself up, giving herself extra life to continue sharing her feelings.

"How could you say you cared for me and not want me?" She wailed.

"Honey, you are our grandchild, yes we loved you—"

The struggle to find the words to say overcame me. I sighed, not willing to mutter another word without proper thought. The tones in the air disappeared, leaving wavering sounds of her whimpers.

"Chloe, sometimes when you love someone, imposing your presence only hurts everyone… You, granddad, me, and your parents so we gave in and prayed until the right time for things to work out."

More sounds of struggled muffles staggered the air, somewhat like the waves of smoke. Again, I attempted to speak, but dared to make a sound until I found the nerve to break the silence.

"It overjoys us both to have you here, we hate to see you go. Honey, in due time, you will learn more about how events transpired."

She strutted around the room as if she avoided my remark. Frankly, I knew that she no longer wished to talk. I concluded that I needed to take off. Maybe she needed privacy? Hopping to my feet, I exclaimed my exit. She hadn't looked my way. I strolled past the dinner table, tapping it as my final stance of leaving.

"Honey, what are you going to do?"

Nothing came from her.

"Well, I figured you might want dinner?"

"I'll be cool," turning her back to me with her arms folded.

"O-kay suits yourself; if you need anything call us."

Leaving the casita, I was an emotional mess. Hurt isn't the word, maybe devastated? Not only am I dealing with my issues, now this. I walked around for a while, thinking — until my phone rang. Hosea, wanting me to join him for supper. I headed his way.

❧

Hosea and I found things outside the house to keep us occupied. He had walked by the casita a few times and didn't see any sign of Chloe; I stayed away. Hosea figured he could say something to soothe the situation. We worried about her leaving so, feeling like she should let us know something. We're happy to have seen her, even if it was only for a few days.

After lunch, he challenged to a game of pool; I took him up on it. He beat me something awful. The parade of the failing muscles started pumping. The routine was in progress. My mind was nowhere near the game, deepened thoughts took over concerning that darn girl, she got next to me with all that yelling and pounding on my table. Life is too short to dwell on things; besides, she means more to me than any old table. I want her to be happy. Before heading to my room for an afternoon nap, I sat at the patio table as I went going some paperwork concerning fibromyalgia. The blue skies. I notice she was coming in with a bunch of bags. She yelled for me to visit. I acted as if I didn't hear her, trying to note her mood.

"Grandma," waving her arms.

I walked over, taking my time, not sure what to expect. I entered.

"Notice you have been shopping."

"No—schoolbooks."

"Ahh, I see."

As she scurried through her luggage, looking for a fresh pair of shoes. It appeared she hadn't unpacked. I watched her work with sadness. Without warning, she shot up with a garment in her hands.

"Look what I have," holding a peacock blue crochet jacket with rhinestones that sparkled like glazing stars.

"Oh, my gracious my jacket, it's still in one piece," removing my glasses, narrowing eyes having a gander at it.

I marveled.

"I had it dry-cleaned beforehand."

"Ha."

Going over my jacket, I noted it appeared the same as when I last wore it. I started dancing as if I was in my fifties again, twirling and eyeballing the coat for a fit. Breaking from the frolic, I slid into it, finding it snug, but not too much. Chloe sat on the sofa, watching in amazement over my joy.

"I knew it would fit because it was big on me back then, the smallest size they carried, I had to have it."

Still dancing and singing to old tunes from my time, bringing back many old memories wearing this coat.

"Girl, nobody believed me when I told them my age. Granddad hated it with a passion. Child folks thought I was in my late twenties, like he was an old man courting a young one. We were a year apart."

"That's so funny, you still look younger than your age."

"Thank you," I bowed, hearing the seams of the coat creak a bit.

Leaving me boggled eyed. God works out even the smallest things in life, which my jacket being one. It was too big back then but fit me now… just a tad bit snug, but it fits.

"Funny thing, he looked good for his age, not a grey strand at fifty-two. Looking fine in his fancy clothes."

This coat made me look like a goddess back when—absolutely radiant. Few things had that effect on this old lady; however, this old jacket is one. Eyeing myself in the mirror.

Relinquishing all those old memories, I removed the coat to head off to supper. Bouncing towards the door, still amused, I focused on Chloe standing in the powder room mirror.

"Honey, did you decide between staying?"

"Grandma… I'm sorry about how I carried out. I guess I let my emotions get the best of me, eh — it's not how I act, I'm sorry."

"Ah, I forgive you. You acted out, but honey, it's best sometimes. I wish the moment was different; but it was what it was. It's the beginning stage of healing."

Grabbing the brush from the counter, I began making long strokes, removing tangles from her long-streaked hair.

"Please don't take off, this is such a blessed time in all of our lives—honey, I don't have answers. Giving up the bristle brush to plucking a few tissues to catch her tears. Her smile emerged like the sunrise, gradual and steady. Sniffles lightened the air with her reddened nose.

"Look at you, why give way to such sadness, tarnishing your beauty? I love you, baby. Listen, I don't want to force you to do anything you don't want to do—you hear," shaking her chin with a firm force.

"I love. u grandma, grandad too. I am just confused. They never talked about you all until now, but I can tell Dad miss ya'll."

"He said that?"

"No, but I can tell."

"We do miss him. I pray you stay; we have loads of things planned for the summer—remember?"

"Ok, I guess I've been over-thinking, I'll be fine."

"Will you be having dinner with us tonight?"

"Yes, the menu?"

"I believe baked fish and something yummy to tag along with it. Well, young lady, I'm off to check on dinner, again make yourself at home, and I will see you in a few."

She stayed.

The wilderness has been used as training grounds for those he has called; campsites revived many weary souls who dare to live on faith. Traveling to Mount Lemmon to camp at the very top of Summerhaven, AZ. A small family-orientated community, which won't be the same once we have our share of it. Our first adventure together; it's our second time, and Chloe's first time going. My memory reminds me of the vistas cascading off the sides of the mountains. Stacked wooden log cabin type homes dangled close to the cliff's edges were just a sight to see. Wonder if things were the same since the devastating wildfires swept through the area a few years back. Going over the memories of our last visit was a great way to start the trip. Hosea recounted our previous visit, giving Chloe a picture of what she had to look forward to. The drive wasn't terrible by any means two hours tops. Chloe was eager to drive the entire way, leaving us to enjoy the scenery. I sat upfront with her, wishing Hosea had since he is better at directing and side driving—he watches for everything.

"Do we toilet paper, Lysol, cleansers, wet wipes, soap—" Chloe stopped me in mid-sentence.

"It's all right — grandma. Relax, we can get everything we need there if we forget anything, besides we are going camping, were supposed to be roughing it," she exclaimed with reserved frustration.

Looking sternly at Chloe to assure that she was correct in her thinking before wiggling into a comfortable position. My stare lingered, hoping she realized the trip would be miserable and unbearable without the things we needed.

"Honey, it only takes a minute to account for the things in question," I stated calmly.

"You know she's looking to go glamping, grandma luxury camping, nothing more. I ain't far from it myself."

Chloe rolled her eyes.

I wanted to rip the bags open and check myself. However, Chloe's expression gave me the confidence that we had a firm understanding.

"Ok, Missy, let's go," I stated, pulling the blanket over my shoulder to keep from getting sore from the air condition.

Hosea and I asked a million inquiries about the campsite amenities; we had to get all the details. Before we camped outdoors; however, we are much older now. We elderly folks need facilities, with running water, real toilets, sinks, beds, all the good stuff needed for comfortable living. Chloe laughed because she made the arraignments, claiming to perceive our needs.

"CHLOE???" I yelled.

I was rustling out of my blanket in dismay.

"Let's talk girl, I pray we have rooms and not just sleeping bags?"

We organized this adventure at the last minute, leaving us with little time to give our request. More so, we stated we needed comfort, amenities, and food. Maybe I should have been more elaborate concerning our needs.

"Relax everybody, I realize all of this. Trust me, please, I have it all under control."

We explained to her we didn't have any desire to use primitive outhouses or restrooms across the world; even though we are young at heart, we wanted convenience; our bodies are not what they used to be.

"Please let the bathrooms be close when I got's to go... I GOT'S to go! Shoot your grandma the same way," Hosea asserted.

"I sure am. Hey, did you understand that, Miss driver?" Making sure she heard him.

"Yes, oh my gosh, T-M-I, y'all," she chuckled.

It has been a long time since we've been camping, Chloe says she often goes back home. However, her first time in the Santa Catalina Mountains—got her excited. We camped here with our oldest son Elijah, who invited us during his college days, about 15 years ago. I'm sure things have changed. We made it to the base of the mountain, thinking we arrived at the campsite. We sure got excited, short of dancing in our seats until Chloe informed us of an additional 45 minutes or 26 miles until we made it to the peak. The GPS did not account for this portion of the drive, making it longer than expected. Hosea relaxed, kicking up his feet as though he made it home to his armchair. Chuckling to myself because he wasted no time returning to comfort. Chloe asked if we needed a restroom break and didn't mind stopping.

"No rush, but could use a restroom break," Hosea said.

"I bet you God would live in a tent over a mansion, what do you all think?" I said.

"That was from left field," Hosea murmured.

"Just thinking of how he loves taking folks from all the worldly things of life, enjoying the outdoors without all the drama and extras," I explained.

"Really? I can see it, He can live wherever He wants, I think it's amazing. He created it all." Chloe exclaimed.

"Ya know, even the Israelites out in the wilderness, he lived in a tent with them. It seems like he brought them to it; he experienced their environment. Isn't that something?" Hosea shared.

"Well, I didn't know that… learned something new today," Chloe said.

"Oh yeah, my Lord stayed with them the entire way."

☙

Entering the road that would take us straight to the mountaintop. The road changed, narrowing down to two lanes, making driving more strategic. The sunlight was refulgently glaring. It was nice and early when we left; if things go as planned, we'll arrive and unpack before dusk. I prodded Hosea to think about building the fire. Worried that he'd forget how, so I reminded him to get to thinking about it.

"Grandma, I'm confident granddaddy will remember how to build a fire."

"Young lady, I wedded that man a hundred years back. He'll forget if you don't get him warmed up ahead of time with his thinking," I declared.

"Woman you the one with memory issues, up there talking all that mess. For sure won't be making the fire, that's for certain, even if my brain left me right now."

"Your right but be assured I can find someone if I need to, you realize it will be an inconvenience and you don't want that. Do ya?"

"Hey Chloe… you ever start a fire? Best to have two good minds, can't count your grandma in that area."

"Why are you getting things all riled up? Your grandma act like we going to have problems; squash those thoughts right here and now."

We had Chloe laughing too hard to talk, heck I was about the same. She looked around the car with her sparkling eyes, trying to catch her breath.

"Whew, you both are so funny. Please stop… please. I can't take it. Do you too always act like this?" She questioned.

"Child, we are on our best behavior, can't you tell?" Hosea shook his head, letting out one robust laugh.

"She does not understand how to act, I be telling her."

I wanted to smack him a good one, but it wouldn't do any good. Seeing he wouldn't know what hit him or who it came from, only leaving him to act out more.

❧

Catalina highway narrowed into two-lanes; we cruised the cascading roadway along the side of the mountain, overseeing the cliff. It's unnerving for me. But Chloe appeared relaxed, not bothered one bit by the declining road. Nor the sweet Christian music that played had us all humming and tapping to the tunes, with occasional singalongs from me. Our eyes were witnesses of the bask array of wildflowers, various rock formations, trees, and valleys down low, changing from forest to desert the further we traveled it seemed as if we were a part of a nature movie. Between the views and music, we rarely focused on the time or my additional need to use the restroom. Chloe turned down the music, asking if I had the fact sheet showing the height of this mountain?

"Yes, I do, my dear… don't they have a waterfall here? I can't remember."

"Yes, three small ones… one of the best attractions," she said.

"Oh, great, we must see at least one."

"Me too, I can't wait," Hosea said.

Fluttering through the paperwork she had in the folder to locate it, "Awe, here it is. Let me see what we have here."

Studying the information before sharing. "The highest peak of the Catalina Mountains is Mount Lemmon; it's 9,157 ft high."

"Wow, we will be in the sky. Frankly, don't think we can get no closer to heaven than that, can we?" I stated, glaring over my specs.

"Sho'll can't, you best hope you don't run into any wild animals like boars, bears, or coyotes to scare you there before your time, woman."

"Why you always trying to scare somebody… can't scare me, acting like a boar yourself right here, right now." As I mean mugged him.

"That look couldn't get any eviler; it scared me too, grandma."

"You recognize you're special, right?" Hosea said.

I whispered to him; in return, he gave me one of the grandest smiles showing his big pearly whites—like Chester, the cat from the commercial—the sunglasses assisted his resemblances.

"See… look how you got Chloe thinking about me?" Bantering with him, I swatted him with my papers.

"I sure am. Who loves the boar who sits in the back, baby?"

Poking at me with his crooked fingers and smacking kisses towards me. I refused to answer him or give into his foolishness. I laid back, taking advantage of getting some rest—Plum Forget I had been informing them on the mountain actualities. The sky just took your breath away as we traveled the winding road. Hosea groaned for us to stop, needing to stretch his legs. "How much further before we reach a rest stop?"

"We are about to reach one in about 5 minutes," glimpsing at her GPS.

"I think we all could use a quick break," I added.

❧

The bolstering temperatures declined; as we ascended into the mountains, making it about 30 degrees cooler and breezy, making it more comfortable. I suspected to pack some heavier garments and thankfully I did. Approaching the first rest area, we scoped out a functional parking space near the restroom. We happened upon the ideal spot near the anchored edge, making it convenient to envision the city and mountain views. The huge cacti stood like soldiers protecting the mountainside. The pictures reminded me of the first time I learned that cacti bloomed flowers, they're beautiful. It prompted me to value the little things in life at that exact moment; they're not enormous flowers, but they make a big statement.

"Are the flowers symbolic in any way?"

"Let me look it up."

"Anything that grows in those dry grounds got to be good," Hosea said.

"Ha, interesting…"

"Yeah, yeah... everything's interesting to you, woman."

"Can I finish? Please," cleared my throat.

"Go ahead, woman."

"The Cacti floral is a symbol of unconditional maternal love because it flowers in harsh conditions. A mother's love can endure all things."

"Once I heard it meant lust and sexual attraction," Chloe said.

"In the army, my buddy said, it meant loneliness and danger. Who knows, all I know is they sure are lovely."

"I agree."

❧

The area we stopped at had port-a-potties, I don't like them. Forced me to double-check with Chloe to assure we had real bathrooms. I found it odd that quite a few folks started climbing the elevations instead of driving. Standing with my hand, shielding the sun from my view—watching them attach gear to get started. I found no sense in it, but to each their own, throwing my hand at his nonsense. The sun sparkled as an invitation to enter the mountains. Strolling over to check on Miss Chloe, I noticed she is conversing with her fiancé Jeremai since we parked. The sight of her smile and radiant face, a glow, appeared every time she spoke to him. Young love, so full of life and hope for a promising future together, praying it stays that way. The happiness one should have when you're planning on marrying somebody. Noticing she finished her call; I moseyed my way over joining her.

"Ready, my lady?"

Before she could answer, I noticed her smile faded, "What's that pouty face about?"

"I'm just feeling some type of way today, nothing major, I'm ready to head on up, how bout you all?"

Hesitation in her reply, "I miss my honey grandma."

She whispered, dropping her head onto my shoulder. Gently racked the hair from her face with my finger. I smiled. Her presence meant the world to me.

"Sweetheart, before you snap your curls, you'll be graduating and married in no time. I want to share these moments with you."

"You're right, I'm so excited," she livened up like her vitamins kicked in.

"New marriage, my grandparents, and my career, what more could I ask? I'm a little nervous I have to admit."

"That's understandable, you have considerable changes ahead of you. Who wouldn't be? I would. Pray about it, don't let it overwhelm you, don't need you stressed out."

"Yea, your right. I care for him so much."

"I can tell, sweetheart. Marriage is a tremendous step; he sounds like a delightful fellow from what I gather. I haven't met him yet, I can't wait."

"Yeah, he is… He's funny, lovable, talented, and charming. Not to mention he thinks I am the greatest," nervously swaying her arms, she rattled on about the love of her life.

"Be prepared, girlie; your grandad has many questions for him. Better make sure he's able to stand the heat."

"Yeah… Dad did already. He was so nervous."

"Sounds like he passed the test."

"Barely," moving us into a deep belly laugh.

"Dad is something else. A genuine character."

"You who he got it from?"

"Yes, Grandad, they act so much alike."

Hosea made some new friends. Sitting on the front of their SUV smoking a cigar, playing with their dog. Fanning my arms to get his attention from afar, failed. His mouth was like a motor revving away. He's always finding someone to talk to wherever we go, sometimes I don't mind, the real question is how long? I glided across the road a different view, glazing over the mountainside giving into the deep slopes and rising hills, which appear to erect straight from the ground. However, the grounds were much lower than I stood. Looking outward, the road we will travel leads us to higher grounds, forcing the valley even lower. Amazed at their endurance to such harsh weather, still standing with superior strength, surrounding mangled grasses covered the ground for as far as I could see, blankets for the cacti roots and refuge for small animals and insects. Giving into thinking how these creatures survived such bolstering weather broke away to occasional patches of snow dotting the landscape. Maybe that's the answer. How do these clusters of snow survive? Walking down the hill, I noticed a small snowman, noting it couldn't be real. Slight nip of the toe. It crashed over, crumbling to snow dust, leaving me darting back to the car for killing someone's snowman. It tickled me but didn't want to stay to see the aftermath of who's handiwork I demolished.

Getting ready to head out, when the air reaped of a kid screaming rattlesnake standing lifeless as his dad grabbed him, bolting him to their van. Before one could blink everyone scattered to their cars or inside the information station, his dad reappeared, waving his gun to locate the snake in question.

"I'll kill him if I have too," he shouted.

Making it even more nerve-racking seeing this man on a mission of a snake hunt or accidental shooting of himself or one of us. The park employee appeared to handle the situation as we pulled off. A thought crossed my mind. Snakes was a symbol of evil, ask Adam and Eve. I shook, just thinking of the evil serpent. When I glanced harder, I cared less to never see another one. The rest of the drive was quiet, commencing to get cooler as we approached the campsite, forcing us to roll up the windows. I flipped through the songs, trying to locate my favorite one. I didn't understand my indecisiveness at the moment.

"Put on any song and leave it be woman," Hosea muddled.

Chloe encouraged me to play anything before granddaddy jump over the seat at me. I turned, giving him a feisty glare. He better not, because I had something for him. He peeked back with his eyes half-bulging out of his head, daring me. We laughed having a good ole time; I still enjoy him as though we married yesterday. We arrived—taking a few minutes to recoup before getting out of the car. I rambled through the papers for our reservations. Chloe waited patiently, chatting with Hosea about some things she planned to do on our visit. Mentioning horseback riding caught my attention, almost snapped my neck to listen. I want to ride a horse; I thought. With no courage in me to let it depart from my lips. My eyes—liven up at the mere thought of riding one, they sparkled, knowing Hosea was reading me like a book. Couldn't hide it, tried, but his nosey behind looked me dead in my eyes, squinting.

"You know you are old. As soon as you get on, heaven's doors will open wide. Stop looking like you are even thinking about it," shaking his head.

"I'm aware of how old I am; you bubble buster. It isn't too late for me to ride. I am tired of people telling me what I can and can't do. Thinking about it even more now, you ain't going to stop me from dreaming either."

My soul knew he was right, would have jumped out and told him so if it could. Instead, it seeped out my heart, making me doubt myself. Chloe disappeared, making her way to the park office. I jumped out to follow. Scanning the area, I remembered the talk—wild animals. Refusing to think any wild animals would be in this area, I pierced through the wooded area, sprinting off to join Chloe. Inhaling a deep breath of that good smelling air did wonders for my lungs until being startled by Hosea, who joined us.

❧

"My, my—well, look at this fine-looking log cabin," taking a brisk walk around back.

He returned, removing his baseball cap, shooing away tiny insects.

"Matea, you ran your mouth the entire time about comfort and looked at here, almost a cabin mansion." I paid him not a speck of attention.

"It's about 1500 square feet and not a mansion, grandpa," she chuckled.

We carried in a few things, check it out before cramming all our belongings inside. The back wall boosted enormous windows that ran from the high ceilings to the floor with polished window frames. They're huge, leaving little wall space along the back. The three bedrooms were perfect for us, even had an extra room for our junk.

"I love it," I said.

Walking around checking it out even more; it's not your average cabin, nor is it like the one we stayed in when our son Elijah brought us up. This kind of camping is my style, pure luxury. The deck overlooked the dense forest and beautiful greenery below, dropping low in the back. We love it. It was breathtaking, making our vacation perfect for the two days we planned to stay. Hosea and Chloe grabbed the rest of our belongings out of the car, taking them to our rooms. Chloe started unpacking while I cleaned the kitchen. Hosea found his way to the TV, taking time to figure out the remotes.

"Hunny, can you please get the fire pit set up before it gets dark?"

He stayed seated as if he was deaf while grumbling. He continued playing with the remotes. Flicking his watch, he realized it was getting late, forcing him to render them back to the table.

"Thank you. I appreciate you."

Drawing in a deep sigh—he threw his hands behind his back as his answer of frustration, I snickered. Preparing the fire, I noted how he arranged the wood, working like a pro. It impressed me that my old man remembered. He might be rusty doing things, but he amazes me every time. It inclined me to say something, but he would get off track and start chattering, getting nothing done. The fire simmered, Hosea sat poking the stick to arrange the logs, crackles and pops splatted from the flames, with trails of smoke floating into the cool air. The glow of the logs gave way to the readiness of the fire to provide warmth to its surroundings. I spotted off the side of the deck, plenty of garbage someone left with flies swarming around it—no telling what was in there. I took a mental note to mention getting rid of it before it smelled even more or attract some unwanted creatures.

"Are we going fishing while we are here, babe?" he asked.

"I have no idea. I know we have activities planned; we'll figure it out. Grilled fish sure sounds good."

"Not for me. I'm certain I want mines dipped in cornmeal and fresh hot grease."

It filled Hosea with excitement, rubbing his hands together and licking his lips.

"Let's flip for it; you know you don't need no fried foods."

Lord, I pray she forgot the oil. I snickered to myself.

Chloe got to work, cutting up fresh fruit for us to enjoy. She had everything arranged on a tray along with refreshing fresh-squeezed lemonade and iced tea. Rendering to our beautiful surroundings, I gasped. Taking it all in by sections, it's too much to view at once, land everywhere. Spotting Hosea, I started walking towards the seating area close to him.

"Are you looking at me?" Hosea said to Chloe.

"Granddaddy, you know I wasn't," eyeing him with a quirky smile.

"Leave her alone, silly man, who wants to look at you?"

"You do," I hurried to my seat, avoiding his drama.

"It's so peaceful here. I want to sleep in that hammock and chill," Chloe said.

"Bet you it won't last long, those bugs and critters out there waiting on ya," snickering like a prude.

"Like?" peering around.

"I saw Anteaters, meerkats and tarantulas, while stationed in the in the military."

"Grandpa, why did you say that to scare me?"

"I ain't trying to scare nobody, girl. I bet you if you lay eyes on those water bugs, big ole dragonflies, and wild squirrels, you would be glad I'd warned you."

"Whatever grandpa, you're not scaring me no matter what you say."

"Girl, that's his second job scaring folks."

"I am a true city girl, but I do like adventure."

Chloe spat watermelon seeds at him, darting them towards his head, stopping when she got him one good time.

"Are you acting like a big kid? You don't want me to get started, that's a warning."

Sitting back in his seat, he pulled a rubber Gecko from his pocket. He flicked it towards her chair. Hearing the thump, Chloe's laid eyes on the object, jumping clear from her seat, causing her to yell. The neighbors came out to see what was going on. Her heart was speeding, causing her to lose her breath. Slowly walking toward the object, she grabbed a stick poking at it. Flipping it around in the bare grass, noticing it was fake.

"Granddaddy, please stop it; you scared me. Dang, you are so irritating."

"What did I do?" With a sneaky chuckle.

She threw a nice chunk of watermelon towards him, missing. He ducked, almost falling out of his chair.

"Let's go walk to check out the grounds."

"Grandma, are you ok with that?" Chloe asked.

"Go ahead, but not too far, the sun is moving on down, don't want you two out too late, don't lose your grandpa child."

I stayed at the cabin, continued getting everything settled. I ran across my journal, massaging the thick soft leather that covered it. The precious lock will be open after all these years. Checking out the clock, noticed 3:33 PM on it. That's funny, I viewed the same numbers in a dream the night before. Wonder what it means?

❧

They made it back just before dawn from their walk, scoping from the opened window. They get along so well, Hosea needed to spend this time with our baby girl. He had taken his walking stick the doctor prescribed for him, only to push things on the ground around and keep him company. Looking at him, his eyes withered, and he lagged, appearing ready to call it a night. We had a busy day with the long drive and sightseeing.

"Now you can play with your remotes. Babe get off those old knees of yours before they hurt," I yelled.

"There she goes screaming, making many kinds of demands, ya know, telling the world my private business," stomping into the house.

Chloe snickered as he changed his mind, "I'll be up there after I get rid of this garbage. It smells as if someone left something dead in there. Besides, I need a cigar. Before she drives me bat crazy."

He put in great effort into ignoring me. Entering the house, Chloe asked for dinner ideas. We brought food for the grill, but couldn't do another thing, too tired. Pouncing on the sofa, laying on top of the pillows with her legs crossed, Chloe peered over the menu.

"Wonder if they have fried chicken?" Hosea yelled through the window.

"You're not getting any fried foods," I replied.

Hosea stomped inside to contribute suggestions for dinner.

"Let's get pizza. Who's ordering? Don't forget those big ole cookies they sell. Chocolate chip and sugar dipped, please," Hosea said.

We ordered from the local store right before closing. We set off to pick it up, leaving Hosea to shower. It took no time to grab our order, stepping fast to return with a semi-hot pizza. Fumbling for my phone as the buzz juggled my pocket. I answered too late. He hung up as Chloe's phone rang next.

"Granddad, you need something?" Listening in on their conversation.

"Go back to the store; it's a grizzly bear out back," he screeched.

"What bear? A real one or a prank?"

"I said a bear — you hear me a grizzly," he started again.

"You're not getting us this time around," Chloe dismissed his message.

Listening in disbelief, "I'm calling the office to request someone come right away," she said.

I listened to see if he'd back down from actions rendered. It seemed to be the truth. Hysterically, he cut off the conversation; the phone went dead.

"Grandma… maybe he is telling the truth," we headed back to the store.

"It may be too dangerous, better not take the chance."

I listened in disbelief, thinking it was a prank myself, I mumbled the entire way of how it better not be. It's best to be safe than sorry. If I find out if this is a prank, there's going to be trouble, I raised my tensed fist toward the greying sky. As we wrestle through the disarrayed forest confetti covered grounds, made it hard to move fast as our feet picked up every piece we encountered. The owner stood out front appearing to have had better days and wife was worse off than him. She turned the sign—closed and glanced her eyes towards us without moving.

"Were closed. See you tomorrow. Have a good night," he slurred out.

Before speaking, we had to catch our breath. Placing the pizza on the rail, breaths returned to normal. Chloe took more time to gain her composure like she was having a bout with asthma.

"My husband is saying that a grizzly bear is behind our cabin, making a bumbling mess of things. He's afraid and needs help, please."

The owner rolled his eyes unenthused. He flicked the sign in a jerking manner and used his shoulder to reopen the door and headed inside. His wife stood with paper bags in her hands, which she dropped to the ground to join him.

"Excuse his manners—been a long day; we're exhausted."

The couple explained that this often happens, with her husband calling the Game and Fish Department informing them regarding the issue.

"They are sending someone to your site as fast as they can, don't feed them or else — trouble."

Our eyes widened as we pierced at each other. "he said it was going through the garbage that someone left on behind the cabin."

Chewing on a toothpick, he spat to the ground, "Ah—that be the problem, can't have garbage just sitting around. Most likely after food. Best to keep the place clean."

"My husband is there alone; I pray he does nothing irrational."

"Call to check on him, ma'am," as he raised one brow of concern.

I let my nerves get to me, too frustrated to work on my phone. Chloe called. "Honey, I'm fine, it's outside digging in the garbage. Tell LP, I love her, eh may be the last time I see—"

His words came across choppy, but I assume witnessing a bear got him speaking with fear.

"Who is LP?"

"Give me the phone. Hosea, please be careful; they said don't leave the cabin and don't feed it."

"It's too late for that, the peoples just arrived. I got's to go," abruptly slamming the receiver down.

❧

In no time, they captured the bear and loading him in the truck. When we arrived, they were pulling off in route to the animal control center, and they removed the garbage. Warning signs were being tacked on the poles in the surrounding area informing folks of the bear citing and a reminder, 'Do not feed any animals.' The sheriff arrived. Walking stiff legged to the cabin, he pinched the top of his hat and placed it on his head. Squinching from the rays and chewing his gum like it stuck to his teeth, "Hosea?"

"Yes, sir."

"I'm sure you weren't feeding the bear or trying to take pictures with it?"

"Oh, no, sir."

The sheriff drifted to the side of the cabin, glancing towards the back. He dropped his head to the ground and toed a few rocks around. He chuckled, "It's been a long day in our neck of the woods, I believe it to be the same bear we heard about earlier. But one can't be for sure."

"On our way up here, we spotted some cat food and piles of blueberries on the road. From the looks of it, bear bait. Earlier we sent a trooper to the area. Someone reported a couple taking photos in a close range with the bear. Most likely the one we collected today."

"You didn't take him in earlier?" Hosea said.

"By the time we got word, it was gone."

"Well, I pray it's him, don't want nobody getting hurt."

"Let's be smart folks, you cannot handle any size bear if he attacks, it's just a friendly reminder—that's all."

Folks gathering to see what was going on. The sheriff gave the other guest the same advice. "Please take heed to the signs," tapping his finger on the sign. He looked around, ending with Hosea.

"Good day sir, any more problems just call," Handing him a card.

❧

Entering the cabin, Hosea gave in to tell his account of what took place, arms in full swing, eyes big, rambling on about the story of the grizzly, along with role-playing. He was outside when he discovered the bear behind the garbage, which horrified him—with a muffled, lazy growl.

"I figured you got rid of the rubbish earlier today?" I exclaimed.

"No, I waited. I went out there and — BAM! That big bear was staring me right in my face—I froze like a statue. Hearing those grizzlies can eat you if you moved one bone."

"Please blink," as his eyes became fixated large glass marbles and sweat poured over his face. "If you don't relax, you're going to explode."

"I'm telling you his claws were big, looking like he'd rip my face off with one swipe. Matted fur with debris from the ground tangled on his strands, as he made growling sounds, waving his arms in mid-air. I jumped, losing my balance, falling to the ground, I could't breath for a moment. Thought I wet my pants, and I got up and ran into the house. I've experienced nothing like it before," heart pumping, languishing him to gasps.

Nonsensically, he rattled on of his encounter with the bear. I enjoyed listening to him, because he was funny as heck. His humorous expressions, stiff movements from one angle to the next, he appeared animated.

"For real Hosea? You undertook a bear, or did you run into the house to call us?" I asked.

"Quite trying to act like this isn't serious."

Took no time grabbing him up, smothering him with kisses and hugs "I love you."

"Yeah, ok."

It seems he'd talked himself into a rut, discovering no alternative to stretch this story any further. "Here's the picture of him."

"HOSEA! This is a cub, not a bear. Well, they can do damage too," I added.

"Awe, he looks cute, soft, and cuddly. He needs a bath though."

"Stop! He's none of those things, could have killed me," snatching the phone back.

Chloe burst out laughing, with me joining in, jerking us both into tears we couldn't control. He was too sleepy and irritated to take part. Exhausted, he called it a night. Throwing his hand in defeat, as we had an excellent belly rolling laughter. He had too much excitement for the day; he got up and excused himself for the evening, touching my shoulder, beckoning for his goodnight kiss.

"You still want to kiss me—LP?"

"Yes, I do, your foolishness of laughing at me and my demise doesn't stop me from loving you."

"Ya know that bear reminded of an Army mate, young fella, cocky attitude a bear attacked him about 15 years ago." Pulling a chair from the kitchen area, with a peculiar look on his face, catching my attention.

"You ok, babe?"

"Ya, ya, listen to this. He was a member of this church; they had accusations of him being a part of this investment group that stole millions from this church and some elderly folks."

"Oh, my, that's not good," I exclaimed.

"During a meeting the pastor had to question him on his involvement, it hurt the pastor to do so. In return he mocked him — calling him 'bald-headed' and other names showing out, ya know, big time. I hear he showed his behind."

"That's all he called him?"

Not too long after, he went on a camping trip with 40 members of his group to relax before the big trial. Out hunting, they met up with two big ole' female bears that killed all but him—no mercy. He lived a short period after that, long enough to look the pastor in his face and ask for forgiveness.

"What a story grandpa, they all got what they deserved."

"What you say, pray he got right with God too," I said.

A thought entered my mind. "The love of money is a root of all kinds of evil. Some people, eager for money, have wandered from the faith and pierced themselves with many griefs -1 Timothy 6:10, NIV."

"You know greed and the love of money have killed so many folks having them doing crazy things and destroyed many marriages too," I said.

"I think I learned something like that in Sunday school. Anything concerning bears in the bible?" Chloe said.

Hosea shrugged. "I don't know. I know this one was a male. Man, I was just thinking even female bears are meaner than the males? I'm guessing all woman species are," he laughed.

"We are blessed nothing happened to you grandpa, but you know you're not right?" hugging him.

He was off to bed talking mess all the way. Chloe speedily turned around, asking if we could begin reading my journal. As expected, I was hesitant, however inclined as she grabbed it before Hosea shut the door.

"I can't believe I have your journal, Grandma."

I looked on as she placed the key into the lock. The pages swirled opening, like a burst of life. Merely looking at my handwriting brought back so many remembrances, I assumed I'd forgotten. Chloe shuffled around, struggling to become complacent on the sofa. I waited — The journey began the reading of my life.

☙

May-1963 ✿ Dear diary, 'Hey child, don't step on those darn caterpillars out front,' mom keeps saying. The aged tree, half-dead, had lots of them; they sure were ugly. Some fury, others not so much, slugging around on all those nasty-looking legs. Didn't matter about the looks of them, they created the finest mud pies in Detroit. Using tin foil pans from the tasty pot pies, we gathered from lunch, gave them a professional look, which was suitable to sell to our friends for a penny. The caterpillars filled the heart of the pies. The cement blocks served as our refrigerator until we started baking, keeping them fresh with the water hose after we had our slurps from the brass spouts. Momma said our ideas may make us bakers one day. It kept us busy from sunup to dusk until she told us we won't ever see butterflies again if we kept on doing it. Nature whispered to my soul. This world would be ugly without butterflies.

June-age 8✿ Dear diary, nothing makes me happier than to escape the madness of constant war in our house. An abundance of bad things happened inside our walls, but still, I loved our home. Mom and Dad are working now. We have some place to call our own, a real big white house. The yard has the greenest grass and a big pear tree, surrounded by the sturdiest gate ever; it was our free babysitter when dad wanted alone time with mom. Today I got the worst whooping with a belt because my friend broke my dollhouse, which ended with her gripping my ponytail and banging my head into a wall. I didn't want it after that and threw it away. Tired of hearing her knuckles crack to the sounds of her hand, grabbing my ponytail as I played with it. The remembrance of my head being banged into a wall. I'm not fond of dollhouses anymore. A few days after, mom encouraged me to write concerning my emotions. I refused to talk until I exploded into wild fits. How could I, with no journal? So, I asked my English teacher should I journal; she opened her desk drawer, giving me a bright composition book. She told me she admired my writing skills, making it a fantastic idea to jot down my feelings. Opening the book, she wrote June 1960 to start my first page, closing it she told me she would miss me for the summer and write much. Her only advice—please keep your thoughts a secret, it's for your eyes alone.

July-age 8✿ Dear diary, I enjoy watching my portable black-and-white TV under the dining room table. Adjusting the rabbit ears covered with aluminum foil frustrated me. My brother was mad at me because I wouldn't let him join me, so he peed in my face as I scrambled away, I broke the antenna in half. Burying my face into the smelly dark-colored psychedelic shag carpet, I cried. Too broken to fight him, or else he'd been beaten badly.

Baking real cakes in my easy bake oven, so tasty and fun to share, Mom bought me Jiffy cake products, which had all the kids begging. I sold them for 10 cents, making them more popular over my mud pies. My favorite was a white cake with maraschino cherries, so heavenly. Sometimes I'd pick the peaches off of our neighbor's tree for my cakes, which tasted nothing like the cherry ones.

I saw Ed The Talking Horse on TV today. Oh my gosh, I love horses. I know they can't talk. They looked so lovely, intelligent, and powerful. I daydreamed of riding one, hair flowing, galloping off into the sunset. Constant whining made my momma nuts. She tells me so, but it didn't change how I feel. One day she pointed out that black girls from the ghetto don't ride horses, only the wealthy white folks did such things. I didn't care about money, but I needed some to buy my horse. Why can't we be rich? How did white people get their money? I vowed to figure it out. I'm going to be rich and black too. Planning on when and how I was getting one. I was keeping it in our garage, just like they did on TV. I set her straight, telling her I'd be rich and have two horses and she should believe in me. Nobody was going to tell me different. She bought me a book on horses and let me sit next to the stove while she cooked; I read to her. Attending a field trip at school to a farm gave me a chance to get close to one. It was a hayride, yet to me, it was life. I wasn't particular of the smell of the enormous glops of crap they left, though. None the less, when I came home, it's all I spoke of. I saw her frustration and wondered why she had little hope of becoming rich?

August-1963, age 9✿ Dear diary, I turned nine years old today. Please note I didn't get a horse; instead, I got a yellow Schwinn bike. It was perfect; never thought about a bike. The big beige padded seat is comfortable with a basket for my babies. I was little, yet my back end recognized the privilege of having good padding. I had never experienced a bell on a bike; it's the grandest part. Today I've resounded it 50 times. It's musical to my ears and a nightmare to momma's — ting-a-ling-a-ling. This bicycle was heaven-sent, motioning me to pure amusement, as my legs twirled each swirl of the wheels produced the most brilliant smiles I ever created. She let me wear my blue rain gear to splash in puddles. I promise never to talk of horses again, but I was still dreaming. Besides, who receives a horse after getting a bike? Yesterday, I was on the porch washing my bicycle—not allowed to leave off it. My dad's friend ran up the steep stairs; I hadn't noticed him until he said 'hello' — pop-pop-pop. A drive-by shoot-out left my parents' friend shot in his butt next to me while we stood on the porch. He fell over similar to a towering tree, with his face rested right next to the empty milk and juice glass containers; dad put out earlier. Extra bullets riddled the house, missing my head by inches. Mom yelled as she argued with daddy about the dangers in our neighborhood. They said I'll never ride my bike again.

August-1963, age 9✿ Dear diary, Today, I sat watching my parents; my mother's is exquisite. With nice shapely legs, I pray I look like her when I grow up. She is pretty enough to be a movie star, but she's our mom. Marveling at her sunny and sassy attitude, always wearing fitting clothes and high heels—her slim body was perfect for it. Nothing was more enlightening than hearing her laugher, which filled any room. Music made her come to life. When her favorite jams came on, she started twisting, turning, bobbing her head, and snapping her fingers disco style. The elegance presented marveled me, so smooth, as if she floated in air. Positive moods filled the house, the house today, like an intense beam of light. I wish it weren't rare to see her like this. A huge afro mingled with brilliant golden rich tints, never a strand out of place. When happy, she's entertaining and amusing. Maybe she should be famous. I'm sure she didn't think so—she hates taking pictures. Dad is quite a looker himself and enjoyed his fine-looking clothes; he was a lady's man before he married my mom, so I heard. It was hard for him to keep a job due to severe depression and oppression, leading him to drinking.

Daddy was a cook in the Army for two years; mom says it screwed up his mind. His food may have tasted good in the Army, but he not good in the kitchen at home. The last meal he cooked was pigs' feet, sugared rice, sugared corn, and unsweetened Kool-Aid — barf. He excused no one from the table until we finished; we fell asleep hungry that last night. Sometimes I agree with mom. Maybe that's why he fought her so often. Did he think he was still fighting? His rampant complaints of racism, discrimination, participation with peaceful and non-peaceful marches, sit-ins at downtown restaurants, and joining in on freedom rides, brought out the rage in him.

We have a picture of him with Martin Luther King, Jr. in a peaceful march on the frontline, which hung on the wall with pride. That was a day he landed in jail, with 300 other protesters. Seen him on the news getting thrown in the police wagon, seeing mom drop her coffee right on the floor.

August-1963, age 9✿ Dear diary, one thing for sure, they looked great together but could get along to save nobody's life. They argued and fought; mom stayed bruised up, with Dad acting as if nothing happened. How could they love each other bruised up? He had his fill of having undesirable items threw on him, such as pig ears, rice, oatmeal, or grits. Each account had its memory, but the pig ears remained the most memorable to me. Hot gooey pig ears stuck right to his chest, mixed with his curly hairs. You heard him scream throughout the house; I hated it happened to him. He didn't even bother to remove them; he just laid on the couch, drifting off to sleep with bouts of cussing and fussing. Seems as if he preferred to ignore what took place. Did he assume they'd dissolve? Not to mention, pig ears are 'yuck.' Given a choice, I rather daddy wear them, then to eat them for supper. He never learned his lesson, the storms kept growing and becoming worse, not to mention the threats he received from Mom's family.

Daddy strolled in the door, swinging the latest album yesterday. This time he brought home the O'Jays. He had a deep passion for music like mom, grinning as he darted to the record player to clean off the needle. Dared to get a fingerprint on his albums. Slowly picking up the arm, flicking the needle, as he took great care laying it on the vinyl disk- the party had begun. He swayed side to side while he read the 8-track package and flicked through the 45's. We had cool tunes in the car too. Times like this brought a moment of peace to our turbulent world, which allowed us a dash of hope that better times were ahead. We enjoyed dancing together, laughing and jeering each other on to decide who had the best moves. Look at my sister do the funky chicken; while I jerked around doing the robot, thinking I could beat her lame moves. Until my brothers chimed in doing the boog a loo and the mashed potatoes. Now they were jamming. Mom was doing her thang all over the place; no name for her funky moves, just swinging and poppin. Mom won hands down, leaving Daddy's eyes sparkling with sheer love.

September-1963, age 9✿Daddy called us in the living room, making us sit down on the sofa. It was his regular speech he told that we had to be better than others in this world because we're black. Each of us sat with widened eyes noting how badly he was hurt. He lost another job to a white man who had less experience than he had, and the anger seeped out in his entire being. Mom tried to calm him down but sat with us and listened as well. Looking at her I saw tears forming in her eyes. Standing tall he said he refuse to give in to being called an Afro-American, because he was born on American soil, he demanded that he was an American. Speaking on the noose he found in front of his locker was the last straw, not to mention all the degrading things they said to him previously. The confrontation with his boss demanding to be treated fairly and stop all the derogatory things being done to him. His boss listened and dismissed him. As he left, he yelled behind him that he wasn't well-behaved enough to stay on in front of the white workers who thought it was funny. Man, he cussed up a storm, slamming doors, stomping, and pounded his fist into a wall. Repeating that they humiliated him and stripped him of his freedom of speech and dignity, before sending us out the room. Creeping in wanting to ask mom a question and saw daddy crying in mom's arms. Nobody knows how I wish there was something I could do to help.

"Is this the same journal your teacher gave you? Listen to those dance names. I can't stop laughing, trying to imagine you'll dance."

"Girl, we were jamming. Do you hear me? I could see my daddy now; man, did he love being the DJ—asking us for our requests and was happy to oblige."

"The book?"

"Nah... transferred the pages over from that old composition book to this one."

"Seem like things calmed down, with loads of dates missing."

"Very observant young lady. Life—too busy living, so I stopped writing here and there. When things got too crazy, I pick up the pen," shaking my head.

"I also stopped putting dates on everything. Not sure why?"

"Yeah, I noticed."

"Don't have a clue why."

"As beautiful as your parents were, hard to believe that they fought so much. Had to be hard on all of you."

"It was."

Come on now, pig ears—yuck! No way your mom threw them on him. Now that's crazy.

"Girl, it was. His howling afterwards was crazy and a sight to remember. I can laugh now, but it wasn't funny back then."

"Yes, it was, I hated the constant war between the two of them. If my parents had changed their ways, they may have lived longer and happier, yup I am sure of it."

"That is so true—you know, to fight your spouse is horrible. Being quick to anger is a huge sin."

We had been intense into the conversation; we didn't realize we were sitting in the dark. The light on her cell phone eased our eyes, bringing life back into the room.

"You had a troublesome childhood, dealing with so much, I don't think I could have done it," quivering from the thought of it.

"Well, it overwhelmed me about things back in the day. However, today I see how much my parents went through; times weren't easy. But you never know how strong you are until you have no other choice."

"What made you feel different about things?"

"Living life did it for me and focusing on their positive attributes. I know how hard it is to stay focused in this evil world and besides, whose family isn't dysfunctional today or back then? Many things we perceive are mere illusions of getting us wanting things we don't have. We went through some things, but overall I had parents—who tried."

"Yea, some of my friends' fathers don't even come around, heck I had a friend who didn't have either parent."

"My dad was a high school drop-out, but he was persistent in getting his GED, and he could talk to anyone no matter who much they rejected him or failure he experienced. He never quit. He taught me how to build a strong character and have the drive to be someone."

Chloe removed the prints of my parents; she had seen none of them before; the moment deemed overwhelming.

"Look at my great grandad walking with Martin Luther King—he's handsome."

"Yes, he was," shaking my head.

"He stood for things, even as he struggled with issues himself."

"They are good-looking," choking on tears.

"My- great-grandparents," whispering.

"My parents never showed me pictures of them," running her fingers across their faces.

"Well, my mother passed when I was a child; my father died while they were babies, so they had no connection with them."

"Look at my mother. Ain't she classy? She showed me how to be a woman, mother, and wife. All those things I hated doing as a kid, somehow it strengthened me."

"My mom couldn't cook and never showed me how."

"Who, Sarah? She can cook, I've seen her."

"Oh- Eh, she showed me how to make greens."

"Now that's something I didn't know she could do."

"Good for her, many women never learn how to care of a family, cooking, cleaning, and caring for kids."

"I see what you mean. I need to focus on the good in my childhood. Thanks, grandma."

"Yup, I had to look at my circumstances from a different angle, focus on the good. There is good in any situation."

"Yes, you're right. I never look at things that way—always so mad at my parents for everything."

"Well, Chloe, one thing for sure, you're grown now. Don't have to deal with the past anymore, forgive them and move on."

"I am thankful to be alive. What if I got shot that day? Wouldn't be here talking to you, young lady."

"Yes, I am thankful too."

"I have more pics to show you before you leave. I'll make certain you have copies of them," Chloe sat just glaring at me, dabbing the tears from our faces.

So full of emotion, harboring pain from lost moments. Never imagined she cared at all. I'll never forget this moment.

"My parents keeping me away made me so angry… mad at you both just the same, angry at everyone."

Looking at her with deepened eyes, understanding her pain and couldn't find the words to comfort her. The hurt wavered through us both. A statement off the back of an envelope caught my eye, "The LORD is close to the brokenhearted and saves those who are crushed in spirit, Psalms 34:18, NIV."

"Real talk, honey. All of it was just foolishness. Forgive us and pray we all forgive each other. I love you so much and don't want pain being part of our future."

Sniffling, working to pull her thoughts together, deemed unsuccessful. I rubbed her back as she had a wholehearted cried. Moments later, her red and swollen face showed her pain. I felt horrible, realizing how much family wars hurt more than the folks involved. It hurts everyone. She continued to struggle through her sniffles, holding back tears.

Gazing over the pictures, holding them to the mirror.

"I see the resemblance between you and my father."

She agreed, forcing a smile on her battered face.

"From the moment I laid eyes on you, I knew you belonged to us. You are just beautiful, and I am looking forward to spending this summer with you, young lady," slapping my legs, I changed the topic.

"I'm so tired; I will call it a night. Hoping your granddaddy isn't snoring like a mountain lion," we both snickered.

"Too late," his roars escaped the room.

"You know, honey, I'm in trouble, I may have to go into the spare room."

"Grandma," Chloe grabbed my hand.

"I want us to go horseback riding—let's do it."

"Girl, no way. I was a kid with those dreams. You know this old woman can't ride no dog on a horse," laughing till tears rolled.

"This aching body won't be riding on nobodies' horse."

"Grandma let's do it. I've never ridden either. I'll be our first time together."

"O-K-A-Y, don't you think we have a vast age difference and I am not 100% fit to be riding?" Chloe grabbed her phone, searching for older women riding horses.

"See, grandma, this 90-year-old woman is doing it."

"No way!" Half glancing at her phone.

"Are you scared?" Chloe beckoned.

"YES, I AM. I have no problem admitting it."

I was frantic in getting my words together, as she showed me more pictures.

"Let me see," grasping the phone as if it could change my mind.

My eyes grow in astonishment; it was terrific to see a woman my age riding horses. Coming to my senses, I smelled madness, and I appeared to be falling for it.

Walking around while she raved with excitement, she had my old bones cracking and rattling.

It seemed as if my body knew we were talking nonsense and began to ache.

"No way, I am not in shape to ride, period. Let alone a horse. Enough of this talk," pushing past her.

"Girl, are you trying to wipe out this elderly woman?"

I stared at the screen with a renewed and opened mind, noting seasoned women with serious ailments riding, so could I. Finding it hard to believe I still wanted to ride a horse. I'm sure this may be my last chance to ride a real, robust, and beautiful horse.

"Remember earlier when I mentioned riding a horse, how you lit up with delight? I saw you Grand—ma," in a comical voice.

"Let's decide tomorrow, okay? We tightened our grasp on each other hand," she held mines tighter.

"Please, grandma?"

"Tomorrow, child, I have to put some brainpower on this one."

She was looking into my eyes, begging for an answer. I speculated how much fun this could be, if I were brave. However, I released the thought as quick as it came.

"Okay, child goodnight. Enough of this foolishness, I'm off to bed."

Move Mountains

The prominence of the mountain tops provides serenity for the spoken truths. A realization I made while lying in bed witnessing the morning gloriously present itself—The sun rose. Birds chirped, harmonizing the incredible feeling of tranquil. The splendor of gratefulness of another day made me excited to get things started. I Grabbed my robe for warmth, snuggling deep into its comfort. I twisted the swiss knobs, opening the double doors, forging in the rays of light, careful not to wake Hosea I'd made my way onto the balcony, taking a much-needed stretch. To my surprise, the snow had covered the top of the distant sky-hugging rocky erections—I'd bet the tips of those mountains sat right in the middle of heaven itself. I stood motionless, studying them; a sigh escaped me as I took in all this before me. God's creations were so powerful; those mountains seemed to have been there for centuries. Gazing across the ridge, I felt blessed to see this day. I could ardor the highlands speaking to my soul in the complete stillness of the morning. I did not understand how to describe the feeling, nor did I know what they were saying, but it brought a calmness to my entire being. It was peaceful—the peace only God can bring upon one. O' Lord, I prayed. The brisk air filled my nostrils as though the freshness cleansed my soul, as it did the earth. It was mystical — soothing. The sounds of the wilderness broke the silence; a faint whisper to fear not the hollowing of what sounded like a distant wild animal—possibly a wolf? Maybe they sought refuge amongst caves of the massif? Leaning out over the side of the balcony, with my body pressing against the wooden rail. Looking downward, I went into deep thought, remembering the many mountains God had moved for me—mighty ones. The ones I just knew were invincible and could have defeated me; He crushed them right before my very eyes. I stood on the lower portion of the rail, as it was wide enough for me to place my feet between the spindles, gazing over the vast area of unlimited forestry with peeks of life speckled throughout. At that moment, I felt a sense of pure freedom. I had no fear — none.

My mind wandered as my prayer ended. Stepping down, I rethought the horse ride, as I hadn't informed Chloe whether I would do it. I wanted to so desperately, but as usual, I doubted myself. Damn it! Pounding my fist on the rail. Why do I always do such things to myself? I'll go to my grave with 'Here lies an old chicken' on my headstone, I was sure of it. Sick and tired of doing that very thing—tippy-toeing through life. I played every aspect as safe as possible. Please, Lord, free my mind to live the rest of my life doing all things possible. Many of my elderly friends just sit around, waiting for the moment. Me? I want to be in the moment — riding high and long, bringing my soul home with a mission completed — horseback riding in my future. I decided; I'm doing it.

A brisk wind chilled my face, forcing me to bundle deeper into my robe, encouraging me to return to my room. A snowflake frizzled past my face, landing on the backside of my hand, resembling glass with the most brilliant design. Then a small flurry occurred. Flakes danced around my face, most unusually holding my hands out to catch the tiny sparkles. The sun gave off an intense glare, with a single ray glowing towards me. My eyes squinted, noticing how strong it was. Funny how it all started after making my decision, leaving me with a sense of strength I yearned for it.

"Babe! What are you doing?" Hosea asked.

He startled me, almost knocking me into the chair propped against the wall. Grabbing the opening of my robe again, snuggling tighter, I laughed.

"I must look crazy, running around chasing snowflakes?" With a despairing look on my face, I noticed they'd stopped falling.

"You okay?" He asked.

"I am. Did you notice the way the flakes sparkled?"

"I noticed, never seen that before."

"Neither have I, it was rather odd."

Standing in the doorway with his arms crossed, propped against the door well. "Dancing like a ballerina, been standing here for a minute watching you. From the looks of it, you were enjoying yourself."

"I was, but glad you are here," I smiled.

"Come on out; I am having a blast."

"Look," I said.

I pulled him closer, pointing to the vast array of nature we saw before us.

"See the beautiful blue stream that glistening like precious gems scattered amongst the waves, an illusion from the sun hitting it."

We glimpsed a small fish jumping happily in and out of his home. The water was clear enough to see the greenery that fluttered at the bottom. Wrapping itself around the rocks that gracefully surrounding the stream.

"Fish—speaking on it, I'm ready to catch some of those babies."

"See the sign… No fishing," I said.

Hosea frowned, "Dang. Let me ask Chloe where the fishing spots are."

Returning, we noticed the other side of the cabin was a dense array of the prettiest red and yellow flowers.

"What flowers are those?" Hosea asked.

"Not for sure, haven't seen them before."

I tried to figure out what type they were but didn't work too hard. I'm just enjoying them. The colorful and plentiful array of butterflies dazzled me, flickering around them.

I hardly noticed that Hosea was dressed and begun preparing everyone coffee. Starving. Put on something for breakfast, while Chloe chattered away about going fishing.

"What y'all think about fishing?"

I shrugged, "We are going, but I don't think either of us remembers much about it," Hosea agreed.

She was so excited. Her eagerness was rubbing off on the both of us, I didn't care too much about fishing. Working on getting things together for breakfast, Chloe ran down to the local store to rent the fishing rods and bait. Hosea quickly gathered stuff we needed and began packing.

"Babe grab our jackets, please; it might get cool later," I yelled at him.

When he had finished, Hosea grabbed his jacket and headed to the door.

"I'll be back; I will check on Chloe."

"Okay, can you grab us a few snacks as well?" I called back to him.

"Sure thing, Babe!"

Finished breakfast; couldn't wait for everyone to come back. Shoot, I was starving! I imagined fishing; been such a long time since I had gone. Still had no desire to do anything that involved worms or bugs, but I will do it. I remembered when my grandma used to take us way back when I was about seven or eight. I had found it fascinating. Those good ole' days of spending time with grandma, and now I was doing it with my granddaughter. I'd only known her for a short time and already was in love with her. I prayed Chloe would treasure these moments the way I had when I spent time with mines.

"We're back, grandma, getting ready to load the car," yelled Chloe through the screen door.

"Okay, here I come."

Tussled myself from the accent chair, much too low for my comfort. Shuffling around, placing things I wanted to take by the door for them to grab. Rambled through the bags assuring we had the worms, minnows, and the tackle box. Good, everything is there; we are ready to go.

"Y'all come on in here and eat, now."

I packed some sandwiches and drinks for us for later. Hosea came in, hugging me from behind, swiping my hair to the side, stealing a gentle kiss on my neck. These stolen moments are always my favorite, as he seemed to know exactly when I needed them—taking a break from moving around, closing my eyes to enjoy his sweet caresses. Chloe rushed in, interrupting, looking for breakfast.

"Yuck! Y'all should go get a room—all that gushy stuff around me, making me miss my sweetie," she said.

Making funny faces, moving around full of blithesomeness. Chloe's attitude was purely contagious to us both. Not to mention the sunshine and warmth that filled the cabin. Had us all in a good mood. Hosea quickly moved behind me, pinching my rear end with much strength before jolting away. I hollered as he grinned, looking mischievous, like a young schoolboy feeling on girls in the schoolyard. I swatted him with the dishtowel, knowing well I was too stiff to do much more to him, forcing him to duck, merely missing the edge of the counter with his round head. He stumbled, losing his balance, leaving him grabbing Chloe as she worked loose, moving around tidying up the cabin before we left — humming her tunes from her headsets. He caught her off guard, almost falling to the floor herself. Hosea walked away, shaking his head.

"Girl, you sure unsteady, grandma bout to kill us both."

"Dang didn't know you still had fun at ya'll age."

"Yes, they can… you better be making sure you and Jeremai stay that way. You never get too old for good lovin'," he stated through his laughter.

We went back to our room to straighten things up a bit and to steal a moment to ourselves. Assuring we took our meds. Before heading out, Hosea picked up his shoes and socks from the floor, tossing them into the hamper.

Chloe yelled from the kitchen, "Don't do nothing in there to get yourselves in trouble," laughing hysterically.

That girl is merely crazy, I thought, laughing to myself, still rubbing my hinny from that notoriety of a pinch. Hosea continued checking out everything so we could leave on time, sneaking around as he would attack again.

"You haven't changed a bit, young man. Remember, you said you got in trouble for feeling on girls in elementary school?"

"Yup, I ain't changed. Got me a young girl, and I'm gonna feel on her butt until one of us is too old," gently smiling.

Pulling me towards him, he hugged me, letting me know he still loved me just like the first time he laid eyes on me. His words sent me into a fit of uncontrolled blushing.

"Oh, how sweet, but you could leave that pinching mess alone. My backside still sore, doggonit."

❧

Finally, we finished loading the car, and we were ready to go. The drive was only about 10 minutes. Still, we loaded the GPS to be safe. Chloe cleaned her sunglasses and pulling her hair into a ponytail, while Hosea secured the trunk. Hosea gabbled on about some guys he met at the tackle shop and was hoping to see them out fishing today.

"Yeah, they said trout were jumping in full force today."

I'm relaxed, enjoying a nice swig of water. Hearing that was a massive disappointment to me, my intentions on having bass. Oh *well, let's see.* Hosea spent no time starting to brag about what he had caught in the past. Far back as I could remember, I was sure I'd never seen him catch a thing. We sat back, listening to Hosea go on and on, just bragging. Still, I held high hopes of eating some good ole bass tonight, if I had to buy some. As we drove down to the lake, I had Chloe open the rooftop. I was sitting in the back this time, letting Hosea help her with directions to Rose Canyon Lake. Hosea took a break from his bragging rights to let us know it would be about five minutes until we arrived. Listened to him chattering on, I looked up through the rooftop opening; the sky was clear blue, with not a cloud in sight. The weather was a little warm for my liking—I just saw snowflakes this morning, now I am about to come out of my clothes.

In no time, we were there. It was a beautiful spot to sit and relax, with a vast array of forestry around to give off a pleasant piney scent. Piercing through the trees, I noticed quite a few were dying or had died. It seemed peculiar to me what happened; it didn't look healthy. The water was beautiful though — calm and clear, you could faintly see the fish swimming around. Locating a picnic table was difficult. Must have been bug season, because bugs loitered on every table. Merely disrespectful to the visitors, almost forcing us to go back for bug spray. Hosea, being an animal- bug lover, gently swiped them to the ground, before fluffy the tablecloth across the table.

"We ain't killing no bugs today, let them live and enjoy this day, too," he chuckled.

At the moment, I felt like spraying him too.

However, we got everything unpacked, set up, and were eager to grab those fish. Passing out the rods, Chloe didn't like the color of her rod—she traded me. She walked away, amused like she had won a bet, glowing as she became familiar with her purple rod. Secretly I wanted the purple one but refused to act like a child over a color. I had an orange one that seemed to shimmer while I played with it. Hosea walks over with his silver rod, looking discontent.

"I don't want this rod. Where is the orange one?" he asked.

"Here you go. Y'all know the color doesn't make the rod work any better, right?" annoyingly responding.

"Nope, but I got the best lookin' one," Hosea said.

Everyone was content, but me. I hated my color but took my own advice. Looking at the container of worms, I closed my eyes — swallowed hard; I reached in, gripping a jiggly one. I just loathe worms, making me wonder why fish like them when they live in the dirt and the other lives in water? Odd. Hooking my worm was not my favorite thing to do. Back when my grandma did this for me. Makin me even more determined to get this nasty-looking creature on the hook myself, even if it killed me. Swearing not to throw up and let a worm put me to shame. Working quickly, I did it; I got it on superbly.

"Whew, I got past the worst part of this trip," taking a break.

Chloe looked at me, puzzled, "Didn't you used to pick up caterpillars when you were a kid?"

"Um, I scooped them up with the shovel for your information, young lady."

"Grandma, you turned into a big girl."

"I don't care what you say."

Chloe hooked hers. I began looking around for Hosea; when I spotted him, I couldn't help but laugh, shaking my head.

"Look at your granddad over there."

Chloe squinted hard.

"Can you make out what he's doing?"

"Nope. He's so busy trying to be sneaky; he didn't notice we already baited our hooks."

"Oh—here he comes!" She bolted.

We both scrambled to make it look like we knew what we were doing and hadn't been watching him. We struggled to cast our lines; I wanted so badly to do it on my own. Hosea pulled out of his newly made tackle box, something he called his secret weapon, which guarantees to bring us dinner, he bragged.

"Who were you over there talking to?" I asked.

"Remember those nice fellas I ran into earlier; they said if we needed anything, just holler. Cool group of guys," giving me a side eye and grinned.

"While y'all over here worrying about what I'm doing, dinner will arrive soon."

Scurrying around getting his rod ready, he was so busy ducking and hiding from us, struggling to get his secret weapon on the hook. As cautious as he was, I peeked over his shoulder to see his big rubbery looking wasp. Something smelled, I knew it wasn't him; it had to be that thing. Peering over his shoulder again, I sniffed harder, found the putrid smell to be his bait — I didn't like it. Picking up trash around the area, I ran across the wrapper for his so-called secret weapon. Vibrant claims to catch some of the biggest fish without the use of worms.

Holding the wrapper, I snapped, "Where're mines?"

"What you mean muggin' me for?"

"Since when do you buy stuff without sharing?"

He shrugged, looking a little sheepish.

"Today… I bought you something—worms. I bought myself a little extra something on the side. If you wanted something special, you could have got it."

"Humph!"

I glared at him before walking away with a slight attitude. I just threw my hands up at him, giving up any idea of winning this fight with him. It was senseless; he'd only aggravate me even more. He saw he was irritating me, and he laughed because it just tickled him to death.

"Y'all say you know how to fish; I'll let you both do what you do and let me do me."

Ferociously laughing while he fumbled around with the smelly bug-looking thing he had as his bait. He must have gone over there to let the guys help him with it. Neither of us said anything; I just let it go.

"Men! Can't live with them or without them."

"I don't know about that; you and granddad look like you can't live without each other."

"Girl, bye…"

Silence filled the air.

"He still makes me sick."

Tired of waiting, I cast my rod. Hosea came over to show me how to do it; I resisted his help—a few tugs aligned me in the perfect position for him to get a firm hold.

He held me tight, "sexy; I like it," I said.

I could feel his breath on my neck, making me relax, getting comfortable in his arms.

He whispered in my ear, "Relax Babe, let me move your body."

Well, we tried it a few times but didn't get the hang of it. I needed a break. So, Hosea told Chloe he would help her. Before Hosea could get started, the guys he met earlier showed up.

"No, no, no, Hosea, you're doing it all wrong," he exclaimed from afar. Moving closer, he beckoned for the rod.

"Well, show us how to do it, Mr. Fisherman."

"Hello, I am Matea, and this is Chloe, our granddaughter," shaking his hand.

His hands seemed sweaty and robust. I felt like he had broken a bone when he released my hand. He smiled wide, taking off his hat, viewing the sky like the rugged type.

"Nice to meet you ladies, we met Hosea earlier — nice fella."

He scurried, securing the rod from falling. "I'm Peter, but please call me Fisherman."

"Fisherman?"

"Yes, I enjoy helping people fish, often you'll find me out here doing just what I am doing today—enjoying the company of cool folks."

"We sure need help — today, hopefully you can bring us a bit of luck. You hear that, Hosea?"

"My hopes as well, Ms. Matea."

"Matea, please."

"That's a cool way to meet new people," Chloe chimed in.

"Nice to meet you," he shook her hand.

Noted Chloe waited for him to move away, found her wiping her hands off on her jeans. The look on her face was worth a million dollars. I felt the same way after he shook mines, yet it wasn't very cordial to us. Hands clammy and sweaty, not to mention broken bones after the tight handshake. He seemed like a nice guy though, very knowledgeable on fishing and had no problems sharing information with us. He was God sent; I figured we'd be out here all day trying to get these rods set up right. Using Chloe's rod as an example, he gave way to showing us the correct way to cast the rods. A few flicks of the rods… we both figured it out, watching him secure our poles. We were all set.

"Thank you," I said.

"You're welcome, anytime," Fisherman responded.

"Nice to meet you both," he grinned warmly at the two of us. Looking hard at Chloe, she smiled, revealing her shyness.

"Well, I must go now; I got my nets in the water, with my buddies over there watching it."

"Nets?"

"Oh — yes, nets. We avoid any bottom dweller, not very good for ya, mate."

"Bottom dwellers… never mind, I understand," Chloe stated with a weird look on her face.

"Alrighty, if you need anything, just holler. Hey, maybe later you all can stop by our camp area for grilled fish? Fresh and nicely seasoned, I can cook some mean dishes."

"Well, keep that in mind, sounds great."

Fisherman walked off, stopping to chat with Hosea. He had already cast his rod. Looked around at all of our poles, it seems like we had spent half our day getting our rods together. It didn't matter, though; it wasn't like we had missed out on anything. Chloe and Hosea had a false alarm on their rods again. Hosea had everyone stand back on my turn, I didn't blame him. I knew my fishing skills were not the greatest. However, with only one swing, my eyes followed until it splashed into a promising spot. Brimming with pride, I rested my rod in the lock and finally sat

❧

The day drifted away slowly as we enjoyed relaxing, fishing, and eating our lunch. I rustled in our bags, finding a few magazines and some puzzles. Setting the table for lunch forced me to rethink the bugs I saw earlier. Instead, we ate our food from our laps. Chloe claimed not to be afraid of any bugs until one walked right up to her plate, scouting for food. Soon after she was sitting next to us like somebody with some sense, plate in lap, bopping to her tunes on her headset. Bobbing my head, "Not bad." I could listen to her tunes as she had it loud as ever. I hadn't thought of what kind of music she enjoyed; I was fond of her sharing it with me. Most young folks today listen to all that rap and cussing. Never appealed to me. The song sounded like a Christian upbeat group; I've never heard it before. It would be nice if she played it in the car on the way back so Hosea could hear. Looking out over the water, it was breath-taking. The sun died down, dropping the temperature down about 15 degrees. I stopped sweating like I was earlier, but still, we were all guzzling water like thirsty vultures.

We'd had a few bites along the way but threw them back in. They were all too small to keep. Chloe and I flicked through magazines, chatting over the things we liked. Her taste differed from mines, but both of us had discerning palates. I ravished over the sophisticated style while she haggled over sportswear. We both agreed on the sweetest shoe candies and purses. We both loved our shoes and handbags, leaving her teasing me over my small feet. While I felt hers were much like my Darcy doll's feet.

"How you get such big feet when you are not that tall?"

"Size 9 ½ is not that big grandma."

"I wear a 5 ½, so I figure I'm just not used to picking up such big woman's shoes as I do now — all over the place, young lady."

"Grandma, are you saying I'm a shoe slob?"

"If the title fits my precious lady…"

"Okay, I'll pick up my shoes. Jeremai says the same thing."

"He calls you shoe slob too?"

"Not exactly, but he complains— big time."

"It is… maybe we can find a group for recovering shoe slobs; I'll join you—you know, for support."

We laughed so hard; my belly ached like my sandwich was doing cartwheels and somersaults. Thinking Hosea was asleep; he added his two cents to the conversation. "Don't let your grandma fool you over there talking all that smack. She is the queen shoe slob. I made her throw out about thirty pairs of shoes last year. She needs to be head of that meeting or seminar ya'lls over there talking about."

I threw a ball of paper at him, smacking him dead in the head, with a piece of candy added in the middle for the extra punch. He didn't budge.

"So, what," he muzzled in a lazy, froggy voice.

Then I threw a handful of pumpkin seeds at him, imposing a response.

"Woman, you don't want me to go back to my school days to deal with ya? Do ya? It won't be pretty," giving off a definite look of trouble.

"You don't scare me."

Knowing full well he could be a mess, remembering earlier today—the pinch. My backside was still feeling the pain from the mind maddening experience. He released his seat to check on the juggling fishing rod. The fishing wire tugged in and out of the calm waters. Hosea pulled his reel in to find his rubbery bug — gone, nothing to show for it except the dangling hook. He stood there, scratching his head in disbelief, then went back into his tackle box to get another crazy looking bait. Hosea cast his reel out, pushing his dead body weight back into his seat — disgusted. He didn't have much to say after losing his bait. The look of defeat lingered on his face and he no longer wanted to fish. The sun made its final grand appearance; it was harsh, even more than earlier. I could tell we were all getting tired. No need of asking, Chloe was up packing our bags and totes. Hosea glanced at her, asking me if I was ready, joining her in her efforts. Chloe showed her disappointment, not to mention an attitude. Flinging things in the bag, jerky movements, and a potty face intensified her mood. Rendering to kicking dirt around the half-dead grass with a vengeance. I was not happy myself but refused to give in to disappointment. Hosea walked around, picking up the trash; he said nothing at all. However, his body language said it all without uttering a word.

Grabbing his rod, he pulled it in. Something snatched his rod back, forcing his limp body to jerk backward. He flung himself onto the rail with full force. He groaned in sheer pain, before witnessing his reel soar across the water.

"Help, somebody — help," he yelled with widened eyes.

He struggled with his words, pushing past his pain. The sound of his strained voice caught our attention soon after. Quickly pulling himself together, he stood firm, trying to gain control of the reel.

"I think I got something. Oh, my side," Hosea moaned.

"Hey, y'all — help, before it gets loose or snatches me away."

Sweat poured down his face faster than a rainstorm as he tugged the rod back and forth. Chloe ran over, helping him while I grabbed the net, stiff and aching. I was of no use to them, and I instantly felt shamed. Hosea's friends, Luke and Peter, came running over to see what was going on, having heard him frantically yelling. They relieved me by helping.

"Holy smokes… looks like a bloody huge one!" Luke called out.

Peter instructed Chloe to keep helping Hosea as he grabbed the net and went dashing into the water.

He yelled, "be careful not to break the line. Pull and walk back slowly," he repeated himself.

Treading the water as he spotted the fish, "pull," he yelled.

Hosea pulled hard with Chloe's help. Finally, the fish leaped clear out of the water, doing a full flip. He fanned his body in a slow wave with his tail flopping side to side. His scales glistened as iridescent gems from the sun rays that cascaded down his sides and flickered off the tail. The waters dotted the air as fallen drops of crystals landed back into the clear waters in which he came. Peter held his hand in mid-air for Hosea and Chloe to wait. Not a soul breathed. Eyes wondered the waters until the line shot off with great speed.

Peter yelled, "reel him in and pull hard."

"Wow, he's grand," I said, as my eyes widened in genuine surprise.

Luke appeared and glanced a gigantic smile at me before diving into in. I squinted, noting his impeccable swimming skills as he graced each stroke emerging alongside Peter. The fish swam fiercely as they worked to contain him with the net as they continued tugging at the line. I stood with my hands over my mouth and eyes glued. A thought came to me: Look at you, loser, can't even help catch a fish sitting on the sideline with your sickly self. What good are you? Who needs your worthless self? It saddened me for a moment. I felt less than. Knowing who was behind that nasty thought; surprised me that I let it linger on.

"We can't, just a minute."

He held the net steady and stood still. Breathing slowly, as he would loss his breath. We watched without blinking and snap, the fish flopped and plopped right in. Taking significant efforts to bring him to the shore even while netted, Hosea kept reeling inward till they met face to face. It took all of them to bring him in.

"Ya'll got a run for your reward—ha," I exclaimed.

"What a whale of a fish," Peter spoke.

Hosea yelled, "We gon' eat right tonight," rubbing his hands together.

"Wonder how much he weighs, grandpa?"

"I don't know, but we shall soon see," holding the bucket, toting it up and downwards.

"Feels about fifteen pounds. Well, know when they weigh it over at the local store."

"Hey, anybody feel that?" Chloe asked.

"What are you feeling?" Hosea asked.

"Raindrops?"

A flash of rain consumed us out of the blue, from sunny to sudden downpour before he could answer. The guys disappeared, running off to their site. We ran around in disarray as we parked farther away. Chloe ripped the tablecloth and placed it over her head, yelling for us to join her. The drops were heavy, like they were pellets instead of rain. Me and Hosea ran around like chickens with our heads cut off in disbelief, viewing the guys as they waved their arms for us to join them. Snatching our important belongs, we sought shelter in their minivan. We could barely see to make it to the van. All of us smashed in, making it feel as if they stuffed us in a sardine can. The keys were in Peter's pocket at their campsite, leaving us with no air. Even bits of hail fell, banging on the outside like it was trying to force entry. It was hot and musty, not sure who contributed the funky smell, but was thankful to get out that crazy downpour. We needed fresh air, big time. All the excitement of catching the fish had taken over any tired feeling, or pain Hosea may have had, but soon realized the feelings reappeared. He ran like a champ but mentioned his side once we settled down and I was still struggling with the negative thoughts laid on my mind. Not to bring up, I was in dreadful pain. The storm lasted 25 good minutes. Hosea pulled out a cigar, stretching it across his nostrils. The entire crew gave him a look which forced him to put it back in his pocket. I realized Chloe and I would never hear the end of this one. The rest of the gang that came with Peter and Luke joined us, bringing some wine and music to celebrate the big catch. They resembled modern-day hippies, spending their days spreading the word and fishing. Not a care in the world seemed to bother them, just appeared happily free and alive. I was proud of my honey, even though his sneaky butt had bought a unique tackle to make it happen. Through all the excitement, I detected something fantastic, urging me to wail out.

"Look, everybody," I pointed towards the sky. "A double rainbow."

Hosea removed his Detroit hat, scratching his head, "Well, I'll be, it's the full double rainbow, never encountered one like this before."

"The colors are so vibrant in hue," I said.

We all stood in disbelief, thanking God for this moment; it was so beautiful. I was in awe, wanting to drop to my knees, but the pain of my hips stopped me. Witnessing one of God's most significant phenomena only happens ever, I know the things he has said concerning me in his word. This reminded me how wrong that thought placed on my mind was wrong. Thank you, Lord, for showing me your ways and telling how worthy I am even in my sickness. The devil was at it again. Your word ran him away. As we stood in silence, the colors faded away. No one spoke a word for minutes after. Peter dropped to his knees, praying. Tears ran down my face, while others just stood watching, till it was nothing left. An experience I wouldn't trade for anything.

"Well now, we can scratch off seeing a double rainbow off our bucket list fellas," I said.

"Yea, I don't have a list, but I'll never forget it," Hosea said.

"Do anyone know the meaning of rainbows?" Looking around for someone to answer.

"Luck? Or a pot of gold? We will be doubly rich?" Chloe guessed.

I wiped the last of the tears from my eyes, grabbing my phone, trying to get the best picture possible before it completely faded into our memory.

"No, it means God's grace. A rainbow first appeared to Noah after the great flood. It was a promise to never have a flood ending humankind again." Peter responded.

"That's very interesting, I learned something new today." Chloe said.

"It was so unbelievably beautiful; I won't soon forget myself. Kind of sad to see it go," Luke said.

Once the excitement had died down, we focused our attention back to the famous fish. The mood of the evening changed. Seems like we all had a distinct feeling of being blessed. Luke grabbed the fish by his tail and flipped it to the side. We got us a bass. Peter worked to force his body into the bucket with no avail, Peter twisted the hook out of his mouth along with Hosea's bait still attached, throwing it to the side and sloshed him with ice. Smiling because I had gotten just what I'd wanted: some good ole bass. Hosea was right; we are gon' eat good tonight, rubbed my hands together ready for dinner. Hosea turned to Luke.

"Thanks, man, couldn't have done it without you or Peter."

"You would have been fine; you just about had it when we arrived," Luke said.

"Naw man, listen, you ran into the water with the net and did your thang, ya feel me?"

"Yea mate, but that's what we do."

"You and Peter are the reason those fish are sitting there. Now, come on, dude, you know ya'll bad with those fishing skills of yours."

Hosea shook him playfully by his shoulders, then stopped laughing and contemplated him.

"Hey — come on over to the store with us, get it weighed, I'll have it cut up and divided. No way can we eat all this."

"No, I wasn't planning on it, sir, but we appreciate the offer."

Hosea looked Luke in his eyes.

"It's OUR fish—plus we shared our double rainbow with you… man, you know you got to—."

Luke stood in silence for a minute, considering it. He looked around at all of us, giving into a bright smile, "Okay, man, we'll meet you up there."

"For sure?" Looking him square in his eyes, "Thanks," Hosea said.

"Yeah, man, let us gather our things," shaking his head, "We'll be there."

❧

We didn't have much to shove into the car, and we were off, the fish being the biggest item. Quickly, Hosea drove out to the local store, as Chloe sat in the back watching the fish and playing with the ice. He was feeling good; you could tell, driving all straight and erect—privileged. His giant being left the car and moseyed into the store. Walking around with his chest stuck out, bragging the entire time we exhibited the store. We had no choice but to listen and gag, as he kept flexing his droopy muscles like he always does when he beat me. He was so happy at this moment; I never wanted it to end. It had been a long time since I had seen him this happy. I pulled out my little notebook and scratched fishing and rare rainbows off my bucket list. I knew it was a small wish to go fishing, but we would never forget the memory we gained today. The guys arrived at the store, assisting Hosea with getting the bucket inside. The owner looked at Hosea with deep-set eyes.

"You got yourself a big one, buddy," rendering a toothless grin.

He hefted up the bass, taking it to the scale. Eagerly, we looked on, waiting to hear how much it weighed. The store owner turned with a smile on his face.

"You got yourself a fifteen-pound, twenty-two-inch-long bass. Before we stake him for you, we usually take pictures of the owners. Whose bass is it?"

At once, we pointed to Hosea.

"Oh, no — It's congrats to all of us!" Hosea said.

"Mighty good-looking fish you all have here, rare to see one this big around here." the clerk stated.

"Thank you, sir, but I can't take all the recognition for it. It's all of ours."

Luke, Peter, and Hosea seemed like their friendship had become a sealed deal, promising to keep in touch. We shook hands and hugged before departing.

❧

We made our fire before the sun went down. The fish was freshly seasoned and placed in a skillet, watching the smoke linger from the fire. The crackles that invaded the air, the fire danced, filling the space with comforting heat. Chloe swiftly flipped the bass with the bent spatula, placing butter planks neatly to melt into the meaty flesh, making it flaky in no time. The butter is homemade here, churned at the local store. It rolled over the fillets, looking like golden tears running down the sides of the grilled fish. Next, we set up the small fryer, as I grumbled the entire time. I try hard to keep my man healthy and it falls on deaf ears. Thankfully, the store loaned out the fryer so Hosea could have his deep-fried cholesterol building favorite foods. Deep down I rightfully love the wonders of fried anything, but in moderation. The sizzle of fresh grease was the best sound to black folk ears, especially during Sunday dinners. I wasn't happy about him having all that grease, but the champ gets what he wants. I cut the bass into small pieces, drudging the filets in the sunny colored speckled cornmeal, assuring an even coat. Slowly, each piece made its way into the hot oil — sizzled to a crispy finish. In no time, we were eating 'high on the hog' as grandma would say. It was delicious, crunchy and crusted into a golden brown with a nice shimmer of speckled grease. My fish was flaky and tender, along with grilled vegetables and potatoes made our meal complete. I sent an invitation to our neighbors — they accepted. Minutes later, their appearance delighted us, and a bottle of wine accompanied them. Meeting them after the bear scare was a sheer pleasure, as before we all enjoyed each other's company. The orange glares of the sun as it molted down the earth, encrusted the clouds as it lowered, escorting in the stars. The evening with a remarkable as I sat folded in my chair, wrapped in the warmth of my blanket. Chloe hugged me from behind, silently wishing her to stop as my muscles cried. I had huge hopes of being pain free one day and today proved to be the day. She laid her head on my shoulder, laughing at the corny jokes filled the night's air.

"Grandma look at the stars."

I looked up, following her gaze. "They were so brightly dancing across the sky."

"Grandma, that one over there is just for you, the biggest and brightest one."

Pulling out her phone, she took a picture of us with the stargazed backdrop. I tugged at her arm and reminded her to make sure I got a copy.

"You know, it's something special about me and those stars. Your Granddad showed me the stars back in the day when we were younger; I'll never forget it, and now I have you showing me. Thank you."

Giving into relaxing in my stadium chair, I stole a moment just studying him. I love hearing him talk, so smart and smooth with his words. How does he know so much? After all these years I've failed to figure it out and yet it enlightens me. I caught him staring back at me and I twinkled my fingers towards him, and he sent a kiss in return. After laughing till we were sore, Hosea called it a night. The neighbors went home, and Chloe and I spent a moment alone. We sat down next to the fire pit to read a portion of my journal as Hosea tidied up the kitchen area.

September-1963 ✿ Dear diary, dad has been in a horrible mood for the last couple of weeks. His argument of how unsafe he felt walking in the park the other day and the lack of care mom received when she went to the doctor. Her argument was moving to a better neighborhood and daddies' inability to maintain a job. They quarreled more than they usually, closer to everyday now. Today I'm sad. Daddy just dragged mom's clear across the floor right past me as I washed dishes standing on a chair towards the basement staircase, merely knocking me straight to the floor, as dad got a good grip on mom, dragging her towards the stairway. I wanted to help her. Pondering it, as I slowly washed a knife — I did the unimaginable. I took that knife, pulling it as a weapon on my daddy. I gripped it steady, ordering him to leave her alone, or I would kill him. Determined not to back down. As it didn't seem like an option. Mixed feelings of love and fear invaded me, not sure which one spoke to me most. Confused and insecure in my convictions, all I wanted was for him to stop. He talked me down to giving him the knife, and I gave in. I felt defeated. I got my behind whooped, leaving my heart ripped to pieces. Hey, no need to punish me; I'd already regretted it.

September-1963 ✿ Dear diary, my parents' quarrel awakened me last night. I listened. I overheard my dad say he would kill my mom if she moved. My eyes widened in fear. Soon after, a gun went off. Multiple shots rang loud, I couldn't imagine what I was about to see. I gasped and abruptly ran to their bedroom door, noting the bullet hole in the floor close to her. She remained standing, lifeless and naked… sobbing. She looked okay, minus the tears and the intense fear on her face. Yet, she just stood. He noticed me and right away, demanded I go back to my room, as he hid the gun under the bed. I fell to my knees at the crack of the door, refusing to move. Please don't die, mommy, I whispered to myself. Fear prevented me from saying anything out loud; I choked my words into my stomach. I prayed. We were all concerned about their erratic behaviors. Nothing stopped their appetite for war. The WAR… THE WAR! I forced myself to look past the black eye she had this morning and her daunting mood. I knew what she had been through. Finally, I gathered the nerve asking her why she stayed? Why you let him treat you like this? She made every excuse before cutting her off. *'I don't want you to keep fighting with Daddy. Can we leave? Please?'* She smiled at me. Reminding me how much I loved her smile, but I didn't today. I felt pity for her as her reply was swift, '*stay out of grown folks' business.*

October- 1963 ✿ Dear diary, today Mom pulled up in a shiny 1953 burgundy Mercury Monterey, loaded with all her house plants, it's been two weeks since our talk. Reaching over rolling down the windows yelling for us to get in, we're leaving your Daddy, she hollered. Music blaring with her bouncing up and down. A cigarette in her mouth, angled to the side, talking out the other side and chewing gum while driving. She looked so happy today, taking a break to flick her cigarette. I imagined this to be the best day of my life. Feet dangling, feeling more significant than ever, I made a difference. She listened to me. No more fighting, arguing, or fear. Freedom felt terrific as we enjoyed the music with her. We stayed with some of her friends; it was cool in the beginning, then four kids abruptly became too much, we had to leave. We moved so many times, forcing me to grow up over-night, becoming her right- hand girl. It wasn't a job I signed up to do, but it happened. I was a youngster myself, keeping children, ages seven, five, and three. Still getting treated like a kid but forced to have grown-up responsibilities. We seemed to have moved every couple of weeks until we ended up homeless. Living at the park or the drive-in when we could afford it. Wiping my backside with leaves while living at the local park was the very day, I regretted leaving my dad. The day I encouraged her to leave him was the biggest mistake I ever made, and it bore deep into my soul. Felt being homeless was my fault. We had nothing!

January- 1963 ✿ Dear diary, Finally, mom found us a new home. Even though we were happy to have a place to stay, no home felt the same as the big white house we once had. It was exhausting taking care of the children while she worked long hours and hung out. Daddy came by often demanding to have her back; she wasn't feeling it. Turning him down, he would become irate, making his visits like the olden days of fighting. He became angry, often threatening her. We moved again, but this time we had relatives who lived close and were my age. I continued to care for my siblings but gained a bit of freedom to go places on my own. Being a kid again was priceless. Freedom tasted so good; I craved more. Having a sample of a normal childhood sparked a rebellion in me quickly. We moved so many times beforehand, I never established friendships, making this the best place I ever lived. I was in 7th grade. She noticed I was staying away from home more often, asking me questions about my friends. Tired of keeping tabs on me, she increased my responsibilities to keep me home more. None of my buddies had the same obligations; so, they would stop inviting me to hang out. I became rebellious, wanting to be a kid.

❧

Closing the journal, she grabbed my hand.

"Grandma, I am so sorry that happened to you," she sighed.

"Girl, it was a long ago... don't be."

"You are a survivor."

"No, I am a forgiver."

"But they passed away, right? Were you able to—"

"Well yeah, they did. I didn't need them to forgive. During my time of healing, I learned to love them for who they were, not who I wanted them to be. Expectations at its finest can set us up for failure, so I mourned the fact that I would never have the parents I perceived to be best for me and loved them for who they were. Because of their death, I found closure for all the childhood mishaps. Writing everything on paper and set it ablaze. It was for me to heal, not them and it felt good."

"Was it a painful process? I mean you accepting them for the way they were?"

"It was. Figuring this out, they both had passed. Mourning them in two ways, their deaths and letting go of expectations. They are not the only ones I had to experience this with. I also had to go through it with my siblings. Past and current painful relationships continue hurt as long as you hold on to expectations. Letting go allows you to be free to love people right where they are."

"Ok, I get it, but I don't think I can."

"Who do you need to forgive? I believe you mentioned forgiving before, is it something you want help with?"

Chloe looked away, "no—I'm fine. Seriously, let's change the topic… ok?"

"Ok, let me say this and I am done. It took me a long time to realize that these experiences didn't happen to me, but for me. I grew stronger each time I went through something, so I can have this very moment to inform you everything that caused you pain, will shape you into the person you're becoming if you learn from it and forgive. Then leave it there, period."

"Humph. I don't know, I'll think it over. Talk about family dysfunction at its finest."

"Family disfunction is a serious disease in this world. It was back then. It is today and will continue on."

"So sad."

"But joy comes from freedom, and the future always holds promises of hope. That's why it's important to let go. Sometimes we cause our own pain by holding on to what was. Whatever is hurting you, it is your job to figure it out. Keep waiting for folks to change and make you feel better—hm, good luck with that."

She chuckled, "sounds like throwing yourself under a bus and waiting for the other person to get hurt?"

"Well—yeah. Funny way for putting it."

"I wish they offered classes on how to be a parent. It would end a lot of messiness."

"It's called the Bible. If folks pick it up and work it, they'd have all the answers they need."

Chloe's grip on my hand tightened, "I had a hard life too."

"Really?"

"Don't care to talk on it, ok?"

"It's fine with me."

"Thanks, guessing I'm still hurt over my past, too painful bringing up old stuff."

"Truly, I understand. Carrying pain from my past was interesting. I put more hurt-on top of hurt until I was bedridden with what they now say is fibromyalgia and it's not pretty."

"I have a friend with it, nobody believes her pain."

"Do you?"

"I don't know… seems as if she's always hurting and not going places because of it, I guess I just quit trying to do stuff with her."

"That sounds right. Many people feel the same way."

"I know it's tough."

I shook my head, looking at her, "accumulating old hurts only weighed you down. Let forgiving be a part of your everyday life."

"Yeah, I know grandma, I've had this major thing happen to me and I don't think I've ever thought I could forgive it."

Draping her hands across the sofa, she appeared to be in deep thought. The room filled with silence.

"Grandma, did you think it was weird that those guys had biblical names today?"

"Girl, yes, I laughed. I did. We had much fun, but those sandals they sported and musty armpits. Whew."

"Yes, the musty smell was horrible, but they were really cool peeps."

Settling into my seat, bustling around striking up much needed warmth. I rubbed my arms. I prayed. Short, but powerful. I needed wisdom at the moment. I sensed something weighed on her spirit. Sometimes we give off the perception of happiness to hide hurt—I saw that in her. Not just the fact that she missed out on having us in her life, but something else. Just couldn't place my finger on it. Not sure what—nor was I going to meddle in someone else's affairs, but He can. And I put Him right on the job.

"Thanks grandma, maybe one day I could get that strong and forgive."

"You can — pray. You may think some things are unforgivable, but you will find the strength as soon as you see the rewards of freedom."

Giving her a look over my spectacles, "It ain't worth it girl, the taste of holding on to mess is like you eating rotten food, while they eat good?"

"Rotten food?" she chuckled. "I agree, I need to work on forgiveness."

"Please do, because it has sent many folks to their grave early because of it. Hurt and physical pain are monsters one should never tackle alone — but Jesus."

"I will."

"Hey, Chloe, start today. We never know when we will take our last breath."

"Come on enough talking, it's bedtime," Hosea said.

"I know—"

She leaned her head on my shoulder.

"Old memories can keep me entertained for days," putting my arm around her.

Hosea peeped his head out, "Woman, you coming to bed or not?"
"Goodnight Chloe."

❧

The next morning, we awakened to a full breakfast brought to us by Chloe. Turned to the news, focusing on a riot on Pelkey Ave. The newscaster's outlandish hairdo fully had attention over what she was blubbering. Resembling a lopsided beehive, not to mention her clothes looked like she got them from her grandma's closet. Chloe rolled her eyes towards me, as an angry black woman jumped to the stage with a huge multicolored afro, fist balled into a ratchet knot with a fierce look of discontent. I haven't seen this amount of sincerity in a long time. She had all of our undivided attention. Inequality and human rights were the center of the chaos, modern warfare. "Are we too hasty to fight?" she yelled.

"No, were not!"

"What do we say?"

"We're fed up!"

"What shall we do?"

"Fight, fight, fight!" The crowd roared.

A man walked by carrying a bullhorn. She grabbed it and stood slowly, scanning the crowd. She gasped for air and continued her stance. The crowd fell silent. She released the built-up courage and hollered with ferocity, "when will the war end?" the crowd roared once more.

Signs flew like flags from around the world, waving sideways, up and down with demands of fair treatment. Signs spoke louder than words in demanding equal healthcare, jobs based on our abilities, save our babies, free our black men, stop police brutality on minorities. The police stood on the other side, ready to take away their rights of being heard. Someone raised a cosmic sign with a fist drawn on it, along with the peace symbol. Shoving it uprising for our people. The music of tired voices being heard, feet stomping, signs flopping, and arms waving rang through the air. Female forces, embracing brilliant fighting tactics at its finest, while maintaining peace.

Leadership harnessed to back down one last time, while officers dropped their gas mask in place one by one. They stood ready as the

Sergeants arm fell. Gas filled the air. Folks hopelessly ran in disarray for relief, as the second attack presented itself of gushing hard forces of water appeared as tidal waves clearing the street like grains of sand being washed to the shore. We trembled lest thy defeat as the arrest began. The news anchorman spoke quickly as he feared for his life. He grabbed a young lady's arm as she ran by. Excuse me, do you feel history is repeating itself? Blood matted her natural curls, as the extra ran down her face mingled with sweat. Seconds of profound whimpers holding unreleased tears, "yes, yes sir, I do," she shivered.

"Do you think—" the reporter said.

"Black victorious woman unites," she yelled.

As she ran away with police on her smoking heels, falling to the ground, arms yanked back with chains slapped across her wrist and drugged to the side. She wailed, embodied in sheer pain. I turned the news off and sighed. "Please sweet Jesus, help them. Please, Lord, lay hands on my people with blessings of strength and protection only you can give. War when it should be love.

"Grandma, what do you think about this?"

"I think folks should stop trying to make people feel their pain and be about change."

"What you mean?"

"Just like we can't make people love us, we can't make other races care about us."

"Dang, that's true."

"We should quietly come together and be about the change. Then emerge with collectiveness and take our stance on a better life. Stop expecting others to give a hoot until we become a threat of taking back what belongs to us. Let's come together with our dollars and buy up property, banks, and other things we need."

"When will that happen?"

"Never."

"You and your daddy used to be right out there wit' em. Eh, now you see things differently?"

"I do. I feel we can show them over talking too much and getting nothing done, but beat up. Sorry, but I am too unhealthy to experience one lick."

Another news flash and it didn't look good. We're facing a monsoon.

"Babe, do you think we should travel with the weather advisory?"

Hosea contemplated as he looked to the skies, a little grey, but still the sun shone.

"Thinking we can beat it, if we head out early."

"I agree with granddaddy; we can check out early and be home by the time it hits."

I was leery. We can't beat nature; they warned people over the weekend to prepare for this. We've been busy and hadn't watched the news since we came. People were out getting gas, water, and food, looking like we faced our last days. We had done none of that. Maybe it's safer if we head out? At least we knew our house better than this place.

❧

The number of trees in this area concerned me.

"Okay, let's go," Hosea announced.

Hosea announced the sun was just beginning to rise. No time to check out the view, which saddened me. Everyone packed up to beat the storm; I stole a minute to see the sunrise on the back balcony as I'd never seen it before. The weather forecast painted an ugly picture of what was to come, leaving us all worried. From here, the skies were beautiful and didn't seem like it would rain anytime soon. Not wanting to take any chances, we headed out. It felt strange; usually, the weather was calm here and spoiled us. The monsoons had a way of reminding us that all fun things ended, forcing us to appreciate how good we had it. It's like life itself. Things would seem to run smoothly; we'd be enjoying all that life offered, then BAM — life would throw us a curveball when we least expected it. The monsoon storms were just like that, we would rather be in the comfort of our own home when it happens. Hosea took to the wheel to be on the safe as we traveled down the mountainside. I forgot how fast he drives, left Chloe clinching the door in secret filled with fear. We talked about the fun we had camping and the memories we'd made; I tried to comfort her because I knew how she felt.

"He drives like a mad fool, road rage and all," winking at her.

Worry set in my face. Glancing the mirror, worry lines settled deep on my forehead, making me look like a prude or a raisin. Had we made the wrong choice of going camping? We had a blast, but were we going to make it home? The 'great' bass conversation came again, taking our minds off the skies that were turning grey with each curve. Chloe's eyes widened as we swiftly hugged the last mountain curve, leaving Hosea looking tensed. With a sound of reserved fear, Chloe chimed in about fishing trading conversation to getting home safe. We still had lots of fish in the trunk on ice. Hosea said nothing much; his full focus was on passing the truck in front of us, who seemed to drive like he wanted to make it home alive.

Making it to the base of the mountain, we noticed the sky suddenly grew dark, like someone flicked a switch. I scanned the radio to find a station giving current updates, stopping at 1554 AM, which blared the latest on the upcoming storm.

"Find shelter, get off the roads as soon as possible," was the immediate advice. I worried. Hosea sped up even faster — with caution this time. Soon after, we saw our first drop of rain hit the windshield. Chloe fell back into her seat with disappointment and groaned. After the few drops of rain, the sky turned yellow-orange and darkened into a grey mist.

"How could this happen? Granddad, please drive safe; you have a precious cargo in the car."

Hosea looked at her through the rearview mirror.

"Hold tight, baby girl—I put them on ice."

Giving him a weird look, "I was talking about—me and grandma."

Chloe pulled herself up and nudged the back of his head.

"Funny fella you are, granddad," Hosea began laughing, but shortened by a massive bolt of thunder.

All of our eyes widened with concern; afraid of what was coming next.

Chloe yelled, "What's that enormous cloud cascading over the sky right there?"

I squinted, trying to focus on it myself, "Chloe, get down," I hollered.

Speaking slowly, with fear sinking into my stomach, "It's coming our way."

Leaning forward, focusing my eyes, I studied the events happening before me.

"A darn dust storm was coming our way. Pull over!" I yelled.

He gave into my command, leaving us sitting with extreme fear on our faces.

"Oh my, it's scary and coming fast."

"Sit back, girl."

As we tried to pull over, cars were racing at full speed around us, ignoring the speedy wind swirls coming towards us. It was getting harder to see. Maneuvering in and out of traffic wasn't easy. Hosea focused hard to dodge other cars to get over. It wasn't easy as visibility became—none. I wanted to help him the best I could without getting in his way. He got over to the next lane, and we could hear a car blowing its horn, slowing down until it passed. I held my breath because it seemed like we could not make it. We could pull off the road onto the shoulder. We didn't have time to rest- it naturally happened. Dust was blowing at alarming speeds as hail pounded the car; lightning bolts and thunder filled the surrounding space. It was like a movie. We all had the look of fear on our faces. Hosea switched the radio station, hearing the newscaster blare out that the visibility was zero in many areas, and there were winds of about forty miles per hour.

"Chloe, grab six bottles of water from the back," Hosea commanded.

He turned to me, "Babe, get the head scarfs from the compartment in front of you."

I couldn't contain my anxiety anymore, hysterically yelling out that we should have stayed at the cabin and followed my first mind.

"What are you talking about, woman? We all agreed that we were going to leave, right?"

"I didn't like his tone of voice—" Hosea gave me a look displaying a funky attitude.

"What are you talking about — woman?"

"Nothin', forget I said a thing."

"Don't say another word," he said.

"What?" I added as he kept piercing at me, throwing my hands in the air.

"Honey, I know it worries you, but we got enough going on with this storm, please don't act like that."

I sighed, turning to look at Chloe, instantly shamed.

"Chloe are you okay?" he asked.

"Yup, just filming and taking pictures with my phone."

"I need y'all to listen- wet the head scarfs place them over your mouth, then tie them behind your heads. Make sure all the windows are up, doors closed, and shut all the surrounding vents."

Chloe face crumpled in dismay, "I have finally seen the greatest storm of my life, and I'm in it."

"You'll be okay, honey, God got us."

We heard shots of thunder loud and clear, jerking our eyes wide open. Looking up, we saw colossal lightning bolts jolting across the sky. It seemed as if the bolts hit the car. The newscaster stated that the winds were getting stronger, reaching seventy miles per hour. Instructing folks whom were in vehicles to bend over in case the windows broke. The car shook as we tried to keep our balance. Chloe laid on the floor, covering her face, as we laid on our sides, pressing the scarfs over our faces. Oh, my Lord, the car shook as though someone was shaking us like a cup full of dice. The car went dark as the storm flew forcibly around us, with dust seeping into cracks. I yelled to see if everyone was okay. I wasn't sure about how long it had lasted, but as quick as it had started, it stopped. The storm was finally over as we waited for ten minutes before moving. Hosea got out, checking out the car; stating everything appeared fine, minus the dirt and sand left from the storm. Chloe breathing became labored with a long gasp. I went back to the car for her purse and she quickly ran, snatching it. We stood confused, wondering what was going on. Quickly pulling out her inhaler, she pushed, taking two good puffs, until she was breathing normal again.

"Are you okay?"

"Yes," she snapped.

Joining Hosea as if nothing happened, she still had her pursed stuffed under her arm. I wondered what was so important for her to act that way. I shrugged it off as I examined the significant hail damage. Everything else was fine.

"I'm—"

Hosea instantly cut me off as his hand came up like a shield.

"Are you seriously about to say that?"

"Say what?"

"Whatever you are about to say?"

"You interrupted me."

"I did, and I already forgave you, woman."

"Wait. What?"

"I already forgave you for the evilness you spit out at me earlier."

"Yeah, you know, you can be a bloody drama queen when you want to be. Trying to act innocent ain't going to work with me, woman — not today."

Chloe giggled.

"You are one too, lady."

"Grandma, I know I am."

"I must admit, I am one too, but the king version, all these women," he grumbled.

"Man, just focus on getting us home safe."

Horses

They prepared the horses for battle, but the victory is His. Interesting poster tacked to the door of the physician's office. A fascinating, powerful black horse displayed on it. Just the reason for this visit. Stepping into the room, ready to move forward with this appointment. Hosea wouldn't think of allowing me to ride without my doctor's green light, so here I am.

"Dr. Michelson, I am planning on horseback riding and wanted to make sure my body can handle it."

I looked at her with intense hope, side-eyeing her as she worked her way around the room. She sat, repeating my statement with a hint of concern.

"Horseback riding? So, let me understand you realize how rough your fibromyalgia has been in the past?"

"Yes, ma'am, horseback riding and a few other things," I said in a firm tone.

I nodded.

"Okay, I would like to mention, according to your past lab work and medical history, that I don't see why not, but getting on a horse… it depends."

"On what?"

"How have you been feeling?"

"Eh, ok."

"Well, how you ride may prove to be of concern."

I scratched my eyebrow, "O — kay… I don't entirely understand."

"If you do a soft ride, you should be fine. but, if you are talking about galloping or fast riding, that may pose a problem."

She tinkered with her stethoscope, then asked, "How do you feel about it, Mrs. Gomar?"

"Scared."

We both started snickering, "I see your concerns; is there a special reason you are doing this?"

"Just something I always wanted to do. I have my granddaughter here; she's been inspiring me to ride."

"How old is this granddaughter?"

"Twenty-five."

"Miss Chloe is visiting and causing trouble, I see?"

"I wouldn't say trouble, but she is inspiring me to do a few things."

"Yes, well, riding a horse is a big adventure; let me glance over your recent labs and check you out good."

Pulling up my chart, studying it over, "Don't be alarmed if you are tender or stiff afterwards; you'll be moving muscles over your entire body you haven't used in a while."

The doctor checked me out. She did the usual things, having me stand, sit, and lean over and a few twists. I felt my nerves become edgy and was sick feeling. I looked past the doctor, noting her medicine cabinets are well stocked and organized, usually they were messy. As she checked me out, I was thinking of Hosea's feelings concerning me riding.

"Have you ever ridden?" Dr. Michelson asked, popping me out of my private thoughts.

"No, ma'am, never."

Clearing my throat as she gave me a stern look of concern. "Let me go over my notes. You are an African American woman, age 68, and married? Married you for thirty-five years to Hosea, right?"

"Yes."

"That's incredible, Mrs. Gomar; I hope to my marriage last that long," she smiled at me.

"You know, staying married this long is difficult, especially in today's time."

The doctor sighed, "You're right; it isn't easy at all; it's rough—been 16 for us."

"Have you ever thought marriage wasn't designed to make us happy, but more spiritual?"

"Explain."

"As you know marriage is a challenge, if we can face them with love and compassion, isn't that being Godly?"

"I can see it, Mrs. Gomar. I would say more holy. As humans, we are selfish, and we walk into a relationship with our ways and it heads us for trouble before it begins. Dealing with marriage issues, we must become more like Jesus."

"Holy?"

"I think so honey, either way, spiritual or holy. It's the same."

"Interesting, but true. Girl, that man has made me crazy and guess what… I made him just as crazy. We both had to change our ways and… I can see it," Dr. Michelson said.

"Chloe, you will find out soon what we're talking about, young lady."

"Well, it sounds kind of scary, I'm feeling maybe it will be too much for me."

"Nah, you will have me, granddad and your parents to guide you, honey. Put Jesus first, you will do great."

"Don't forget keeping your love life spicy."

"Spicy? What you know about that, Mrs. Gomar?" Looking at me funny with a quaint smirk on her face.

"Don't act like you don't know how to keep things spicy if you don't get you some books on it. Never too late to start," I snapped while rolling my eyes.

"I do, but it's not everything, because a marriage built on lust in the sheets will fall quicker if that's all you have going for you."

"Oh, so true."

"Yes."

"My granddaughter is getting married in a few weeks, and she is here finishing up her last semester of her master's program. I am so proud of her."

"Oh, great! Congratulations."

"Thank you, yes."

Dr. Michelson completed her exam, "Well, for your age, Mrs. Gomar, you are doing well, considering — I don't see why you can't go riding, just be aware that you may be down for a while, because of your fibro."

"No falls, young lady, or that will be a whole different story. You know us seasoned folks don't heal as fast?"

"I will, but I ain't gonna worry myself with nothing negative,"

She stood up to leave but stopped in mid-step, "Make sure your warmed-up, your joints beforehand, and I think you will do just fine," tapped me on the shoulder.

"Someone will help you, right?"

"Yes, ma'am, they are going to help me throughout the ride, they claim horse riding will be therapeutic and healing."

"So, when is the big day?"

"Big day?"

"The day you will ride?"

"Within a few weeks, gotta get my nerves up."

"Beautiful, I will see you soon, and want to hear about this horse ride and pictures."

❧

Chloe fumbled with her pencil, taking a deep breath, "Hey grandma."

"I'm ready," giving her two thumbs up.

"Yes," she exclaimed.

Interlocked arms, we walked out, happy to have the doctor's approval to ride. I know I'm bat-crazy for even considering it.

"I'm riding," I whispered.

Oh, the scream Chloe let out sent me into a shock for a minute. I never told her I was sensitive to noises, but I enjoyed the moment. Hosea will have a fit! Taking a deep breath, snuggling deep into the car seat while waiting for Chloe to get settled. She asked a thousand questions; I wasn't giving into her whimsical demeanor. The poor child talked so much; her hair came loose. She cut herself short to pin it out of her face, but once it was done, she went right back to chattering.

"Grandma, I can't believe we're do it," she said, with bright eyes and a smile out of this world.

"I don't know, I have to talk to your granddad," giving her a grim look.

Chloe looked me in the eyes, saddened, melting my heart like pieces of melting wax. She ran out of things to say. She groaned in exasperation.

"You know granddaddy will say no, with his cranky ole self."

I just sat quietly, listening to her babble on as she did when she got excited. Chloe squealed, and I laughed to myself, feeling free and liberated — *I will ride a horse, a — horse.* That child knew she could get anything she wanted. But this time, it wasn't for her, or nobody else. It was for me. I needed to live my fullest life before it was too late. I have another event I'm about to scratch off my list.

❧

On our way home, we stopped at the horse ranch to get more information on riding. The ranch was off the major highway, but not by much. The long, winding dirt road kicked up much dust; it was troublesome to see. It resembled a dirt storm, leaving my car looking a hot mess. I had Chloe roll up the windows and close the vents to lessen the chance of all that pesky dust getting in. The air was extra warm and dry, which made the dirt that much more prone to blow; we could get valley fever out here in all this dirt. It felt like we were in a western movie—the only thing we didn't have was cowgirl gear! I laughed to myself as we pulled up at the ranch. Getting out of the car, Chloe hugged me tight; I savored every minute.

"Okay, child, loose me—I can't breathe, and it hurts. Girl, you get that hugging from your granddad."

I gently grabbed her arm, with her squeezing me tighter before I could pull her from around my neck. Looking around, finding it was nothing fancy. In the back of the ranch were the stables, it's mesmerizing. Reminded me of watching old westerns on my old black-and-white TV when I was young. The stalls were neat, fully lined up with horses. The primary area was a half empty store, which sold horse stuff. Rodeo looking clothes, horse riding videos, snacks, and small trinkets with their ranch logo on them was the complete setup. Everything had a rustic look to it, not appealing to my eye.

Wandering off into the stables where the horses themselves seemed to act as if they were looking for someone to rescue them from boredom. They best believe I was on my way to do just that. They were beautiful, each one of them in their way. As I approached the first one that caught my eye, I felt we made a connection. She was so soft and friendly, seemed like she had something to say to me. I wished I knew what it was.

"Good morning, Mrs. Gomar," said a young woman who worked for the horse ranch, breaking my attention from wanting to learn horse language. I studied her as she bounced around with robust energy. Cowboy boots with spurs carried her around the barn, like she had no care in the world. Curious how she knew my name, but I was impressed with her entire being. Sunny attitude with a pearly white smile, exchanged a firm handshake to giving the horse a nice smack on the hind side, "She is beautiful, isn't she?"

"Yes," as I looked back at the horse with an immense smile on my face.

"My name is Anna and I'll be assisting you today."

"Well hello, nice to meet you."

"Are you ready to ride?"

"Oh, heavens, no—not today. We came to get details about riding. I'm excited, though, and can't wait. Do many people my age come to ride?"

"No, we don't. Most young folks, as yourself feel they can't ride, but that is so far from the truth."

She reached up and stroked the horse's mane as she spoke.

"We have a local senior group that comes in to feed and groom the horses; it has proven to reduce depression and anxiety."

Wringing my hands, thinking of questions to ask, "So, you figure I would be alright riding… I am 68?"

She swung her face back to me, staring me in the eye, "You don't look it at all. I'd never guess it."

"Thank you, but I am, my body sure knows it," I blushed.

"Rest assures you will wear a helmet and other gear to keep you safe. You will fine; we will assist you along the way."

She gestured while holding onto the horse and continued talking.

"This beauty you are looking at, Mrs. Gomar, maybe a little rough for you."

Reaching my hand to her lips, wanting to pet the beautiful horse.

"She is so grandeur and strong."

"Magnificent warrior."

"Excuse me, you called me?"

"A magnificent warrior, it's what comes to mind when I look at you."

I laughed, wishing it were true, but it didn't sound bad—I'd been called worse. Anna amused me; I like her. She was a very charming young lady. Anna went on about me being a warrior, a brave heart, riding at 68.

"Keep reminding me of my age, make me more and more nervous each moment about riding," I gazed around.

I didn't know what she saw in me to think I could be a warrior, but it made me stand taller. Maybe it was the fact I will ride in my 60s. I shrugged it off; I won't let it bother me. Walking to the other side, I spotted out my next horse.

"Now, missy, this horse you are admiring is not the one you will ride. Say hi, Shallow. She is an Arabian mare and can be a rocky ride," Anna explained with a scrunchy face.

"She's one of the oldest horse breeds on this planet, and they love speed and lots of activities — one of my favorites, but I am a trained rider, and she is tough for me."

I followed Anna to another stall as she pointed out an unusual horse.

"The one you will ride is over there; his name is Stormy, and he is very gentle and exceptionally trained. He is a paint breed, with a color called tobiano, a lovely arrangement of brownish spots on his white body."

Standing firm, moving his legs as if he were marching in place.

Anna nudged me, "Give him a touch."

He was very playful, soft, and enjoyed flipping his tail in circles.

"Hey! He butted me with his head," looking dazzled and perplexed.

While massaging my shoulder, I figured he was being funny.

Anna chuckled, "Yes, he loves to play."

I walked a few steps away, looking back at him, daring him to do it again. I don't know about him; he is a little too feisty.

"He's innocent, just loves joking around."

"Today, you will spend a little time with him to get you two acquainted. I'll have your brush and feed him a bit, just to make you more comfortable. You want to get started?"

"Yes, that would be lovely."

While she gathered the materials I needed, she introduced me to the horse next to Stormy.

"Now, this angel is Castaway. We have also trained this horse to handle children and beginners. Like yourself, young lady. We also use him for the local senior citizen center for special events; he goes there a few times a week for senior therapy sessions."

He didn't impress me at all. Looking around the stable, I felt uneasy, but not in a bad way; I needed to adjust to my new surroundings. Listening to the horse noises was comforting, hearing them grunting and neighing was soothing. Getting restless made me remember my trip to the farm as a kid. They seemed like children, fighting for attention. I was nervous about being in a stable, to begin with, but I loved every minute... especially being around the horses, minus the smell. It was forcing my urge to puke. Being sensitive to smells was dreadful, another one of fibro's wicked sidekicks. The air reeked of manure, not to bring up these pesky flies, I assured myself I can get used to it like everybody else. Crispy golden hay was everywhere, with workers effortlessly sweeping it back into the stalls and barreling high levels of poop to its destination. Wondering how many horses and riders walked through these stable walls seemed interesting to me? As I scanned the wooden structure, I noticed small cracks in the woodwork, allowing bits of the sun to seep through. Two big barn doors allowed even more light in when a gentleman opened them wide to transport a few more horses to their rightful place. He pulled each horse to a stall, hurriedly closing each door behind him. The horses appeared as perplex as I did, noting the rush.

I was ready to brush Stormy, but the horse across from him was highly interested in talking with me—he left no doubt about it. He forced his head over toward me, neighing and showing all his dingy teeth. I looked him dead in his eyes, trying to figure him out; he had intense eye contact too. A bit too nice for my liking, I trotted back to brush Stormy. He was kind of challenging to work with, as he kept moving and turning away. Didn't seem interested in me, and I decided I should see the other horses; I just wasn't feeling this one too much. I spotted the horse across from Stormy again. His name tag said, 'Legend.' He was beckoning me to come to chat with him, so I did. He was beautiful, appearing to be friendly and playful and robust.

"Look how happy he is, curling his lips, slightly exposing his teeth," Anna pointed out to me.

"It means she likes you, lady."

I blushed.

He was a sweetie pie; I enjoyed him. I hadn't known horses could move their mouths around like that. He looked like he was trying to talk to me while looking me dead in the eyes, sort of like Mr. Ed the Talking Horse. His color awed me, as he was charming and the softest hair I'd encountered. A white horse with no spots was stunning with rarity like no other horse in the stable. Quickly grabbed an apple from the bin, asking if it was permissible. He was so gentle, kind, and such a funny eater. Holding the apple in my hand, I could feel his hairy lips tickle me.

❧

"How about this one?" I inquired.

"Hm… Nevertheless, I believe Stormy is the best option for you, Mrs. Matea."

"Although you formed a great bond, he rides rough; he wouldn't be good on your body."

I understood Anna's concern. Looking around, I became annoyed wondering where Chloe disappeared too. I hadn't noticed her for a while now, and it hadn't dawned on me as Anna and the horses kept me distracted. I was ready to call it a day when I noted her absence. Walking out of the barn, the warmth of the sunlight touched my face, reminding me to flip my old lady sunglasses in place. As I continued scanning the grounds, I set eyes on the most splendid horse I'd seen. I studied it from afar, praying that it would be appropriate to ride. My insides screamed with excitement that this horse was the one. Please, let her say this horse is okay to ride, I became fixated to find out.

His color was beautiful and appeared to be reddish tone. Smaller than the other horses I had seen. I returned to the stable looking for Anna, before losing sight of the horse, I couldn't find her. I didn't feel comfortable walking up to the horse without her. Waiting seemed daunting, so I walked around speaking to anyone who crossed my path, but my eyes remained on that horse.

Outback, I saw an arrogant young fellow, geared up, came bouncing through the stable with high confidence, stepping up to the horse I had my eye on. He grabbed a saddle and threw it on the horse's back and adjusted it. My eyes widened as he jumped on, riding into the training area.

I ambled over to the wooden gate while searching for Anna and Chloe. Approaching the gate, I noted how he managed this horse. Chloe caught my eye as I flapped my arm profusely to capture her attention.

"Over here," I yelled.

"Whew, sorry about that. I had a call and looked around the store while I was up there."

Anna appeared.

"Forgive me, ladies; I took a horse upfront and handled a few things."

I returned my gaze to the beauty in front of me. Anna came closer and signaled the guy on the horse to join us.

"She is a beauty, isn't she?"

"I want to ride her."

"Ok — that's a problem, it's not one of our horses."

"Chloe, what's your thought of this one?" I asked.

"Eh, it's an excellent choice for you. I like it," as she went back to playing with her phone.

As usual, full of life and so energetic, but I could tell something bothered her. mind else where, and it wasn't horses. I shrugged it off, turning my attention back to Anna.

"I would say she is brown, but her color seems more reddish than brown, or could be a mixture of the two?"

"Ah, yes, her color is sorrel, a reddish hue. Her name is Amazing Grace, but we call her Gracie. She got her name from her previous owner, who says that an amazing double rainbow appeared after her birth."

"Oh?"

I could feel my eyes sparkling with tears that had welled into the corners, clouding my vision. Everything about this horse mesmerized my entire being, and it wasn't as nice as the white one. Her tail was so full and flowing.

"That makes her even more special."

"What?"

"Her beauty, name, and the double rainbow. I'll take her."

Chuckling, "she's not for sale. The guy riding her owns her and brought her in for training. I spoke with him and he says let him know the day and time and he'll accommodate you."

Everyone watched, noting how well her training was going. She showed off accomplishing jumps with ease, tail flowing behind her as her trainer galloped around the yard.

"Grandma, your eyes look like diamonds, looking at him ride."

"Yes. That's the one."

She was right. That horse did something to me, and it felt incredible, a soothing feeling come to me as I watched the young man ride 'Amazing Grace.' She had my full, undivided attention. Taking a short walk over to her owner. Anna introduced me to both. He jumped down, trotting her over, meeting us halfway. Stoking Gracie's mane awed me. He was a nice fella who saw my love for Gracie. He explained that he rarely allows strangers ride his horses. But stated something told him I was to ride her. Holding her tight by the ropes, he asked for the day and time I wanted to ride, and he'd be there. He looked me in my eyes without blinking, "I am sure you will be good to her, no creature named Amazing Grace isn't worthy of love and care, besides if you don't, you'll answer to me."

Gracie huffed, as though she knew we were talking about her, Anna laughed. As you can see, she has a lot of personality and charm."

"Yes sir, thank you. Don't worry."

"I was kidding, you'll be fine, right Gracie?"

"She has trained to work with elderly people. She is shorter than most of our horses, she will be easier for you to get on. Honestly, I believe she would be excellent for you; she is full of life and very calm and friendly," he said.

"I love her fur; she is so soft and shiny. She isn't as talkative and outgoing as Legend, though. That's a good thing; she'll focus more on the ride and can stand still for long periods."

Anna exchanged words with another employee, pulling Chloe and me to the side, making room for the trainer and a few others with him.

"The guys were coming in to check the horse's water and tidy up the stables and put the horses away. It is roasting out here; we've been busy keeping their water fresh and full."

"We are going to call it a day, I'm tired."

"Did you want to visit the gift shop and putt around for a bit? You might see something you like?"

"No, it's been a long day, going to all it quits."

"Mrs. Gomar, it's easy to get tired around here, trust me."

Chloe chimed in, Grandma, I'm tired as heck too."

Preparing to leave, Chloe stopped short in her step.

"Hey, wait—I didn't pick my horse," she pouted.

Anna allowed her to go back in to choose one. These young folks always on those darn phones can't handle business, always preoccupied. She hustled around the stable, stopping mid-step as she pointed to the first one in the stable.

"I want the black one over there."

Anne nodded her approval. "Wonderful choice for you, girl. His name is Popcorn Kernels."

"I love his name, and his mane is so fluffy," Chloe beamed.

"Yes, we all get a kick out of it too, we call him Popcorn — we enjoy keeping things simple."

Anna giggled as she played with Popcorn's braided mane.

"Sometimes one of the gals braids his mane before she rides him. Some folks around here are so funny."

Chloe played with his braids.

"Are you going to let me ride ya, Popcorn?"

"You know, he is a fun horse; you might get him to do some tricks for ya. I can ask the gal to braid his hair for you on the day you ride?"

"Okay, that's what's up—a natural show boy. Sure, I love the braids."

"At least you are getting excited; I was worried about you.

"You don't have to worry about me… I'm all good."

Anna opened her appointment book, looking for her next availability.

"I have 10 a.m. open for Tues or 11 a.m.? Which is good for you? Remember, no weekends or holidays, ladies."

"I need a few days to rest and exercise to loosen up my joints and rattle my bones."

"Grandma, you better not rattle your bones too much and shake something loose."

"Girl, don't you know it? this old woman is doing new things. I need to keep my old bones in shape."

"Hm, 10 AM—is that okay with you Chloe, I know you have school one of those days?"

"That's fine."

Chloe, "I'll have the driver transport us, is that okay?"

"Awe, thanks."

"Anything else we need to set up?"

Chloe smiled. "Nope, I can't wait! Okay, next week. I'm ready to ride!" She started dancing around as I joined her.

"Wild horses can't drag me away from this moment."

"We're getting ready to rock the world."

"Okay, ladies, see y'all next week."

❧

We made it home in no time; the entire morning drained us. Pulling up, Hosea stepped outside, and he couldn't wait to ask where we had been.

"None of your business! Mr. nosey," I answered to him hastily.

I yanked off my glasses, watching Hosea like I saw a ghost. "What the heck are you wearing?"

"Well, it's the same answer you had—none of your business."

Chloe chimed in to tell us how comical we were. Closing the car door, I began strolling towards the house.

I couldn't take it another second, "you look like a fool, what do you have on a clown suit with no reason for it?" I asked him.

"No, but you have to talk about my working clothes?"

"Yes, I was gone a few hours, now look at you."

"No, more like all morning, and for your business, I look like a hard-working man—"

"So, to get things straight, you have on a sombrero, fishing boots up your legs, a tackle vest, and short pants, doing hard work on what?"

"Don't matter no how," taking off his hat, looking up the sky.

"Do you know what you look like?"

Stopping just shy of the front door, before he could answer the question, I noticed my flowerbed was dug up. I shifted to him with a massive grin on my face.

"Oh, look at you. I've wanted that area to be cleared for years. Hosea, did you dig my flower bed up?"

"Yeah, I sure did. Bout time, ain't it?"

"Oh, you're a headstrong man. I have a surprise for you later tonight," I winked at him

Chloe looked between us, perplexed, "Like what, grandma?"

"Girl, get out of grown folks' business."

"Oh my gosh, yuck!" she yelled, storming away.

Paying her no mind. Walking around humming my favorite tone, stopping to think how happy I was at the moment. Hard to contain myself as I pondered what herbs I was going to plant in that very area. It was the perfect space for it, too. I decided to plant some cilantro, parsley, tomatoes, and some peppers, making a mental note of what I needed to buy. Or should I plant florals? I scampered into the house to jot down notes before I forgot. I loved gardening but hadn't been able to get him to dig the flowerbed up for me for years. That fishing experience had changed him, even if it was only for a minute. He keeps a smile on his face ever since it happened and hasn't stopped talking about it. I should have taken him fishing a long time ago.

Hosea caught up to me and asked again if everything was okay, "Yes, everything is fine."

"Well, everything ain't okay with me, woman. Y'all left here to go to a doctor's appointment, but you been gone half the day."

He stopped me and placed his hands on my shoulders, looking me in the eyes. "I was worried about you and thought something had happened."

"Okay, fine, we went to the horse ranch."

I pulled away and kept walking with a pep in my step, hoping to break his attention from the subject. "Wait just a minute, let me make sure I heard you correctly… You went to the horse ranch? For what?"

Chloe popped in, brimming with great excitement, telling him all the details. "We're gonna ride, granddad! You wanna ride too?"

"Oh, no. I'm not crazy enough to think I'm not too old to be riding no horse and break none of these battled up bones," while looking at me without blinking.

"For sure, you need not be riding either, but I'm sure you got Chloe thinking you ain't sixty-eight years old, you need to keep both feet on solid grounds."

I folded my arms, standing my ground. "I knew you'd have something negative to say. Go ahead, try to discourage me from doing what I to do!"

He seemed to be ticked off, big time, "So, you're gonna ride, huh?"

I nodded, "Sure am," I replied.

"And you are going to give me that raunchy attitude and think I won't say something?"

I wasn't taking any of his negativity personally, as he just stood there, looking stunned, while playing with his beard. Within seconds, a smirk of a smile appeared on his face, like he was up to something.

"Oh, heck yeah I'm going… but only to take pictures and to be there just in case your old butt falls off, somebody got to be a witness."

"There you go, jinxing me before I even had time to try," I told him in a sassy tone.

"Okay, I'm gonna shut up about it, but don't say I didn't tell ya so when you go flying off into the sunset after that dang horse kicks your tail off."

We all started laughing. I didn't like what he was saying one bit, but instead of getting mad, I figured I might as well laugh because getting mad never does any good.

"Well, at least horses are good with the Lord."

"What do you mean?"

"You know that story in the Bible, where that man Elisha was in battle, and God sent those chariots of fire to battle?"

"I didn't know where you were going with this, should I prepare myself?"

"That's just to let you know; he's gonna be working behind the scenes for you too you might need that army yourself!" He explained with a loud maddening boisterous crazy laugh.

"You just remember to pray; he'll be working behind the scenes, keeping you safe too. Only I know what I want to do to you right now."

I said nothing much after that. I knew my man was a special one.

However, I couldn't help but think back on the biblical story and decide he was right; I hadn't thought of it that way. I thought back on all the battles the Lord had helped me with throughout my days. He did just that—fought behind the scenes. Simply put none of the battles were mines to fight.

"Whatever you got going on in the head woman, share it, or put it away."

I threw my hand up at him. He just stood staring at Chloe and me, making us quite uncomfortable, "So, when is the big day?"

"Grandpa, it's next Tuesday at 10 a.m. They're going to call the day before to confirm."

He shook his head in disbelief, "Did we pay up the life insurance policy yet?"

"You know you're a fool, right? I can't stand you right now."

"I'm done with you; you know I'm right and you are wrong, while you are playing."

"Yeah, yeah… I'll be there. I would not miss it for the world. My wife, riding a horse at sixty-eight for the first time. Hilarious!"

His big smile turned into pure laughter while walking off, shaking his head, disappearing into the back yard.

"Grandma, don't let Grandad change your mind about riding."

"I wish he didn't feel that getting old meant you couldn't do things."

❧

April- 1964 ✿ My grandma left her keys to my mom's house. We stood outside, waiting for her to dump her purse out for the last look. Frustration radiated from her face. Grandma asked me if I would go into the milk door to get her keys. She held me by my shoulders, looking me square in my eyes, I swallowed hard, looking around at everyone waiting for my answer. Gaining the nerve; I agreed to do it. The deadbolt lock needed a key on both sides, so they gave me instructions on what to do. I slid through the milk shoot on the side of the house. Once inside, it was dark; I yelled out in fear. Hearing the voices encouraging me to move forward. I trudged down the hall toward my mother's room. Inside, I saw the keys lying on the dresser. I grabbed them and froze. Not one finger moved. Within seconds, I saw her as if I was dreaming. She was so serene. So peaceful. The voice which only could belong to her echoed in my mind as she sat lifeless on the bed. Disbelief raged through my mind, reminding me that this couldn't be true. The message: I'm not coming back, I am ok honey, and please take care of grandma and help her with the kids. Just as quickly as she came, she disappeared, and I fainted. I remembered someone touched me and I went crazy. I begged her to stay. Moments later, it took four men to get a hold of me. I cried, screamed, and flung things, finding myself hurled into the car. That was the last visit. Pain sank into my heart that very day. I didn't know what it meant to feel that kind of pain, which nestled in my broken soul. My eyes sunken from the flood of tears that streamed from them. My siblings needed me to be strong, but how could I when I was too weak to hold myself. I took the blame for everything that happened; I stepped into a deep ball of guilt. Every day I longed for her, trying to make things right. Could I comfort her by saying I'm sorry? If I didn't mouth off about the kids, could it have changed things? I wanted to take so many words I sent into the universe back. Guilt embraced me like a thief. A role in her death I believed played left me feeling ashamed. I vowed to silence, refusing to never hurt anyone again. Do folks understand when the hurt just seep from your swollen eyes, pain released through salted waters pointed to the skies? When no amount of force can hold them in, can my soul be leavened? As much as I deplore crying, I'm thankful God counts each tear and stores them in jars in heaven. The fragility of a broken heart and its tenderness is an experience only those who love deeply will one day treasure. Please Lord, don't let my heart harden from the evilness of this world for nothing lasts. Protect it and keep it safe with you, for I know my father this too shall pass.

Chloe quivered with grieved eyes, "Grandma that had to be the saddest day ever. That's how my great-grandma died?"

"Yes. One of the saddest days of my life. She died of a massive heart attack at 32."

I stared into the pool water, thinking back on those memories. The little waves sparkled as if it was a gazing into my past as a movie played back to me.

"I still remember what I cooked that day, rice, string beans, and hamburger. I mixed it together and called it goulash."

Chloe frowned, "That doesn't sound good," laughing as I described my flavorful dish.

"It was delicious, straightforward to make. Girl don't hate on my cooking skills. Grandma has to get you on that; we were happy to have food."

Making funny faces at her. Forcing laughter was comforting for both of us, as we were both still fighting back the tears; it lightened up the atmosphere. "You know, Chloe, I never talked about my feelings about her death. I withdrew into myself, locking out the entire world. I don't think I ever healed from her death until I was in my fifties."

"Don't lock up your emotions, talk to someone you trust or professional help. Mental health is important, take care of yourself."

"Good advice, prayer helps too."

"Yes, it does. No one encouraged us to communicate our emotions; Think about how past hurts affect our future relationships."

"Yeah, I can see that."

"Later I learned my dad lost his mother at sixteen years old, and my mom lost her father at sixteen. What a nasty cycle of pain. Looking back, you learn how pain continues to hurt generations. I don't believe either of them had helped to support their grief, and the experience continued into our generation. We were hurt."

"Grandma, I don't know how I can live without any of my family. I'm so thankful to have you both."

She placed her feet in the water, swishing them around, "My great-granddad seemed mean."

"He struggled but was a good person, plus the death of my mom changed him."

I shrugged, watching her feet fidget in the pool. "My dad died young as well; only fifty-one years old. Drugs and alcohol just tore his life and body apart."

We sat in silence for a while, just watching the moonlight tickled the water. The stars shined bright, with one twinkling more brilliant than the others, no matter how much we stared couldn't figure out the reason. Maybe it wasn't our business to know.

"Well, lady, I must turn in now; it's after 9 p.m., and it's been a long day. Didn't you have homework due tomorrow?"

"Yes, I do. Thanks for reminding me—school calls."

Hopping to her feet, grabbing her belongings.

She turned to me and said, "I enjoyed you today, grandma. Thank you for sharing your life with me."

Couldn't have kept the grin from my face if I had tried.

"I love you, my granddaughter. Thank you for finding my key. It brought the best gift ever to me — you," I blew her a kiss.

Tomorrow was the big day.

My nerves ran over my body like ants, so irritated it was like I could scream. We had all laid around relaxing over the last couple of days; it was the big day. I started my exercises again, as it had been a few weeks since I had done them. Like my doctor suggested, I needed to make sure my body was ready for this adventure. If you asked me, I thought I'd never be in shape, but I can at least soften up some of this stiffness, Richard Simmons had a girl working out. I could see Chloe swimming and Hosea, talking her ears off. I would not complain; it was the day that the Lord had made, and I was too busy rejoicing.

Excited and ready to get it over with and scratch this to off my list. It was a hot one and kind of gloomy out, which was different for Arizona weather. I had to find suitable clothes for riding in the heat. It took me a while to pick out some things. I was all set. This should do it—comfortable jeans, a cute t-shirt, and some gym shoes. Spent half the morning seeking comfort, believing this was the best choice. Threw my clothes on the armchair. Deciding against showering and took a bath instead. Throwing in some Epsom salt and took a pain pill. They had given me that advice at the ranch, and it was a good idea. Scurrying for water, Chloe came up, informing me that the lady from the ranch had confirmed our appointment. She disappeared down the hall. Hosea couldn't stop making me laugh, walking around and telling corny horse jokes, so I closed the door on him. I wasn't sure if he was trying to ease my nerves or make them worse! Robed and ready to get dressed, when I heard a knock on the door. I figured it was Chloe because Hosea had no reason to be knocking on our bedroom door. Opening it, who did I see standing there with a funny expression all over his face? Hosea.

"What are you knocking for, crazy man — here comb your hair?"

His soft fine hair sticks straight up like folks holding their arms up in a robbery, but today his hat made him look as if he had a shag.

"Swimming the other day, I mentioned to you to get your hair lined up. Now we are about to go out, and you're looking a mess."

"I sure do look like I got a shag, might bring it back in style, nothing wrong with that," patting his hair in place.

"Nobody don't want shag season to come back. You'll just look crazy that's all. Next time you'll take my advice."

Giving him a look as though I could just knock him out. He couldn't hold his laughter in either. As I was just about to say something smart to his old butt, Chloe jumped from around the corner.

"Surprise!"

"Girl, you scared me half out of my robe! I'm trying to put myself together, and you and Hosea out here foolin around, making it darn hard."

Grasping my belt, I tugged on it tight. Hosea stepped forward and I swatted at him.

"Here you go, attacking me with kisses."

While fighting him off, Chloe sat some beautiful bags on my bed.

"What's this for?" Inquiring in sheer shock."

She was bouncing around full of exhilaration. "SURPRISE! It's from grandpa and me."

Looking around, I noticed these are the bags you get at those fancy department stores. I was too excited to open them, deciding to open them when we returned. Informing them we didn't have time, but they insisted that I open them up. They both assured me I needed to open them before we left. Letting loose a deep sigh, I gave in. It's been so long since I had a gift this big and exciting. Wondering what it could be?

I'm soaking in this moment in for a minute or two. Hosea rolled his eyes. "Quit acting like I don't buy you nothing, woman."

"No, I didn't say that. I said it's a big and thoughtfully wrapped package."

"Now, you know—."

Giving him the evil eye before changing my mind on saying anything mean, even if it was in joking manner, also softened my look. "The more you keep talking, the more time it's going to take me.

"Okay, you got me, babe. Let's see what's in there, got to get this party started."

Almost forgot I had an appointment, with all the excitement. I reminded them both that the driver would arrive within an hour and a half. We had to be ready to go when he comes.

"Hurry, Grandma, we have little time! Open your gifts."

The first box I opened was so beautiful, light pink, with an enormous bow on it—too lovely to just rip it open. I needed to savor this moment. This surprise was just blowing me away. I seemed to go too slow for Ms. Chloe, so she helped me out. A t-shirt. It read: 'This grandma walked rainbows to ride Amazing Grace.' The body of the t-shirt was a pretty blue, with colorful glitter on the rainbow portion. I loved it. The next box was periwinkle blue, with a huge bow, and a yellow accent flower—small and dainty, embracing it. Shaking it, listening for anything to rattle off inside. Chloe laughed, saying that I wouldn't be able to tell what it was by shaking it. I pulled the bow, ripping open the box, and saw some jazzy looking jeans, which also had glittered pockets. I held up the jeans; they appeared small.

"You think these will fit me?"

"There jeggings grandma, they stretch to your shape."

"You sure?" Feeling it would have to do a lot of stretching to fit these hips.

I looked up at the two of them; I was beaming with happiness, "Oh, how did you know my size?"

Hosea stood in the doorway, waving his hand, with such a toothy smile on his face.

"I know everything about you, lady."

He had me frantically blushing. Finally, the last box was bright yellow, with a considerable-sized sunflower tied to it. A real one, too. I found it was heavy as I positioned it on the bed to open it. When I saw what was inside, my jaw dropped.

"A pair of riding boots! Oh, my… I hadn't had riding boots since I was about fifty and was still looking good in them."

I always had to get the ones for big, voluptuous legs.

"Thank you for remembering.

Looking at Hosea, he shook his head. I loved them; they were so fancy. I was thankful they had a zipper up the back, with delicate brass accent pieces against the black leather. I partook in a deep sniff—nothing like the smell of a fresh pair of leather boots. I started tearing up; this was so thoughtful of them.

"Shucks, I can't believe you did all this for me! You probably just didn't want to see me going looking like a hot mess; well, I don't blame either of you."

Throwing my old clothes to the side, I worked eagerly to get my new pieces organized. I looked up and saw they were still standing around; I began pushing them both out of the room. At the door, Chloe turned back.

"I'll help you get ready."

"Okay, come on, missy. We have only a little time."

Hugging Chloe as she reentered the room, still thanking her.

"It was mostly granddad's idea; he knew how much this meant to you and wanted you looking good."

Thoughts of running to kiss him again, but time didn't permit it.

"I am so thankful for both of you."

Standing back looking in the mirror, it amazed me how much I looked like a professional rider. I'd never imagined this happening, that I was as old as an ancient mummy. We both scurried down the stairs, but I needed a minute. Wearing new riding boots left me feeling a little stiffer than usual. As I was stretching my riding boots a bit, the driver arrived.

❧

"Good day, everyone, nice to see my fine people looking marvelous, chiefly you Mrs. Gomar," Mr. Richardson said.

"Good morning and praise you for your kind words."

He is always so positive and courteous. Professionally dressed in his entire-black work attire and a cap. As usual, he has it pulled tight to his head, one could barely see his eyes, unless he takes it off to wish us well upon leaving. He's been with us for the last seven years and does an admirable job. I was happy to see him today. His driving comforts me, takes his time and gets us to our destination on time. Occasional peeks into the rearview mirror, gives him an idea of times to chat. His soft-spoken, even toned demeanor engages in the most interesting conversations intertwined with laughs makes the time run away. Hosea loves to challenge him occasionally with off the wall topics as he is always on point with his responses. Opening our doors. His smile gleamed with gentle crow's feet gracing his eyes, which always seemed at peace.

"Welcome my good folks."

We replied to his warm greeting. Finding my place in the back of the car proved challenging to move because of these darn jigging's and stiff boots. Hosea was too impatient to wait for me, so he sat upfront.

"Special occasion, ma'am?"

"Yes, Chloe and I are riding a horse today."

"Well, I say… wonderful. I give you both my blessings. Mr. Gomar, you're not riding, Sir?"

"No, I came along as a witness, but I am excited none the less."

Mr. Richardson gazed the rearview mirror, faintly smiling. "You sure picked a beautiful day, ma'am. Not too hot out today, nor a cloud in the sky, and the sun is perfect. I'm sure you will do great."

"How true, I hadn't thought of it too many things on my mind at the moment, thank you for bringing that to my attention."

"Not a problem. Are we listening to any sounds today?"

"Do you have any classical?"

"Grandma, do we have too?"

"No, we can pass. Helps calm my nerves."

The ride was quiet, with occasional sounds seeping into the car from outdoors.

"You okay, babe?"

"I'm fine, thanks for asking," my hands were rambling around anxiously.

"Grandma, don't be nervous; you are going to do great."

I felt unease; I used the travel time to pray. I knew everything would be okay, but the time spent in prayer helped to confirm things were in place for me, and that I'd be coming home in one piece and with no scratches, dings, broken bones, or dents. By the time I said amen, my mind had drifted into a mode of gratitude for this very day. I would finally get to ride a horse, something I had imagined ever since I was nine! She was the second horse I had fallen in love with and was excited about riding her.

"Y'all don't forget to take a picture of me riding from the good side."

"All your sides look good to me—especially that backside." Hosea relished.

"Here you go," rolling my eyes.

"Just make sure you take some decent pictures, so I don't end up looking like a goon."

"Grandma, I can't even imagine you looking like a goon, ever."

I couldn't help but laugh at myself, "Whatever — You haven't seen none of my old pictures then, have you?"

"Oh, hush, grandma. I bet you ain't taken a terrible picture in your entire life."

"Okay, okay. But seriously, I would like to share this moment with my friends and family, ya know? I want to make a nice photo album, so please take well-thought-out pictures."

❧

Upon entering, my memory prompted me of the smells, which is not the best part of this adventure. Hosea complained of the odors. He soon quieted down, when the barn employee reminded him, he was in a stable. Giving him a haughty look. It was apparent he didn't like the way the employee had said it to him, and he instantly copped an attitude and nearly stepped on a pitchfork, stumbling backward, forcing him to pull his frantic composure together. Chloe yelled for him to stop, and he did, just in the nick of time. Then I saw her through the window; I gasped, there's my Gracie. She is just as beautiful as she was last week—but, wait; we didn't ask for three horses. Anna walked up with the extra horse, exclaiming one was for Hosea. I figured he might have changed his mind. His stance became full defensive mode, making it evident he had no desire to ride.

"Oh no, I'll pass, thank you. I just showed up to be a witness, offer prayers, and take pictures," he said.

Looking serious, but entertaining. A stable guy came up informing us he wouldn't mind taking our pictures if we wanted him to. Hosea quickly dismissed him and insisted that he would take the photos. Chloe and I got ready for brushing and feeding our horses, to get acquainted before riding. Anna began instructing us on the correct way of tending them.

"Okay — ladies, stand in front of your horse and extend out the back of your hand to let him smell you; this technique is the 'horseman's handshake.' It helps the horse to become familiar with you."

Gracie was amusing as she smelled me, as she released a kooky, whiny pitch, as her lips quivering in midair.

"What's all that noise about?" I asked while caressing her.

Anna smiled. "She likes you; keep up the wonderful work," giving me a firm smack on the back.

The horses were happily neighing and grunting, which seemed to fill the air like horse songs. Hosea stood next to the stable, and every time I looked over at him, he was shooing away spiders and webs. His fear of spiders usually sends him into fits. Today he was rather calm, as there were some big ones around here. Anna brought in some small steps to assist me in getting on with Gracie. They were very accommodating in helping me with my health issues. I became overwhelmed with my riding helmet. Hosea helped me secure my it in place, as I enjoyed his closeness and his desire to assist me. It was a minor task that meant so much to me.

"Is it tight enough?"

"Wait, it's snug. I can't breathe. You trying to kill me before I ride?"

Quickly, he loosened it and checked the clamp. As he tugged on the straps, it became more comfortable; I turned back to Anna, waiting for our next instruction.

"Okay, ladies, once we help you get into the saddle, try to relax. The horses know when their riders are stressed, so—we need you to loosen up. We'll assist you in a few techniques to help you out. Remember to take deep breaths and slowly let it out. Positive self-talk gets rid of anxiety and jitters and is very important in helping you stay encouraged."

They geared up the horses with blankets and the saddles, then double-checked our helmets. Anna announced for us to make sure we didn't have any purses or scarves, to avoid any injuries, and we had none of those. Finally, they were ready for me to get in the saddle. After walking up the steps, I placed my right foot into the stirrup. Taking a deep breath at their command, I threw my leg over but missed the saddle. I sent pain up my leg.

"Agh," I moaned and took a deep breath.

Couldn't lift my leg high enough, hitting my it on the saddle hump. Not to mention my painful hips. Feeling embarrassed, I was hesitant to try it again. Luckily, the young man behind me said, "I can help you if you like?"

I peered at him without a response. Spent time pondering if I could do it myself? No doubt I needed a boost. With these tight jegging's on, I gave in and accepted his offer. He had me relax my leg and checked to make sure everything was okay. Anna came over, holding the horse secure, and whispered motivational encouragement as she stood close.

"Do you have any pain?" He asked.

"No, no pain."

It reassured me. Hosea joined the guy in helping me get on. He patiently waited, asking me to let him know when I was ready. I concentrated on positioning my body and relaxing my muscles while taking deep sighs.

"Okay, I'm ready, but gradually, please."

"I got you," he stated.

One good shove and my leg flew over, forcing my butt into place instantly.

"Whew. Thank you, Lord." I exclaimed.

I sat for a minute, flexing a few muscles to make sure everything was still working correctly. I slowly placed my feet in the stirrups. Now, I was ready. At that moment, I felt like a real horse rider. The smile on my face was worth noting; I thought I might have competed with the sun, I simply glowed. I was so excited and happy. Watching Chloe as she got on her horse with ease. Moments later, though, she made a sour face. Telling Anna, "I don't feel so well… kind of nauseous."

Anna asked if someone could grab some water. We waited as Chloe chugged it down.

"Whew, I feel better, thank you."

Anna explained how to hold the reins, while Chloe finished getting herself together.

"Ladies, be careful not to pull too tight; straighten your backs to prepare for the ride."

We started walking the perimeter of the ranch.

"Slow and steady," Anna repeated.

Even though we were going slow, I felt like I was on a racehorse, with my hair flowing in the wind like a champion rider. In reality, none of that frolic happened as we were toted around with loads of help, but it felt really good. Grace was so beautiful, like one of those horses in a romance movie. Chloe and I worked hard to get to aligned with each other, and after about ten minutes of practicing, he rode. Getting on, he needed no extra help, other than the stairs. They had brought him out a beautiful black one; it looked healthy and more beautiful than our horses, with Hosea looking like he was a champion racer. His horse's name was Fierce. Funny, because his mom called him that in a joking manner. Making the name of his horse kind of symbolic. Hosea talked so much smack about being the best rider as soon as his butt hit the seat; we could barely stand it but were excited that he joined us.

Being beginners, staff led us, with ropes attached to the halter of the horse. We were practicing how to handle the reins and control the horse. Grace was easy to handle; she rode beautifully. Chloe and Hosea, they seemed to do well. Seeing Chloe give Popcorn a nice kick to move faster, being a braver than I. Watching her handle, it, I tried and chickened out. I noticed Hosea had come to a bit of a gallop. Me? I continued slow and steady.

"Whoa, whoa, whoa." I cried out to Grace.

Hosea pulled his reins back, "Atta boy," he said.

Petting Fierce for listening.

He had done well. My guide came over, asking me to loosen the grip on my reins and to relax. I agreed I needed too as my body was stiff as a board and my shoulders ached.

Yelling out, "Look at me now, baby!"

Grace seemed to ride much better after I did few breathing exercises and loosened up. Anna called out, "Okay, everyone, you are doing great. We're going to let you all ride without our help to see how you do."

We all looked around nervously as she announced it. Hosea even galloped past me.

"Show off," I yelled to him.

Chloe trotted ahead of me next, smiling as she passed. I wasn't trying to impress anybody — slow and steady; I continued.

"I see ya, I see ya," Hosea said, laughing as he passed me.

"Don't get so happy over there," I called out as he waved back.

He began hovering around the training equipment, trying to slow down.

"Okay, good. Folks let's take to the trail," Anna yelled.

Frantically waving her hand in the direction she wanted us to go, the final stance left her arm pointed straight out onto the trail. A few guides rode before us, and the rest trailed behind. The mountain views on the narrow trail were breathtaking, with sounds of nature lingering in the air. The path was about four and a half miles out and the trees aligned the path creating much needed shade. A vast array of trees resembled a guarded path. Peeking through the trees, you could see the beautiful arrangement of mountains in every direction. Through one area, the mountains seemed so close, looked as if we could touch it. One bird made the weirdest sound. Like it was looking for a mate, Anna rambled on, explaining details along the path. Halfway through, we stopped to take in all the beauty. The sky displayed a beautiful, vibrant blue that met the reds, oranges, and greens and filled the peaks. Too early for a sunset, but it sure looked like one forming. The three of us sat on our horses, taking in the wonders of this moment. Our guides held on to the ropes, enjoying the views.

Breathing in all that fresh morning air reminded me of the morning dew I enjoyed as a kid. I still enjoy it, but it seems like as a child, I took time to notice the small things, not so much now, he's always busy doing too much. A note to self, take time to appreciate the little things in life. The area below was steep, with small animals darting in and out of the greenery. Watching them scrabble around, living life in the great outdoors was serene.

"Hosea, Chloe… look at that rabbit."

Pointing in its direction. I was almost bluish, never seen one like it. The animals cascading across the trail did not bother the horses. Couldn't say the same for us. Chloe was watching the trail like a hawk, like a mountain lion would appear. After the run-in with the bear, Hosea wasn't at rest himself. They both were fearful of the array of animals that crossed our path. I knew they were ready to move on.

I looked out yonder and thought, Mom, I've finally ridden a horse. The regret of not riding had disappeared; threw all the crap I carried with me concerning any pain from my past down the side of the mountain. I wish I could save it and relive this day over. Mom, I am riding, I out loud until it took my breath away. Everyone clapped and cheered. I wanted to share that with her; I had the feeling she heard me and so did they all. I knew God was there because he had brought me here. Another promised granted. The sun glistened so brightly; like he heard me. I did not regret how long it took for this moment. My only regret would have been if it never happened. It was perfect timing — God's timing, with some most amazing people around me.

"I could never forget this day, grandma. God is so amazing," Chloe whispered.

"What you say. Yes, he is all the time."

Turning to Hosea, I released one of the biggest smiles, felt like my face couldn't take another inch of expression.

"Thank you, babe, for this special day. I would have never done this without you or Chloe."

"Hold on; it's more to come," they chimed in.

"Wait a minute, don't be coming up with too many crazy ideas, now."

I was enjoying myself but felt tired and achy. There's more to come? I pushed it out of my mind, trying to continue enjoying the trail, before stopping at a spring. The sound of it was very soothing as we approached it. I listened to the trickling water, splashing at the end into a substantial downpour. I noticed a small waterfall with a rainbow around it.

"Look at the rainbow and a waterfall, ya'll." Pointing with sheer awe.

"Grandma, this is your second amazing rainbow."

"I need to give her a few lottery tickets with all that luck."

Getting everyone's attention. The horses needed to take a drink, so we loosened the reins to slow them down. Gracie neighed as I petted her. I could hear the other horses huffing and panting. While Grace chewed pieces of crabgrass and apples, I fed her from my pocket. I couldn't stop smiling as I fell in love with him all over again, watching Hosea ride his horse like a perfect gentleman. He was so bothered by me and my safety; I admired that about him. He rode up front, blowing a kiss my way.

I told Chloe, "Bet you Jeremai would have loved this. Advice for the day, never stop dating. Always appreciate all the things your spouse does for you."

"He will one day soon. Thanks for the advice."

❧

Sounds of trotting filled the air as we all gazed over the area. The guides talked amongst themselves. Chloe was having a blast, but I realized that she was missing her sweetie, and it showed as I watched her. She was beautiful. I appreciated her pushing me into this moment. I swear I would have never done it. She was everything I dreamed of in a granddaughter. We made it to the end of the trail, and we rode the horses into the stalls. Getting off the horse was challenging for me; I had gotten stiff as a penguin while riding and pain was radiating. Dang it. Old age and fibro are a monster. My mind felt like I was in my 20s, ready to jump off. However, in reality I wasn't and had to be strategic about getting off. The same guy came over and slowly nuzzled my leg past the saddle, helping me get off quicker than I thought. Hosea seemed as if he was stiff. Chloe hopped off without a blink of the eye.

"Oh my, I think rigor mortis has seeped into my muscles. I am stiff as a board, walking like the tin man."

Hosea walked like a penguin for a minute or two, he tried to stretch, but his body had given him a run for his money. He joked around singing cowboy songs since it forced him to hobble around for a while.

We about died laughing, "Granddad, your drinks are cut off," Chloe heckled.

"I ain't even had one yet, just might be the problem."

He laughed uncontrollably, hitting his knee in pure amusement and eyes filled with tears. Hosea walked around the stable, telling joke after joke. He had everyone laughing; suggesting he play in a comedy show because he was so hilarious.

"Ya know, that's not a bad idea. Hosea, you are a star."

"No, grandma, I think you should," giving her a quizzical look.

"Who you supposed to be then?"

"A visitor?"

"Girl, hush! You could be the producer, all the brains you got."

I stopped to say goodbye to Amazing Grace, giving one last look in her eyes. I kissed her on the forehead. I needed a moment with her because she would never know the impact she had made on my life. I rode you, gal; thank you. As we prepared to leave, I noticed that I was stiff around my hips. Hosea came over, hugging me, and made sure I was okay. I laughed, giving him the biggest kiss. I was so thankful for this moment.

"I know you like her."

"Yeah, I do, but it's time to go."

I rubbed her one last time. Tears clouded my eyes, refusing to let them fall.

"Goodbye, Amazing Grace."

We were hungry for some food. Rubbing my hands in anticipation, this meal was going to be good. Brunch looked fabulous; they fixed it up nicely for us. We wasted no time digging in, gobbling down salad, burgers, potato salad, coleslaw, and drinks.

"Excuse me, everyone, we have a special gift for the Gomar family," Anna exclaimed.

We looked at each other, "what it could be?" I said.

"We have a ribbon for each of you, for today's ride."

She looked directly at me, "Mrs. Gomar, we have a trophy for you, for being so brave to live out your dreams."

Shock hung around me like a halo, with my mouth hanging wide open — I covered it in disbelief. Everyone broke out clapping as I walked to join Anna.

When they settled down, she continued, "You have inspired us. This trophy is a token of your courage, wisdom, and strength."

There I stood balling like a baby, fighting hard to pull myself together. After a moment, I honorably stepped to the mic, glanced the room. Few people were in attendance—about 20 folks. It was more than enough to make the occasion special. One I'd never forget. It didn't take many people to make this a grand token of love. I cleared my throat and began speaking:

"At nine years old, I became a horse-loving gal. I differed from many girls in my neighborhood, as my dream of riding turned into a bicycle, and their dream of a bicycle never turned into a horse — inside joke. None of my playmates ever wanted to share in my desire to ride a horse. Instead, my yellow Schwinn bike, with a big bell on the handlebars and a padded seat, became the envy of the neighborhood. I wanted so badly to show them horseback riding and how grand they are. My bike replaced my goal of ever riding a horse until today, which shows me the importance of patience and faith that things meant to be will be. Folks my age gave into the fact that they are too old, and it became true for them because they believe it. It would have been the same for me if I would have listened to myself and not my granddaughter who showed me all things are possible. Bike riding was very therapeutic. Now, I have learned that horseback riding is because a horse's heart beats and can love you back. Amazing Grace was wonderful; she taught me much in the little time I spent with her — thank you."

I paused, wiping tears from my eyes again.

"Let me scratch this event off my bucket list. I am thankful God answered my prayers. Thank you for the awesome crew who helped make it happen and for this grand event. Your patience, kindness, and generosity will never go unappreciated. May you all live your dreams."

We took our last picture, all of us with Amazing Grace, Fierce, and Popcorn Kernels. The image would hang on my office wall, right next to my desk—proof that I rode!

The Canyon

The carvings from water are evidence of brokenness and judgement—The reminder. Our son's flight touched down in Vegas last night to join us on a trip to the Grand Canyon. Chloe was so excited, uncles she hadn't met before. Nervous wasn't the right word for this girl. It's been a long time since we had these three together. Jez is stubborn as a mule, fixed in his ways. I called him as I planned the trip and he was dry, answering each question with a short response which eventually lead to him saying no. Chloe tried talking him into coming, but he came up with every excuse not to. She seemed bummed out at first but didn't let it weigh down her excitement. Walking past the mirror, she glanced at herself fixing her hair and checking her makeup. I was getting worked up myself just listening to her. Watching her from a distance as she fluttered around the room, looking over their pictures, with occasional outbreaks of who was who. The front desk called informing Hosea that they were here and were being let up. A light knock at the door sent Chloe racing across the room, opening the door with a face that glimmered like famous folks stood in the entrance.

"Girl let them in, standing there like someone half frozen like they somebody extraordinary."

"Granddad?"

"Dad? Hello, we are," Asher gave Hosea a quick eye.

"What I'm just saying, let all of you in."

"Well, hello, uncles, too many to identify separately. Let me try."

"Whatever Chloe… You are gorgeous with those big ole eyes," Asher said.

Smiling at him while holding his hand, "Thanks, Uncle Asher?"

"Yup, that's me. Never thought I would hear you say these words."

"What words?"

"Uncle Asher," he laughed.

She teared up and wiped her eyes, "me either," forcing a smile.

"Give me a hug, girl," Elisha stated as he walked towards her for his hug.

"Hey, they are not movie stars, just your uncles."

"I know. Come on now—this is a big deal for me."

"Oh, my goodness, I got all my boys here… well except Jez."

"I hate it too grandma, but let's enjoy the ones who came… ok?" She wiped the hair from my face.

"Girl last time I saw you—you were brand-spanking new."

She twisted side to side, just blushing.

"Yes, let me inform you I'm all grown up now," blinking her eyes.

"You are beautiful and look different from I imagined. Do you still have that strawberry birthmark on your back?" Elisha said.

"Eh — uh, no. I don't have a strawberry birthmark. You say it's on my back?"

"Yeah, when you were born, your dad took a pic of it and showed me. He was excited because strawberry ice cream is his favorite."

Chloe appeared nervous after Elisha asked her, then the rest of them stated they remembered as well.

"I think I remember that too. Kind of red and puckered up like a real strawberry. It really went away?"

"Well… I haven't, eh no it didn't. I still got it."

"You know when you had on the bikini last week, I didn't pay it no attention."

"Hey all this talk about me. Shoot, I got me some fine uncles; I know y'all are all taken, right?"

"Hecke no, I'm not about that life yet—too young. But your dad and Omar are," Asher said.

"I ain't either, no time for that drama just yet. Been there, done that — I'm good," Elisha sat, shaking his head.

"Ok, I hear you. So—what have you all been up too?"

"Nothing much, baby girl, happy to be out here to see you, mom's and pop's," Omar stated, giving her a big bear hug.

"Dang Omar, you are taller than everybody here, and you hug just like granddad. All tough, like we about to wrestle."

"Speaking of him, hey Pops," walking over to him, giving him a handshake and a slap on the back.

"Hey, my man, I'm so happy to see all of you and going on this trip with us. You better go see your mom's you know how she gets all dramatic about you boys," Hosea said.

"Right, where is she?" Elisha said.

"She went into the room; you know, to tidy up."

"Oh, ok, sounds about what I need to do, been moving all day and the flight."

Knocking on her door, "Well, hello, look at you. Did you have a problem getting here?" Matea said.

Hugging everyone, "see you all have spent a little time with Ms. Chloe, who is about to get married in a few weeks," clapping my hands.

"Yeah, Chloe, you didn't even say anything about the big day yet." Omar said.

"So, when do we get to meet this cat you about to marry?" Elisha curiously asked.

"Soon, here he is," pulling out her phone with pictures.

"Girl, you beat us finding somebody, you a bad girl," Asher stated, leaving Chloe blushing.

"You'll slow… better find you somebody or enjoy watching me do my thang," Chloe playfully dancing around.

"Wow, we haven't even been here but a minute, and you're already starting mess."

Hosea informed everyone that the folks would be here around 2:00 PM to take us on a tour to the Grand Canyon. Everyone groaned as if he could have just canceled the entire trip.

"What's with all this moaning and groaning, you'll tired already?" Hosea said.

"Dad, we ain't that young no more, we just got off the plane last night and up early—man, I tired as heck."

"Where is your dad, Chloe?" Omar asked.

"He couldn't make it… but you have me," smiling with a widened grin.

Elisa began clapping, "Look who bailed out again… the notorious Jez."

"Don't start. We have a wonderful day ahead of us, and we have Ms. Chloe. That's a blessing," I added.

"Yeah, man, he has his reasons, and I'm happy to have you all here," Hosea quipped.

"Dad, it has been a long time since we've gotten together—even us. It feels good, ya know? Have to do this more often," Elisha said.

"It sure feels good; ya'll just don't know how much me and your ma miss all of you."

Everyone agreed, sitting around talking, we saw the sun creep into a full beam. Clouds so fluffy they appeared like substantial cotton balls lingering in midair. I started tidying up a few things; if I sat still, I would fall right to sleep. Offered everyone something to drink and disappeared into my room, focusing on nothing but the bed. Asher knocked on the door.

"Ma, you got something for dad's back? It's bothering him."

"Ya, give me a minute."

Entering the Livingroom, Elisha is standing on Hosea's back with his legs bent backwards like he was in sheer pain. Asher joked around saying nobody else wanted to be a part of his shenanigans, which may leave him in the emergency room. Hose's words seemed as if he smashed them out from his jerking body. Each step taken, he moved like he was a living rug. I stood watching, as it was too late to stop him. I grumbled reminding him the last time he had somebody do that he ended up in urgent care thinking he broke his back.

"Oh yeah dad, you let that big dude stand on your back and you swore he broke it."

"What you have to go and bring that up for? There you go telling all my business."

"Dad, we were there, Asher said he heard your back crack… Jez called the ambulance,"

"Yeah, this is not the same thing," as he got up from the floor.

"That dude looked crazy. He had that black shoe polish looking paint all over his head and mustache, and he was over 300 pounds. Remember?" Elisha fell out laughing with tears running.

"Oh yeah, that crazy-looking man related to us?"

"Naw, he was my co-worker for your information, he lost all his facial hair and we called him uncle Fester. Thank you, my back feels better."

"All man! that's messed up," Elisha laughed with his fist covering his mouth.

"Be careful who you talk about, it can happen to you. He was my boy until he retired."

"Change the subject, sorry I brought it up. Your dad is getting an attitude."

"Y'all should have seen your dad dancing in the streets last night, just like he did when we came here the last time. I got him on video."

Hosea sat on the chair, leaning back easy, propping a pillow behind his back with Asher, helping him get comfortable by putting his feet on the ottoman.

"Ask him why his back hurts?"

"Woman, don't start on me about last night."

"I'm just saying… dancing as if you were 21 again, and it caught up with, that's all — just like the old days."

"We had a blast last night with granddad dancing and having a blast. You got to watch the video," Chloe stated.

"What — Pop's, can still dance?"

"What makes you think I can't?"

"I don't know, maybe your age."

"Oh — my back, I'm old not dead, fool. Boy, don't get me started," he groaned.

"Alright, well leave you alone."

It was still early; the guys laid down for a while, asking me to call for a wake-up call so they wouldn't oversleep.

"Hm, it's about 6:30 AM. I have them call about noon."

☙

I peacefully slept until abruptly awoken by them loudly talking and joking around in the living room. Ripping the door open, everyone stopped instantly, looking like they did when they were kids, always wrestling and arguing over sports crap, except Chloe joined in. Broke everything in the house that could be broken and today I see things are about the same, but they're grown. Asher fell over onto the coffee table and smacked the glass to the floor. Everything seemed to move in slow motion until the glass shattered and he fell besides the mess to the floor. He released a robust laugh, letting Elisha know he wasn't hurt. I stood with my arms folded without a mere blink, wondering if they'd every grow up.

"Get the mess up please." It's time to head out. I began complaining as to why they waited so late to wake me for the tour. I was starving!

Elisha said, "Ma, we will get you something to eat, don't worry your beautiful self."

"Awe, that's so sweet of you. I have to take my medication; I need food to go with it."

"We'll get you something from the restaurant. Get dressed and well go down there."

"We got to take care of Momma," kissing me on the forehead.

"I love you, ma."

"I love you too."

Everyone got ready so I could eat something in the restaurant attached to the hotel. I found it hard to shake the tired feeling, and maybe it would be wise to drink some coffee, which I rarely drink. They had a few good choices on the menu which appeared tasty.

"Brunch was not bad; actually, I enjoyed it."

The shuttle pulled up; the staff loaded our luggage while we quickly picked our seats.

"Has anyone been to the Canyon yet?"

Looking around, Hosea stated, "I don't think they have."

"No, this is my first time. I'm excited too," Asher exclaimed.

"Well, that makes this trip even more exciting—plus we have a baby girl with us."

Scanning the booth looking at everyone, "This makes me happy, thanks to everybody for helping me scratch this off my bucket list."

"Ma, I might get me a bucket list going. Shoot, you got me feeling like I need to live more myself."

Look at my sons, handsome, ambitious, and healthy from what I can see. Everybody is so busy nowadays. Look at Hosea sitting all proud with his sons like they were trophies he had won. All that hard work paid off.

So did those prayers. My man sure enjoyed them as they grew up. I wish Jez were here, but we have Ms. Chloe, who makes up for it. We made our way to the Grand Canyon and were excited.

❧

We were announcing our plans for the day, which starts with the Jeep tour set up for us, which will last about four hours. We will stop for lunch in the last part of the trip; we'll have a helicopter ride for another two hours. It was a quick tour of the Grand Canyon because we old folks couldn't see being in for us just to say we had been there and mark it off our bucket list. Hosea had a towel on his head tied to fit and sunglasses.

"Why you always gotta look weird when we go out, huh?" I asked.

"Woman — you must forget where we live? Folks don't watch it could get a heat stroke out here."

Everybody chimed in, taking shots at Hosea, but he paid nobody no mind. However, Asher took up for him getting them off his back. Asher was close to Hosea, always willing to fight for him no matter what. They didn't care; usually, the jokes include him as well. Laughter filled the air as we waited for our jeep to pick us up till, we couldn't breathe. The heat stopped us after a while, leaving us gasping for air. We sweated like condensation on sweltering windows moistened with steam; even our shirts became wet. I'm sure it was hot enough to melt wax, with no relief in sight. Elisha returned with cold water for everyone; what a deliverance to our parched mouths. Omar splashed half his bottle on his face for quick relief from the heat. Watching in despair, it became a pattern for the others—except Hosea and me. I don't play with water like that—unless it gets a smidgen hotter. However, soon after riding about an hour in the jeep, Hosea was the main one not sweating to death. The joke was on, for sure we'd never hear the end of it.

The south rim of the Grand Canyon was indescribable; no picture could explain its beauty. It took our breath away as we stood, soaking in everything we never imagined. For a minute or two or three, we stood silent. God sure created a wonderous world. We stopped and stood on a ledge while the tour bus driver gave full details on its existence.

"The Grand Canyon became an 1893 forest reserve, and in 1919 they declared it a national park," the driver bolstered.

No telling what year God made it before folks came around claiming it. I stood there for a moment soaking in God's gift, yes; I cried.

"Ma, I know you love those colors."

"Who knows the biblical reasoning behind the Canyon?"

"I do, Ma," I stated.

"Really… let me hear it."

"It has something to do with Noah's Ark and the great flood."

"Your right," looking at him in shock.

That young man always astonishes me. Knowing he isn't into religion; I pray he keeps seeking God.

"Yes, he's correct. They just lost a case preventing us from speaking on religious things and took down all the signs regarding religion," the guide said.

"They can take a sign, but they can't take the evidence," I said.

"Well, my lady, you are correct in your thinking."

The driver stated as he walked back to the jeep.

"You always fascinate me on the arrays of colors you love, ma," Elisha said.

"You know it; I am in awe looking at the layers of white, yellow, green, and… hmm looks like pink. The colors tenderly interwoven and blended to perfection hung against the eroded walls."

"It's amazing," I whispered.

"Yeah ma it is," grabbing my hand.

Taking a minute to note that my son held my hand. Thinking it hadn't happened since he was a kid, back when life was hustle and bustle, being a left-behind parent, who owned up to the promise of caring for my children. It was moments like this that proved my hard work didn't go unrecognized. I felt love. Laying my head on his shoulder, all I could do is think how amazing it was that God blessed me with my sons and how nothing in life compared to it.

"Did ya'll know that the lines represent timeframes throughout history?" Hosea mentioned.

"Naw, Dad, I didn't know that," Omar said.

"I didn't either," Chloe exclaimed.

"It's about 17 million years old."

Reading the brass sign, Chloe mentioned two climbing rocks to our right.

Scanning the area, Chloe and I noted a couple. In disbelief, we looked on as this slender young lady climbed a boulder to take a picture which over hanged a cliff.

"Oh my, I pray she doesn't fall!" I squinted.

"Are they for real?" Chloe watched.

Our eyes grew enormous, watching in fear. The young lady slipped and was too frightened to move, looking as if she would fall right over and it was a steep fall. We gasped. I flung myself into Hosea's chest, burying my eyes. Her husband worked effortlessly to help her. Hosea yelled for the guys to see if one of them could help. Her tour guide ran over to help, but she was too frightened to move. She appeared too scared to even open her mouth; it was like she was frozen to the rock with sweat drenching her face like an intense rainfall. She was ghostly pale as she turned her face our way. Her visor toppled over and flew down the side of the Canyon. Almost proved to be her fate. The dry 100-degree heat forced everyone assisting her to amble, yet they never stopped. My breathing became labored as I watched them work effortlessly to save her. The thought came to me: *Jesus is the rock and foundation do not fear.* Comforted, I wanted badly to tell her who needed this message the most.

"Dang, they didn't read the sign that says, keep off the boulders, do not climb or stand on them. It is right there!" Omar stated.

"Folks never read those signs, this becomes a regular occurrence," the tour guide responded.

The crowd grew, many with their hands over their mouth in disarray. The whispers and hackles mired the air. The lady appeared to be in her late twenties, finding her face had taken on the color of pure purple and most likely sun burned. Finally, she'd been saved, and everyone stood clapping, cheering, and mocking the poor limp woman. She only needed compassion and prayers, but few saw like wise. I'm sure she felt grateful and foolish at the same time; however, she appeared too shaken to tell which. They led her to the jeep so she could recover, and I went to her. Trying to speak proved difficult for her, as her husband assisted, "My wife says Jesus told her he was the rock and to hold on. She said he was with her."

"Really?"

He asked, "honey, are you sure that's what you heard?"

I touched him, "I heard the same thing, I can assure you she heard it."

"Funny because we're atheist, we don't believe."

"After today I believe she will and pray you do too. He saved her life today."

"Thank you."

He turned and walked her to the ambulance. I prayed for them both. Walking back to our tour guide, I wiped the sweat off my face and noted the biggest, brightest double rainbow as my face met the sky.

"Grandma look… another double rainbow," Chloe yelled out, pointing out to the heavens.

"I'm looking," scurrying over to her, while waving my hat.

This is the second rainbow we've seen this summer. It was amazing, yet couldn't get a decent picture, so Asher took a video of it instead with his phone.

"Ok, that's what's up, baby bro. Try to get all of it."

I just stood in amazement. You know, it appeared right after they rescued the young lady. Glancing his way, I noticed her husband looked outward at it, dropping his head.

"Thank you, everyone, for helping us; she seems fine, just shaken up. We are just thankful she's ok."

Shaking his hand, Hosea comforted him, "Man, just help her relax and calm her nerves."

Not too long after, they quickly sped off, as I stared them off and out of my view. We pulled off shortly after that to have lunch.

❧

Going over my notes. Next, the Upper Antelope walkthrough I'd pointed out earlier. The helicopter rides next. None of us had been in a helicopter and we were excited. What memories we are about to make. Folks around us were raving about seeing the Upper Antelope Canyon tour, making it sound even better than the pamphlet. Stepping closer to the chatter to understand what we were in for, I'm so nosey. Looking for the guys, Chloe told me they had gone to the shop to browse around. The driver asked that we get ready to roll out and gather everyone. Walking around searching the multitude of people for them, I pulled out my phone with a finger on the numbers. They showed up. My mouth dropped wide. They all had on towels draped around their heads and mesh shirts. Each one of them had on the same mess Hosea did.

"Ma don't say a word. We're hot as heck out here," Omar stated.

"Well, you won't be sweating, let's go."

Chloe wanted to be just like them. Elisha picked one up for her and helped her braid her hair and placed it on her head.

"Who taught you how to braid?" she asked Elisha.

He looked at me and laughed.

"Grandma?"

"Yup."

"Come on, you'll, it's time to go," I yelled.

They warned us of possible flash flooding and that had me worried a bit because we're too old to be running from water.

"Did anybody hear about the flash floods they could have in the Antelopes?"

"No, Ma, I'm reading about it now. They claim we have nothing to worry about, that it is rare nowadays," said Omar.

"I didn't know about the water issue. I will inquire more about it. I'm not up to jogging from nobodies' water," Hosea said.

I had the couple next to us, laughing away. I was wholeheartedly speaking from my heart. "I don't need to be around any flash floods; neither do any of you."

I addressed my concerns with the tour guide; they assured us all that we had nothing to worry about; they have equipment that lets them know if it's safe to go through—finally made it to the Upper Antelope Rim. It's purely made of sandstone, similar to a cave, and tight in space. The guide continued to speak. He said nothing concerning the muggy air that filled the space, making it hard to breathe. Getting to the center of the Antelope, the space opened up so we could see the beauty of the walls. We were comfortable and able to breathe, making it more enjoyable. My mind was running a mile a minute thinking about how I could describe this, as it's was breathtaking. Taking pictures proved useless; they all came out dark or blurry. A guy standing next to me was a photographer, advising us we needed a unique lens to get any quality pictures. Hosea noted he took some of the most vivid angles.

"Your reflections are bouncing off the walls," the man pointed out.

Showing us the lens and camera, we needed for quality photos, especially in this environment. "Ok, ok. Hey, how much do you charge if we asked you to take a few pictures of my family and send them to me?"

He looked at us, shrugged his shoulders, "Nothing, we'll exchange numbers and go from there."

"Thanks, sir, I owe you big time. I'll treat you to lunch," sealing the deal with a handshake.

"Thank you," he gleamed.

The pictures came out beautifully, with all the fantastic colors embedded within the background. The walls displayed striations of oranges, crimson, yellow, and some brown marbled together in complex patterns made up of the sides of this sandstone cave.

"It's called Tse` bigha'nilini, the place where water runs through rocks by the Navajo's," the tour guide stated.

It was noisy as sand blew off the walls we couldn't hear.

"Who name is that?" I replied.

He laughed, "No, it is what we call the walls 'Tse` bigha'nilini'".

"Ma, what did he call the wall?"

"I don't understand neither, best to get it from him if you want the right answer."

This place was so exciting; I had to just stand in one place to take in another one of God's wonders. Hosea grabbed me, kissing me. I called it a sandcastle kiss; he held my hand to keep up with him. The tour guide was babbling away with some interesting facts about the Antelope. He did an outstanding job. What an adventure — as we headed back to the jeep.

"Are you all enjoying yourselves?" I asked everyone.

In return, I heard silence.

"Hello, are you all having fun?"

Everybody started speaking at once, "We are having a blast," Chloe exclaimed.

"Yeah ma, it so much to see in one day."

Asher flumped into the seat as if it exhausted him.

"Boy, move and let everyone else go in, the youngest one in the bunch and the most tired?"

"Come on, Ma, age has nothing to do with this," Asher said.

Scooting over, we all piled in ready for the grand finale—the helicopter ride. I had been trying to get Hosea to take me on a helicopter ride since we first met. Thinking it would be romantic and a perfect stance for a date. Somehow this seemed better than what I had planned. I'm with my family, and that meant more to me than the world.

"Thanks for having us on your trip, so cool being with you all. Been a long time," Elisa said.

"I love every moment too. Got my hottie, my sons, and granddaughter, I'm in heaven."

"Are you trying to make me blush?" I said.

"I am."

Me—sitting there blushing, looking like a brilliant red rose, I was at a loss of words, which was rare for me. It saved me from sticking my foot in my mouth, which I usually do. I enjoyed every minute of this trip.

"Thank you for making this happen, honey, this means everything to me," as I snuggled deeper on his shoulder.

The ride to the helicopter was further than we thought. No complaints from any of us, as we were enjoying the air-conditioned ride. It gave us time to rest for the next part of the day. We were getting tired, though; I dug into my fanny pack, pulling out some b12 shots, offering them to whoever wanted one. I think we all needed some help with energy. We could hear the whirling of the propellers of the helicopter with increasing sound as it came closer. Hosea looked up, noting that it seemed like it was the helicopter we would ride in. It hovered, jerking side to side looking for a clear landing spot. Our tour guide requested us to move to the area closer to the rocks for safety. Chloe and I huddled together, pulling the others into our circle. The wind blew around so hard that it was difficult to see. The closer it came, the more the winds picked up the debris, swirling it around. The guide asked us to cover our mouths and eyes and stood in front of us to assure we stayed back.

"Sure, it makes me feel like I'm back in the military. I had some good times in there," Hosea said, struggling through the wind.

"I sometimes forget you were in the military dad, you never talk about it," Omar stated.

"Yeah — I know, nothing really to talk about. I enjoy talking about the memories I have with you all. I hardly think about those days of hard work and low pay — seven years I gave them. Life has been much better since then."

"Thanks for your service, dad. I appreciate your hard work," Omar said.

"Can't forget Elisha, he did three years."

Smirking, "Thanks man for your service."

"Shut up," laughing loudly.

You can tell Hosea felt some type of way hearing the words from his son. The smile on his face spoke volumes.

❧

The helicopter landed; the noise was too much to hear. Not to mention the whirling wind that continued as we tried hard to listen to instructions. We introduced ourselves to the pilot, Mr. Carter; he's an older, friendly guy with a charming smile. Hosea asked many questions, assuring we were in expert hands.

"How long have you been piloting helicopters?" Hosea boldly asked.

"27 years, sir," beaming with pride.

"Oh, you good, just making sure you knew what you were doing."

"Not a problem, sir," tipping his hat.

Boarding the helicopter wasn't bad as I thought it would be, Elisa and Asher helped me with a little push, reminding me of horseback riding. We worked getting our ear gear, sunglasses, and seatbelts on, we were ready to go. Chatter filled the area as we snapped snaps and made sure we had everything we needed.

"Ready for take-off?" Mr. Carter yelled.

"Yes," In unison.

Off we cascaded to the air. I was holding Hosea and Asher's hands tightly.

"Dang mom, you are cutting off my blood circulation."

Releasing my grip looking at his fingers, he was right.

"Yeah woman, I might lose a finger or two dealing with you, remind me of when you were having Asher."

"I'm sorry. I was just a little nervous."

Shaking my head. The rest seemed to take the lift off fine. It amazed us all the views from up here. Those propellers were blazing away, as the pilot did some fancy moves, kept us entertained. The sites from the sky were beautiful, not to mention peaceful. First, we visited the Horseshoe Bend, which was interesting. The waters from the Colorado River incised meander through the rock, making its shape into a 270-degree horseshoe shape. The water from the river looked mystical and green… at some angles, it was hard to view. The pilot curved the plane, so everyone got their pictures. Mr. Carter seemed to enjoy talking in his mic. The comical fella told jokes and crazy stories about his family and how he became a pilot, very patient in answering all of our questions. Hoovering over the Horseshoe Bend, he explained that it was rich in hematite, platinum, garnet, and other minerals, it's too beautiful to believe. He made a few comments before whirling off.

"Hold your towels and wigs were off to the Tower Butt," Mr. Carter stated.

Flying and hovering over our location, we safely landed. There we were, standing on a tower in the middle of the Grand Canyon, 5,000 feet above the ground. I was past scared and drew in breaths like a machine was passing out small amounts at a time. Not to mention I dare move a toe and wasn't even if somebody paid me too. The rest moved around like we were on a regular sidewalk. Poking around and taking pictures, we stood on a solid rock which resembled a skyscraper with some amazing views. The pilot walked around stopping in front of me declaring that he had the secret to better breathing.

"Trust God," Mr. Carter stated.

My eyes widened as I bust out laughing right in his face.

"I'm sorry, really I am."

"What you don't believe me?"

"No — I do. I was prepared to hear something else, but you hit me with the obvious."

"Good, or I can offer you a paper bag to help you."

"No, I'm fine, I practically forgot about my breathing just talking to you."

"Good. Let's join the rest before you miss these beautiful views and pictures."

I walked around but nowhere close to them, my breathing guided me through the safe zones. The sites were so wondrous; you felt close to God standing there. Viewing landmarks such as Glen Canyon, Lake Powell, Kaiparowits Plateau, and The Grand Staircase. Chloe and the boys stood as close to the edge as they could, taking in the views and pictures. My nerves were about shattered, I stayed in the middle of the tower, quiet and snuggled close to my best friend, Hosea, who joined. He encouraged me to stand with the group to take a few photos, promising me he would stay close and I did. Last, we took one picture alone and I'll never forget it.

❧

Later that evening, Chloe and I sat by the pool, thinking I had gotten away with reading the journal. No, she didn't slide it out of her pocket. Shaking my head, "Girl… I am too tired."

"You read while I listen — deal."

She chucked, "I know you thought you got away from it, didn't you?"

"Yes, this old woman sure did. You're not tired?"

"Nope."

She rolled over on the sofa, beginning to read.

The Journal- ✿Life after my mom's death

My grandma- Mrs. Cozi Mc Carthy took us in at 55 years old. She had only one child—my mom. However, she accumulated 4 of us as a bonus package. As a small child, I loved visiting my grandma. It was a different way of living; I remember her throwing together oatmeal cookies or pancakes when we visited. She never had store-bought cookies as we grew up in the 60s; people still made home-cooked everything. Funny, because her house always smelled like bananas, even when she didn't have any.

Around the age of seven, grandma's house was rarely fun anymore, either we'd been left there by our parents or sent there for help. It was nothing for my parents to drop us off on the porch with precise instructions of sounding the doorbell when they tore off, and that's what we did time and time again. She ignored us until we played with the metal mailbox cut into the front door, making a loud clanking noise with occasional yells, sent her cussing as she made her way to the door.

She had the tolerance of steel when handing my homework, especially my timetables. My mother had no patience to teach me anything, and it usually turned into violent fits when she tried. The smacks and rage she displayed left me stiffened with fear. I wanted nothing to do with numbers. No matter how much grandma tried, she couldn't rid me of the fear of the hostile stance mom gave before she sent me to her.

"Mama, I'm sending her to you. I can't do anything with her."

Was her favorite line when she had enough of me; it was often. My anxiety was through the roof because of it, leaving me frozen with the fear of math, which required me to partake in special ed. My grandma would search around the kitchen in her multiple junk drawers, searching for a rubber band for homemade eraser for her pencils. It was a routine of hers. Placing one good rubber band wrapped pencil behind each ear, she was ready to teach.

Grandma made sure no one interrupted her when she moved her TV on a cart into the living room—arranging the rabbit ears antennas, along with two hard bangs to the side to get the best picture blink in so she could watch her soaps—both day and night. She would listen to radio mysteries while in bed. Laying in total darkness was intriguing and relaxing. The suspense of a sudden scream to awaken one's senses to solve the mystery, often proved fascinating, after we would tune in to local police calls.

She always had big cars that seemed hard for her to handle, which may explain why she drove slower than molasses dripping out of a cold jar. Driving, she put on her AM radio and listened to her favorite Christian radio station… 'Martha Jean the Queen'. She sang and hummed the entire time while tapping the steering wheel like it placed her in a deep trance. Pressing my feet on the floor, pretending that I could make her go faster. She never talked or allowed us to talk while she drove, figuring her nerves were bad.

Grandma Cozbi was a dynamic woman who suffered her the loss of first husband a few months after buying a house and remarried years after.

She had a set of twins from her first marriage, losing her son at birth and my mom at 31. I could only imagine the strength she had to have. To this day, I don't think I could have survived what she had been through. My mother's funeral came fast, allowing us to only view her body—four kids, badly stricken with grief, so young that we barely understood what happened. For me, I thought I had found her as I stood by her casket admiring her yellow dress, but wait, her hair wasn't right. I started walking around telling folks they had her hair all wrong, assuring that it's the best they could do. I wondered, Is this my mom? I gathered the nerves to touch her, quietly standing next to her I slowly forged my finger into her body, finding she was hard as a rock — with a lousy hairdo — it wasn't her; it couldn't be.

Grandma brought some normalcy to our lives; we had matching clothes, food to eat every day, and a reliable, quiet roof over our heads—best of all, her and granddaddy didn't fight. That November, we had our first Thanksgiving meal; it was something we'd never celebrated at home. All the food that we cooked left me in disbelief that I'll always remember it. My mom never celebrated the holidays, except Christmas, when we had the money. The greatest thing my grandma ever did — she introduced me to God. The church became my family. I joined the choir, getting my first taste of singing solos — couldn't sing worth a darn, but they sure made me feel good when I tried. We washed cars to pay for spiritual trips in different states to learn more about His word. Those events gave me my thirst for travel and taught me to let go of worldly things.

My sister and my relationship became even more broken; her mental and sometimes physical abuse was a nightmare. Our relationship became torturous to where I will do anything to get away. Finding it hard to understand as I watched her cunning ways entice others into her smear tactics against me. The room we shared decor resembled the existence of two different people overwhelming a small space. Wishing I had her as a friend, and she would change, I gave in to her tactics more than I care to remember. The times she left me feeling like a victim from someone who should have been my closest confidant. Instead, it feels as though we would always be enemies, and for my soul, it's best to walk away, but when? My grandma and I seemed to have lost our special bond after my mother's death. She'd appeared to have taken it well, but in reality, she was in survival mode, proving time after time it was useless talking to her about my feelings. With my sister resembling the exact likes of my mom, it doomed me, making me feel invisible. She sat on her throne well. The tension in the household was immense, with the wars between my sister and me, kept my grandma in the middle of constant bickering matches, as I always sat on the losing end. Giving in to whatever she wanted, I despised them both. Yet I knew, as a young lady, that isn't what I wanted for my heart.

I sat back watching my sister today, trying to figure out if I should continue to love her and make myself miserable. Or do I yearn for the day to walk away, never to see her again? I despise saying this — she looks just like mom… but doesn't act like her. Or did she? Everywhere we went, the family flourished over her as if it would bring our mom back. No one ever thought about how their careless actions made me feel. My sister loved the attention, soaking in all the admiration of looking like someone who wasn't kind to me, made me even more depressed. More like sick to my stomach–Dealing with deep depression, a broken voice, I remained withdrawn most of the time, I couldn't disappear, but I was invisible. I was a lost soul in survival mode.

By the time I became 16, I had experienced so much that I was ready to call quits on life. Grandma shielded me from what she saw best. Life was quiet, too quiet- in short, just dull. Oh, how I loved to run, but after-school activities were strictly forbidden. I enjoyed running the most; it gave me the freedom to take my mind off the world. None the less, I never ran, expect for the rat my brother chased me down the street with. It didn't count. Our dysfunctional family was essential to me; however, being around them was painfully unpleasant all the time. To add to the painful experiences, I had already encountered. I was gang-raped, forcing myself to hold my pain inside as though it never happened. Even rape didn't force me to share my emotions, only sent me into a more profound depression.

"Wow, I don't know what to say. First, your mom passes away. After you deal with issues at your new home? Grandma, I just can't believe you got raped?" Chloe said.

I sat shaking my head. Hearing that story again was painful, not to mention sharing it. Those days were so hard on me; it was hard reliving these moments, especially to my granddaughter, who barely knew me.

"Yes, all of that happened before I turned fifteen and I held it in for a long time. I am a survivor, so they say."

"I am so sorry that happened to you," with a weird look on her face.

"Hey, I'm concerned, why the face?"

"What face? I'm thinking that's all."

"Honey don't feel sorry for me. I forgave those boys so long ago. I think I was in my late 30s when it all crashed down on me; I could no longer hold in pain and wanted to heal. Ya know, let Jesus handle the rest."

She frowned, "It took that long for you to face it?"

"It did. Thought I had put it behind me until I saw one of the guy's and crashed. Told nobody until your granddad showed me, he was worthy of hearing."

With teary eyes, she shook her head. She was quiet, just sitting there without saying a word. The tears streamed from her face before looking at me.

"Grandma—"

"Yes, honey?"

"Your sister makes me glad I am the only child, Yuck."

"She makes me wish the same thing. But — what I need from you is prayer. Till my last breath my prayers are we will heal, change, and become close."

"Why would you want to be close to her?"

"Nothing will change that we are sisters and —"

"What?"

"I love her."

"Why do you think you should change when it was her?"

"I want to be free to trust and love her, I've made mistakes too and am not perfect. Only Jesus is suitable for that title. Hurt people, harm people. I'm sure I could have been a better sister, I'm confident I can because I'm not suffering anymore."

Sitting quietly.

Breaking the silence, "I was raped before," she quivered.

"What — When?"

"In high school, eleventh grade."

"Did you tell your parents?"

"Yes, it was horrible—but it's not something I want to talk about."

"Oh, honey, you don't have too, I'm here if you want to discuss."

"Okay," she sniffled.

I hugged her, "I am so sorry."

"Look to me, baby girl, forgive them and let God handle these evil demons. They have theirs coming, oh yes they do."

"How can you forgive that?"

"Pray to release old hurts, baggage… pain just eats at your heart. Rips your spirit to pieces. You don't want that. You can't handle the hurt alone, pray."

She just sat in silence.

"I was so full of hurt. I had to forgive each of them. I had to face the pain. Couldn't have done it without God. He held me, instructed me, and along the way… he healed me."

"I'll think about it," wiping her face from the fallen tears.

"Forgiveness baby is the key to life. No matter what you go through, forgive. God deals with all the things that need to happen to whoever may harm you. Ask Him for courage."

"I've been hurt before, a few times. I don't know if I can forgive them."

"Oh yes, you can," clasping her chin.

"You can forgive them, write it down and face the problem. Pray for direction and let it go. That's all you have to do and throw it away. Whenever the thoughts come to your mind, forgive them. Soon it will go away."

"Ok, I will."

"Don't carry these past hurts into your marriage. You need to be free from anything that can hold you back from loving him freely."

"I love you grandma, I needed you so long ago... glad I got you now."

Laying her head on my shoulder.

"I love you too."

"Girl, I have to go to bed. I'm drained and as you can see, time waits for nobody, not even this old lady and young girl who need their rest."

Sandcastles

A house built on sand quickly passes away, but those build on rock stays forever. Hosea slid through the house, grumbling about how fast time flew. All that lip flapping he was doing didn't bring one-minute back, just wasted energy. I was still flying high from riding and wasn't ready to come down, after all it only took me forever to make it happen. Still in disbelief that I had ridden a horse. Spending days getting pictures printed, canvas placed on the wall, certificate mounted, and hours of blabbering to all my friends about my special moment. I can't believe a week had passed. Still tired and sore all over gave me a hunch that maybe I shouldn't have ridden, not to mention the worst fibro flare, leaving me bed bound for three days. Regret crossed my mind a few times. However, the feeling of accomplishment overruled. It was a great feeling. However, I couldn't deny that it had taken a great deal out of me. Today, Hosea announced he had the weekend set up for us; excited, but probably could use more rest. I pushed on. No time for extended beauty rest and fretting over pain. Seeing a difference in both of us since we were doing things with Chloe. I figured living by ourselves; we had let old age take us hostage and had gracefully given into it. He asked Candace to prepare breakfast and pack us a lunch; she started right away. Waiting around, we helped her, while Hosea went off to handle some business. Feeling like a kid again, I was excited to see what his plans were. My soreness forced me to move like a snail. As we chatted, I shared my summer's desire list with the ladies. Chloe laughed.

"Grandma, you only have a few things listed. Besides we've done some of it already."

"Uh—I know… I'm working on it. Besides its things I want to do this summer, not looking too far into the future."

"It looks like a good start to me. Just a few months ago she mentioned it and had nothing planned. Good job, Mrs. Gomar."

"Candace, do you have a bucket list?"

"I do. No time or resources to do them. However, I know the good Lord has plans for me."

"Well, we'll just have to do something about that, let's see what the future holds lady."

Scrunching my face while I thought over them. "For sure, I can't be a ballerina anymore; bones done dried up."

Chloe hollered something loud, spat her tea across the room.

"Why do you laugh?"

"Grandma—heck, no! A ballerina?" Chloe shook her head, laughing at me even more. Bringing herself to tears.

"What about learning a new dance? Maybe salsa dancing? You and Mr. Gomar can do that together?" Candace said.

"Don't think I can do it! I'm too stiff. Especially after riding a horse, I think it taught me a lesson on doing too much."

Chloe shrugged her shoulders. "Well, if you think you can't, then you won't be able to. Be positive, grandma. And no to ballet."

"Maybe I should do some soul searching — ya know. Figure out the things I can do," feeling frustrated.

Candace chimed in, "Matea, I am so happy to see you and Hosea enjoying life again. The things you guys have done these past few weeks have been a blessing. I see a big difference in you both."

She gave an immense warm smile to Chloe.

"You think it's because of me? I thought you all had things planned before I called?"

"Chloe, we needed you here a long time ago; look at the two of them. They didn't have a thing planned before your visit," Candace said.

"It feels good being here."

"Oh, thank you, honey. It has been a blast."

She was right; doing new things had made us feel so young again. We needed some spice back in our lives, just didn't know how.

"Chloe, we are so happy to have you here."

"Yeah, I agree. Should have a long time ago, but I'm here now and that's what's important," she smiled.

I admit I was so ruffled on the inside; I was close to bursting at the seams with joy. We hadn't had this much fun in years. As we finished packing lunch, Candace worked on breakfast.

"Candace, breakfast was delish. Girl, you sure know how to cook," Chloe said.

"Thanks, glad you appreciate it."

We helped clean things up, eager to see what Hosea had in store for us. While waiting, I chuckled to myself. Shoot, it might be awhile. Lately, he's been moving slower than me. I figured horse fever might have settled in his old bones. In the short, it already felt like we'd known each other forever and had become comfortable around us. Rambling, she shared details on her education and things she had done over the years. Elaborating on a few challenges she had overcome in her younger years, I leaned over the side of the sofa with my body propped against the armrest. Sipping juice, I watched her mouth move like she was one of these energizer bunny's that kept going. My granddaughter had the gift of gab for sure, which I don't. Her background was full of awards, noting she was fluent in Spanish and French. It impressed me; as she was a brilliant young lady, much like me in my young days. Her parents put a lot of work into her. She loves sports, cars and healthy eating, going for workouts faithfully. I enjoyed stealing glimpses of her, watching her feisty demeanor with a rattlebox mouth. She had so much going on this summer, spending time with us, finishing school, getting married, and finding a house soon after. I'd be a mess if I the same. But young folks seem to handle things much more naturally than us old people. All that would have sent me over the edge just thinking about it, but it didn't seem to faze her at all. Suddenly, her phone rang.

Covering the mouthpiece, "Grandma, it's my mom concerning the wedding. I have to take this."

Speaking in a low tone, she dashed off. I checked on Hosea. Headed off looking for him in his usual spots with no avail. I was oblivious to what my husband was up to, but knew he was doing something in the garage. Hearing him rattling up a pile of noise through the hall walls. Picking up my step, I grabbed the mail and shuffled to join him. Vaguely hearing him talking to someone; it wasn't Chloe. Being nosey, I listened. Hm, maybe our neighbor from down the road? The mailman? We don't get many visitors up in the mountains; there aren't many who will brave these steep roads. I shrugged and straggled to the living room to get cozy and gaze outside. It was a beautiful day, but hot enough that a pair of Chloe's jelly shoes melted by the pool. He must have seen me moving around, appearing at the front door, holding his finger up for me to give him more time. I threw my hand up and went back to what I was doing. He reappeared soon after, beckoning for us to come on out to the garage where he kept his old cars. They haven't been moved in months, but he spends most of his time cleaning and waxing them. Chloe jogged back in time to join us.

"Is he ready for us yet, grandma?"

She was moving nervously. I eyed her, trying to figure out what was up, but decided against asking. She'd tell me later, if she wants.

"Yup, he just yelled."

We headed out, and Hosea immediately started chattering. His love for cars will keep him talking.

"Okay, baby girl. You about to see my toys. My second loves."

Chloe's eyes went wide as she saw them both.

"Nice cars—wow! I didn't know you had these; how did you know I love cars?"

"I didn't, but Glad you like."

Hosea smiled as he rubbed off any print he saw with his dusty rag. I looked around, noticing he cleaned his man cave thoroughly. Piercing at the floor perceived, he had the garaged waxed. Nice, shining like new silver coins. All his tools nicely hung in his tool chest like they're supposed to be. Years of blaming the kids for taking his tools are over; no one at home left to blame. They still came up missing. For years I haggled him about the tool issue. Now we knew the real problem. I'm impressed, noting he has been doing a lot of the things he had on his list. I think we have to make more fishing trips. Pointing to the car Chloe leaned against, he rattled to off the details, believing a girl wouldn't be into cars. Chloe was on a mission to show her skills.

"This baby here is a 1979 Chevy Malibu. I bought it brand new that year, right off the lot. Not a spot of rust, nowhere."

"Okay, I see you granddad—sweet."

Walking around the car with her flip-flops sounding like they suctioned to the floor with each step, I disliked the sounds they made as she pranced around. I thought I would go crazy. She tried hard not to touch the cars, as Hosea dared anyone to leave a fingerprint. Hosea nudged her.

"Get inside, get a feel," flaring out a grand toothy smile.

"I'm scared to touch it; might leave a print."

"Girl… get inside. How do you think you will drive it if you can't touch it?"

Giving her a quizzical look, "Get in the car—woman, quit all that crazy talk."

Jogging around to the passenger side, she quickly jumped in, "Nice!"

"I love my cars?" He laughed.

Marveling at its incredible shine, she gazed over its specs.

The interior was unblemished. Not even a scratch, rip, or discoloration anywhere. Looking over the dash noted some wear on the radio, but that's it. She hopped out and strode around the car, mentioning his color choices.

"Black, clear coat, with pink faded flames and a chrome bumper? What made you choose those colors?"

Hosea rambled, "Ya know, it was the only car with headlights I like."

Walking to the front of the car, he pointed out the dual headlights.

"These beamers are limited. Not all Malibu's have these lights, so black and pink it was."

He made a show of pumping up his upper arm weighted tendons, "Young woman, color don't form no man."

Stopping in mid-step, glancing over the car. He shrugged, "I still love it."

Chloe chimed in, informing him how much she knew about cars.

"What you know about this car?" Jogging over to the driver's door, she popped the hood. Hosea stood in astonishment but played it off.

"Anybody can pop a hood; what ya know about what's under there?"

Studying the engine for a minute. Hosea talked junk about girls not knowing nothing about cars. She stepped back, taking a hard look at him, then focused again on the car details.

"Okay, it's an 8-cylinder, 4-speed? Right?"

His brow went up, "Okay, you might know a little something-something. However, I believe it to be ladies' luck."

"Whatever!" Rolling her eyes, "clean engine too, granddad. You know you need to hand this puppy over to me," she chuckled, crossing arms as she egged him on for feedback.

"Good luck with that, girl; your granddad has turned down some hefty offers on this one."

Giving him an even harder stare, "Come on, think about it long and hard."

Then she hit him with her sweetheart's face, "For little ole me?"

He frowned back at her, clearing his throat. "I paid four thousand dollars for her brand new—worked hard for it, too. Drove the first engine plumb out of the car; oh yeah, enjoyed every minute too. Had a new engine put in, only 17,342 miles on it."

"But it's not just pink; it's blasted pink with a black — faded to a grey fire design on the sides—and chrome fender. Just perfect for your precious, only granddaughter?"

Hosea uncovered the Mustang, ignoring her as he grunted.

"Now, this baby right here…"

He trailed off, looking hard at it with sparkles in his eyes; he had a grin that would enliven any darkened room. "This right here is my other love, she sure has been good to me."

He gave it a good, swift wipe. Suddenly, he bent and looked closely at it, snarled, "I know ain't no scratch on my vehicle?"

Swiftly he pulled out his rag and wiped until it satisfied him. The car was okay. Chloe, "Now, this one right here, I bought in 1970—ooh wee, still love this baby right here! I think I paid about fifty-five hundred fully loaded for this one."

Chloe circled the Mustang, admiring it as Hosea rambled.

"I had it repainted two years ago to the original color: grabber blue with black stripes down the sides."

Chloe climbed in the driver's seat and waved her fingers for the keys. Hosea looked a bit perplexed but scurried over, giving them to her. She started the car and revved the engine. Vroom-vroom-vroom.

"Sounds good, granddad," she popped the hood, got out and studied the engine.

"It holds a 351ci V8 engine, looks clean. No leaks and the oil look fresh."

She peered in at it; her eyebrows raised high. "Hm, they converted it to an automatic?"

Pulling her head up to see Hosea's response, and she froze—just staring outward.

"When did you get here?"

Without waiting for an answer, she jumped him, both legs locked around his waist. Embracing his face, kissing him like tomorrow wasn't coming no time soon.

"Surprise!" Hosea yelled.

"We saw how much you missed him, so we asked him to join us this weekend, he's been hiding out back."

"Jeremai… no wonder you haven't been returning my calls, when did you get here?"

"Late last night," he said, smirking at her.

"Yeah, over here trying to creep up on me, I see."

She was blushing hard, swirling around. Smacked him with a huge kiss, "I am so happy to see you."

"I missed you too," Jeremai stated.

He nudged her, "You ready for the mini adventure? Your grandparents planned a trip to Mexico for the weekend, and we've never been."

He kept smiling at her while she pranced around with excitement, "I love you."

She filled him in on the cars Hosea was showing her. Busy talking a mile a minute, telling the details of the vehicles. I entered the garage, focusing on the young man Chloe seemed so fond of. Hugging him like a scarf around his neck, she introduces her fiancé Jeremai to me, quickly pulling herself together.

"Hello, Jeremai, I'm Chloe's grandmother. Nice to meet you."

"Wow, I see where Chloe gets her good looks from."

"Thank you, I try hard to keep my beautiful face up," Hosea said.

I hit him with my tray. "He was talking about me, fool."

Hosea shook Jeremai's hand. "Hey, man, I'm Hosea."

"Nice cars, sir."

"Thanks, we just finding out about our baby girl knows a little something about cars. I'm impressed."

"That's one thing I love about her, sir. My girl loves her some cars."

I studied him as he walked around talking to Chloe and Hosea. Handsome, which I figured he would be, Chloe's exquisite taste wouldn't stop at her man. Delicate, smooth brown skin, pearly white teeth, about six-foot-two, slim stature, and well-manicured all the way around, down to his polished brown shoes. Looking studious. Noting he couldn't stop touching and smiling at Chloe, which was a good sign that he was happy. Glad to see who made my granddaughter flourish enough that she agreed to be his wife. A million questions were lined up for him but felt we should wait until we got on the road. Jeremai instantly took to the 1979 Malibu as Chloe did. He walked around inspecting it, then dipped his head in the window, glancing over the interior. Looking excited, Jeremai told Hosea, "man, this car is sweet. I had a newer model, but I sold it a while back, sir."

"Hey— cut the 'sir' stuff; it's old. Got enough of that feeling going on already," Hosea snickered.

"No problem," while licking his lips, he released a faint chuckle.

Jeremai gestured to the Malibu, "How does it run?"

"Like a wild animal. Purrs like a kitten and drives like a beast—need I say more?" Hosea offered him the keys.

"Here you go, start her up."

Instantly, the car cranked, grumbled a bit and came to life. Jeremai agreed that the paint job was sweet.

"One of my buddies said back when, what man would drive a car with pink on it? I thought to myself, I would, and bought it right on the spot. Don't no pink do nothing to my manhood, you feel me?"

"I hear you; I would have kept the paint the same myself. Looks smooth with the black interior."

Jeremai revved it a bit, "Man, this sounds good."

As he glanced with a smile that filled the space between him and Chloe as he caught her eyes gazing at him, left her twirling her hair. She winked at him.

"Wanna take it out and get a feel of it?" Hosea asked.

"Heck ya," Jeremai broke his eagerness to make sure it was all right.

"You sure, man?"

"Yeah."

Removing his suit jacket, he tossed it to Chloe. Hosea shooed him into the car.

"Man, we ain't got but so much time," glancing his watch.

Jeremai walked over to Chloe, giving her a gentle hug around her waist, and kissed her.

"You doin' okay, sweetie?"

"Now I am," she said, smiling and gazing into his eyes. She looked around nervously.

"I'm going—" she said.

Reminding Hosea to please take it easy; that man would scare the daylight out of dead folks with his driving. For a moment, I became concerned but dismissed it. He always seemed to make it back in one piece; I trusted him. The power of a praying wife does wonders. I threw my hand up and waved them off. The car sat idle, rumbling for a minute or two, then Hosea opened the garage and blasted off. I sent Chloe a text to remind Hosea and Jeremai to be careful with those mountain curves. I always swore that man's driving would drive me crazy. I wonder if he knew those curves were tricky. Many of the folks have ended up cliff hanging, flying around those corners. Back in the day he would have a drink or two before riding out, I'd be a worried mess. Just waiting on the police to come knocking at the door. Lord knew he wasn't going anywhere before his time—so that stopped me from worrying and blessed to settle my nerves. I watched them till they disappeared.

They'd been gone for about thirty minutes; they were back because I heard Hosea zoom into the driveway doing a 360-degree turn and screeches. I hated it, because he always left all those darn marks in our driveway. Not to mention, one day he had almost run straight into our house. I came outside, fussing, waving my hands for him to roll down the window. He knew what was happening, driving slowly, progressing to creep into the garage. Chloe rolled down her window, immediately telling me all about how crazy Hosea drove. Jeremai got out, looking half dazzled himself.

"Man… I thought my driving was bad," Jeremai said.

"You took that cliff like it was nothing," Chloe chimed in.

"I don't scare easy, but you had me for a moment. Man — that was wild."

"I told y'all he drove crazy."

"Grandma, 'crazy' is an understatement."

"Y'all talk smack, but I got you back in one piece, didn't I?"

"Barely!" Chloe exclaimed, still bubbling with the adrenaline.

❧

Driving to Rocky Point beach in Mexico, we'll be staying a night, Jeremai opted to drive, with Chloe giving him a small fight about it. While we set up the GPS Hosea had trouble finding our location. Sitting in the car, listening to them argue, was not the way we wanted to start our mini vacation. As she quieted down, he pulled her towards him, kissing her on the forehead, "I'm only here for a short while I would love to do the driving. Look babe, you can relax and see the sights. Okay?"

Chloe hesitated, but gave in. She surely acted ugly, fussing and throwing her finger in his face. We couldn't believe this was the same person. Well I had gotten a taste of this anger when she got here. Finally, her blown fuse died down and the chatter stopped as she focused on her breathing. Managing slow breaths, she grabbed the back of her head, bobbed up and down a few times. She placed her hair in a pony and gave in, throwing him the keys and rolled her eyes. Hosea booked two rooms for our stay. Jeremai and Chloe freshened up before we left. Noting his jogging attire proved much more comfortable for the ride. A few things slowed us down from leaving as early. Jeremai forgot his passport, forcing us to go back after being on the road for fifteen minutes, and Hosea forgot to add Mexico insurance to the car. As we waited, I tried locating the directions once more.

"I found it; it seems like it is one main road and one highway."

"I can do that, about 211 miles, making it three hours—no problem. Are you ok, my lady?"

"Yup, let's go," she said with a lingering attitude.

By now, Hosea was off the phone, assuring us that the Mexican insurance was good to go.

"Okay, let's rock-and-roll."

Hosea gave him a stern look. "Driving in Mexico differs from in Arizona. Police out there is, you know the story," he grumbled.

"I'll be careful, for sure — no choice with all this precious cargo," smiling at Chloe.

"Alright then, lets zoom" Hosea clapped his hands.

"It's about 10:00 am, we best get to moving, don't want to be on the road at night. Wait one sec—let me inform everyone that highway 85 doesn't have many rest stops, so get it all out now."

Chuckling to myself, knowing Hosea would be the first to go. Before the first roll of the wheels, he began elaborating on cars. My man surely will talk forever. He pulled himself towards the front, hugging the headrest to make sure everyone could hear him. I sat in the back, rolling my eyes because once you got him started on cars, it would never end. I gently nudged his shoulder. Asking him to sit back to let them get comfortable and breath. I could tell he got a bit irritated, but he sat back.

"You'll have plenty of time to talk car stuff, okay, babe?"

He said nothing, just stared out the window, ignoring me. The road wasn't very scenic, as it was mostly dry lands and cacti. Miles onward we saw nothing but heatwaves and occasional tumbleweeds cascading across the roads. So, we made our own entertainment, Hosea went back to talking about cars, kept the conversation going strong. Until Chloe needed to go to the restroom, she seemed flushed, saying she was nauseous and hot. It didn't take long for her to hobble to the restroom with Jeremai's help. He dipped inside the store to get her a ginger ale, soda pop, and salted crackers. Not long after, she felt better. Reaching the border, a stocky-looking officer waved for us to pull up. He stood tall with a face that looked like he was going to give us troubles—giving his pants a forceful shift by his belt, revealing his gun walking to the back door of the car, giving Hosea and myself a long hard-core stare.

"Driver's license and passports, please," shifting his head towards the front of the car, then his body followed suit with a tin man walk to the front with his hand stuck out.

"Here you go, sir."

"So, you two are from Michigan?"

"Yes, sir."

"My hometown… welcome and have a good time — Mr. Jeremai," chewing his gum, giving into a weak smile and a nod.

We were on the road again. After a while, I struggled to listen to Jeremai's rap music, but it was hard to pull up the nerve to ask him to play gospel music. We always had a rule that the driver controlled the radio, but all the foul language was killing me. I didn't want to be any different with him. I closed my eyes and tried to sleep, but it became impossible with Hosea, who faded out before I could. I hated it when he would fall asleep first because he always snored horribly loud. At home, that darn c-pap machine helped, but then blew out air that made my shoulder joints hurts. Not to mention the loud noise it made. I called him Darth Faker as he looked like him with the mask on, all bound up at the face. Chloe looked back at us, then whispered something to Jeremai. Soon, I heard the radio station change frequently. Then Chloe plugged in her phone. The oldies but goodies played blazing tunes from our old days, bringing back so many old memories.

Hosea loved a good deal of music, and rap was one, but I never liked it. I warned Jeremai to look out for border patrol; they rarely came out, but when they did were worse than tax collectors. None of them knows a word of English until they heard dollar signs, thus become as fluent as water running out of a facet. I snuggled back into my seat, rocking to one of my favorite jams. These young folks know nothing about decent music. Everytime they switched the station before I could enjoy a beat. At first, I said nothing, letting them have full control over the music, but I was getting quite irritated by the constant flicking. No, they didn't switch off my song 'My Guy by Mary Wells.

"Why can't y'all let the radio be?"

"Oh, grandma, you like that song?"

"Well, yeah. It was a jam, don't you agree?"

"I've never heard it before. We'll play it for you, though."

I saw Jeremai make a face of disgust, but quickly drew his attention to the cars speeding around him. Hosea was still snoring until he abruptly woke himself up, asking how far we had gotten.

"About another twenty minutes," Jeremai said.

I released them from having to listen to my music, before dozing off myself until a putrid stench hit my nose. The old gizzard had horrible gas, which filled up the whole car. Like a sappy poison, out to kill us all. Of course, he thought it was funny, as usual, telling us it was the ice cream he had earlier.

"You know you shouldn't have had no darn ice cream; your lactose intolerant."

He had the most prominent, cheesiest grin on his face. I glared at him with sickness in my stomach.

"Where did you get ice cream from?"

"I'm a grown man."

I nearly growled, "Where, Hosea?"

"When we went out riding earlier."

"He sure did, grandma; no wonder he ate it so fast,"

Hosea shrugged. "I didn't want to hear your mouth about it."

"Well, that's why we all gotta smell your enjoyment."

No one had a problem opening their window. We had to let all the cold air out and let pure heat in, just to get relief from the stench. Boy, did we let him have it. We complained, hoping to embarrass him not to do it again.

"Gone with that look before I do it again. Oh yes sir, I will."

"Better listen and believe because he will."

After that threat, nobody said anything. Now, it was Chloe's turn to be the noisemaker while she slept.

Jeremai yelled, "This is how this beautiful woman sleeps."

I yelled back, saying, "Yup, she sleeps like a bear fighting a coon."

Those loud and low pitches sound like growls. She makes Hosea sound quiet.

"How do you sleep that racket?"

Jeremai laughed. "Give her a while; once she settles down it gets quieter," he said.

We sat in amazement just how loud that child can snore.

"Ooh wee boy, how you get rest with that howling going on?"

"It's a battle every night, granddad."

"Well, look who's talking?"

"You know you love somebody when you deal with all that noise."

We sat around talking over Chloe's bear growls, which seemed to get louder by the minute.

"What we gonna do with this child and her sleeping?"

Nobody had a clue.

"I guess we'll let her sleep for a few more minutes before we wake her butt up!"

She woke up on her own a few minutes later, looking strange, like we had kidnapped her. We got a kick out of that. The music played in waves of familiar songs that sent me back in time, reliving moments of joy and sorrow. I leaned back, enjoying the melodies, while Chloe and Jeremai talked.

"Chloe, you thought I lied when I said this was the least scenic route; absolutely nothing to see for hours."

"You are right, grandma—boring."

"Jeremai, what type of work you do?"

Hosea straightened up to listen; he's been waiting to hear.

"Mrs. uh — grandma?"

"Grandma is fine; we family soon."

"I am an FBI agent for about seven years now. I work in the cyber-crime division, solving online crimes of all types—especially fraud."

"Sounds like fascinating work."

"Yes, most of the information are high-security issues. It's hard when you can't talk about things issues pertaining to work, not even with your spouse."

He looked over at her, taking her hand.

"When I'm stressed, she always makes things better, even though I can't give details."

Looking out the window, seeing the sign on the side of the road. Noted we had arrived.

❧

Hosea made his way to the restroom first, as usual. I swear, my man has to potty at every stop. As we talked mess about him, guess who beat him there? Everybody. I'm not fond of public restrooms, noting Chloe wasn't giving up on soap dispenser. Tossed her the hand sanitizer making way to my stall when the soap escaped and splattered her shirt. Appearing flushed, she washed her face and straightened her hair. The forged smile and weakened eyes proved she wasn't feeling the greatest. Refreshing her makeup, I waited around contemplating the things I wanted to buy. I wished I had a way to take back some of their garden pieces; they were lovely. Tall glazed vases rimed the store in assorted bright colors, Mexican style decor is always a delight. I enjoyed touring the store. Noticing Hosea trotting my way, I waited for him. It was scorching out, heatwaves filled the air, but didn't seem to bother the bugs. Seemed like he slowed down to the speed of a snapping turtle in the tropical sun.

"Hurry, man. I ain't got all day to wait for you."

He grinned at me with his pearly white teeth; that hadn't changed since the day I first met him. We both aged, but I still saw the young man I had fallen in love with. He better be glad I love him, or better yet, I better be. Something special about being in love, it's like experiencing your first kiss every day. I was starving, demanding we try their steak quesadillas. It was a small stand which appeared to be family owned. A vendor stand sitting on side of the store with small children working like adults. They impressed me with how well they took care of their duties, just wished they wore gloves. Admiring the entire family, even the mothers who carried baby's backside and breast fed out back, took turns creating the soft wraps. The shaven'd steak and chicken slices sizzled on the grill with bubbling fat, intermingled with colorful peppers and onions. The aroma danced like belly dancers twirling around your nose. Pure steak smells were calling me over. I put in a Mexican dance step towards the iron pot which sat on an open flame held a large portion of rice, being stirred with a long wooden spoon by a young man about fifteen. Watching the vendor generously spread a three-cheese blend on the homemade soft shell, returning it to the grill with a flip, then smacking it on the plate for the next customer. The smell danced in the air until it entered our nostrils, drawing me to whip out my money without thinking twice. Well — until we saw the flies swarming around the food, without no one swatting them. The pesky flies even swarmed around the grill. That never happens at home. Hosea put his foot down, determined to find food elsewhere. I agreed, following him down the strip to see what else they offered, but found nothing. Others complimented how well their food tasted, made me feel as if I'd give it a chance. Hosea commented that he would not eat any food with flies swarming around, period. Letting a couple go before us once we made our way back in line, they purchased and ate their food right on the spot. Hosea grabbed my arm, pulling me close, "Look at that fly land right on that steak and the nerve of it walking around."

My face frowned, watching a mess of flies taking their opportunity to join in. Glancing at a couple enjoying their food, I walked away. Chloe and Jeremai were still shopping, so I caught hold of him, steering them back to the car so we could move on. We didn't need a thing but gave the two love bugs a minute to shop around before noticing they were behind us with food on the stand. Chloe raved about how good the steak was, taking a huge bite, passing to Jeremai.

"You'll didn't see those flies on the food?" Hosea asked.

"Yeah, but the fire will cook all those germs off its good granddad."

"I wanted to try it until I saw a bunch of flies, and it became a 'no' for me."

Jeremai hunched, taking another bite, "It's Mexico, seems like flies and food go together in these necks of the woods. Besides, I'm with Chloe, it's the best steak I've had."

Chloe beckoned for me to try it, giving into a bite. The shell shattered, releasing a nice crunch, making it hard to handle. The gooey cheese held its pieces together. Pieces of steak pulled outward, taking more than I had planned. Pushing it into my mouth, I savored the taste with each chew. My eyes rolled as I imagined it would taste amazing. I shook from the goodness. Only thing missing was the tomato.

"Oh, oh my… this is good and tender, wow."

"I'm done! Kisses are off. You'll up here eating fly meat," holding his hand to my face blocking my efforts.

Chloe ran over to him with her lips puckered out, chasing him for a kiss, while he shooed her away until the prescription sign caught his eye. Quickly, he made his way to check it out. It's a no for me, last time I purchased something for acne scars, I got burns all over my face, took months for my skin to come back. Couldn't resist the urge to see what he wanted to purchase. The explanation was long concerning the various pills he was purchasing, but I already knew — Viagra. He gets them for his friends down at the rec center. Old men still chasing dreams and pockets getting lean.

"Previously, one of the old coots took a few of them, ended up having to get a shot right in his pecker almost died of a heart attack! Couldn't get him down. Wonder how he explained that in the emergency room?"

"Grandma! Are you serious?" Chloe exclaimed as she yelled out in laughter.

I nodded. "Yup—Hosea was feeling mighty low when it happened and had nothing else to do with him."

Chloe and Jeremai were dying laughing. I was pretty choked up myself. Hosea returned, immediately knowing the things I had been saying; I still had tears in my eyes and about peed my pants from laughing.

"Dang, getting old is most definitely not for those trying to stay sexy."

"What does that mean?"

"Some of my friends tell me each sneeze or laugh, their bladder explodes like a balloon in a water fight. Happened to me twice, don't even leave you with a moment to catch yourself."

"They have something for that," Holding a bag up.

"I'll wait. I refuse… and lose my sexiness, tchah!"

Chloe gave me a look of concern. "It's not that bad, they have some nicer styles, for sexy grandmas."

"Nope, not doing it… so put them away," shoving the bag to the shelf and walking away. Chloe caught up with me.

"Grandma, it's not that bad. When you are ready, they'll be there."

Making our way to the car, we headed to the hotel. I wasn't feeling the greatest closing my eyes for a while, with Hosea yapping about me eating fly food. I was feeling tired. I hadn't done these many things in one summer, ever. But I'm having the best time. While resting, I barely heard the conversation, until Jeremai exclaimed we had made it to the hotel. I popped up like a jolt, ready to get the heck out of the car. Chloe and Hosea will have to stop with all these car rides; my knees can't take it too much more. I used to say I would stay young forever and growing old was all in the mind—that was a bold face lie. I was getting older by the second and my body would not let me forget it. I couldn't pretend that the horse ride didn't still have me sore in all the unused places. I was old and needed to face it before it got me in big trouble. Standing outside, trying to warm up from the fidget air condition in the car, had my bones aching. Hosea and Jeremai were in the line to check-in, with Chloe sitting with our luggage. I joined her.

"How do you feel, young lady?"

"Great," she said, poking the gravel with a stick.

"I'm happy Jeremai came and drove."

"What? All that fuss'n you did, now your happy?"

"Yeah."

We sat quietly. I warmed up, giving into stupid heat from a freezing car made me feel worst. Can't handle abrupt temperature changes too well. Throwing down the stick, she started looking for the guys.

"Ya know, you mentioned appreciating the things our men do for us, and you got me thinking—"

"About?"

"Being appreciative and being loving woman to my man. Ya know — not always quick to be a hag and control. I am ashamed of how I acted today," she said.

"Really?"

"Yeah, I am. Thanks grandma."

The men appeared with everything under control, with the room key in hand, asking if we wanted a snack. We declined. Hustling to our room before the evening sat in. Constructed of mustard-seed colored clay on the outside. Melodies rang the air by three middle-age guys wearing all black, played a guitar, nothing like previous times of them wearing sombreros and ponchos. Look like a pop group we see in the states. Stepping inside, the vast array of colored tile work that adorned the walls and floors enlivened us. Music played through the speakers, with Chloe grabbing a sombrero, pulling Jeremai to dance with her in the isle. He resisted, but gave in, dancing her right to the room with us tailing them. The rooms were much like an authentic adobe housing, giving us the real feel of their richly colored culture.

We settled in and made ourselves at home quickly. We changed into our swimwear. Everyboy beach ready — except me; I was ready for bed. Pushing my old rattled bones on, pain twisted around my body like a snake. Chloe thought the most of my bathing suit as I modeled it for her. She helped me pick a two-piece skort set, one to cover everything, and even helped hold the important stuff in place. My suit was a very colorful display of marvelous yellow, gold, orange, and blue, that went well with the decor of the hotel. I twirled around as my aging body would allow me. My bold sunglasses brought out the sexy in me as I threw my head back, claiming it. Winking at Chloe for her approval. My gold flip-flops were sweet and kept me grounded. She laughed while covering her mouth in amazement.

"Look at my sexy grandma go, granny, go granny…," she chanted.

"Girl, I ain't finished—look how this sarong nicely twisted around my neck, creating a drape that gracefully enwraps my ole tired curves."

"Perfect grandma."

Flinging my body in different directions, showing off. Chloe joined me in modeling her swimsuit. We pranced back and forth, taking turns in the mirror. Chloe wore a cream and gold crocheted bikini. She was beautiful.

"I like." I admirably stated.

"We're going to be too hot for beach, shutting it down," she yelped.

Hosea and Jeremai stood in the doorway, laughing, clapping, and egging us on.

Hosea blurted out, "Yeah, you still got it, now cut all this foolishness out!"

You look nice, grandma… it fits you well.

"Heck yeah! My grandma still got it!"

Jeremai pulled her up close, telling her how radiant she looked. He didn't lie. She did, just beaming full of life and a blast to hang around. I was still recovering from being embarrassed from the guys catching us parading around in our suits, caught dead handed having too much fun. Exhaustion ruminated from my body moving like a slug as aches went through my entire body from reaching for my straw beach hat. I staggered, bracing myself against the chair. I refused to give into my crappy feelings, so I placed the finishing touch on my head and looked fabulous — we headed out. The beach was a few steps from the hotel door; we appreciated that. We assumed the sun may have gone down somewhat, but it wasn't the case.

The sand was beautiful, crystal white with shimmers you could see miles away. It was silky fine, like grains of sugar and inviting until it hit my feet. Dry sand and my toes don't mix well. Every few steps I'd wipe the excess sand off my feet. I stopped when I saw how far we had to go. Frankly, didn't know which was worst: my dried soles or my tired, achy body. Could I make it?

"How many times you going to wipe your feet, woman?"

"Leave me alone, I hate dry feet; it's a creepy feeling."

"How do you go to the beach and not get dry feet?"

"Never mind me, I'll get there," with a steady creep forward.

The beach, we finally made it back, and we were lucky, it wasn't pack as usual. We were free to pick almost any spot we wanted, so we move in close to the water. The vendors half drove us crazy, pesky people who all sold the same crap came one after another. Chloe allowed a young girl to braid her hair. She quickly set up shop with beads and other accessories and got right to work. Chloe relaxed and chatted with Jeremai while the girl braided. I just relaxed. Regardless of the way I felt about dry feet, the sand was beautiful. Chloe flung her cover-up on the blanket, grabbed Jeremai, whisking him off to the water. I watched them until they drifted off into the clear blue waters. Hosea wanted to do the same. I gave him a look back that told him to sit back and chill. I needed a nap and leaned back, covering my face with my beach hat to catch a few winks. After about twenty minutes passed, I pulled my sun hat to the side to reveal one eye toward the beach. Going back to my sleep position, I met eyes with Hosea. He looked bored, wanting to go to the water. I tried to ignore him, how could I? Giving a deep sigh.

"You wanna go out?"

"Yeah, been waiting for you to wake up. Come out and all you do is sleep?"

He had walked a bit before me, stopping to grab my hand, tugged me toward the beach to get me moving faster. I resisted but still moved more swiftly. Reaching the water, I placed one toe in, jerking back. Too cold. Hosea grabbed me, holding me in place as the waves crashed into my feet and legs. I hollered as he laughed, reaching upward — he kissed me.

He helped me flutter around the waters. Chloe and Jeremai caught up to us as they were goofing around, splashing that darn water in my face. I hadn't planned on getting wet and messing up my hair, but you can't tell some folks nothing nowadays. She walked around with hair that didn't kink; white folks' stuff. My hair didn't play that and would curl up into beady balls like those in a cotton field—well, maybe not be that bad, but still. The water felt so good, if you could get over the rocky areas under your feet. They didn't hurt but made you cautious. The currents were becoming rough, making it hard to stand in place. It was a perfect exercise, keeping myself upright, but I was ready to find my seat again. Hosea enjoyed himself, laughing and talking to folks that passed by, helping kids and women stay on their feet. I beckoned to him to go back. He agreed. On our way back, he grabbed a stick. Positioning himself, holding steady like the wind could topple him over with his rickety knees — he braced himself, drawing our initials in the sand with a big heart encircling them.

He's such a romantic. I wasted no time grabbing him by his face and smacking him dead on the lips.

"Love you," I whispered while looking him square in his eyes.

"I love you too, babe."

Folks passing by and admiring our relationship left both of us purely glowing. Chloe and Jeremai stood behind us, egging us on to kiss again, we did. He doesn't know I'll never tire of kissing him.

"We want to be like y'all when we grow up and get grown and sexy."

"Girl, you can be like us now; always keep your love alive and learn to more like Jesus in your relationship."

Hosea whispered in my ear, "If they know best, they'll stay young as they can and be like us now."

We both laughed and chilled as we watched the sunset.

"Best go back to our room. I need some rest."

He agreed. Chloe and Jeremai stayed at the bar and chilled while we old folks headed in for the night.

❧

The next morning was so beautiful… it greeted us with bright sunlight that bounced off the colorful walls, as if the glares were tapping our faces as a wake-up call. I knocked on the door to their room, with them barely saying much. Happily, seeing Chloe and Jeremai made it back last night. My vision distorted from the brightness, I waited for my eyes to adjust. Making my way to the coffee, couldn't figure out how to work it. I was too tired. Hosea dug deeper into the pillows, hiding from me and the rays. Moving the pillows forced him to wake up, he was grumpy. I let him grumble; knowing dog on well, it was time to get up. We had to check out soon. I started packing, calling room service for coffee. I was still feeling bad. *I hope I am okay…* as concern wavered my mind. Trying to ignore the sickly feeling as I packed for the ride back to the States.

❧

We stopped for a bite, getting out the car, I noticed we each looked like we had fought wild bears through the night. Chloe was wearing sunglasses to hide her dark circles, from what seemed like a lack of sleep or a hangover. Jeremai complained of a bangin headache from smacking back tequila shots at the bar. Hosea and I were just old. We all sat quietly during breakfast.

"What the heck y'all do last night?" I said.

"Y'all look dreadful," Hosea said.

"We don't look any better, babe."

"Y'all want another night here?" he asked.

"You'll still tipsy from last night?"

"No, granddad, we're fine."

"Yeah, okay."

He shrugged and dropped the keys next to her on the table before he got up and walked away. We stayed another night to rest. Driving in Mexico was nerve-racking enough, traffic was hefty. Chloe and I scoured the town for a room. Calling places left and right, eventually snagged two rooms at a nearby hotel that resembled an old Mexican Villa, very nice. Things are so modern nowadays, didn't even seem like we were in Mexico. Looking out of the villa's window, people filled the streets buying all kinds of things. I decided on naptime for me. Not too long after getting settled, I was asleep.

❧

The following morning, I awoke ravished; I searched for food. Slowly, everyone joined me in the kitchen.

"Grandma, are you okay?"

"Yes. Why do you ask?"

"We we're worried about you; you slept all day until this morning, and it's not like you," she rubbed my shoulders.

"Maybe you should take it easy for a while when we get back," Hosea said.

I agreed, I was more tired than usual, and it was getting to me. The others seemed fine and well-rested. No matter how tired I felt, I still had an outrageous appetite. I wasted no time getting breakfast down. Before we knew it was on the road again and reached the border. It was unusually busy today, with many cars going across. Time went fast, then slow as we waited to cross the border. Soon we were traveling back home and were in the United States again. Chloe read my journal alone. I was too tired to join her; she had my blessings.

❧

The Journal- Mexico ✿We surprised our sons Elijah and Asher with a visit to Tucson; we hadn't seen them in ages. We stayed a few days with them, then headed to Mexico for the weekend. It was in June, and about seventy-five degrees with soothing, bright-blue skies. The visit to Mexico was charming because of the weather, not to mention the fresh blue waters and fine sand. We rented some RTVs, four-wheelers and dirt bikes. After lying around our hotel, chatting, we were ready to hit the beach. We hopped into our swim gear and headed off to enjoy ourselves with our sons, twenty-nine, and the other eighteen. The beach was relaxing and peaceful. We splashed and ran around like two teenagers; Hosea even wrote our names in the sand to show the world we had been there, until the tides reminded us that our visit was only temporary, washing them away. We basked in the sun while shielding our faces with big sun hats. Later, we were excited and ready to ride the ATVs. Reserved but gave in to the excitement. Hosea and I shared a four-wheeler, while Elijah and Asher chose dirt bikes.

Off we went into the city, dodging cars, whirring past houses, and sanded areas. I hadn't been on an RTV since I was fifteen years old, bringing back old memories of being a kid again. The breeze cascaded across my skin like gentle reminders of being alive. Riding the sands, Hosea took full advantage of his ability to drive fast. Screaming with excitement as we drove between this rocky area. All of a sudden moving in slow motion the wheel hit a rock. I could see our ATV rise to the air, ending with everything turning black. Awaking to Hosea standing over me waiting to see if I was okay. I had passed out and had been pulled out of the sand after they flipped the ATV back over. Seat-belted in, I was buried deep. Walking around dizzy, trying to figure things out. Repeating, "Did anyone else die?"

Hosea grabbed my face and held me close to him.

"Babe, you're okay? Nobody died," he said.

I scrambled to get my things together, as everything had fallen out of my purse. A man approached us, informing all of us to get our RTV up before the Policia came. He seemed to be of Mexican descent, with a nice haircut, looking relaxed as he gave orders of what we needed to do to get the RTV up. He never gave his name. Standing on the rock we hit, he asked me to help push the RTV from behind while Hosea pushed the gas. Hosea gave the RTV some gas. Flinging sands escaped the twirling wheels and darted the air meeting my body as it cascaded back to the golden grounds in which it came. Standing drenched, literally, like a chicken floured for a deep fry. Face, hair, everything ruined. The struggle to scream for Hosea to release his foot from the peddle rang throughout the air and fell on deaf ears. Finally, the madness stopped. He never heard my cry and failed to realize the heightened troubles that we faced this day. wiped the sand from my eyes. I was a mess and stood lifeless, in dismay of everything that had been happening to me. Once more I wiped my eyes and focused on the man who stood on the solid rock. I felt a sense of urgency to thank him. Who are you? I whispered with no reply. He yelled for help to push the buggy from the hole in which it dug. I looked up at the man again and tried to get to him. Something knocked me down as my face met the sanded grounds. I had fallen to my knees as if I were in prayer. I raised my head and stated.

"I just need to hug and thank you," I said to him weakly with my face returning to the sands.

"Get up," he said.

As I lifted my arm, he drew me to my feet and hugged me. The hug felt amazing and comforting, a surreal touch. This mysterious man brought me peace at that very minute. He got on an RTV and rode away as I watched him until he disappeared. I stood staring until Hosea broke my attention. He soothed me. Witnessing to this day, I felt like I had touched Jesus, himself. I could never forget. Never. The day it happened; it seems as if it gave me a new life. It was hard to explain. I've tried, but no words could describe the feeling I had at that moment. I walked away a different person. Hosea kept asking me if I was ok and I was… just changed. He said I acted peculiar. I was different; I felt the tranquility that only Jesus can produce. He took me to the local restaurant to get cleaned up. Servers laughed wholeheartedly as we walked into the local restaurant. Fingers pointed as the news spread about the accident. In fill the bottom of the basin the silvery sands sank, as I glimpsed my face. The day I felt Jesus.

Assessing the damage on the new RTV, found to have a cracked fender. They tallied the damages of a hundred American dollars to cover the cost of repairs. Our ride back to the hotel was a quiet one. Thinking about the incident the entire way home reminded all of us how brief life is. Thanking God, we walked away without harm. I'd never felt so blessed than I was at that moment.

Spent a few more days in Tucson; it was a hard goodbye. I cried, as usual; it was just too hard to break away from my young men. Driving to the airport, I felt time seemed to go faster than usual. I informed Hosea there was no way we could make it to the airport. Not to mention, he had to use the restroom. I shook my head because we had to stop, no way around it. Reentering the road, I informed Hosea he might as well slow down because there was no way we could make it and take the rental back too; we only had twenty minutes to do everything. He kept driving. I sat back and relaxed; there wasn't any sense in worrying about it. Still, hadn't looked not sure why. We made it to the car rental place — no problems turning in the car, then we jetted over to the shuttle. No point rushing now, so we sat back and chilled, waiting for the driver to come. Neither one of us still hadn't looked at our clocks. When the driver arrived, one young lady boarded and appeared to be in a rush. "Man, he never takes this long to leave. I'm going to be late for work," she stated.

Made it to the airport to check-in. The long line wrapped around the entire waiting area. Still we relaxed as if everything was going as planned. A heavy-set lady with a full-bodied hairdo wearing a security uniform came stepped from behind the desk. She marched like a soldier with no eye contact to anyone. She stopped and scanned the line. Pulled out a pocket watch and pierced it. In a base voice she yelled, "all folks flying to Detroit to please step out of the line and stand right here." Double stomping the floor for the spot for folks to stand. Within seconds, we formed a new line. With a few folks in front of us, it moved fast. It encouraged us. The couple in front of us flung their bag on the scale. It was overweight. Security pointed to the sign of what they owed for their bag. His wife stated she wasn't paying anything and unzipped the luggage and he followed suit. They snatched out belongings and threw them back and forth to rearrange their items to avoid paying an extra fee. How this could be? Still hadn't looked. Another officer flagged us to come over to his scale and threw our bags towards the back and shooed us toward our boarding area. Wasting no time, we ran to our gate, out of breath. Finally, we noted the time, we had 20 minutes to spare. It stunned us.

"How could this be, babe?"

"I don't know."

We both were in disbelief—there was no way, yet here we are getting on the plane, I dropped asleep. I dreamt I was in some kind of burned-down airport with injured people all around. Injured people were everywhere, and I was afraid. A lady looking like an angel walked up to me, holding a hot-cross bun. "He's are looking for you. You — with all the colorful hair," she smiled.

"Who?" she didn't reply.

Instead, she beamed, "They told me to find a woman with colorful hair, just like yours. You know — beautiful oranges, golds, and browns in her hair."

She gazed at me with a pleasant face.

"Who's looking for me and, where am I?" asking again.

She still didn't answer, she just kept smiling. I took the bun, and she pointed in the direction she wanted me to go—I walked. Moving around, I saw so many hurt people crying, holding small children. I was fearful but kept walking. The damaged airport appeared as if a bomb or something similar had hit it. Occasionally, someone would run past screaming, searching for a family, or just sitting around crying and consoling others. Then I turned the corner and saw him. "Hosea," I yelled.

Running over to him, I hugged him with all my might.

"They found you?" he cried.

"Yes."

He kissed me—and I woke up. I slept the entire time I was on the plane, waking in only enough time to get my things together and leave. Grabbing Hosea, I wanted to be first off, the plane. A tall guy threw his arm across the aisle, stopping me in mid-step, and held it in place.

"What the heck?" I couldn't believe how rude he was. He slowly got up and looked down at me, sort of daring me to force past him. Taking up the entire aisle he just stood firm. Allowing everyone in front of him to get out of their seats. And waited for them to exit. The nerve of him. Too short to give him smack behind his head, instead he got it to the back. I cussed and fussed, even called him a few names. Yet, he didn't move a muscle. During all that yakking, he just looked at me with a blank stare. I ran my mouth all the way off the plane, giving him the finger as we departed. We made it to Detroit.

Later that evening, we were home relaxing. I was overtaken by an odd sensation, then the small voice. In the still of my heart, I understood the message, clear as day. You know, you need to learn patience; they waited on you to board the plane. How could you feel you should have gotten off first, without waiting for others? I stopped moving around, feeling some way. It bothered me. What? I said to myself. Whispers graced my ear again, repeating, those people waited for you; you know you both were late for that flight. Learn patience; you'll need it on this journey.

The next morning, finding Chloe having breakfast, I joined her.

"Candace, can you make me a veggie omelet, please?"

"Sure thing. A — veggie omelets?"

"Yes, thank you."

"Whoa, healthy eating too?"

"Yes, you're going to see more changes of me, time to get this ladies' life together," I smiled.

"Well alright then, veggie omelets coming right up."

Quickly, Chloe exclaimed, "So, grandma, you've been to Rocky Point before and got hurt?"

"Um, hm, I did."

Chloe's eyes grew enormous.

"You and granddad were in love back then too?"

"Yes, we were."

"Ya'll was in a nasty accident in Mexico, right?"

"Yes, in Mexico. Funny how life is—this old bird is still going strong. Can only thank the Lord for it."

"Who do you think the man was?"

"In my heart, I felt it was Jesus."

"Really?"

"You would have had to understand how I felt that day holding him and the peace I felt. Tears ran down my face, it felt so good. When God speaks, you feel it. He lets his presence be known."

"Wow, I have chills just talking to you about it," she said.

"I get teary-eyed when I talk about it. The dream I experienced seemed like a light hell and given a chance to live again—had me thinking differently about life."

"No way. Is that why you wanted to go back there?"

"Yes, I wanted to see that place again, where I felt I touched Jesus. It will always be a special place for me."

"Awe, I can understand why. It would be to me too."

"Right after that, I changed. Let go of so many of my bad habits, repented my sins, stopped cussing, let go of pork, crab legs, lobster, shrimp, and any bottom-dwelling fish, got re-baptized, joined a church, cut out negative folks, I started my complete life over again."

"Yeah, I understand… all the things He says don't eat in the bible. Does letting go of all that make you feel any different?"

"Nope, just following his request of our lives. Our father made every creature in the world, on land and in the sea. If he says don't eat some things, who better to tell us? Him? or a man?"

"Very true. I felt something reading your journal, like it was a testimony. I'm so glad you didn't die; I wouldn't have had you here today."

"God had been so good to me; I'll never be the same, and He tells us to spread the word of His goodness."

"So, did I tell you, you looked hot in your swimsuit? You were such a busy admiring mine; I forgot to tell you, Ms. Soon to Be Mrs. Jeremai—You looked fabulous,"

Chloe smiled, "thank you, grandma."

"That Jeremai is a keeper. We love him, and we have informed him he had better take good care of you, or else."

Chloe shook her head, chuckling at me as she got up to get her day started.

"Honey, one more thing—don't forget to have patience and put God on your mind more often and pray for any and everything, especially over your marriage."

She can ruin her house or lift it up... only the wise will recognize the difference. Today was a stressful one, Chloe and Jeremai had a massive argument over the phone this morning. Highly irritated, I stay out of her realm. The bickering was nonstop; she walked past the refrigerator, cascaded the shelves and slammed door, and banged on counters. I braced myself as the windows and my nerves rattled. She roamed the house like a beast, devouring the air with her vicious words. This woman breathed in fire; spitting out flames that jetted behind her. Stomping through the dining area with her phone smashed to her ear, she stopped to give off an insulting joke and moved on. "I just want to punch him in the face and watch his blood pour out, I hate him," she stated.

I didn't sense whom to extend my loving emotions to him or her... I was saddened to see her carry on like this. The feedback from the voice on the phone continued egging her anger on, and she feasted on it like a gourmet dinner fit for a king. Girl this and that and the other filled the air as she excoriated him in every way imaginable. I saw myself in her, always running to my friends to talk out my problems, only to find later I'd eat the fruits of my words. Especially when they were repeated back after deciding to make up with my old man. Noting in this short time, this man could make or break her. I, too, had moments in my younger days, but this old lady learned to keep calm and not let Hosea get next to me. And if he did, I responded with love. To face someone with endearment is difficult, especially in the mist of adversity. It takes maturity and a prayerful heart to be successful at it. I'm sure whatever he did, nothing would make her feel better than getting back at him. That's exactly what's she's doing.

The reward feels good momentarily and can savor the soul. But who's job is to revenge? Only the Lords. What happens when we do these things? Besides, what does the bible say? Many times, this exact same behavior left me looking like a complete fool. Surprised to see the word fool, used so many times in the bible. I almost feared he was speaking directly to me and now my granddaughter.

"Uh—Chloe, may I have a minute with you?"

She covered the mouthpiece, "Grandma, I am on the phone, can it wait?"

"Well—no, it can't."

Her voice sounded pinched, as if she was restraining herself.

"Just one—one?"

"I'm busy, I see you later—ok?" appearing annoyed.

"Suit yourself, young lady… I'm going out for a minute."

"Whatever."

"Chloe."

"She is so annoying right now. Talk about getting on my nerves," she whispered as she disappeared into the backyard.

It has rubbed off. Now I'm annoyed, and I wonder why I never had a daughter. Experiences like this may be the answer. It reminded me why I don't get involved with people's drama unless they ask. Even then, I only ever give neutral advice. I've dealt with my son's negativity when they were living with me; it never worked well with us, always leaving both sides full of anger. Besides, they slandered no one, as she has in the past twenty minutes, I've listened to her. My heart wouldn't let me rest unless I said something. I must remind her how powerful her words are, saying dreadful things all morning. She only became more irritated than she was talking to him. These friends of hers seem shifty, wishing they would give her some helpful advice to soothe the argument instead of adding pure petroleum to the fire. I can't blame her friends; she seems to be okay with the support she is getting.

❧

Driving briskly, cutting those curves, taking in more fresh air than I could breathe in. Finally, I'm out of the house. It was refreshing and freeing until I noticed I've been driving for a while and still haven't found my regular flower spot. Wait a minute. I've passed the Shell gas station twice now, scanning the route as I wondered if I'd taken a wrong turn somewhere. I barreled back in the opposite direction, but nothing looked familiar. Let me turn here. Whipped the corner and turned left on Card Rd. That should do it. Another five minutes into the drive, I came to the realization I was lost and had no way of remembering how to get back on track. Struggling to get my thoughts together, I grabbed the phone in efforts of figuring things out. Sweat beading on my forehead with a pain shooting down my back, body riddled with stress. Could feel the buildup around my chest and back area. Deep breaths taken in, relaxing myself with positive words. I can do this. I am worthy. I am going to be okay. The final deep breath gave way to using Siri or the GPS. Why hadn't I tried that before? Gripping the phone, I pulled over. The next struggle, remembering the name of the shop.

"Ugh, Siri, show me the local nurseries."

"No nurseries in this area, do you know the name?"

What is the name of the nursery? I struggled to remember the name.

"Paul's? No. Larry? No!" All the searches proved wrong.

Dang! Banging my hand on the steering wheel, I cried uncontrollably. How did I get lost? I shop here all the time. Nothing looks familiar to me, scanning the area with a look of confused fear. I gave in and I called Hosea.

Out of breath and sweating profusely, "Bae, what is the name of the shop I buy flowers at?" Wiping the sweat from my tense face.

"Oh, are you talking about Joe's nursery over there on Conners street?"

"Yes, that's the one."

"You okay?"

"I am. Thanks babe, I'll be back soon."

Quickly plugging in the address, Siri unemotionally garbled out the directions until I met face to face with Joes nursery. Bright colors on a sunny day, full of life and new buds, I grabbed a dozen of assorted perennials for the spot Hosea dug out for me. I am in a blah mood today, but the buzzes of the bees enlightened me until one landed on my arm. Beautiful… I admired the bee as I glanced over its body until my eyes spotted the stinger, startling me. My eyes widened as my arm flew around as if I was boneless. People eyed me like I went stark mad. Breathing fast,

I scurried to compose myself, piercing back to assure it wasn't retaliating. Seems like we've had more than usual this year. Annoyed by the darn bee was an understatement, I must admit they're pretty amazing, but not on me. The cashier beckoned me to place my items on the counter. Before I began, I spotted what looked like the queen of bees, "Gracious words are a honeycomb, sweet to the soul and healing to the bones, Proverbs 16:24 NIV," came to mind.

Next thought was Chloe—how can I help the poor child see the power of her words? All that bickering around the house was just nonsense, pure evil. Tore the poor man's soul out of his body with mere words, spoken so harshly that we all felt the sting. Why can't we realized this until our tongue has become a weapon that hurts those around us? Sad, but true.

Watching birds leap around the birdbath, I never assembled. For the past month it laid in a disarrayed pile, but the sprinkler filled it just enough for the birds to enjoy. The fond sound of colorful birds chirping and the sun peeking in and out of the fluffy clouds livened my heart. Hurrying in my works before the heat started blazing upon me like a furnace. Hosea brought out the garden tools just in time. He was always helpful doing things to make my projects easier. I've felt much better since the trip to Mexico a few days ago. Followed the doctor's orders, relaxed, and drank plenty of water like a sane person. We needed rain, speaking of water. The ground was hard as a rock, digging proved fruitless. My frustration level reached one hundred, not to mention pulling and tugging at the water hose, dragging it along the way, bringing half the yard with me. More mess to clean up, but I didn't miss a chance of getting my bright blue rain boots wet with a good slosh in the mud. It was soothing. As the ground moistened, I peered over the plants for instructions, seeking the best placement for them. The rattle of the plastic containers being massaged by my garden gloves broke away to the promise of fresh growth to my florals. That's if I don't kill them as I have in the past. My green thumb has turned purple, dipped them in the fertilizer to bring them back to life. I then popped my plants in their new home. I needed more and had already tired.

"Chloe," I yelled.

"Yes?" With the phone still attached to her ear.

"Can you please help me dig a few holes?"

"Give me a second; I'll be right out."

She appeared, grabbing the garden gloves as she moved a few extra things out of the way and calculated how many holes we needed. Then began tugging at the now semi-softened, rock-hard dirt. After excusing herself for a minute, reappeared with plant food she'd found in the garage.

"All this work, you want to make sure these babies have nourishment," she said.

"I hadn't thought that far, just excited to have some pleasant colors around the yard. She was right."

"The ground is still hard; let's wait a few more minutes."

Sitting like two bumps on a log watching the water roll across the cracks as it made its way through the earth; it seemed like we were watching a nature show in slow motion. Two chipmunks scurried across, sipping the water and taking baths like we had opened a private watering hole just for them. Chloe just burst out crying out of nowhere. One chipmunk froze in front of her, snacking on an acorn as if he was watching a movie.

"I'm calling off the wedding; It's over!" she blurted.

"No way, what's going on?"

"He doesn't listen to me; we get in huge arguments over anything he doesn't care about or doesn't affect him."

She rambled as I listened, allowing her to get it all out.

"I have the worst mother-in-law ever. He won't say anything to her about how she treats me," whimpering.

"Not the mother-in-law drama," rolling my eyes.

"She shot down all my ideas for our wedding, and he supported her even though I disagreed."

"Okay, do you want to talk about it?"

"He wants me to let her have her way and disregards what I want. It's my wedding and not hers!"

I rubbed her back; "awe, it may not be as bad as it seems."

"I don't want her input. Period."

As she had finished screaming her concerns, tears flooded her face, again. Her eyes were beet red, face swollen, and hair disarrayed. Mascara ran down her face like a car, burnt rubber tracks down her face. Honestly,

I didn't know what to say to comfort her; I had been through that same situation with mines, and it didn't end well. I prayed for the words to comfort her. When she looked at me with those big, puffy eyes, my heart melted.

"Baby, you got to wear waterproof mascara if you will let people get next to you," pulled a tissue from my pocket, dotting the runs.

"Honey, join me on the patio in a few minutes; let us get out of this blistering sun and chat."

We collected the scattered tools into a neat pile alongside of the porch, turning off the water—meant I was finished for the day. The full set of the beaming sun had come upon us, bringing on an incredible amount of bolstering heat.

"I don't know if I can help you, but let's see, okay?"

She agreed, and within a few minutes, we had met up again on the patio.

"First, let me say, I understand. I have been through the same mess myself, and trust me, it's interesting—mother-in-laws. Not all of us are bad," I laughed.

"Yes, that's true, grandma."

She was still whimpering, seemed ready to rattle on about it again. I stopped her, shaking my head. "Have some tea, freshly brewed right here on the sunny back porch. Had to beat a scorpion off the top of it, earlier. He may have added some extra flavor—not," laughing as Chloe's eyes widened.

Yet she drank, eyes rolling and bobbling around. Sounds of pure goodness came from her.

"Welcome to Arizona living, ha," laughing loud.

"Ugh… She—, sighed. My mil has been excluding me from family functions after I spoke to her about the wedding. Times she invited me, it was uncomfortable as you could tell she didn't want me around and other get-togethers he went alone, saying he wanted to avoid trouble."

"Have you spoken to him about it?"

"Yes, well — I spoke to her about it along with my concerns about the wedding, and it turned into a shouting match."

"When did this happen?"

"About four months ago."

"Jeremai said?"

"Nothing to her but told me that no one disrespects his mother. After our heated argument, he exclaimed that I highly upset her and was ashamed of the things I said."

"Interesting."

"He said nothing about the statement she made about whooping my behind for having the nerve to say anything to her about anything with her all up in my face."

"She got in your face?"

"Yes, it was crazy. I wanted to hit her but respected her too much."

"Well, that's a good thing. Fighting isn't the answer."

"What about how me and the things she said? I wanted to beat her good but was still trying so hard to do the right thing. She let it be known she was the queen bee, and I was the intruder."

"This is not good Chloe."

"No! It's not fair at all. Today he relayed the message he needed time to think things over because he was loyal to both of us and on nobodies' side. Funny how he needs time away from me but talks to her every day."

"Oh, Honey."

"He cared less about my feelings and babbled on about how he hated his mother being upset. Afterwards he got in his car and left for hours, refusing to talk to me when he came back. We've been going on like this for months."

"I am done. How can I respect him when he doesn't stand up to his mother?"

"Yeah, it's a tremendous problem," rolling my eyes.

"One more thing, his cousins came to help with the engagement photo shoot. They claimed not to have a picture of all of them. So, I let them get a picture. It turned out nice. The bad part is they made copies of the pic of them and passed it out to the entire family, the only picture taken without me. His mother raved about the photo and never put one up with me in it. Again, he said nothing."

"Wow, they did that?"

"Yes, Grandma… I can't."

"I'm wanting to punch the whole darn family in the face, let's go. Who you want me to hit first?"

Chuckling, "grandma… fighting is not the answer, remember?"

"Naw, but we can burn their house down. Let me—"

"No, not that either, want to go to jail?"

"Nope, but something needs to be done. I'm mad for you, fuming like thunder balls. I heard you, honey, all morning, rambling on about it."

This iced tea is so refreshing, almost makes you forget how hot it is, wiping the sweat off my face.

"First, honey, we have to become humble. I know we all want to prove that we are right, and they are wrong, right?" she nodded.

"But, listen to this: the problem doesn't just lie with them. You have the power to change lots of things."

She wiped her mouth, looking as if I'd lost my mind.

"Hear me out, okay? When we get upset, one becomes irrational, not able to see the entire problem. Just lost in our feelings, that never helps us solve anything."

"I guess," she muttered quizzically.

"What do you want her to do for the wedding?"

"Nothing. We have it under control."

"You assume that she wants to be a part of the wedding, it's also her son's event too."

"I guess."

"Do you think you can compromise?"

"I—"

"Yes, you can. Let her do apart and pay for it since she offered. It seems only right."

"But—"

"Now the problem. There is a certain amount of respect that you both need to have to each other."

"She treats me like she wants to drive me away so it can be the two of them."

"That's a terrible, however a lot of women go through this, it can be worst when he is an only child which is the case for Jeremai and Hosea."

"Oh messy, messy situations. That's where Mr. Jeremai will have to choose, if she is not willing to respect your feelings… period."

We continued chatting, sharing advice on how to handle the monster-in-law she had to deal with. Sharing ideas on how she could handle the ferocious beast she had set out for her. She sounded like a mother afraid to be replaced by his wife or just plain jealous. Not to mention he's the only child, that's a tough one. Poor relationships like this can cause the marriage to be strained and eventually break down. Not to mention the trolls that helped her be who she was. I'm sure she played injured in her endeavors, forcing her side of the drama to prove herself right. Praying things work out before the wedding. The echoes of laugher, tears, and occasional hugs even hollered a few times as we enjoyed ourselves.

"She is just an evil grandma; I can't stand her and her canting ways I will never accept them."

Her response gave way to her emotions, she was all over the place. The conversation at hand did not change her stance on the subject as her emotions hadn't budged.

"How was she before the engagement, and what about his father?"

"Not bad, rather nice until he asked me to marry him… then she turned into the ice queen—cold-hearted and pure evil. His dad doesn't say much."

"Has he talked to her about it?"

"He's useless in dealing with her, goes along with whatever. I think his nonexistence of helping in the matter is giving her more power."

Her anger sat in, leaving me helpless in my endeavors to liven her spirits. Deep down, I knew what she was going through. After dealing with my mother-in-law, I had to cut off our relationship because she refused to change. Sadly, it remained strained until she passed away. I'm guessing we all have to change, I tried. Some folks she slandered me too often called trying to help us to no avail. Making me feel like I had lost control of my marriage, and my husband went right along with appeasing her in her madness. I couldn't help thinking things could have been different if he would have to step up to her drama, demanding that she change or else. It didn't happen, and change was not her desire, so I broke it off the entire relationship. It was ugly and sad. In my time of growth, I found that situations like this prayer works. Depending on human help does nothing. I wish I would have known the power of prayer during our relationship; I know things would have been different. It would have been God's way and the best way if I would have included him on my journey. Lesson learned the hard way, but I learned it.

"This is when we ask ourselves, can we fix this problem by ourselves, or should we let God? Trust me, I believe you have the answer to that question."

"I don't understand."

"Can you fix it or change it? If it's yes, then do so. If it is no, then we accept it and deal with it or walk away and let God handle the problem. Not easily done, but doable. Sometimes, we have to work on ourselves first to handle problems in a marriage or better yet an engagement."

"What do you mean?"

"Prayer works for the things you can't change, worrying only steals from the moment. Pray over your man and your mother-in-law and let Jesus fight the battle. Besides, you can walk away without a messy divorce and no children. Honey, try to work things out first or if you walk away, you will handle future issues in your next relationship spiritually."

"True," she nodded.

"That crusty ole devil himself, out to kill and steal anyone's happiness that hasn't set their feet on solid ground, forcing us to open our eyes and be on the watch, if you love him prayerfully fight for him."

I paused, staring off at the mountains as I took a nice long swig of iced tea.

"Sit down and have a one-on-one talk with him well before the big day. Get a good understanding of how you both will deal with his parents and if possible, try counseling."

"Your right. I need to do that."

"Communication and effective listening are a must for any marriage. Without it, we will lose."

"It's so hard to talk to him," deeply sighing.

"If it's like that now, what makes you think things will change later? Sometimes God will use your man, family, and friends as a sign someone is not for you. Do we always listen?"

"No, I've been thinking the same thing."

"Girl communicate now with him and don't force the marriage if he isn't willing to work things out with you. If he can't hold a meaningful conversation now, then you should call it off."

"Grandma, I'm so scared."

"Don't be, Jeremai is a smart man. I am sure if he wants you to be happy, he will work on issues that pertain to your happiness, better yet your happiness as one. Explain your feelings and listen to his concerns—you both will be fine."

"Talk… not argue."

"I can do that… I hope," she sighed.

"In the tween time, work on yourself. Become one who is slow to anger and more than willing to gain understanding and quit tearing down your man behind his back or to his face."

"What?"

"I heard ya all morning talking about that man to your friends—stop."

We sat in silence.

"Do you have faith the size of that tiny little mustard seed?"

"Yes, I do."

I held out a little bottle, sprinkling some in her hands, playing with them, "they sure are tiny," rolling the specks around her palm.

"Instead of trying to fix others, always try to work on yourself first, you know that old sayin'… why do you look at the speck of sawdust out of your brother's eye and pay no attention to the plank in your own eye?"

Her eyebrows shot up, "grandma, I did nothing wrong."

"First problem I see that can be worked on… tearing down your relationship from the inside out. Yeah, it was messy, telling all kinds of folks his faults," faintly smiling.

"What if he did the same to you?"

She stared into her lap, "It would hurt."

"I have done it too, thinking I was getting advice—wrong. Keep all folks out of your business, including your parents and us. I had to learn that lesson the hard way. Oh wee, it wasn't good, I tell ya."

"Okay, never thought of it that way. You heard me today?"

"Who didn't, do you think we were deaf?"

"No."

"It was terrible the things you said, not only that you carried on something awful, I believe you felt the worst afterwards than you did talking to him. And your friends…"

"Grandma—"

"Get some praying friends, ones that will give you spiritual advice."

"O-kay."

"You should sit down, think about all the things you have rooted in your life—past hurts from exe's, childhood traumas; any unpleasant experiences… sit down and work on anything that you shouldn't bring to this marriage," giving her a playful swat on her arm.

"I know you ain't going to do it, but you will if you want this to work. You want to start this marriage off right. Never stop forgiving and praying."

"I have talked to him already about this; he gets so defensive!"

"Girl, all that drama, yelling, and having fits — it does not work, a complete waste of time. Speak your peace calmly, pray about it and be patient. God moves in mysterious ways and working on your marriage and family is no different. I have seen God move some of the most stubborn men and mother in laws."

"How you know that's how I talk to him?"

"I hear ya! No wonder he closes his ears; I'd close mine too. You will find no man wants to be with a sour prude… a woman full of anger will drive a man running for the hills. He'd rather sleep on the rooftop in a corner than with a brawling woman."

"Yeah," she giggled.

"Wives should live in a manner in which her ways show him the path to God himself. Guard his heart safely and give him peace of mind. Even when he ain't worthy, it doesn't go unnoticed."

"Well, if I can, there's still my mother-in-law."

Slumped in her seat, she fiddled with the mustard seeds.

"I can't believe you have these; they are so tiny," she said.

"Yup, and I give them out to folks who need a reminder."

"You sure reminded me."

"Back to the wedding, what if you have a son, and his new family doesn't include your side of the family?"

Chloe looked at me, "you mean in their wedding?"

"Yes—not pretty," I sighed.

"Marriage is about unity, bringing two families together. Many miss that point; tearing spouses away from their families hurts everyone involved—lets change that."

"I can see that… I'll try to work with her."

"A man is to make his wife number one—period. Agree on a few things she can do for the wedding; embrace it. Don't be one of those bride zillas. You are too beautiful on the inside and out to be that person."

I leaned over to whisper in her ear, "Don't be that person."

I grabbed a bottle of red wine to bring more joy to the conversation. Before long, we chatted the afternoon away.

"What do you think about me canceling the wedding?"

"Rubbish!"

"You're right; I love him."

I played in her hair, "yeah, I am sure Mr. Jeremai will do right by my baby girl."

She shook her head as she poured us another glass of wine.

Shaking the bottle, she chanted… "More, more, more!" she exclaimed.

I directed her to the wine cooler for our second round, just as Hosea came out back to check on us.

"Well, look here—," Hosea stated.

"Intruder alert, intruder alert," she muffled at him as I waved my hands, shooing him off.

"Go on! We havin' girl talk out here."

"Okay, okay, I'm gone, man bashers alert. Don't want to hear none of that stuff, for sure."

Threw his hands up and shuffled away. When Hosea disappeared, we settled with our glasses full again, I couldn't stop staring at her.

A goofy grin overtook my face, shaking my head at all the memories flooding back to me. Pure war… with someone I cared about—my mother-in-law, bless her soul.

❧

January, 1978 ✿ Dear Journal, Ooh wee, he was a fine look-in' man. He came in my life at a point when I no longer wanted to be in a relationship. Saying he fell in love with me the moment he laid eyes on me at the Mexican restaurant where we met. Funny how he told me I should have married him first, would have been no second go-round. I chuckled so hard; how would he have known? I was out celebrating my best friend getting a new job. He was waiting to get a carry-out, watching me from afar. We were having a blast that day; I was thirty-two years old and rarely had time to get out of the house. I was a single parent going to school and working two jobs, with no help. My sons were staying over at a friend's house for a sleepover, so I was free. We were all crammed into a booth, hackling about guys and who was dating who. Many assorted drinks flooded our table, along with fresh food to entertain our palates. Not one of us had a care in the world. Bone-chilling cold outside for the past week, huge piles of snow left us stranded in our driveways; we all needed to be away from those kids.

I missed hanging with the girls. I wasn't close to any of them except Jersula, but I had hung out with them before. A live band played with the lead singer looked like someone off the streets, dressed in ragged clothes. His sidestep singer wore a three-piece suit, the total opposite of the lead singer. They drugged their instruments across the floor, making all kinds of racket, diverting our attention over to them. My friend Jersula yelled, "Why ya'll over there, tripping with all that noise?"

We tried our best to shut her up but failed. One of the band members shouted back, "Who over there got balls to be in our business?"

Jersula replied, "I do, you jive turkey?"

Oh, we hee-hawed. The look on that man's face was priceless! But she was embarrassing.

"Who you callin' a jive turkey, chump?" she yelled.

We all died laughing because he didn't know Jersula's temper, and boy, did she have one. She jumped across the girl next to her and pushed past the next one, grabbing a glass of water with one hand and working her legs at the same time. She walked up to him and asked him again if he had something to say and dumped the water right in his face. The argument began. His band members stopped working to support his wimpy butt and seeing that we all ran over to stop a fight from starting.

"Girl, I know he ain't mean-muggin' us, who is he scaring?"

We mean-mugged them back, with extra attitude.

The band leader looked over at Jersula, shouting, "Stop dipping in my Kool-Aid, fat pig."

She threw another glass of water right in his face and lunged at him. This had us all wrestling to get them off each other, felt like we were fighting each other. We pulled Jersula off him and began walking away, but they stayed eye-locked until we got close to the table. We cut into her immediately, asking her what in the world had gotten into her.

"You could have gotten us killed," I said.

Fixing our clothes and hair after dragging her from a fight, she had no care about any of it until the manager came over to our table, asking us to leave. We all looked at her while requesting the bill with visible attitudes.

"Humph, got us kicked out?" One lady smirked as she gathered her belongings.

We all had an attitude, and the fool was unwilling to accept fault. She held her head up high, blaming it all on the guy. We just shook our heads in shame, as she had never known boundaries, but as usual, we had her back. Standing around, waiting for our bill, Hosea walked up, asking if everything was okay. We all looked around at each other, saying we were fine, wondering who he was.

He extended his hand to me, "Hi, I'm Hosea, and you are?" grinning.

"Matea."

I was blushing; this cat was smooth. Looking around at all of us,

"I kind of overheard you all got put out, is this right?"

"Yes, and it concerns you—why?" I asked.

Giving his answer in a smart tone, I gathered my belongings, waiting for the bill to come. He retrieved the bill from the server piercing over it.

"I got it," he told us, then pulled the manager over to the side, steading his eyes over my way.

"Hey, what are the chances these beautiful young ladies over there can stay? I will cover the bill and send my man over there our sincere apologies."

He handed the manager the money for the bill, along with a nice tip. The manager stared at him, giving him a long, firm look of seriousness with eyes that could kill if he tried any harder.

"Hey, tell the band I'll buy them all a drink as well… we cool?"

"Yeah man, we good," band leader replied.

Next thing we knew, he was thanking the manager for letting us ladies stay… finishing with an arrogant smile. The manager grumbled and walked away. We thanked him for his help, and for paying for our bill. He asked if he could join us.

"I paid the bill, right?" He asked with this smirky grin while licking his lips.

He was a good-looking guy, dressed to a tee. He impressed me. However, he would never know it. As I stared over at him, I said to myself, look at him looking all professional with his two-piece black suit on, fitting him in all the right places. He pulled his jacket back, placing his hand on his hip, revealing his fitting mock-turtleneck sweater waiting for us to have a seat. We girls stole a moment, leaving us giggling and chattering like we're in high school. As I walked past him, he grabbed my arm.

"I want this beautiful woman to sit next to me if she may?" I giggled, looking around, face reddened.

"Okay, but no funny stuff."

He chuckled and then introduced himself to all the other ladies at the table. He held a pleasant conversation, occasionally catching him admiring me off and on. Not too long ago gone through a nasty divorce; I wanted nothing to do with no man. The same ladies who sat with us tonight were the ones I had vowed to that I would not date for a very long time as they'd consoled me. I wasn't interested in dating; it was nothing personal toward him. Telling some of the craziest jokes and enjoying ourselves, I realized it was time for me to turn in. I got up, excusing myself- saying goodbye to everyone, including Hosea. Quickly, I scattered away. He rushed to get up just as quick, saying his goodbyes. He ran to catch up with me while I was getting in my old white beat up truck. As he shuffled over, he started calling my name and flagging me. I continued settling in my seat, ignoring him.

"Hey, how you just going to leave me here, knowing I was there trying to see you? When can I see you again?"

"Can't," I scoffed, giving him a side-eye, "I really don't think so."

"Why not?"

"I'm not interested in dating at the moment."

He stood there, propping my door open with his arm while leaning into my truck, just staring at me. He took his eyes off me and stepped back.

"This your truck? Didn't think a cutie like you would drive an old truck like this. I would picture you driving a car or something different."

"I don't think I asked you for your opinion, did I?"

"Naw, you didn't."

Leaning back in the car again, smiling. Giving him a good looking over. He was handsome. Deep brown chocolate skin, oiled; trimmed mustache, wavy hair with a side part; dressed to impress, all crisped up; and smelling -oh, so good. Need I say he had some sweet, thick, tempting lips? I snapped my thoughts back in place, pushing him out of my truck and closing my door.

"Come on, now; I just want to call you sometimes, woman." Rolling the window up, the dang knob broke off in my hand.

"That's what you get with your evil self."

He repaired the knob.

"Goodnight," I said, then drove off with my car sputtering and coughing down the road.

About a half a mile away, I whipped around the corner and turned back. Pulled into the lot and gave him my number.

"No dating!" I yelled.

I adjusted my rearview mirror to see his response. He just stood there, smiling, watching me drive away.

❧

February,1988 ✿– Dear Journal, He didn't call me right away. I figured he wouldn't call me at all the way I had acted. I had changed my stance and prayed for God to send me someone he wanted me to have and not some knuckle head that I wanted. None of my choices never turned out well and tired of doing me. I still didn't think he was the one, I didn't think God had already answered my prayers. However, he called me about two weeks later. We talked for a while before I informed him, I had recently divorced and wasn't interested. Telling him, it was nothing personal; it just wasn't a good time. Giving off a good chuckle, elaborated on the ladies admiring him. how one of the other ladies I'd been with that night all thought he was charming and would love the chance to talk to him.

As he remained silent for a while, he responded, "Oh yeah?"

"Yeah."

"What would you say if I told you I only want you?"

Then I was silent. Hosea kept showing interest in me; I heard him loud and clear, but I needed him to listen to me just the same.

"What do you like so much about me? You didn't even know me when you saved us from getting thrown out of the restaurant, so what's up with that?"

"Let me come over; I'll tell you in person."

Sighing, I noticed he was not taking no as the answer.

"You know, I told you I wasn't ready to see anyone."

"Yes, I heard you, and I respect that. Just give us time; you'll change your mind."

"Us? What does that mean?"

"Yes, you and me… give us time."

We had a pleasant visit, truly enjoyed ourselves, laughing and talking about all kinds of things. He was a smooth talker, but very respectful, and I enjoyed his company. I had made some refreshments for us, and he praised me on how good my fruit punch Kool-Aid was. Loudly I laughed, telling him it was just Kool-Aid, making it sound like it was the best he'd ever tasted. I marveled at him; he amazed me, but I refused to let him know in any way that he did. Looking at him move around, and his lips, so lovely and full! Such a beautiful color to them, moist and soft looking. That man had a beautiful smile, with big, bold white teeth that shined like he had gotten them polished and finished with a sparkle. He was short, which was cool; he was about five-foot-seven and carried a bit of extra weight. He impressed me. Finally, he called it a night, I was getting tired- both of us had to work. Walking to the door, he turned and grabbed me, holding me close to him. Then he kissed me. Oh, my- his lips were so soft, like I'd imagine them. He was firm in his hold that I gave in to the kiss. For the first time in my life, I felt stars and sparkles from his embrace. You know, like in the movies. His hands were magical—as he touched me, I felt feelings I never had before. Our eyes locked as we stared at each other for a minute. He just knew his love was one-sided until that first kiss, the one that blew my breath away.

Suddenly I yelled, "You have to go!"

Pushing him out of the door, he stated, "Yeah, I'm so—"

Can't believe I slammed the door before he could say another word. Next thing I knew, I was lying in the back seat of Jersula's car, wondering, how did I fall in love in one night? With one kiss?

She was driving and yelling, "I told you, you would find someone. All that talking you did about wanting no one and, girl, I haven't ever seen you like this before."

"What am I going to do? This is crazy, but it felt amazing!"

"Girl, he'll never talk to you again the way you acted; you know that, don't you?"

Groaning, I covered my face.

"Nope, I wouldn't talk to me either."

I sat up and leaned against her seat.

"I'll figure out a way to let him know, but how?"

I waited for him to call me first since I had practically pushed him out of the door and I'm sure he thinks I wasn't interested anymore. However, a few days later, he called holding a generic conversation. After a while, I asked him if he had a girlfriend and why I wanted to know?

"Last week, you were all like, you don't need no man because of the past losers you dealt with."

I sighed, rolling my eyes, as though he could see right through me.

"What you call me for?" I chuckled.

"Because I wanted to. I never said I didn't want you as my woman; you said you don't want a real man. You live in the past if you want and lose a good, hard-working man. That's why I called. I'm trying to tell you I would love to be with you."

I took a deep breath and said, "What if I said, Okay?"

There was a momentary pause, like he couldn't believe his ears.

"Are you serious?"

"Yes, but let's take things slow. I'm still not sure if I'm ready for another relationship."

❧

March 1978-✿ Dear Journal, within days, a love affair out of this world began. I took the words to take it slow and threw it right out of the window. He was so romantic and attentive that I enjoyed every moment. I'd woke up to special gifts scattered around the house and enjoyed each one of them. Sneaking around to see each other, as I had the boys and never had a sitter. He had his son every weekend. So, our late evening adventures began when they were asleep. We couldn't get enough of each other. I worked two jobs, one during the day and the other midnights. I practically worked around the clock, was at school, or had my kids. We both worked a ton of hours and it was almost impossible to get together. It became frustrating. One day, he called me and told me to quit my second job.

"I'll never be able to see you, woman, if we both are always working."

The next day I quit. I was feeling alive for the first time. Before I felt like I just lived; Now I felt vibrant and amazing. I was just mesmerized by our new romance. He spent all of his free time with me mostly, sharing a few dates to include the boys. The beautiful dates he planned were something I wasn't accustomed to. We introduced each other two different cuisines. The funniest food he introduced me to a giant lobster, something I had always wanted. You would think if I'd wanted it so badly, I would have known how to eat it. I had a marvelous time figuring it out. Our favorite past-time was watching the sunset come up. He loved to cook, and often would cook up some sumptuous meals. Honey, that was the ultimate turn-on for me — a man who can cook, I was sold. Soon thereafter, we moved in together. He would cut the boys' hair and cook breakfast. He was like he was a short-order cook.

"Maybe you shouldn't give the boys so options like that, I'll never be able to do if you leave."

"I ain't leaving. So, I say things should carry on as usual."

We were so good together, hardly ever arguing. We were in love; the touching of fingertips, holding hands, countless hours of being tangled in each other was so amazing to us both. Long talks on any subject were like foreplay to our minds; we longed to hear each other's thoughts and opinions. Things were so exciting that I paid little attention to my body until the exhaustion kicked in—the verdict? Pregnant. I'd never thought about having another baby while buying and selling a house. And three kids already? Our kids were teenagers, and here I was, pregnant and starting all over again. Reality set in after our whirlwind love feast came to a complete stop. We had a big decision to make. Hosea wanted no more children, nor did I. But it happened. He put his foot down that this was not a good time to have a baby. For a moment, it devastated me. Then, I called him right back and told him I was having it. Nothing more to talk about. Asher was born right after we purchased our first home together, and we did these things within a year. Two house notes, daycare, four children, two car notes, and the other bills that came along with it all was a lot of added pressure for a newly created family. Not to mention, the struggle the kids had with moving and the blending of the families. The many issues we faced in our marriage early on; appeared like something destined us for failure without our knowledge. It just kind of happened as we lived our daily lives without God at the head. We dealt with hardcore racism, as we had moved into a predominately white neighborhood, and at our jobs. We faced vehement opposition from the kids' schools. Too much family and friends' involvement, no spiritual guidance, kid issues, our issues, financial issues—you name it, we dealt with it. But nothing worked out for us until we put God at the head of our lives. Period.

❧

"Wow grandma, look at you." Chloe laughed so hard she had tears rolling.

"What?"

"You played hard ball, big time."

"You think so? I was just trying to get myself together, girl I wasn't thinking about no man."

"From the sound of it... I don't think it worked."

"Humph."

"Look at you grandma, you know it was a project stay single failure."

"Girl, you know it was. That man was too fine."

"Your friend--?"

Rolling her eyes. "She is the one who gave me the wisdom that I shared with you today. I got rid of her. I replaced her with my good friend Shilo, who passed away. Spiritual advice anytime I needed it. What a true and loving friend."

"Ok, ok, I hear you, maybe I'll find one when I attend church."

"Come with us."

"I may take you us on that?"

"I'm going this week. I attend every Sunday and I see you dodging me when I get ready to ask you to join us."

"You noticed that?"

"Sure do."

"Okay, I'll go, but I really don't think I'll like it."

"Well, before you assume, try it. Besides, it just may save your life, young lady."

"Save my life?"

"Yes ma'am… spiritual food keeps us encouraged on this journey called life. Helps you to make better decisions."

"Well then, for sure I'll go. I'll check you out later. Got homework."

"See ya."

The Surprise

You laid eyes upon me before you wrote my name in your book and called me wonderful. Chloe had been sleeping more than usual and had been complaining of her feet and hands swelling. She came into my room, lying across my bed, moaning about her fatigue.

"How have you been sleeping?"

"I don't know… we've been doing so much lately."

Chloe appeared ok; I had noted she wasn't as cheerful as she had been, thinking maybe she and Jeremai were at it again. As tired as she may have been, it didn't keep her from hanging out and shopping with her classmate and doing research for school. Doing all of that, I didn't worry about her too much. I wanted my hair washed and asked Chloe if she could do it for me later.

"Yes, ma'am I will, I'll be home by 5 is that good?"

"That will be perfect! I should be done by then."

Starting the adventure of cleaning my closet out today. I stood in the doorway with my hands on my hips looking towards the end of the long walkway; it was a mess! Having a walk-in closet is a blessing, but why did I have to fill it up to the brim? Stuff everywhere. Clothes, shoes, and purses I no longer wanted. Laughing at myself because it included things from every phase of my life, back to the 70s. Might even have that nightgown my mom gave me the year she died and my 8th grade shoes I found cleaning out my grandma's house. I hardly ever threw anything out unless it was ugly or damaged. My neighbor is going to help me. She always claims if I gained the tenacity to do it, she would help. This time she put her foot in her mouth because I took her up on her offer. Any minute, she should be here, looking at my watch. Candace is going to set up a pleasant lunch, making it a girl's day in. I pulled out my old radio to give us some inspiration, along with two chairs because we are both old. Michal is about five years younger and a pleasure to have as a friend. Almost like a sister. The first thing I pulled out was my old jug of moonshine. Really, it's red wine I made awhile back and kept a jug in my closet to hide it from Hosea. He drank all my wine, and he wouldn't get to this one. The only problem, it seems too fermented for anybody to consume. I couldn't tell, tilting it to the side. As soon as it hit the floor, the settlements ran rampant throughout the jug. It took me forever to make that last bottle. We just may try some tonight; I figure if it kills us, we won't remember, right? Plus, I think alcohol never goes bad. I laughed to myself as I dug into the back of the closet. The closet was tremendous as a room, lots of shelves for my shoes and hanging space. Now I just need to gain some order in here. Some stuff I hadn't worn since- shoot, I had a figure and a life. Why do I look like the monarch of hoarders? Michal arrived and came right in.

"Woe missy—you got a lot of stuff," she exclaimed.

"Girl don't come over here to talk about my mess. I told you what it was like before you said you would help."

"I know, I just didn't expect this kind of chaotic. We need a Salvation Army truck posted out front and just throw this crap right out the window."

"Lady, you ain't fibbed not one bit."

"Let's get to work before I change my mind," Michal shouted.

"Hold your horses' woman; I had some snacks and wine served."

"Hey, you want to go to the movies this evening, you and Hosea?"

"What's it about?"

"Some slavery movie that just came out."

"Is it the one comparing southern slavery to modern day slaves?" I quickly replied.

"Yes."

"I don't know, girl… I have plenty to do."

"What? Not the activist lady?"

"You know you are a mess, yes I love helping my peoples."

"Now ain't that the truth."

"The movie starts with the slavery dealing with the Israelites and their freedom. How the southern states freeing the slaves, moving to Jim Crow laws and other manipulative means, redlining in all areas of life, and now they are locking up our men in greater portions. Don't even mention us killing each other."

"It's just sad?"

"Sometimes it seems like we're just moving backwards no matter how hard we try."

"Dang, they just killing anyone moving with brown skin and using modern tactics of invisible chaining of our people, what could we do?"

"See the movie, maybe we can learn how to make a difference."

"I don't know... you know I'm selective on what I watch."

"There you go, girl, let loose sometimes."

"Let me watch the preview and I'll let you know. Too much going on in these movies now a day to just be loose, missy."

"I just wish more leaders today focused on really helping people and not corruption."

"I know what you mean government, church leaders, and many of these charities designed to help are taking instead or not doing nothing."

"Think about it, we listen to all the evil in the world through our music, movies, and books we read, and it all kills us off starting with our minds. Tell anybody to pick up the good book and do what it says, and you've committed a crime," she shrugged.

"Times so bad today, I just want to see something that's not sex, using the Lord's name in vain, cursing, or fighting. Now you know telling some people today to read the word is an insult."

"What you say! Well-you can't watch or listen to nothing nowadays, cuz everything got all of it, even kid movies."

"Look, when the Israelites were freed, you know how they stayed in the wilderness because of their sins. Would you think that maybe blacks have similar lives?"

"Now I have thought about that. You also got me thinking about Lot's wife looking back."

"Yes, she turned to a pillar of salt... they say she's still there."

"Oh my. That looking back is a mess."

"Yup, we all about materialism, listening to the wrong folks, and being captives to debt. Why do we have to have the latest gym shoes and cars and nowhere to live? Or the car chained to the house?"

"We need to do better; I rode past a line the other day out the door of a gym shoe place. My nephew told me the new Jordan's came out. I wish they would line up for church the same way."

"I wonder, how did we get here? Back in the day we used to own some thangs, now we have nothing."

"Really, I don't understand either. It's very frustrating. My grandma always said we have back slid into a far worst times where we've lost our motivation."

"What if looking at slavery movies is the same as looking back, as the bible says? You know, like the Israelites?"

"It's possible, girl, but surely our folks got blessings coming if we hold tight."

"What if the answer is us moving together in unity and creating our own?"

"I agree and stop all the rioting and get to planning how we can flourish a community on our own. Really, I'm tired of trying to make some unworthy folks care about us. Screw em."

"Ha! It will never happen. We can't stop grumbling, criticizing, and pointing fingers to save our lives; if we do—it just might make the world a better place."

"So, there goes the blessing."

"Girl, all this talk, and we ain't did a thing, so are you going?"

"Maybe I'll see what Hosea says."

I divided my closet into four sections, just to make it easy to see where we start and finished. I let Michal chose what section to start. She went right for the wigs.

"Girl, I've been knowing you for over ten years. I ain't seen you wear a wig, ha," glancing at me sideways.

"I know, I hate wigs but wore them to keep my colleagues off my back about natural hair on the job."

Michal was looking at me like I had lost my mind. Her eyes protruded out her head and appeared blank. Looking at her hilarious facial expressions, I pushed past her to keep my momentum.

Look, I had them on a shelf nice and neat, at least I've been dusting them. Piercing over the mannequin heads, I took them down getting a closer look.

"I've endured so much racism within my job; it wasn't funny — over my hair. A few times I almost got fired fighting white folks about wearing my natural hair on my job. You can put them in the donation bag."

Goodbye wigs and the horrid memories that go along with them. I found some pictures of me wearing one of my wigs during a riot back in the day, showing them to Chloe.

"You didn't look like yourself."

"I wasn't, felt like an imposter, giving in to demands just to keep my job. I almost got one of those hot pieces knocked right off my head, debating with a white guy on a job concerning my hair."

"Eh, oh no. I know you gave him the business."

"You know I did."

"What if we owned businesses and told white folks we don't want their straight hair representing our company? Ya just don't fit into the culture… curl it or else!"

"Now that one… I ain't never heard of before. Now would be something."

We both screamed as she continued stuffing the wigs into the bag. I paused and looked at them as we pitched them into the trash. Old memories flooded my mind of all the mess I took over my hair. Made me hate my own God given curls and made me a prisoner to their demands. Those days are long gone, and so is this crap. Ready to live for today nowadays. Michal went over to this big bag neatly hanging in the back of the closet and brought it up.

"What's in here?" Michal asked, hauling out a garment bag.

"My wedding dress and vow renewal dress, you can toss them for donations."

I had them packed to give to my granddaughter one day, but it never happened. Chloe's wedding is in a few weeks, and she already has a dress. My worst thought was the gown would be ruined or yellowed from the 18 years I've contained it. Laying the dresses across the table, I deflated the garment bag; I gasped as the bag folded. Looking as if they graced my body yesterday. Beautifully appearing before my eyes, the one I renewed my vows in was mesmerizing least to say. The cream-colored bodice resembled grandma's famous custard pie and joined waist point with a glorious sapphire blue and cream tulle which flowed into a full-bodied skirt, a fitting for a queen. The intertwining of the mixtures of the cream and blue hues created a harmonious array of amazing colors. Jazzy crystals popped like twinkling stars, along with the most adorning embellishments, which blended well with the ocean and sandy background. Looking over the lacey covered top of the gown with cascading lace that delicately hung from my shoulders transitioned to the back of the dress embracing dainty floating buttons. Gracing over the skirt, I fondled the split that showed more leg than I wanted, forcing me to laugh at the efforts it took to keep important things covered. The love of the splendor of it and hate of the stressed it caused existed before I stuffed it into my suitcase, which ended the day I wore it.

The challenges caused were unreal; the worry came right out of me, riddling me with daunting daydreams of having a trash the dress event. First, the crystals I placed on the cream-colored bodice were discoloring the lace. Nothing worked at removing the dirty look, which wasn't much, but I noticed it and didn't like it. I prayed. Next my seamstress altered it and appeared perfect until I found slight cuts around the waist that weren't there before. Searched the fabric stores and found a beautiful ribbon of crystals that matched the dress perfectly, similar to a belt. Glued it on, covering the tiny slits until the glue gun slipped and made another problem, a hole. Tried it on finding it was too long and I struggled to walking in it. This time I prayed and cried. As the wedding theme was moon and stars, I made it work by covering the hole perfectly. My seamstress went on vacation and I took a chance of fixing my length myself and it proved to be too much. I hung it in the doorway and sat and stared at it for hours. I cried, prayed, and said screw it with only a few days before our flights, I had had enough. I left it alone until… she called. Telling her my dilemmas, she came right away and fixed it a day before taking off she handed me my gown. I never tried it on until the moment—but God. Second, we could find nothing Hosea could wear to match the colors. Month of searching before finding the one suit that fitted perfectly, and it cost more than we could imagine one week before. It blew me away by how wonderful everything turned out, just amazing. This dress represented a Cinderella moment and a marriage that had many blemishes from the mistakes we both made. It was a symbolism to trust in the only God who took what I thought was a mess and turned it into something incredible. No one saw the problems I felt would glow bright in the dark. Instead, we shined, and everyone experienced nothing but our happiness. I don't think I ever looked as beautiful as I looked that day, and grander than I ever thought I would have. Truly, no other day was as magical as the day I remarried my best friend.

"This is one classy get up… is this the one you wore on the pic over the fireplace?"

"Yes, that's the one. But enough of hoarding it. Someone can wear it and look as splendor as I once looked."

"I'll take it out of bag and place it on your bed."

"Ok. I could at least show Chloe's what her grandma wore on her special day."

Reminding myself to grab the shoes. They had turned a light yellow, but yet sparkled. I didn't place them in a shoe bag, and it's bound to happen. The toe of the shoe had a display of crystals and pearls wrapped around the ankle, I put them with the dress and the heel snapped, as I cried laughing. Michal continued digging in the closet until she came to see what was wrong.

"What happened?"

As I leaned against the bed in tears with one foot twisted and the other holding me up.

"Dang it, I broke my shoe, bout to kill myself. Help me up."

"Have you heard of dry rot? The stuff you have is junk," rolling her eyes.

"Do not store up for yourselves treasures on earth, where moths and vermin destroy, and where thieves break in and steal… For where your treasure is, there your heart will be also (Matthew 6:19,21, NIV)," I said.

"Girl, your closet is in the past, just like you said. But — you know… I love you and happy to help you get rid of this mess. Your helping me do mines next."

"I see it concerning money too."

"Hm, yeah. They just buried old Mr. Walters last week and his son found money stuffed in his lounge chair while they were moving it. This man sitting around eating cat food with thousands right under his behind. You go figure that."

Going back into the closet, she pulled out some of my fast girl clothes from back in the day. Stuffing them into the bags, until she noticed they were from the 70s. My mouth fell wide open, looking at my old clothes. I wouldn't be shocked if they fell apart before our eyes. We both fell out laughing.

"Not my leather-look, hot pants, bell-bottoms, miniskirts, and halter tops," grabbing a few more pieces out.

"Oh my, you were hot-to-trout," she cackled, holding my pants to her waist.

"Yes, honey, nobody couldn't tell me a thang."

I giggled at her stance of fitting into my old jeans, strutting around flinging her head back about to break her neck. The patchwork across the top which had a funky appeal to it.

"Child some thangs not meant for everybody, your shape and them pants… it's a no!"

"Oh my, I agree, not flattering at all, but they fit."

Not sure why I don't like that style as I did in the past. The air between us floated horrible tunes as we sang with laughter. An occasional blast from the past comments that entertained us for hours. The radio blared an old song Michal said she loved back in the day. 'Rubber band man' got us poppin' our fingers… the fun began when she darted to collect two pairs of bell bottoms, throwing me one. We boogied down as we held the pants to our body's. Enjoying each second of having a genuine friendship, I felt like a teen again. Oh, we sang loudly until Candace peeked her head in the room with widened eyes.

"Are you all ok in here?" she asked.

"We're wonderful," I replied with my body pleading for oxygen.

"What in the world do you have on, Michal?"

"Bell bottoms and I tell you; I'd have to pass on these jokers. They look terrible."

"I agree, carry on ladies," Candace said.

"Girl, I was a mess back in the day."

"I see. Hard to believe you still have this stuff."

"Me too."

"Are these go-go boots?"

"Yes, they were sweet back then, with my tights, miniskirt, and a fat afro."

Twirling around and dancing just having a blast going through this stuff. Funny because I don't miss the old days at all. Lesson learned, and I survived. But it's time to get rid of this old stuff, tired of looking at it, and besides, this girl isn't the same and will never wear them again.

"How crazy does this look?"

"Way crazy," giving me the eye.

"What would I look like in hot pants at 68?"

"Put a pair on, let's see?"

"Bet you would love it, but it ain't going to happen."

"I'd be snapping pictures like crazy."

"You ain't never lied about that; you know how old you are and those clothes?"

She laughed until tears ran down her face, couldn't control herself. Looking over at me, she ran into the most serious face like she hit a brick wall which forced her to gain control. I stood frozen with a serious, stern look on my face.

"It ain't that funny! Syke," I said.

Then we both fell out into uncontrolled laughter. Pulling up the olive-green wing back chairs, we flumped into them, gaining our composure. We just stared at the ceiling.

"Girl, we've been through a lot in our lives and look at us now."

Complaining it was hot, I threw her a funeral home fan for relief.

"Oh my, a funeral home fan, what you trying to say?"

"Yup, don't look at it, just cool off."

Looking around for another one, I noted she flicked the fan oddly. Seemed like she was moving slow motion as she stretched out her legs. Lifting a few bags to see if any was under them, a thought came: "Dear brothers and sisters, when troubles of any kind come your way, consider it an opportunity for great joy. For you know that when your faith is being tested, your endurance grows. So, let it grow, for when your endurance is fully developed, you will be perfect and complete, needing nothing (James 1:2-4 NIV)." I stopped looking and sat in utter quietness, closing my eyes and thanking God. Looking back, I noted he kept his promise in every part of my life. Nothing seemed like a hardship as it had been in the past, thank you, Lord.

"Baby, we are diamonds! You know how much pressure it takes to make a mean gem? I'm two carats myself."

"I'm 10 carat myself."

"Whew, I probably need to check my blood pressure after hee-hawing and jaw jacking all day long with your crazy butt."

"Yes, that was a workout, for sure."

She shook her head as she continued stuffing them in the bag. Chloe returned, joining us. Looking like someone had hit her by a speeding tire, just as she did earlier — resting her weary body on the bed.

"What's wrong, Chloe?" Michal asked.

"I don't feel good."

"Uh—still? Maybe you should go lay down?" I said.

"Yea, I don't think I can do your hair today, is that ok?"

Before I could respond, she picked up my vow renewal dress.

"Oh, grandma, this gown is sweet."

"That's the dress your grandad, and I renewed our promises in the Dominican Republic- Punta Cana about 18 years ago."

"I kept it for my granddaughter, but she already has a dress."

"Can I try it on, I love it?"

"Sure, you can, I was much bigger than you though."

She rushed into the dress before we could blink; it was big on her, but it looked better on her.

"Wow, girl, too bad, you already have a dress."

Michal got up and pinched the sides. She figured out what we needed for it to fit.

"If you take a little off the sides and taper the shoulders, I think you may fit it, the length looks good."

"Can I have it?" with widened eyes.

She twirled around; her face lit with a smile from ear to ear. She is taller than me, but the dress drug on the ground slightly on me but fitted her perfectly lengthwise.

"Look at my beautiful granddaughter," staring at her; I noticed she appeared to be glowing more than I've ever seen.

"It's mines now… right?"

"What you going to do with it?"

"I don't know yet."

Shrugging my shoulders as I tossed the garment bag for her to return it to its old home. Laughing to myself because even she didn't notice the imperfections, which I focused on. I dared not show her because it seemed to be part of the beauty of it. Showing her my original dress, I married Hosea in, didn't appeal to her as much, but took it. It was a long cream-colored dress with lots of beading; it was heavy. The dress fell right above her ankles. Michal went to the kitchen to get cups to taste the wine. Disappearing around the corner, I sat back in my chair watching Chloe eagerly put the dresses away. Funny, because my first choice was to wear black when we first married. It's my favorite color, but his mom thought it was too harsh and I respected her idea. Thinking back on life's choices, it's cool respecting folks' wishes, but ultimately you have to do what makes you happy. Living only once in a lifetime, we find that if we live according to other people's wishes, we'll never live for ourselves. Choosing to follow God is one, folks can tell you about Him all day long and if it's not your choice and we force them into the relationship, just won't be right. Michal appeared with three wine glasses, laughing and gabbing on about the afternoon. Her natural hair bobbing around searching for the wine jug, she flung pieces of clothing towards the bags in frustration and laughter. With a deep breath, she flounced into the chair.

"This stuff looked better in your closet than out here, stuff everywhere like it exploded once we opened the door."

"If we drink nothing will get done, that's for sure."

Michal showed Chloe my 70s clothes; they had another hardy laugh.

She tried a few items on, saying they were ripping in certain areas as she laughed. I also noticed that she had gained some weight, especially in the butt area. Girl, those clothes are old as the mountains out front. She laughed so hard at my wigs before trying them on and hurling them back into the donation bags.

"Grandma, how could you—I don't think these were ever in style?"

I couldn't even reply looking at that child's face, instantly moving away not to fall into another fit of laughter. Not to mention playing in my old shoes was just as fun. The styles have changed so much. Plus, I've worn none of these things in so long. Just as I was speaking, she put on a pair and the heel broke right off.

"Girl put them old thangs in the garbage," Michal said.

She kept going back to my dress as it fascinated her, sitting on the bed and just staring at it.

"Grandma, I hope I look as beautiful as you did on my wedding day."

"You will, sweetie—but better."

Michal appeared with the jug, stopping to shake it up so we could get all those grape settlements at the bottom. Pouring it, the room filled with the scent of pure aged grapes.

Before taking a sip, Michal asked, "You didn't smash the grapes with your feet—did you?"

"Girl—I would never!"

"Ok, just being safe by asking," she chuckled.

We sipped, finding it sweet and flavorful, nice and smooth, warming to the gut- but delicious.

"I taste raisin?"

"Yup, good taste buds—girly."

We were no longer working but lying around talking.

"Nice label," Chloe said.

My neighbor made them for me. She wanted a bottle, so in return, she made me unique labels to put on my jugs.

"The labels are creative. Look at you are being fancy," Michal exclaimed.

"Grandma, I can't believe you made wine?"

"This old lady had done many things."

"What happened to working ladies?"

"This is so much more fun."

They both scanned the room with the clothes disarrayed all over with Chloe and Michal looking special with an array of clothing on. I had the oldies but goodies playing, snapping my fingers, as we sat around talking mess about the good ole old days. Taking turns trying on old junk, modeling, and dancing. I got up, doing the robot with some old bell-bottoms on that barely zipped, with my shirt covering my little pouch.

"I done got fat."

"And old…" Michal belched, "that's what happens when folks talk too much," laughing hysterically.

I continued to strut my stuff across the room; it was too fun to stop.

"Nobody does it like me in this colorful tonic and fly hat."

Chloe laughed, pulling herself to tell us to chill; the girl seemed like she was going to pee her pants if she didn't stop laughing soon.

"How y'all like me now?" Chloe strutted out with one of the ugliest wigs I've ever owned and a fox fur shawl with its mouth as the clutch hugged my neck with my grandma's old red purse from the 50s. Not to mention those thick-soled shoes, I couldn't stand.

"Those are platform shoes, right?" Michal asked.

"Yes, girl… you look like a hot mess that flew into the 2000s from the 70s. Ooh- wee."

We all had tears flying off our faces. I couldn't take it, not a second more.

"Please don't say Hosea has old stuff like this too in his closet?" Michal fuzzily chimed in.

"Heck yeah, but he doesn't want nobody going through his belongings. He even got some pants he had dry cleaned over 30 years ago; they are so crispy they looked glued together. Not to mention all his 70s, 80s and 90s stuff too."

"What? Girl, no."

"That's what happens when you get a huge walk-in closet- it seems like we become hoarders. Embarrassing as it may be, I still love seeing my old stuff," chuckling out loud.

A few moments later, Chloe started looking pale, not to mention whining a lot in-between her bouts of laughter, lying around rubbing her stomach. Instantly she got up, darting into my bathroom. All you could hear is her heaving. I knocked on the door.

"You ok in there?" I yelled.

Michal and I assisted her.

"Girl, did you eat something bad? Maybe it was the wine," Michal asked.

"Don't be blaming my wine on her stomach issues; she was feeling bad before taking the first sip."

It was an awful episode too. Chloe appeared she would never stop. Becoming hot, she laid her face on the side of the commode.

"Girl, you may have almost killed your granddaughter with that old wine, look at her with her face on the toilet," Michal stated.

"Shut up with that foolishness, since you said it- you may be first. How do you feel?"

"I feel great about to eat some more of these delis snacks and enjoy another glass," hysterically laughing, sticking a grape in her mouth.

I sat on the bed looking at my dresses. Jumping up suddenly, I asked her when her last period was? She rolled over, sitting up to think about it.

"Your pregnant?" I asked.

Chloe looked at me and sobbed forcefully. Blubbering words through her tears.

"Not now, not before my wedding! Oh my gosh, what if I am a grandma? Michal?" looking hysterical.

"We're not ready for a baby right now! We have plans- major ones!"

"I can't even drink if I am…? Oh my gosh, I just had wine. I couldn't be, could I?"

Looking around at us, "I can't afford to gain weight, not even a pound grandma!"

"Honey, a pregnancy test will ease all your fears; you could cry for nothing."

She had the look of hurt and fear on her face.

"I promise if you are, you will be ok. Honey, don't worry until you find out."

"Let's go get a pregnancy test," Michal said.

"Grandma, I'm too scared to find out."

"Girl ain't nothing to be scared about, shoot what's done is done! Let me grab my keys."

We piled into the car to run to the local drugstore to grab a pregnancy test. Michal drove like a speed monster in a racing contest. Looking frizzled, I informed her Chloe was not having a baby and encouraging her to slow down. Looking at the clock, it was 3:33 in the afternoon. There goes that 3:33 again, I thought.

"Michal, I think you drive worse than granddad."

"I should have warned you I love to speed, hope ya'll don't mind."

"Too late now, we in here fearing for our lives."

"Girl stop that mess; I have seen you drive too," chuckling.

We rushed into the store, recovering from the worst drive ever. Few folks were in the store, waving at the colorful cashier. I stopped for a minute to see all the colors but figured everybody got their style. But really, she looked like an unkept circus clown. Scanning the products in the aisle, figuring out which one would have what we were looking for. The next isles over; I found Chloe just standing, looking blank.

"Young woman, grab the one that says the least amount of days after her missed period."

"How do you know about this grandma?"

"I had my days."

"I know I had mines, ten times, and so glad it's someone else turn to be here," Michal said walking up behind us.

We both stopped looking, staring expressionless at Michal.

"What?" Looking clueless.

She picked the one that tells you if you are pregnant, even after one day of missing your period. Shoot, I don't even think we had the things when I was haven't needed one in so long — amen. I just knew it almost instantly with each of them I was sick as a dog.

"Well, let's go see what's going on with ya, young lady," we grabbed five different brands.

Marching to the register as if we were joined at the hips. We encountered the colorful lady.

"Five of them?" The cashier cackled.

"Yes."

"Okay, I say she already knows, don't you, Chloe?" Michal said.

"No, I pray I'm not, but something is wrong."

As she grabbed some Tums, two candy bars, and a bag of chips, she rarely eats junk food, which got Michal, and I eyeballing each other knowing the answer already, but we still had hope that maybe she wasn't.

❧

When we got back home, she wasn't ready to take it. I highly encouraged her to do so. I guess she was trying to prepare herself because she kind of already knew.

"Are you going to work on your closet anymore, grandma?"

"No, I'd rather do the pregnancy test, come on woman, let's do it."

Michal whispered, "You know she is, she does too. Get ready, great-grandma—child," as she rolled her eyes.

I waved my hands for her to stay quiet, as she prepared to leave to get ready for her movie. Michal asked us to call her if we needed anything. She scurried off, yelling that she would be back to help tomorrow.

"Chloe, are you ok in there?" I shouted.

"Yeah."

She came out of the restroom.

"I'm pregnant. All five were positive. Grandma, I'm not ready."

Her face turned beet red, with flurries of tears flinging from her face. Amid her crying, she threw up again. I had some water and crackers brought up to comfort her.

"Jeremai has already told me he doesn't want children for a while."

"Girl that man loves you, he will love that baby too. You all are about to get married; honey doesn't worry."

"He will do the right thing, just be patient."

After crying till she couldn't cry anymore, she asked me to read the next section in my journal.

❧

The Journal- New Life ✿ Being a newlywed, I found myself pregnant at 18 to a boy I didn't love. Just starting classes at the local trade school, after contending with grandma for her taxes so I could get monetary help for my classes. Not even weeks after starting, I got sick. Today, I was nauseous on the public bus. Looking out the window trying to determine should I jump off or ride it out. With only two miles to my stop, I went back and forth in my determination until it happened. Pulling the line, the bell rang, I jumped to my feet and ran to the door. Sweating profusely, I darted out the folding doors, diving my head into the bushes, and my lunch exploded out of my limp body. Wiping my cheek with my coat sleeve. My eyes drifted down the road while my mind cursed the miles I had to walk. The sun was no joke as it felt each step would be my last, but I continued until I made it. Standing at the traffic light, feelings that I would collapse right where I paused. My gut churned like I had eaten something greasy, leaving a malice taste in my mouth. As the green light transferred to red, I rushed across the road. The intentions of making it across the nausea stopped me in mid-step. And I hurled. Not just a typical episode, but one which left me uncontrollably heaving and gagging. Seems like my stomach wanted it all out, but why in the middle of the road with a road full of cars watching me like I was a drive-in movie? I peed my pants and part of my food stuck to the front of my coat. Looking at the cars as I pulled my head up, the feeling of embarrassment wasn't enough to describe my feeling. My walk turned into a scuttle to a full-blown run until I made it to the restroom and wept. It was my fourth week of school and already I questioned my desire to continue. Last night scrubbing the clothes in the tub tired me. I got the plunger and almost threw my back out trying to get them clean. Yet I continued and added more detergent, making it even harder. Loads of homework meant nothing to this boy as we argued half the evening over him turning off the radio so I could study. Storming out, I swiped the tickets from the windshield and flumped myself into the backseat car along the wall in the alley. Local bums leaned against the car yelling over each other, holding forty ounces and sharing toothless grins. Annoyed, I threw my jacket against the windshield, hiding myself as tears streamed. I stayed till the streetlights came on, which was the time I continued to keep from my childhood to come inside.

❧

As the teacher spoke, her words ran past me like the dust in the wind. My main thought was how slowly the clock ticked and the sickness I felt. The bell sounded as I ran for the bus, eager to get home and sleep. Each step felt like I carried cement blocks, exhaustion riddled my body. Running across the street, the gaze of the cars made me wonder if they had been there previously and witnessed the barf episode, I was too sick to care. Yet it crossed my mind. Truly, I felt like it could be a repeat, but it didn't happen. This was the third day I had similar events, but none as bad as the days before. The bus ride was long as my eyes drifted past the world in a flash. Feeling as if life was being sucked out of me. Ringing the bell over three times, made me wonder what was wrong with the bus driver. I weakly yelled for him to stop as he passed my destination. I'd made it to the front when he abruptly stopped, and I was almost flying through the window. I swallowed and composed myself and stepped off the bus, almost falling to my face. Like he threw me off with a vengeance. Walking home, thirst came over me and my tongue felt swollen and thick. Held back by my backpack and purse proved too heavy to carry another step. I stood in the hot blazing sun and look over a weeded vacant lot which appeared to never end. My backpack dropped from my shoulder and I tossed it as best I could and watched it grace the air until it disappeared, but not far. I'll be back to get it, I told myself. Three blocks to go. Walking through the roughest part of the hood didn't matter to me. Everyone seemed invisible as I stepped slowly to the next step until I reached the rat and trash infested alley and collapsed next to the only step.

Barely seeing the face of the man who carried me to my apartment, as I phased in and out of consciousness. I couldn't help but wonder how did he know me and which apartment I lived in? More so, how did he get in my apartment or know who to call? Waking up in the hospital was a huge surprise, not to mention my husband ticked off that I had a strange man in the apartment. Never thanking him for saving me. How rude of him? How ungrateful? Next, he cussed out the nurse who came cheerfully to open the curtains for some much-needed sunlight. Calling her every name under the sun she let in, then had him put out permanently. Listening as I laid there witnessing this mess, praying the stranger and nurse knew how grateful I was. Not being able to eat or drink anything for over six months, weighing only 88lbs at seven months pregnant. Lonely as I laid in a darkened room silent for days to come but had no fear of nothing. Not knowing I should pray, yet in my heart I knew God was where I was and somehow things would work out. Needing my baby to be who he was going to be, I couldn't help him or myself. I just laid. For a while he fought on his own. My poor body, with a sunken stomach rejecting food, but kept my soul inside. Food tube was in place as I watched the white liquid keep me full instead of the burger commercial that ran across the screen. The first time my phone rang, I listened to my aunt and uncle give me a speech on getting an abortion because they heard I could die from this. Listening to the sickness on the other end made me wish we could trade places, but I loved my son too much. The nurse gave me a spiritual magazine after I shared with her the call. The verse on the inside of the cover spoke magnitudes. "Wow to those who quarrel with their Maker, those who are not but potsherds among the potsherds on the ground. Does the clay say to the clay say to the potter, what are you making? Does your work say, the potter has no hand'? Woe to the one who says to a father, what have you begotten? Or a mother, what have you brought to birth? This is what the Lord say—the Holy one of Israel, and its Maker: Concerning things to come, do you question me about my children, or give me orders about the work of my hands? (Isaiah 45:9-11, NIV)

The day became beautiful when they removed the tube and were given mashed potatoes. Next, baked chicken. Days after they told me I could go home, and heaven had opened up for me as I survived hell and came back. Still weak, I climbed the stairs as the elevator was broke to meet an eviction notice on the door. No children allowed was the reason. How do you get over being kicked to the streets from a battered roach and rat-infested apartment with paid up rent? Didn't see that coming, yet it was a blessing. The nurse gave me life every time she opened the curtains. I wanted life right now from the tall windows that touched the 10-foot ceilings. Pulling the old battered brown shade, flopped and flipped around and fell back in place. Tried again broken. I missed my mom and needed her badly.

The remembrance of being a new mother was hard, but it was the most beautiful experience I'd imagine. My baby meant the world to me. Never had I babysat a baby or even held one. Here I was, a brand-new mom with no support, I learned. God showed me everything I needed to know from the milk gorging my breast without a clue of knowing it was nourishment for my son. The pain that struck my tender breast with sticky milk running down my body, left me crying for relief until my grandma had me place a cloth diaper over them. Later, pulling my skin off my breast posed another problem. My tiny apartment was the training grounds of a woman determined to improve his life, making it better than mines. God provided me with all I needed as I made every mistake on earth with him, but we survived even when I hadn't learned to pray yet. He kept me. My husband was so more lost than I, giving no support to either of us. Manhood never struck him, and he had no desire to become nothing more. My first job was 3 months later, I worked and took care of my son. Grandma would pick me up as I jumped from the window daily. Drop him off with her and walk to the bus stop to go to work. Thankful for my grandma; she helped whenever she could, which wasn't often, but sufficient. Without her, I had no one. For a long time, I struggled, and he made it worth every moment. Motherhood forced me to feel love.

❧

"Uh, hearing this again brings back so many memories, motherhood."

"Yeah, then you think of my dad and how he treated you."

"I think more about how my husband treated me more than anything else."

"Uh, I pray Jeramai doesn't change."

"Everyone changes, but your prayer should be to grow in love. Love conquers all."

"I'm afraid to have a baby, looking at your life—it's hard."

"It was, but it built me, made me strong. Don't be afraid of nothing-child. You have a complete team to help you along and a loving soon to be husband and the dear Lord, honey."

"Thank you, Jesus, for giving me my grandma… please help me too, amen," she said, "Grandma, wait just one second. I want to ask you something."

"Yes, dear?"

Chloe swallowed hard. Clearing her throat, she chuckled.

"Grandma, will you be my bridesmaid for my wedding?"

"What?" With widened eyes looking around the room as if a stranger sat before me.

"Who me?" Pointing to myself, looking like I had lost my mind.

"Yes, grandma, you!"

"Mrs. Matea Gomar, will you be my bridesmaid?"

"Girl, that's for young folks like your best friends and peoples like that. Not old coots like me in their 60s, looking all wrinkled and broke down."

"Grandma, stop, you are beautiful—well?" She smiled.

"Girl, you are out of your mind. Your granddad and I will be there, wouldn't miss it for the world, but a bridesmaid—no!"

"Please," holding my hand, rocking side to side.

"Honey, I don't have a dress to wear and it's in a few weeks. I'm flattered though."

"Dad said he would order you a dress and get measured, so it's a yes?"

"He knows about this too?" shaking her head.

"Yes, and Mom too."

"Just don't go Bridezilla, I can't take that at all, messiness."

"Yes, ma'am," she saluted.

The doorbell rang, I excused myself. Noting before I took off the room, she appeared anxious, and it made me ponder my acceptance of being her bridesmaid.

Will Things Change?

His image radiates in each of us, so why do we learn to hate instead of love? This morning we headed off to shop for my dress for the wedding, and I must admit—I'm thrilled. I received the invitation in the mail today; I have never seen an acrylic glass-like invite before. Smokey colored, with some fancy writing inscribed in gold.

"Oh, la la simply posh, missy… I love it!"

"Thanks, grandma, I'm excited, can you tell?"

"I can, it's going to be a grand day."

"Mom really likes my choice too."

"You have great taste, I'm keeping mines forever," I relished.

"I hope so—I felt they would make nice keepsakes. Did you see the stand?"

"Stand?" Going back to the envelope, I noticed it. It was set up in no time.

My eyes enlarged, "Fancy, perfect for my mantel."

"Show me your gown, young lady."

"Ooh, Ma just sent me a pic, I can't wait to get into it," clutching her phone, fingering through the photos.

"Nice, is this the back?" I exclaimed, strolling over to the picture, working to figure it out.

"No, it's the front."

"Do you have a stock photo?"

"Hm… no, but I think ma has one."

"Gold… hmm. You know cream and gold represents wisdom to those who seek Him, prosperity for he knows the plans for you, elegance because our Father only wants you to look your best, and eh- happiness once you marry your best friend keeping your grass watered will create it abundantly. Nice choice, you're going to look grand and I'm about to jump out my shoes I'm so happy for you."

"Did you just make that up?"

"Yes, well—some of it, anyway."

She stopped and stared at me, "that was lovely. My dress has a meaning… I think I may put it somewhere on my bridal shower."

"That would be lovely."

"Yes, I still have things to do. It's crazy all the effort it takes to plan a wedding. I am thankful for my mom helping me."

"Thanking God for mom and dad. I love em."

"Just think… a fairytale wedding for my princess. Girl—you are going to look luxuriously wow. Everyone is going to be amazed at this incredible gown. The glowing sparkles seem to be bling bright. You might have to offer sunglasses," I snickered.

Gazing over the picture of her dress, I admired the color, noting she had a bold attitude and classy. Loving the confidence and spunkiness in her. My girl. The sheer sleeveless gown is faint cream with gold appliques around the bust area, and the ends of the skirt. Talk about 'bling'. Many crystals embraced the bodice, which appeared heavy and much for her tiny frame.

"Is the dress heavy?"

"Yeah. Didn't think it would be, but I'll manage," as she chomped her apple.

Looking at the second picture, the gown hung lifeless and without shape from her closet doorframe within her junky bedroom. Not the most flattering angle of it. Proving difficult to envision the full beauty of the dress in this environment. Wondering to myself if it too revealing? I enlarged the photo to gain an unobstructed view. Still gorgeous, however, the train just ran everywhere. Wondering how it would look with her shape — is it too much? I forced any doubt right out of my mind; I knew it would be perfect as God's hand laid on the entire event. I must wait till the big day to see it. Picking up the clutter from the table a thought came to me: The king's daughter is all glorious within, her clothing is of wrought gold (Psalms 45:13 King James version). What a thought, I couldn't wait to rattle it off to her.

"What a perfect verse and it fits my dress so perfectly… I'm going to cry," fanning her face.

Flicking my watch over, I didn't realize how late it was. "We don't have time for tears, let's go."

"Before I forget, do you have a dress form or hanging mannequin? This beauty shouldn't be hanging over a door. Especially with—."

Shaking her head, "the messed-up room? I knew you would mention that," as she rushed into her shoes.

"You know me well. How about a picture with you wearing it?"

"You don't like it?"

"No-no, it's not that, just can't fully picture it. I want the full effect; it appears to big for you. Did you get it measured?"

"Yes, I have a last fitting, but it may fit since I'm expecting. Great eye grandma, it was kind of loose on me, but who knows."

"The train, it's detachable?"

"Yes, it would be difficult to walk around during the reception if it didn't."

Running back into the room she grabbed the phone, "You must see it in person—as you stated the pictures does the dress no justice," gazing the over it again, returning her phone to her pocket.

"Are you sure you want your old granny in your wedding?"

"Stop! Yes, and please — let's go before you change your mind."

"I just want to make sure, honey… the age difference with the girl's worries me. You know how young ladies feel about old folks."

"For sure don't worry, it's my wedding and I can do what I want." Gripping my hands tightly, "Grandma, I wouldn't have asked if I didn't want you to. I do. Really, I do."

"We have to get going for our appointment, or else we will be late."

Walking to the car, Chloe complained.

"It's fiery out here, dang on it. What's the temperature? Hades?"

I looked at her and laughed, "You think this feels like hell? Better gets your life right before you feel the actual hell."

"Dang grandma, are u serious all the time?"

"Nope, did you forget you are in Arizona in the summer? It's about 120 degrees and that ain't as hot as it will get, girlfriend."

I hate shopping, but this was so exciting no way I could refuse. My life story forever a bride and never a bridesmaid. Three-time champion. Well, that is about to change because of my granddaughter, has made me a bridesmaid. They centered her wedding around some of my favorite colors, black, gold, and cream. And she didn't know it. They are hers too. Tapping my fingers nervously, again I pray I can find a classy gown and some shoes that don't make me look ancient and are comfortable.

"Oh my, what the heck I'm going to do with my hair—maybe a wig?"

"No—you should get your hair curled in an updo, it's so long. I'm going to have mines curled and hung to the side."

"Maybe some pin curls will do?"

"Do you think granddad will walk you down the aisle? He will have to wear a matching black tux, what're your thoughts?"

"Creatively ask him, he hates wearing suits and can be resistant beforehand, so don't get your feelings hurt if he acts out."

"How bad can he act?"

"Ugly!"

Before she could respond, the small jewelry store display window instantly caught Chloe's attention.

"Oh, my—grandma, look at this," grasping my hand, dragging me into the store before I knew it.

It was a charming store with about two customers and three sales associates inside. Honoring their 25th anniversary with a special sale going on. Chloe peeked through the jewelry cases to see if she could see the piece she saw in the window while I stood by. In mid scan, she turned to me and beamed.

"I got to have it, grandma, come help me."

"Honey, you grabbed me before I could see it."

"Hm, it's black, cream, and smoke-hued gems on an exquisite collection of earrings, bracelet, and necklace set that would just go perfect with my dress."

Wondering how long this would take. Not one staff member paid us any attention. Becoming more frustrated by the minute, maintaining my composure while she shopped, I watched. My insides were comparable to a steamy hot pot of greens boiling on high. Chloe searched for the articles she wanted. The two customers left. But no one approached either of us while she scanned the cases. Glanced at my watch, noting the hour was 2:00 PM. Slowly I pierced my watch as the minutes ticked by as they dispersed simultaneously, leaving only one associate on the floor who appeared too busy doing nothing. Eventually, she disappeared. Chloe look around about 10 minutes as my mind drifted off to the many accounts of racism. I was sick of it and ready to pound my fist on the counter when a white customer mingled in. She was taken care of promptly.

Chloe said, "pardon me. I was here first," appearing displeased.

The clerk said, "someone will be right out."

"Hello, may I help you?" With a hideous smirk, as another salesclerk approached her.

I didn't appreciate none of this. Chloe quickly stated that she wished to view the jewelry collection that was in the window as she described it. The sales lady stood looking rather indifferent, immediately telling her that the collection was out of stock.

"Can I purchase the set in the window?"

"Sorry, but we don't sell displays."

As she conversed with the saleslady, I noted how long it took for them to wait on her and was not interested in selling her anything.

"How much is it?"

"Let me see… for your information, this is a costly set?"

"Okay, how much is it?"

We both were past agitated as I continued to look on. Chloe showed a side I'd never seen. She was just extremely agitated, and she gave them the business. I didn't fault her, because I wanted to as well. All this drama was not something she wanted surrounding her special day. A thought come to me, "Shameful those who judge by mere appearances but judge them correctly (John 7:24, NIV)." Surely that was happening to us and was ready to move on. We can take our money elsewhere. They didn't deserve one nickel from us and beckoned Chloe to leave.

Holding her finger to me to wait, clerk found another set comparable to it, to use as a quote. "$5,000," as she waited for Chloe to review the item, again she appeared unenthused and distracted.

"Hmm, do you have a book with a picture along with the cost of the item? The stones, are they genuine?"

"Yes, they are real. It shows in the pricing of the set."

Her eyes pierced at us with an evilness that bore deep. Making you want to say forget it on her face alone—her intentions were clear as day, Chloe flatly refused to entertain her attitude.

"I want it, but I'm not comfortable with the estimate. You just used another piece to price it and…"

Before Chloe could finish, she cut her off, telling her again that it was an expensive piece, while shoving the pieces back in the display. irately Chloe told her that the price was not the issue; it was how she came up with the pricing and her funky attitude that bothered her.

"Miss, if you can't afford the piece, it's best to find another store that sells costume jewelry."

Chloe looked up from the display case, immediately telling her a thing or two with choice words. Being unmoved by Chloe's argumentative stance, she slammed the display case.

"Finished?" the salesperson commanded.

"What's with the attitude? I told you the problem was the way you found the price, not the darn price itself."

"Did I not give you the price? Take it or leave it—the end."

Chloe went off again. I grabbed her arm, nudging her to leave. I whispered, "Control! Your wrath is becoming great and they are not worth it."

This time we took the lead, however she stopped for a second taking a breath.

"Screw all of ya'll—just acting like this because I'm black?"

The women shrugged her shoulders, stepping back, "I don't get into the race, not part of my job," with a smirk embedded on her face.

"Yeah, I saw you helped the white customer with respect."

"Same service you got."

Before Chloe could respond, I stepped in, but calmly.

"Ms.? What is your name again?"

No response.

"May I speak to your manager?" I calmly asked.

She stepped away, disappearing into the back. In her absence, Chloe ranted, cutting them up one side and down another. The young lady returned with her manager, who was a white male, probably in his 30s, who stood like they came out for a fight. "I want to make a complaint. First, time to get serviced. Second, a white person walked in and got serviced right away. Third, the rude behavior, who does this?"

Another white couple came in and immediately the clerk approached them. I eyed them and continued speaking.

"Look at their fine service," looking at him with disgust.

Overhearing their conversation. The guy stated he couldn't afford the ring they showed him but given options to help him.

"We had to ask for help even though we were standing here in broad daylight and I can tell you we're not ghosts or is the problem we're merely shopping while not white?"

The couple gasped and said nothing. They passed on their purchase but stayed to watch. They chattered amongst the three, hearing the words 'disgrace and how dare them' poisoned the air. Lingering stares pierced right at us without a break, with their faces of hatred like we were the problem.

"Wow, they had options of layaway and credit and we weren't," Chloe stated.

He blinked violently and cleared his throat, "Okay — look—the problem is the one question they asked you many of times… can-you-afford-the-collection, if not don't waste our time?"

"I'm shocked that you allow your staff to be rude and condescending. This is a fact because I'm sure you heard the entire conversation."

"Frankly, you are acting just like them," Chloe said.

"I did, and yet you have not answered… you are wasting our precious time? Please ladies leave."

The couple started complaining that we were disturbing their shopping experience, and they felt we should just leave—instead they left and slammed the door behind them. White privilege at their finest as we watched them exit. This entire experience was uncomfortable and embarrassing, a plain mockery.

"I felt my employee handled the problem and we would hate to call security. You are making the environment uncomfortable with our other guest, not agreeable ladies," vigorously shaking his head.

"Well—you might not give a care who we are, but—I will tell

you, anyhow. We are personal friends of Mr. Warren, president of the Millionaires Group on the mountain in Grand Valley's Way."

He boisterously laughed, "I'm positive you don't know him," in a grotesque voice.

My eyes fluttered, "Well, call him! His number is (480) 299-4800 and I'll wait."

He picked up the phone and his secretary answered. His face turned magnificent red as he apologized, returning the phone to the base without speaking a word. Asking if he could help us himself in making a selection?

"No, thank you as I have noted all the names that worked today, including yours, Mr. Copenhagen. Wondering why you failed to ask for him? However, no need to answer, I will inform my circle of your hospitality. I will not stop until I see this disgraceful business closed."

"Madam, I am sorry; I wish you would have informed us beforehand."

"You were told appropriately. Our presence should have been enough, thanks anyway... but no thank-you. Just in case you forget who we are, I am leaving my business card, you will hear from me again," we walked out.

❧

"Grandma, you were calm in there, how did you do it?"

"I prayed and asked for the right things to say. And the ability to keep my cool."

"Must have been a powerful prayer, cuz I couldn't have done it. I wanted to tear the place down."

"Oh, my old ways were terrible. That's how I know you can and will change if you really want to. Pray for strength and guidance, ask and you will receive. He will give you strength."

"I have to practice that, big time."

"Honey lets a stop for lunch, I'm famished. Do we have time?"

"Actually, we don't—sorry, we have to go straight there," she still appeared dismayed over the situation.

"Don't worry about that situation for one second. Once I talk to a few friends, you will have your set from somewhere else. So, clear your mind and get ready to help me pick my dress. I don't want any stress around my dress, or my shoes, or my..."

"I get it, grandma," chuckling, "Hey, did you really know that guy you mentioned in the store?"

"Nope, not as a friend, I have his number because he owns the house next door to us and his secretary asked us to contact him if we needed to. He is the one I told you broke my office window and had a problem with blacks living next door," I winked my eye.

She looked at me with a huge grin on her face and we burst out laughing.

"Ooh, you're a brilliant lady."

"Sometimes," I smiled.

"Are you ready to pick my dress, so I can look spectacular on your special day?"

As we headed over to the boutique. Walking. The sun beamed in full blast, trying to fry us like an egg. I kicked a pop can, bending over to retrieve it as I felt tension in my lower back. Stress aggravates my body badly, I needed to hurry to our destination before I went into a full episode of pain and stiffness. Chloe chattered on about the heat, full of complaints like I wasn't in the same environment. It was too much for her to handle and wasn't helping me either. However, she was sweaty, like water pouring down a stream. Sipping water by the gallons to cool off, but she remained cheerful. Finally, we made it. The lady who greeted us made the entire trip worth it. Her huge personality graced the corner and instantly brightened our day, as if she arrested our tension and threw it out the door behind us. Her eyes were intoxicating, forcing us to toothy smiles to return the favor.

"Hello, I am Ms. Dasher—welcome… let me set up in your room and get you ready to look your best for the upcoming event."

"Thank you, nice to meet you—I am Chloe and my grandmother, Ms. Gomar."

Her floppy hairdo made her look as though she had a busy day, but her personality was refreshing. She fumbled her way to her seat amidst us, seeking every detail of Chloe's wedding without missing a beat. I fell over the hills crazy about her, as made us feel comfortable and appreciated. The shop was glamourous, looking over all the fascinating articles they displayed, before she led us to the spa—which was part of the consultation. *Treated us well, short of rolling out the red carpet and her staff was just as stunning.* Sipping champagne and finger sandwiches… we loved the complimentary spa. Talk about getting pampered. I felt relaxed after the massage while sitting in white robes; I tried on dresses. Sadly, finding none fit my style. Mrs. Dasher brought out five more items to try on, displaying them on fashion racks, with a benevolent smile. I adored all of them except one. She insisted I try it on. I looked at her with much doubt but agreed to give at least a try. Of all the dresses I tried on, the one I least liked, was the one that made me look like a movie star. I owed Mrs. Dasher a big apology and did so with a nice tip. The dress was floor length, golden lace, which delicately cascaded off the shoulders… I got so many compliments on it from other customers and her sales team. We fell in love with it.

"What about your pumps, grandma?"

"Girl don't think I'm one of those young girls with the shoes. I can't wear high heels anymore."

Cutting her eyes at me, "I meant granny shoes."

"You're not hurting my feelings. I want to be comfortable, but cute."

"Heck, if they sell my size here, I always had such a tremendous problem finding a size 5 ½ shoe."

"Oh my gosh grandma, I forgot how small your feet are, you have nubs," She laughed.

"Girl ain't nothing you can say about my feet I haven't heard already—their cute though and don't stink, so don't even go there."

"You do have pretty feet though—mines stunk and was sweaty earlier."

"Ewe- never have I had that dilemma. I must have a comfortable cute shoe that fits, with a low heel not just because I am old… health reasons too—women."

"Give me a second," Mrs. Dasher said.

Quickly reappearing with the most delightful pair of gold-colored heels about 2 inches, gorgeously encrusted with rhinestones that shined like her hands were full of glittering gems.

"I don't have them in stock; however, I can order them, they will be on the doorstep within two days."

"Better yet, Chloe. I'll have them forwarded to your house."

"Ok, we are all set."

The mirror showed a dazzling queen—ha. Gold was so great next to my skin that I couldn't believe it was me. All I needed to do was get my jewelry and have my hair done.

"Hosea won't know who the heck I am."

Chloe blurted out, "I don't recognize who you are, what happened to my grandma?" Looking around eagerly, we all had a hardy laugh.

"You better make it home by midnight."

"Girl bye, or else what? Still movie star status." Admiring myself in the floor-length mirror.

"I can't wait. I'm so excited."

"Your eyes are gleaming, Ms. Chloe," with a smile that could lite up a midnight sky, "I love you," I whispered.

We blew kisses.

Quickly we removed our thoughts off ourselves and back to Mrs. Dasher. She couldn't believe I was my granddaughter's bridesmaid.

"It's the first time I've heard someone doing this," with tears in her eyes. "It's such a beautiful gesture,", she said.

"Please, Ms. Dasher—stop, you're moving us all to tears."

"She is my only grandchild and like my best friend."

"Awe grandma, I normally state that… now I got you saying it."

"Well, it works both ways, right?"

"Yes, it does."

"Can you have everything altered and shipped by say Friday of next week?"

"Let me find out for you. Yes, I can—maybe earlier?"

"That will be fine, but no later."

She gave us lovely gift bags full of goodies. I was feeling worse by the minute; maybe I needed to lie down. I couldn't shake this feeling, had me concerned. But none the less, I realized God had this too. I loathed Chloe had that experience as we planned a portion of her wedding, but the memory we were having was one we would both remember forever.

❧

Later that day, we sat in the sitting room, admiring the mountain views. The sun was slowly fading to its resting state. It had done its job of baking us half to death today and still had a brilliance going down. I love God's creation of the sun, how its radiance enhanced the mountain and city view during its transition. Not to mention seeing big and little creatures that scanted through the mountains seeking refuge for the evening. Chloe leaned back, making comments about her and Jeremai living in our casita. I loved the idea; it gets so quiet sometimes. She wanted to read the journal.

❧

The Journal✿ Dear Journal, today was a difficult one; it is a point in time where I had to reflect on racism and career inequalities that has altered my life. I needed to heal, but how could I in a world full of hate I yet faced today? Fighting has taken a toll on my mental and physical health. Today I walked into work forgetting how I made it there. Scribbling in the time I realized the clock was off by an hour, but I wrote the time I thought it to be. Blaming their clock and not my own insufficiencies. Walked into my office and stood in the middle of the floor and cried. I've had enough and felt God talking to me today to journal my thoughts, as he had in the past. It's taking me a minute to gather my thoughts because it has been a rough road. As tears flood the gateway of my memories, I focused on my grandma's past stories about living in the south, only to move to the Midwest to still face racism. Our ghetto's hold black's captives, preventing them from getting a better life, finding barriers that chain many of us in modern-day prisons. Not only the ones that house bars of holding our people back, but the invisible ones that lie deeply nestled in structural layers that are buried too deep to address. Facts don't lie, and truths hide the complete picture that the confinement of our folks ranks highest in the national penitentiary system. The misconstrued fact is the shackles don't end in prison, it's only the tip of the problem and what we can see as a whole. The other pieces of overt racism is the unfair treatment in where we shop, student loans, housing loans and demographic barriers, and the lack of funding for small businesses seem to keep us bound. Finding ourselves lost in the wilderness for how many years? Buses barely taking us around our communities, leaving us stuck with no means out. Riding around in circles nowhere near the outer bounds of the city where better jobs and schooling exist and even when we get there we are held back with unequal pay and horrendous treatment no other has gone through. Those who are afforded to break out face the harsh realities that we are not good enough and face even tougher treatment. My father was an activist who kept us updated on things going on within the city. Catching the bus and walking miles to go to work and the same to get home had him feeling defeated. The stories he shared of the privileged frequent spats, slurs, and trash throwing made the daily rituals even harder. I hadn't seen these issues firsthand until I ran out into the actual world—the real one. The ones that hated blacks and as history has it, they have incorporated creativity to keep bound us. My parents always had white friends that we visited often, attended mixed catholic schools and churches; color never seemed to be an issue. I hadn't known anyone had to fight because of race. However, being young and naive behind the scenes was a lesson I would soon learn myself.

Today I relinquished my job. The secretary ordered me into the manager's office because I wore my natural hair—a neat afro. I knew it would be a problem because they had written me up for it not too long ago. It was my God-given hair that grew out of my head. I prayed about it weeks before I gained the nerve to quit. I examined the long hours of getting my education, surviving an abusive marriage to becoming a single parent, raising black young men, creating a new family, working two jobs to keep food on the table in hopes of a better life. To only find a brick wall of white faces demanding how I could wear my hair, yet they wanted to touch and run their fingers through it. *Don't touch my hair!* The countless screams that ran through me whenever they were brave enough to try it. Many asked if they could and the answer never changed. No. Who could never understand my fight, treating me less than a human because of my everyday stance? I was wearing my hair the way I wanted to—period. My boss informed me that the white people in the office found it offensive and seemed threatened by my curls. So, I had it braided. That too met adversity. They just wanted it straight and orderly. Following her statement, she asked if I could wear straight hair to match the company's culture? Before I could get out of my seat, she also asked if I would not wear braids. For a few weeks, I followed their rules and was angry about it. How many times have I come in here and addressed their retched behavior towards me and was shoved back out the door in which I came? The unfair pay with greater education, no advancements, no health insurance, slander, racial and sexist jokes, derogatory things left on and around my desk, lies told on me and the unending write-ups that graced my employment folders, was some things I experienced. Reaching out to several advocates, finding no one who would support my issue, one of the advocacy agencies I contacted spoke to my manager and things got worst. I worked with itchy wigs, making it too hot and unbearable for me to function. I was not too fond of wigs, refusing to press my hair, so I figured I'd wear my own regardless of how they felt. No one cared about any degrees or experience most of them didn't have, or how less they paid me. I worked longer hours proving myself worthy, only to submit to issues with my hair. Today was the day I didn't care, not one morsel about their feelings. I became fed-up of the sexism and racism that engulfed my entire life.

My career sucked the life out of me, microaggression, sexism, and pure racism that affected me every day. I had to work harder, prove myself to be competent, to be the girl that everyone needed, and it meant nothing. When I couldn't figure things out, I was the one getting wrote up without a second thought. Leaving work, I sought to leave the issues that crushed me on my desk; mentally, it never worked. Going home was no better. Trying to provide better education and housing for my children proved more mental anguish for me. My sons were dealing with racism in their schools, making me fight for their rights to quality education and fair treatment. I also had to deal with racist neighbors who used microaggression trying to force us out, but we stayed fighting a ferocious battle. The immoral behavior lingered over to what doctors we could see, the stores we shopped for groceries and clothing as clerks gave you the invisible shoulder of shopping with black faces. Scoffing at you because you wanted better food and services, feeling they were only the only one's deserving.

Every time I thought about leaving, I'd be angry at the thoughts of it. My family needs kept me coming, while I pushed my needs behind into a dark hole that even I couldn't reach. Why should I leave the job I've worked for nine years? My mental had the final say and kicked me out the door. Then my family felt I didn't fight hard enough, I should have reached more people, I should have demanded my rights, none of them walked in my shoes. I had to ask myself who was I fighting for? I believe I received my answer the day I walked into my office, not knowing where the heck I was. Mental breakdown—A look of blankness, with coworkers making snide remarks as they passed my door. Laughing and cracking jokes at my expense. They wanted me to fail as they gave their last efforts of making sure I'd never come back. Not understand what day it was, or who I was left me feeling depleted. The final blow as I walked through a crowded room with one male coworker who snarled and spat towards my shoes. I stopped and with a blank stare, wanting to knock him to hell itself, but I continued towards the door with my belongs.

Making it to my car, I sat for a minute as the numbness wore off and allowed me to drive. My ride with him was incredible as I rolled down the windows screaming, I am woman songs with the wind blowing through my fro. I felt I had done something big. Riding past the local restaurant, I'd figured I get dinner as I had no energy to cook. Walking in notice all the wait staff standing at the register with a 'wait to be seated' sign. And I waited. They giggled and spoke as I wasn't there. I addressed them and they walked away until a white couple came in and escorted with a seat. Marching to the car, I wrote their address to file a complaint. They stood in the window looking into what I was going to do. I drove away.

Needed a break, so I took off several months before job searching. Even if no one understood or supported me. How could you leave such a well-paying job? I risked losing everything- I knew Hosea couldn't afford the bills alone and felt he wouldn't see things my way for leaving—he didn't. My best friend encouraged me to file unemployment benefits. Securing a free lawyer and turned down the agency's acting attorney was my plan to win. The lawyer quit the day of, saying he didn't know racism was involved. This wasn't his specialty and would cost to use his partner. The only support I had was my friend, with no attorney. The judge supported the company, slamming me for having no representation.

Why can't I stop crying? As we sat in the car, she said nothing. I asked her thoughts, she babbled for a minute ending with you lost. She asked me how I felt after I quit? Free, but afraid of failure and what others thought. Feeling as if I was weak for not fighting more. Walking out I felt I had support, people to fight with. Others in the office experienced similar treatment, none was from my office. Collectively I gained courage, feeling strong in unity, built my faith around the team. All were ready to sign documents, speak of their experiences, yet when the time came there was none. Feeling knocked down, who could win after that? I became one nappy tight coiled colorful haired angry black woman who had much to stand for, but nothing to stand with. I screamed until my throat became numb and, in the end, who felt dumb?

❧

"That's a shame, grandma; all this because of your hair—?"

"No, it wasn't. It was everything, but the issue of my hair was a distraction from the main issues."

"Not that it mattered, just curious."

A Bible verse popped on my screen. "In the storm, you lost sight of God. Your focus on what the evil one presented around you as the tossing of the winds. The eyes you laid upon Me turned to the tactics of the enemy and sadly I watched you slowly drown, waiting for the invitation to assist (Matthew 14:22-33 NIV)." What a statement, thinking to myself. Not my thoughts for sure, knowing the One who always spoke volumes to me. I noted that during that time I had taken my eyes off the Lord and it was horrible. Busy trying to take on things on my own and it was too much. Instead, I turned to humans, who were just as weak as myself.

"Grandma?"

"Uh eh—yes. I'm here."

"Are you okay?"

"Yes, hon I am. You were saying?"

"This pic of you is epic, but—the wig."

"Girl, that was when I called myself joining a group of young ladies rallying on women's rights."

"Really… sweet."

"Ya know, today kind of took me back to those days," I sighed.

"I feel you. It was tough. But you handled it well, really you did."

"I've grown since those days, where I felt I had to show up and show out. Today, I pray and let Him take over."

"Well, one thing for sure, I took notes. Your calmness and quick thinking spoke volumes."

"Really?"

"Yes, I've been listening to you. I am a work in progress, look who I have as a role model."

She forced a smile on my face. Maybe it wasn't for nothing after all.

"Yeah, those wigs- they were ugly," snickering.

"They sure were- they had the nerve to like them better than my real curls so I could mix in with their culture. Honey, I was just plain stressed out."

"Wow, your right, I have dealt with a lot too at my job and family life, grandma."

"Really? Like?"

"Being a woman in the science field. Gets bad sometimes. Heck, after reading about your life… I find mines pretty lite."

"Don't compare! If you feel uncomfortable, it means someone is inappropriate—period."

"Hair styles and types are still a big issue today."

"You know I read something recently finding it hard to believe that folks still going around worried about another person's hair? They have learned nothing in all this time, that different hair types exist?"

"Well, they still feel threatened by us, especially my dad. Still can't figure him out."

"Really?"

"Yeah, so many issues to deal with when you are mixed. The black, the white, the world is confused on who I am. Really mom raised me as a white person and dad just saw me as black, especially in the summer months when my skin became somewhat golden."

"Jez has a problem with you?"

"Eh, No," shaking her head.

Placing her fingers between her eyes pinching them closed. "No, I was thinking of something else. Forget I said that."

"Hm okay, forgot that statement, was thinking about a friend of mines."

Taking in a deep breath, I understood her feelings. Been there myself looking over my own skin. Noting how neither side of the culture world accepted me for who I was, and I wasn't mixed. Just lighter than most and darker than others. She elaborated on how she hated looking white because deep down being questioned if she was really black always hit her hard. Feeling like she wore a costume pretending and if she didn't embrace the truth, they swore she was an imposter who couldn't be either.

"Honey you are not alone, too me you are a beautiful young woman who is just that."

"Thanks grandma."

"None of your uncles thought race issues to be real until they started living, folks always accusing them of not acting black enough."

"They dealt with this too?"

"Chloe, we all have… things haven't changed, just done quietly."

"You are right, never thought about it. We need more leaders to fight for everyone to be equal."

"Who wants their house burned down, families tormented, and fearing for their lives to save folks today? They made examples of our leaders in the past; don't you think?"

"Yes, they made that very clear."

"That precious baby you are carrying will have to face all these things we are talking about unless something changes."

"I know, I fear that."

"Don't, be strong and brave, raise that little one to have values. Make sure he knows God and pray. We are living in some bad times."

"Yes, we are. I admire you," leaning in to snuggle.

"Thank you, young lady, I admire you too," giving her a brisk smile.

"Ok, off to bed I go, you'll have me up till next year if I let you. Goodnight."

The Wedding

Upon this day, a man is prepared to leave his parents becoming one with his wife. We arrived safely. Our first time in Hawaii; location right here under our noses, we're excited to get started. Traveled many parts of the world, but never Maui, Hawaii. The wedding is taking place in a historic venue, with a waterfront reception. The wedding planners met us at the villa to welcome us, they were lovely. This is sheer paradise. The weather was perfect, with breathtaking florals and greenery everywhere. It was everything I imagined. Hosea quickly found the bar as he waited for others to arrive. It wasn't a big wedding; more like an intimate one with about 25 guests. Looking around for Chloe, I didn't see her, Jeremai, Jez, or Sarah. None of our family seemed to have arrived yet. Joining Hosea, I ordered a glass of papaya juice with a hint of grenadine topped with an orchid. Finally, the wedding coordinator announced the rooms were ready, and they delivered our luggage. The wedding—two days away, this Friday to be exact. Looking over upcoming events, hair, and nails Friday morning. Rehearsal and lunch on the beach Thursday afternoon.

Taking a sip of juice, "Hmm, this is good."

"Mines is too, bourbon and a cigar."

"I'm sure it is."

Giving up alcohol hasn't been bad at all; well, it would be impossible if I didn't have help. Times like this I struggle somewhat, just because I'm used to drinking at special occasions. Hosea wasn't helping any, but prayer did. For the Lord knows our struggles and cast them over to him. Our room was lovely; she had purchased a block of places to keep us all together. The floors are just amazing, hardwood, and high gloss, with maroon drapes and bed covers. The cream wall opened to a wide view window peaking over the lagoon down under—with crystal clear waters for as far as I can see.

"Hosea, come see the water," I beckoned.

"Oh my, what a view."

"Babe that looks like a tree-lined cave with a swing over there—"

"Interesting," trying to make it out.

"You gonna let me swing you?"

Blushing, "I might," giggling like a young teenage girl.

Outside the retracting doors, we had double chaises and side chairs in a small private setting. Hosea got comfortable sliding into his bedroom shoes, hopping right into bed, dropping them right off one by one.

"Awe, the bed is so comfortable," with his eyes rolling.

Inviting me to join him by tapping my side of the bed with a weird smirk on his face.

"Let me finish hanging our clothes before our wedding attire gets wrinkles in em."

Texting Chloe to see if they had made it to their room, and they had. Knowing that everyone made it—it eased my mind. Finishing the clothes, I hopped in right next to him and snuggled close. He sniffled me as if I was a fresh rose; he'd just picked leaving me feeling specially his. I loved it, snuggling deeper into his chest. Hosea and I went straight to sleep. We old folks needed rest before everyone started with the wedding demands. I couldn't wait to see her; it's been a few weeks. I slept well until hearing a knock at the door. Chloe and Jez were making rounds to check on everyone, giving us the schedule for the evening. A few more hours passed when I rolled overlooking at the clock; it's 3:33 PM. There it goes again.

"Wow, Hosea get up- we are sleeping like we ain't in Hawaii," beating him with my arm.

Hastily moving around, I made it to the door, looking down the hall, noticing everyone was gathering to tour the area. With heavy eyes, I got all the information and started getting ready. Looking over at Hosea, who hadn't moved from the spot, I initially tried to wake him. They disappeared down the bend of the hall as I worked to get him up. Grumpily, he strolled to the restroom to finish his stance of reviving his tired body.

"How long was I asleep?"

"About an hour in half."

"Give me a minute to get myself together," he moved to the restroom.

Finally refreshed, we searched for everyone at the beach. Briskly walking, I could barely see through my sunglasses, checking them out, they appeared oily like someone had smacked me across my lens with a salmon filet. I fumbled for the lens cleaner in my beach bag, running straight into Sarah.

"Well—hello Sarah, how are you?"

She looked as if she had seen a ghost, with a bit of arrogance blended in.

"Matea? I'm good and you?"

"I am well, thank you."

"Congrats on the wedding."

She smiled. I don't particularly appreciate when people smile when you ask them questions and say something, instead of answering. Her condescending attitude hasn't changed, nor did we think it had. It was our first time seeing her in 25 years. She looked the same; you can tell she was older, with a few fine beauty lines and too much makeup. She was still pretty, but also full of that nasty soul-quenching attitude. I hugged her and shared a few generic words before walking away. Hosea wasted no time wondering why I even spoke to her, "I thought you didn't like her evil butt? Humph, for sure, I wouldn't have hugged her."

"Stop, Hosea! I forgave her a long time ago; you need to too."

The devil sure was busy had us both starting troubles. We also spent time with Chloe and Jeremai before things started. Hosea was not happy about one thing I said, quickly copping an attitude sitting with the fellas to escape me. Honestly, I didn't care not one bit; I got a nonalcoholic Pina Colada enjoying the waves, nuzzling the sands back and forth, admiring the beauty of Hawaii. It was so soothing and carefree for the moment until I visualized grumpy Hosea, who sat right in front of the views I was trying to see. The sun shone. The rays were a blend of hard yellow, gradually blending into a faint orange. Listening to the chatter of everyone signing up for excursions was uplifting. People were excited; I had my share of being adventurous this summer, I'm sitting this round out and playing it safe by keeping my behind on the ground. I could sit here all week, without thinking of nothing but keeping the sobering drinks coming, laughing to myself. I can't take it anymore; I placed my hat on my head with my dark shades... drink in hand, strolled over to Hosea as if he wouldn't know who I was. Abruptly pulled a chair up, staring at him before giving an apology.

"Sorry for snapping at you," I quietly said.

"What you say, I didn't hear ya?"

Clearing my throat, "I'm sorry," giving into a soft kiss on his cheek.

Seeing Chloe chatting with a few of her friends, she seemed distant, sad, and not glowing. I know she's worried about the baby. This should be an auspicious time of her life. Pregnant with her first and a charming husband to be, he stood by her smiling like he had won the lottery. The devil stays busy ruining anything he can get his hands on. Turning around, she caught me staring at her and waved, blowing me a kiss. I blew one back as she resumed chatting. Looking around at everyone bashing with happiness except my princess.

❧

The next day, we followed fellow senior citizens joining them on a glass-bottom cruise. It was beneficial, saw a lot of animals under the crystal-clear waters. The tour guide hung off the back of the boat, straggling a bucket of bait. He dumped them. Fish swam, surrounding the riverboat with unobstructed views of them fighting for their share of snacks. Nice seeing sea life up close in their natural habitat.

"You know, babe. I haven't been feeling well for a while. The doctor said I was fine."

"I noticed you've been complaining for about two months," he said.

"You notice every dog on thing."

"It is my job, woman. You still don't think I love you? I do—just like the first day I met you. Yeah, we both made some foolish mistakes here and there, hell, even some doozie's, woman. Yes, I notice everything I need to notice. I even appreciate how good my lady looks today."

If he tried to make me blush it worked. He made such a great effort to make me feel beautiful and unique. Won't watch a romance movie to save both our cotton-pickin' lives. That man has been good to me, and I thank God for him every day. I snuggled under him, getting comfortable. He always makes me feel so good and relaxed. I can tell I relax him too, get mighty anxious when we spend long periods apart. God has been good to us—oh, yes, he has.

❧

We made it to the rehearsal. Thank goodness it was brief. The venue was lovely, people were working hard for the big event, Chloe and Jeremai's Wedding. They impressed me with the crystals; they didn't use them sparingly either, gasping at its elegance. I love the look of jewel-like diamonds hanging from the sky, which is what the display appeared like as they attentively hung from the ceiling. She has astonishing taste; she's my granddaughter, even though her dress worried me. Encouraging myself to walk around seeing what else they were doing, Hosea found me and redirected me into walking with him on the beach. We just relaxed and enjoyed the calmness of the waters as I drew our initials in the soft sand. The waters brushed them away as I tried to take pictures. Jez called Hosea to meet with him to go over some things. Chloe ran over while joking around, "Grandma, I will be a married woman tomorrow. Can you believe it?"

"Yes, I can, and you're going to be beautiful. Are you ready for your new journey?"

She started at the water, with a bit of sadness on her face. I asked her again, with her getting slightly more excited this time—say she was. I saw something different; something was bothering her. I just knew it, but I left it alone, allowing her to tell me on her own. She rattled on about the decorations in the venue. They are lovely.

"Aren't they just gorgeous, just the way I imagined?"

"I can't wait to see the big picture."

"Me too, your granddaddy pulled me out of there while I was trying to see all I could."

We held each other's hand, laughed, and smiled while staring off into the waters.

"I love you, young lady."

"I love you too, grandma… what would you say if a bride wanted to change her mind?" Looking into her heavy eyes, searching for answers.

"What's going on?"

"Do you have a good reason to do such a thing if you are talking about yourself?"

"I just—I feel I may make a mistake by giving my heart to someone who doesn't feel my feelings and our baby is most important."

Abruptly we were cut off as she jumped up, zipping off to speak to one of the wedding planners.

"Grandma, I have to go… I'll see you later."

That evening, Chloe texted me, asking me how to calm her nerves. I text back, telling her to focus on the wedding and relax, but she wouldn't have it. The last message was to meet her at the bar downstairs at 11:00 PM, I did. We talked about everything and anything. Time seemed to zoom away.

"Girl, you are a mess, and I am going to be looking like a goon tomorrow. I let you have your way because you are getting married."

"Ok, grandma," we ordered our last round of virgin frozen Pina Coladas.

A toast to the big day, "CHEERS!"

❧

We find favor when love ties three together. Today's the big day; our baby girl is getting married. I was so overwhelmed with the event planner pushing me around. Woman, I am an ancient lady who needs a moment. But I just kept up best I could, without verbally complaining. Surely the look of distress wore on my face. I got my hair and my nails done and met up with the gals for group pictures. I saw the ladies sitting on the bed in their robes and wondered how they would take pictures if they're not getting dressed? Sarah joined in to watch and help Chloe prepare for her photo shoot. The event planner stopped to tell me her name; she was tired of me calling her Ms. Event Planner.

"My name is Ms. Kane, good to meet you."

"Nice meeting you too, Matea, Chloe's grandmother."

"Okay, I need you to go into the restroom and change into your robe for pictures."

I looked over at the ladies and wondered who takes pictures in their evening wear? I took the robe and changed but was reluctant. I informed

Ms. Kane that I wasn't comfortable with the idea. Maybe I should skip this part—giving her back the robe, appearing half concerned, half irritated. "I'm an old lady," with a stern funny not funny look on my face. Gazing over her shoulder, Ms. Kane gave me the cue to take my place. Did she not hear me? Chloe caught a glance of me, beckoning me to come on over. Not to mention all the young ladies chimed in, making it even harder for me to refuse to be a positive part of the event. I forced myself across the room, trying to smile as if I was excited. Waving at all the chuckling young ladies, pulling up some excitement to fit in. Ms. Kane looked back at me briskly with her headset sideways.

"Okay, in the back you go, will that work for you?"

"That will be wonderful—thank you."

Reluctantly dragging myself over to the young ladies, joining in. They were all so beautiful with their freshly painted faces and hairdos. I was looking good too. Ravishing skin tones blended in as they embraced each other uniqueness. Smiles and giggles filled the room like a pleasant mist of the finest perfume. Sitting down, a quick wave of regret flooded my mind. I know I didn't think all this out when I accepted the offer to be her bridesmaid. But pushed it out of my mind as quickly as it came. This is what it means to be a bridesmaid taking a deep breath; I gave in. Seeing I'd done nothing like this before. Chloe bounced around, handing Ms. Kane a bag. She peeked inside, asking me to join her in the powder room, immediately I followed her. Chloe knows her grandma, forcing a smile on my face larger than all the other ladies—pajama pants.

"Yes, hurry—put them on, rush, rush."

"Thank you, Chloe must have known that I would feel uncomfortable," she smiled.

Before I knew it, I was enjoying myself. The robes were black with a hint of gold to accent the voluptuous cream roses embedded in them. They were short with a tie waist—mines added black pants to match. We also had black fur slides—we looked like real divas. Chloe wore a cream solid short robe in the same design with cream fur slides. She picked a bunch of lovely ladies to share her day with, and I was one. They sure knew how to have fun. We took many pictures as a group and watched as Chloe took some alone—she looked fabulous. My favorite was the pose we took as a group with champagne-filled glasses with confetti thrown in the air. They did a superb job of catching the moment. The one picture Chloe posed for included her dress next to a claw tub with gold feet, my favorite. However, her excitement over that one almost tripped her into taking a bath. Waving for me and Sarah to join her.

"I think this may be my favorite pose," she began frowning for a minute.

"What's wrong, Hunny?" Sarah asked.

"No frowns, sweetie," I said.

"My stomach looks bloated, wonder if they could retake it?"

Sarah immediately ran over to the photographer requesting him to retake the picture, scanning through the poses for the one she wanted to be retaken.

Looking back over the proofs, I agreed with her, "It seems like the little man wants to to be here in this moment."

"Yeah, look at him," admiring her Little belly.

"Look, the two of you," I whispered.

"I love you, grandma," she whispered back.

"Ma, that's okay, I'll keep it the way it is."

"You sure?" Sarah said.

"No, it's fine, the Lil one wanted to be a part of this day."

"Okay, let's continue," throwing her arms into the air.

Ms. Kane abruptly appeared back into the room, swooshing us out to get dressed in our wedding attire. She took us to the dressing room, where we eagerly assisted each other with our attire. The photographer effortlessly worked to get great poses. How can I be tired, and it was still early? Dragging around the room like I could collapse on the floor and sleep like a baby, but I continued. Looking for something to moisturize my lips, I ran across a b12 shot. I needed this badly to help me get through the rest of this day. It still tickled me I was a bridesmaid. It was a pleasant experience so far, especially for such a glorious occasion of my granddaughter's wedding. None of the ladies could grasp Chloe having her grandma as a bridesmaid. I enjoyed listening to their amazement. Heck, it amazed me. Was so happy to be a part of her day, I must admit I would never forget the experience. The ladies took turns fixing their makeup and hair in the Hollywood lighting, wondering how long before it would be before we started? It seemed to take forever. Ten minutes later, the planner stuck her head in the dressing room, letting us know the wedding will start late. "We're running into a slight problem, we'll let you know soon what was going on."

"Excuse me, is everyone okay?" I asked, knowing she was pregnant and could be sick.

"Oh yes, Mrs. Gomar, everyone is fine. Just be patient with us. I will be right back."

The other ladies were getting antsy. To lighten the moment, I began telling stories of the quirky weddings I'd witnessed. Quickly running out of events to share, so I included them.

"Who wants to next?"

They looked around at each other before Chloe's best friend Eve gave in. Sliding out of the room to check on things. Quietly closing the door behind me, I rambled into the hall, noting Sarah and Ms. Kane were leaving her room with a look of concern on their faces. I squinted to focus on them more but could only vaguely see. Ten minutes more past since she first told us that the wedding would be late, she appeared again. This time with a more serious, worried look on her face. She announced they called the wedding off!

"Off?"

I turned and went into deep thought, Oh Lord, what have I done? Did I encourage this child to stop this marriage when she talked to me yesterday? Before I make assumptions, let me ask for more information.

"Can I see her?"

"It might be best to wait; she's with her parents at this moment."

Plopping down into my chair, with all kinds of concerns. I became determined to find out what was going on.

"Is she well?" I asked.

"Yes, she is fine. Their working on things as I speak."

All the ladies began chattering, getting riled up. Eve abruptly jumps up, "I need to speak to her now," she demanded.

"Eve calm down, please have a seat, please let them handle this."

As she returned a funky look, which I ignored.

Demanding to speak to her myself. Stomping to her room, Eve followed without my knowing, running right into me when I abruptly stopped. I gave her a sickening look because that child was getting on my last nerve.

"You just couldn't wait, could you?"

"Sorry, grandma Gomar, I need to speak to my bestie."

Knocking three good times, the door swung open, "Grandma."

"What the heck is going on?" I blurted out.

"I just ran past your mother; she's upset, dabbing her eyes. Looks like she's been crying."

"Girl, I got you, where is he at?" Eve asked.

"Hey Eve… he—"

"Why hasn't the wedding started yet?" I asked.

Hysterically crying, Chloe spewed out, "The wedding is off grandma."

"Jeremai is on his way down, Eve, can you come with me, please?" Sarah said.

"I can't marry him, even if he says he wants the baby now. They have been so evil to me lately," she yelled.

"Girl, it's probably stresses of the wedding and a new baby… Come on now, Chloe."

"Sarah, do you think this is just cold feet?"

Eve came in, wasting no time with the drama and going on and on trying to convince Chloe to move in with her, ready to pose` up and fight.

"STOP! I can't take it anymore, Eve. I have listened to your garbage all week—didn't they ask you to step out?"

"You too," she replied.

"Mrs. Gomar, can you please step out as well—Sorry," she hesitantly stated, "Jeremai is here."

Jeremai stepped in the room, saying nothing. He remained silent as he scanned the packed space. Folks appeared like a can of sardines stuffed in every area, however, they became quiet with his presence. Hands embracing snacks and sounds of bickering once lingered in the air, but now they just stared. The only person missing was Chloe, who sat in the restroom. Standing in the doorframe gripping the doorknob, his presence spoke for itself, tall, masculine, freshly shaven, and a solemn face of sadness seeking answers. Looking around, he cleared his voice, erecting himself taller, "I need a moment with my wife—please."

A few left instantly drifting past him like scattering ghosts, with one grabbing some snacks before leaving. Eve blurted, "she ain't your wife yet," picking her nails and wildly smacking her gum.

"Eve?" Jeremai said.

"Yeah?" blow, bubble, pop went her gum.

"Can you—"

"Chloe and Jeremai need this time to meet, please everyone—out," Ms. Kane yelled while pushing folks past him.

Eve was the first to go.

"Thank you," he stated.

I informed Chloe he was there, and she went into an argument mode before I could say a word. Eve peaked inside, encouraging her, with Ms. Kane shoving her back out.

Looking bewildered, "Chloe, you are going to upset yourself, calm down."

I stopped taking a deep breath; this is much for an old lady. Sweating from all this excitement, not only was my makeup a mess, but the updo was also taking a hit. I asked Sarah if it was okay to speak to Chloe for a moment. Asking Jeremai, if I could have a moment, he agreed.

"Chloe," I yelled.

She appeared slowly from the restroom, looking gorgeous, but robed.

"You know those hormones we get when were pregnant?"

"Grandma, somehow, I don't think it is this time. I wish I knew what to say to Jeremai, I'm at a lost."

"First things first—what transpired?"

"Mrs. Alcott told me Jeremai was mad about the pregnancy saying it disappointed her. On top of it, Jeremai has been acting as if he is not happy since I told him."

"I thought we cleared this up before you left Arizona?"

"What about the talk I gave both of you?" The poor baby looked a mess with tears streaming down her face.

"Me too until I got home. He asked me what options we had concerning not having the baby. He wouldn't go to first appointment. Is this how he is supposed to treat me before I make the most important decision of my life?"

"No."

"How can I wed my best friend who says they love me but reject our baby? Would my best friend do this to me?"

"Here—wipe your nose, you got stuff everywhere… child."

"You know Jeramai is the one you should be speaking with, right? Tell him how your feelings."

"Yes, but what to say?"

I took notice to her concerns, asking her if she wanted my advice. Through her whimpering, I sat in prayer for a minute to put the words in place to comfort and help her.

How crude of a woman to say such things. I was ready to punch both right in the face, but I chose prayer.

"Don't walk into this marriage destined for divorce. Clear this mess up now. Talk to him, and tell him how you feel, if he doesn't value your feelings—."

"Okay."

"Look, I'm not here to decide for you. I am letting you know whatever you decide. Your family is here to support you."

I pulled her close to me, letting her know it took an extensive set of ovaries to push fear aside and demand respect or walk away from the lack of. We both chuckled.

"Extensive set of ovaries, grandma? For real?" With a soft smile grew on her puffy face.

"You said it that way, not me. Got me laughing harder than ever. Hunny, you think you are the only woman who saw some bull crap coming before her big day and wanted to cut it off before they walked down the aisle?"

"No," poking out her bottom lip.

My mind strayed off. I saw myself in her, but I was eighteen; I was frightened. I wish I had the guts to call off my first marriage, instead I listened to everyone, except my own feelings, my heart pains, and it scared me to death to stand up for myself and I didn't. No one who cared about my feelings, not even the folks who attended the makeshift wedding. A room full of strangers watched me make the biggest mistake of my life. Not one of them was there to help me clean up the mess of an unfortunate marriage afterwards. Just waves of good luck to have an enjoyable life tingled my ears as I cried silently. She would not end up like me if I could help it. As I listened, she has valid reasons, but she needed to talk to him. Lord, we need ya. No matter how badly I wanted to see her walk down the aisle today, God knows I did. But the fact remained, she had concerns that were hurting her. We could push her feelings under a rug to make everyone else happy- not going to happen. Jeremai's side of the issue left us all with a lack of understanding. She needed to hear him out. He hadn't been saying much because he hadn't had the chance. None the less, we must hear what he has to say.

"Who wins here, you or the devil? Be a wise young lady; he is about to step in."

"Grandma—."

"Yes?"

"Thanks," she tearfully smiled.

Sarah entered the room to let us know Jeremai needed his time. "Thanks, Matea, for helping. This is a big mess. I hope soon they will clear things up," Sarah said, piercing her watch.

Mrs. Alcoy walked past as if she didn't see me. She wasn't friendly. Seems to be a woman full of pride, you know the kind with a chip on her shoulder. If she didn't think she was better than everyone, she sure acts like it. Coming back into the room to have a seat, finding myself overwhelmed, this is crazy. What kind of family are we getting into? What mother doesn't want their grandbaby? I joined Mrs. Alcoy instead.

"Can we talk a minute?" I asked.

"About?" Blinking wildly.

"What do you think about the kids?"

"Humph, it's a mess. I was thinking he should have called it off."

"What is going on with you and their relationship? You understand, once a man gets married, he is to leave his momma? Just like you did when you married your husband, right?"

"Is that any of your concern? Putting my marriage in your mouth."

"Come on, let's straighten things out, right here."

"Oh, I guess you're the one to set me straight, huh?" Rollin her snooty eyes.

I saw the tension getting tight. Quickly, I had something hit my mind. This is not the way things should turn out.

"We family now or soon to be. Right?"

She backed down, relaxing a bit, "Ya right," taking a deep sigh.

"Look, Chloe feels like you are not respecting her feelings concerning the wedding and other issues."

"What?" looking shocked.

"She didn't like my ideas for the wedding; I know that. I told her I would pay for some things if she wanted me too. I have just been so excited to do my share of their wedding."

"Yeah, that's what I told her."

"Oh, my goodness, I just knew she was okay with things. She should have said something."

"You are right. We wouldn't have this problem if she had," we both bust out laughing.

"Girl, I wish I would have spoken to her about her feelings, I guess I got excited. I've waited for this day Jeremai would get married, I just wanted to be a part of it. Everything seemed to be about them, leaving us out."

"I understand, I've been there. She allowed you to do things you wanted, right?"

"She did, I appreciated it."

"Well, one more thing."

Mrs. Alcoy copped an attitude, turning around to listen.

"The baby?"

"You know Jeremai is not ready for a baby now, the wedding, his career, their plans?"

"I don't see him having a choice; the baby is coming whether anybody likes it," she had a look of disgust all over her face concerning her precious grandbaby.

For a few minutes, neither one of us said a thing, just stood in a room filled with substantial feelings.

"You're not ready… to be a grandma?"

"I don't have time for this mess?" she snapped.

"That's what's going on today; she's hurt about some things you said about the baby."

"Yes, I spoke with her, telling her how we both felt."

"You were wrong in doing that. If he confided in you, it should have stayed there. How can you say you love your son, with you treating his other half this way? After this day, they will be one!"

"Are you done?"

"No, love doesn't hurt! If you love your son and Chloe, be a part of their lives. Not the problem. You will gain a daughter and instead an enemy. Do you know you can lose your son if you don't respect his family? Show wisdom, not hate. We can all be a big happy family. Now I'm done."

She spread her arms out for a hug and I embraced her. Getting ready to leave, Mr. Alcoy stood at the door. "I'm proud of you, honey. Matea, this is a good way to start our new family, everybody working together to help this young couple stay together, well if they can work things out."

I have an idea, follow me.

❧

Everyone was getting tired and wanted answers, not to mention the guest who were firmly letting me know they would leave soon; these folks are on vacation. Where here in Hawaii. She assured me they would be right down. It would have been nice to have information about what was going on. I tell you; young folks nowadays get so riled up, hard getting everyone to relax. Someone knocked at the door; everyone got quiet. The knob turned, and eyes were plump. The door flew open; it was Hosea.

"Awe man," the crowd roared, throwing their hands at him.

"We thought you were Chloe and Jeremai, dang on it."

"I was at the bar having a few laughs, too much going on for me. Ya, feel me?" Hosea said.

"Yea, me too. I'm bout ready for bed and some relaxation."

The door gave way to the entrance of Chloe and Jeremai, and nobody noticed.

"There they go," a guest announced.

They were holding hands with smiles on their faces that lit the room, a good sign. Jeremai formally dressed, with Chloe still robed.

"Thank you all for your patience. We appreciate every one of you here," he looked at Chloe with a brilliant smile.

"We're getting married in a few minutes as soon as Chloe can get dressed."

"We apologize for the delay," Chloe said.

Jeremai walked over to Chloe, "May I?"

Reaching out for her hand, "I want to tell my beautiful lady that I am sorry. I was wrong in every way; it would honor me to ask you to marry me again. I love you woman and can't imagine life without you."

"Yes," blushing.

"Mom has something to say," Chloe's eyes grew large.

"You two are so good together; I got beside myself. Please forgive me, daughter in love."

"I forgive you," hugging her tightly.

"I have to get dressed—we have a wedding."

❧

We all made it to the site; we waited for the cart to pick up Chloe, the officiant (kahuna pule, Hawaiian holy man) they call him. He walked in with Jeremai and the best man, his friend Abram, a nice-looking young man. Chanting (mele) as they took their places. The parents and grandparents of the bride walked down next and escorted by ushers to their seats. The men elegantly wore all black, with black ties with a sheen to them. Their boutonnieres were cream and gold, with crystal accents. They looked fine. Fumbling for our spots in the procession line, I grabbed Hosea and held tight—my man was looking good, the finest out of the group. He didn't give Chloe not a drop of a fight about wearing his tux, like I figured he would.

The violinist played, closing her eyes, visualizing the song of interest. She appeared poised, as if she could collapse at any moment. Dressed in a pale golden dress with florals around her waist and her hair tied into a bun. Gracefully holding the wooden instrument which quivered as she strung heart-piercing sounds. The tunes of pure love rolled through the air, compiled by her delicate strokes of the strings, brilliantly orchestrated with richly deepened notes displaying immense power through the noise that soothed our minds. Her impeccable skills mesmerized and intrigued everyone. Leaving us swaying our heads, many with closed eyes taking in this enjoyable moment. The directions of the bow blended the sounds into a song that depicted our witness of two people becoming into one—a sonata by Bach pacified our souls. She replicated notes from a historical legend with passion and proved perfect for this special day.

First the brides made walked alone, Eve who caused all the trouble. She looked gorgeous though in her attire and was happy to see her quiet and smiling. The couples walked; with us being last in order which gave me much time to notice Chloe still hadn't arrived. Each one strolled, arms interlocked. Scanning the crowd with radiant smiles shown to the guest as the couple met at the front, they released and took their stands. I know this girl didn't pull another stunt and not show up? We walked—slowly breaking our locked fingers to move to the opposite sides of the room, taking our place. The doors closed. Everyone awaited. After five minutes, the doors remained closed. Jeremai tugged at his collar with a small look of concern. He gazed at the room and tightened his stance of patiently waiting. The conch shell blows brought attention to the sacred moment; the doors cascaded, revealing darkness. Chloe stepped into the blackness, creating immense light—she was breathtaking. Leaving nothing but muffled 'awes' bouncing in the air.

Pictures did no justice for the gown—wiping the old image from my mind as it proved useless to remember. That young lady made that dress spectacular or the other way around… it doesn't matter. She looked like a queen. The body of the gown was gold encrusted with stones with a plunging neckline with double straps one hanging from her shoulders, accented with gold embroidery around the bodice with floating buttons, crystals glared like diamonds from every angle, exhibiting pure radiance. A royal train ran for minutes behind her. The sleeveless gown hugged every inch of her shape — so fitting and romantic. Chloe's breast filled the cups gracefully as her tiny waistline made a statement we'd never forget. The dress was nothing without her soul, bringing it to life. Chloe's shoes were gold, but you could barely tell because of the glare from her dress. Her hair lightly curled, with a loose twist holding her hair out of her face. She accented her hair with dotted crystals. Her small bouquet of cream roses twined with diamond accents. Eyeing Jeremai, his face was indescribable. That man was shocked—wait, is he shedding tears already? He sure is. Chloe stood still at the door. Glancing around the room, her eyes sparkled. She held her head high, back straight, posture correctly maintained—she walked. As she walked halfway alone, with Jez stepping out to greet his glowing daughter. He smiled, whispering how beautiful as looked. She replied, "thank you". Placing his arm in hers—he stood tall for the entire room to feel his pride and joy. He walked her down the aisle, transferring his hold to Jeremai.

Jeremai whispered, "thanks, man, I'll take good care of her—I promise, sir." Jez shook his head, fighting tears back as if his soul depended on it. He took the side of Sarah, who was also fighting tears. Rubbing his back in efforts to stop each other from crying. We ladies all had on gold different styled lightweight dresses, about ankle-length. The weather was perfect, about 80 degrees, with a mild wind to keep us fresh. Blessed to have perfect weather. We all had on gold shoes with rhinestones across the toe and heels. The young ladies wore high heels, and I had about an inch heel and very comfortable. Look at my grandbaby. Jez and Sarah stood tall and proud as they should have. They look fantastic as well—they raised a beautiful young lady inside and out. No words could describe this experience.

❧

The Wedding Has Begun ✤ Kahuna pules presented the tray of lei for the exchange. Jeremai took the white ginger lei (pikake lei) and placed it around Chloe's neck. Chloe took the Maile Lei and put it around Jeremai's neck, bending down to help her.

"Parents of the bride and groom, please stand up," stepping close to the alter.

The parents' place the lei around Jeremai and Chloe's neck. Jeremai and Chloe presented their in-laws with a lei and the entire wedding party.

They played the 'Hawaiian Wedding Song,' as Hula dancers entertained us, with their bare feet and strolling bodies—twisting and turning effortlessly. Their arranged movements provided energetic entertainment. Cascading across the floors with gigantic smiles, emitting boundless energy with graceful moves. The brilliant colors of yellow, green, and bright orange flickered around the entire venue, forcing smiles on each of the guests. Drums and chants filled the air like boastful sounds of happiness. As fast as they started, they stopped.

"The Vows, please," looking around the room.

Sarah got up to present Chloe's with her scroll of vows, and Mr. and Mrs. Alcott handed Jeremai his. Scripted on heavy brown paper with a slightly burnt edge, as they unrolled each revealing handwritten calligraphy writings.

"Jeremai, please present your vows to your beautiful wife and cherished mate," Jeremai opened his and read.

'To my beloved Chloe Diane and our baby, your love is like the sun after the rain, which has brought rainbows into my life… as I gaze upon your face, it refreshes me like a tender blossomed rose, which is vibrant and beyond beautiful. As I have grown to love you, I have found the true one that I can honestly say loves me unconditionally past my flaws. I'm imperfect, but perfectly in love with you. I promise to love you with my entire being, may our new life be an example of devoted love to each other and our child for all the world to see. I'm sorry—I love you, baby.'

Sarah dabbed the tears from Chloe's face. Kahuna waited until they approved him to move forward. Sarah nodded; he proceeded.

Her eyes sparkled, filled with tears. She held onto the scroll, shakingly she opened it.

"Chloe, please state your vows to your cherished soulmate," he smiled. Sarah wailed out as we assured, she was ok. Jez comforted her,

He nodded for the mister to continue.

"Continue, please," Kahuna said.

'Jeremai Elvis, I fell in love with your soul, and it has blessed me to feel and experience authentic love. It is such a feeling that I have ever grown to know, I'll never forget. As we become a knot of three, me, you, and God—may we bask in happiness forever. I tried to find the most creative words to describe how much you mean to me, but none of them did justice to describe our love story. Today I promise to love and cherish you as if tomorrow will never come. Your love makes me feel like the most beautiful girl in the world and can do anything I put my heart to because of it. I vow to be all I can from this day forward. I can't wait to spend eternity with you and our baby. I love you.'

The minister took a koa wooden bowl, filling it with water from the sea.

"Who gives this beautiful bride away?"

Jez and Sarah arose; in unison, they stated, "We do," returning to their seats. "A poem read by Eve, written by Chloe," Kahuna said.

True Love

Love is an experience of the heart which entangles the souls of two fragile humans, once met will never forget. How blessed is he who finds such treasures that leaves a flame in one's soul? We often take for granted the feelings of heaven when trouble comes. The gift of true love is not for the faint because it's packaged in hard work, pain, and endurance and will need the waters of His word to become completely nourished. Is one ready for the challenge or is the mind clouded with roses and chariots and unable to withstand the fire and rain when one's beauty and health may soon fade? Life's journey takes unchosen paths twisting and turning into the wilderness of the unknown. In the truth of spirit, from the day you are born love becomes the solution to all problems. As the years past forming the wisdom of life's experience of understanding love in a world of hate will be the mission of those who are not faint. As this love story begins, it will turn bends, and head back again. May love lead this journey which begins today till death pulls us apart.

Jeremai & Chloe

Eve smiled as she tips back to her place in line.

"Who has the rings?" Kahuna says.

All Chloe uncles stepped up to handing their rings over.

Jeremai nodded at them as a silent 'thank you.'

They dipped the rings in the sea water and stood with heads bowed as Kahuna prayed over them.

"Thank you," they returned to their seats.

Jeremai and Chloe walked over to the table with help from Ms. Kane. They each held a glass of sand (Chloe/cream and Jeremai/gold) and poured them into the vase, mixing them with a golden spoon.

"This is a symbol of what was; once the grains of sand are mixed, you can no longer be separate—you are now one. You may kiss your bride!"

Wow, what a kiss, bent my granddaughter back, and wouldn't let go. Kahuna cleared his throat.

"Ok, save some for later," he grumped, leaving us all laughing, and clapping filled with happiness.

Off for pictures and to the reception for the guest. Chloe wasn't feeling the greatest, nor was I. But I more so concerned about her and the baby. Jeremai was very attentive to her. His mother tried to fight off her attitude, but she said something smart to Chloe, and Jeremai checked her right in front of everyone. No one said a thing because she needed to know her place and hear it from him. We all wish we knew what she said, but it was not our business and respected that. Lots of pictures, as we were all tired. Couldn't wait to see them, I know one was going over our fireplace. Finally, was off to the reception.

~ The Reception ~

Everyone was enjoying cocktails, strolling hors d'oeuvres, and the live band when we entered. Locating our seats arrangements on the etched mirror. The wedding party chattered, admiring how beautiful the mirrored sign looked. Reaching all over the place, we appeared as a bunch of groupies trying to be the first to find our names. Examining the ceiling was a giant metal frame, which hung greenery ropey florals, loads of crystals, and a million pin lights. The crystals beamed rays in all directions, sparkling like stars. The complete venue boasted elegance. The place held two long tables with black tablecloths; gold drapes cascaded to the side with the sliding glass walls opening to the beach. Greenery graced the four pillars in each corner of the room. The chairs were black with cream cushions, and cream-colored florals tied to the back. Tables were complete with gold glass dishes, gold silverware, and satin cream napkins. Each plate held a green leaf with gold writing revealing the menu and seating number. The centerpieces embraced mini cream, and gold sprayed roses with candles. The venue didn't need many decorations as it was beautiful as it was. It had a Roman romantic appeal to it, lots of ivory body-sized statues that blended in so well with the theme, not to mention the opened wall to the private beach which had black umbrellas and gold chairs at each table. Walking around her 4-tier cake. I was speechless, gazing at it from every angle. Hosea and I just stood staring for a few minutes because it was one heck of a cake. Sarah walked by asking if we like it and we're enjoying ourselves?

"Yes, you did an outstanding job."

"Thank you, glad the day has finally arrived, minus the drama everything turned out great."

"I agree, what do you call this style cake?"

"It's a crystal cave cake, with strawberry cheesecake on the inside, Chloe's favorite."

"Beautiful."

She laughed and mingled with us as she cascaded to the next guest.

Studying the cake, we noted the all black with gold marbled fondant cake appeared to gap open with sparkling crystals forming out of it. The lower tier set on a crystal, antique chandelier cake plate. The unique cake stand was an excellent choice to hold her cake. The cake table had gems and gold pieces scattered all over it, resembling rhinestones and rock candy, black and gold. The topper formed their initials in gold.

✧*Mr. & Mrs. Reinhart*✧

Everyone's attention, please, allow us to formally announce the entrance of Mr. & Mrs. Reinhart. Everyone stood and clapped as they gracefully joined us, making their way to the dance floor, where they went right into their first dance. Chloe cried, with Jeremai gently kissing her. They took the train off, making it easier to flow in her moves. It was a slow song but seem as they practiced well for the dance. In completion of their dance, they made their way to the cake table. They gripped the crystal cake knife, cutting their first slice of strawberry cream cheesecake. Jeremai took a dab of frosting and placed it on her nose, kissing it off. Chloe chuckled, giving him his bite of cake. As they proceeded to their seats, everyone again gave them a standing ovation.

Chloe yelled, "let the party began," twirling her bouquet in midair as they continued to their places.

❧

Jez and Sarah walked over to us, talking about the wedding again. Hosea and I studied everything for a moment.

"You both did an outstanding job; somebodies got wonderful taste," we beamed.

"Thank you, it was tough. Especially with Chloe gone," Sarah said.

"You can't tell, everything is so perfect," I replied.

"No, things went rather smooth, it was hard to decide without her," that's all, she forced a smile.

"But you made it happen."

Everyone began tapping their glass for the couple to kiss. They looked so good together. Jez got up, giving his speech. Clearing his voice, he held a glass of champagne the entire time he spoke.

"Congrats to you both. Time spent with this young lady has been very special to our family. Thank you, Chloe, for your presence and adding Jeremai to the circle."

"Jeremai, take care of our precious jewel."

"I will—I promise."

He held the mic for Sarah, and she declined and smiled.

"That's all he is going to say to his daughter. Sarah didn't say nothing." I said.

"Yeah, it was a kind of generic, but hey maybe their tired," Hosea shrugged.

The best man was next, "Jeremai dude… when you first met Chloe, it didn't take long before you said, man—I think I'm in love. It came when you said it would never happen. You made the best choice, man. She came into your life, but ours as well. Chloe, you made such an impact on all of us with your beautiful personality. For real, if you can change Jeremai, you can change the world. Love you and continue to be who you are. Congrats on finding your family."

"What did he mean by that?" I said.

"About what?" Hosea responded.

"Congrats on finding your family and Chloe's face when he said it."

"I ain't pay it no attention. You are thinking too much."

The maid of honor was last. "Chloe, my girl. I can't rescue you from your man anymore. I knew it already, but your grandma told me for sure," Everyone laughed.

"Girl, on the real, this wedding was amazing. I am so happy for you; you have been my best friend since the 7th grade, and here we are now sharing the best day of your life, and I'm going to be an auntie. I am so excited. We've been like sisters forever and will be unto the end. I'm honored she chose a great man and blessed to be with your new family. Love ya, bro, and sis."

Chloe whispered, "I love you back," Looking like she swallowed a canary.

"She must talk about us, when she said new family?"

"What new family?"

"Are you listening to anything?"

"I'm trying, but you are talking too much."

Instantly, Hosea stood up to speak, and I slowly stood beside him. He didn't warn me before he did it and wasn't sure what I wanted to say.

"I see blessings all around each of us today. Family! The first time in forever, we have our family together, and I'm proud to have you all here. Be good to one another and keep God in charge. Please don't do it alone—It won't work. Keep folks out your business, including us."

❧

Dinner was delis; we had a choice of steak or Maui fish, with many sides to accompany the main dish. As soon as we completed dinner, they passed the cake. Never have I tasted such a moist and tender delicacy. Delicious- tasted like they made it from scratch. As we enjoyed our cake, the Samoan fire dancers began their show, twirling a war knife effortlessly. It was intense and included beautiful fire dancers. When they were done, we hit the dance floor, and we danced—yes, we did. Jeremai asked his mother for her hand; they danced, with Hosea pulling me to the floor. Jez joined in with Sarah, and Mr. Alcott snatched Chloe to her feet. After a while, everybody joined in. She had a smile on her face, most prominent than I ever seen. Next Chloe danced with Jez, who gave her a run for her money. I could see she was tired, but she handled him. I was too tired to do anything but sit down somewhere, like someone who had some sense. Until Hosea and all the men came and got me on one song, Mariah Carey. They sandwiched me in a circle, busting all kinds of moves around me. I showed them a thing or two. Hosea had to make some crazy dance moves, then Jeremai and Chloe joined in. They did me in after that I couldn't move another muscle. The wedding was a success and ended at midnight. They're married ~ tied in a knot of three and surrounded by love.

New Beginnings

They will rise and call her blessed. Flicking through the mail, I noticed one being from my doctor's office. Going through the rest of the letters, I dropped them on the table to go over later. Meet with a few friends for lunch and cancer came up. Interesting discussion of how speaking life over matters is important for healing and practically everyday life. Our conversation moved over to how we needed to get in shape and take better care of ourselves as we are all getting older. A few of them talked about eating healthy, exercising, supplements, and drinking more water. The laughs and chuckles had us spitting out our food and drinks as we sat in a small local American Bistro. Candle lights danced on the tables with a single dainty calla Lilly in a small vase. Our waitstaff had just brought our drinks to the table, and I was the only one who had a virgin one. The response was a kind of badgering because they were raising the voices over me, giving up alcohol. It shocked me. The ladies chattered on about how crazy it was for me to give up pork, bottom dwelling seafood, drinking, and artificial sweeteners. As the conversation went on, my girlfriend Delilah was armament that I had to be the craziest person on earth to believe that food God created shouldn't be eaten.

"Why are you mad because of what I chose cut out my diet?"

"Girl, gone with that mess, bless your food and eat whatever."

"I'm just sharing things in my life that I am changing as I listen closely to God."

"What did he say?"

"I had been getting sick after eating it, and the smell was getting to me. Further, I had mercury poisoning a few years back off shrimp. Can't believe I didn't give it up then. But he didn't let me forget."

"To each their own, do you—boo. I ain't never giving up none of it."

"But I mean, doesn't the bible say all foods were now are acceptable to be eaten?"

"I don't think so, but it's my choice and why am I arguing with you over it?"

"I'm just saying, even Jesus made wine… what's up with the drinking?"

With a side smile, "because I want to be compliant when the Lord speaks and that's what I am going to do."

"Do you girl, I'm eating bacon… excuse me waiter, can you bring me an order of bacon with my lunch? Thank you," rolling her eyes at me.

"Oh, and another drink for the ladies and uh—one virgin, thanks."

I shrugged my shoulders at her request. I couldn't care less. Her attitude was grotesque and would not let her get to me. Rebecca joined in saying she could never give up pork, especially not bacon for nothing.

"Girl, you are good, not me," asking for a piece of Deli's bacon.

Crunching right in my face as she fluttered her long lashes, relishing the taste. "Hm, delis," Rebecca said.

"Do you think you are a better person than us because of all the crap you gave up?"

"Why would you say that to me? Did I ever say or imply I was? Further, did I say anything about you when you gave up stuff for religious or for any reason?"

"Nope, but you still didn't answer the question," Becca said.

"Well—I am not better than anyone else for any reason. Further, I couldn't care less what any of you eat or drink."

"Frankly, I'm not permanently giving up pork and especially ribs? I have let it go for a minute because the local meat packing plant had a salmonella poisoning and I stopped eating it until it's over. After that it's back on and popping," Batya said.

"What if God asked you too?"

"Girl, he wouldn't ask me, he knew I couldn't."

"Well, I feel like he asked me, and I thought I couldn't. I prayed for help to let go and never had a taste for it afterwards. I still cook it for my family, but I don't."

"Good for you lady, not me, and it's a—no, for letting seafood go too," as she laughed and crunched another slice of bacon.

"I'm shocked at each of you. I've always enjoyed your company and friendship, but all these comments are rude. I would like to remind you of the words you speak… listen to life you are speaking over yourselves. You never know what God will ask of you, be careful what you say, might come back to bite you. I've had my share of bites. Enjoy the rest of your afternoon, bill please!"

"Come on now, don't take this out of context, we were just talking," Becca said.

"Yeah, I know, see you'll Sunday at church."

Driving back home, I felt stressed and anguished thinking about the ladies. I remember a small restaurant near my home refused to offer an artificial sweetener that I liked. The day stands out to me because I asked the owner if he could add it on and he refused. We had choice words over it, and I moved on, never went back. Days later, I was at an auto parts store and the cashier was talking to a coworker, telling him how the same sweetener caused cancer and other major health issues. He elaborated that his family member had crystals on their brain found in an autopsy from the sweetener. Listening in on his conversation, I felt something as if God was speaking to me then, but I joined in explaining how I used it because I was diabetic, and it tasted good. He went on and on about it to encourage me to stop. Just like them, I didn't listen and continued. Until God spoke firmly, "let it go!"

I heard Him, bagged it all up and threw it out. It was when he had me let go of pork. I'm never looking back; I don't care what no one says. Driving home so preoccupied with my afternoon with the girls, I didn't notice, not even the weather outside. I sat outside to note of it and still hadn't after I sat out for thirty minutes. Instead, doubt set in my mind, moving to my heart. What if He didn't ask this of me and I was being foolish? Why did I share this with anyone and not just keep it to myself? Does He really care about me this much that He would say don't eat or drink certain things? Why hasn't he told them or anyone else I know? I didn't share that he had me give up other worldly things, such as designer clothes, snakeskin products, cheap cuts of meat slaughtered unjustly, and my wasteful ways. Running my finger across my phone searching for biblical quotes on these issues only gave me a firm trust me in return. Why me... I cried, then I prayed and moved on with my day. Then I answered my question, why not me? My prayer was to hear God and knowing the Holy Spirit wouldn't tell me nothing wrong, I left it at that. The thought came to me, "By their fruit you will recognize them. Do people pick grapes from thornbushes, or figs from thistles (Matthew 7:16, NIV)?"

❧

Six months went by; Chloe is doing great with the pregnancy; they both are healthy. We're excited to find out the gender of our precious little one. Chloe looked terrific, so big and plump, like a huge blueberry. She appeared to be ready to have this baby already. Hosea and I could not make the gender revealing; we're saving our trip for when she got closer to having the baby his birth. After the summer, I slowed down, going back to our healthy living somewhat. As promised, they had the gender reveal on Facetime to include us. We loved the little one already; just hate being so far away and not see our only granddaughter and great-grandchild grow-up. Unless we get a surprise visit before the big day, let's see. I went through the old mail while we waited. Opening the letter from my doctor from six months ago, read please come in for your annual breast exam. Immediately I picked up the phone and made the appointment, not sure how I missed that. Hanging up, Hosea was still running around ducking and dodging fake passes.

"When is she due again?"

"Uh—It's late March, hm... she is due in May."

Hosea was in and out of the room, getting prepared like we were watching a sporting event, popcorn, sport chair, and.

"I know it's a boy," can't wait to throw a football around with the young fella.

"Come on, woman, tackle me."

I was trying to join in his shenanigans with him, shooing him away. Sort of like you beat on flies. I rolled my eyes at him because I feel it's a girl. He always wants to bet on things, this was no different, "I bet $500 it's a boy," he sneered, "hand over my money."

"Gone with that mess. I'm not betting on our only great-grandchild."

"Why—not, don't be a prude?"

"Because we are only going to take the funds out of our account—right?"

Couldn't look past the goofy grin on his face, "always got to be so serious. Woman—you just scared to lose."

Wildly laughing as he walked away, reappearing with a football jersey on. Had me laughing so dang on hard, I almost burst and peed my pants. I still think it's a girl. It's time to find out the gender: the revealing method—a paint bomb.

We set up our computer as they were about to start.

"Hey Y'all," as they hovered around the screen waving.

Focusing on the background, I noticed they were outside—with snow on the ground. Their parents were prepared to throw the paint bomb at them. I thought it was very creative and fun. I hope they hurry, so neither of them got catch cold. Jeremai and Chloe were wearing white outfits standing in the line of fire, holding each other like their lives depended on it, probably trying to keep warm. On the count of three, they threw the bombs- POW, POW, POW… what a spattered mess. The screen bounced around as if it fell. When all the excitement toned down and screen back in place, we have a—BOY! Their outfits had vibrant hues of blue paint all over them. What a mess. It was so cute; I loved it. Oh my, I think Jeremai is the most excited, jumping all around—yelling, swinging arms in the air. While Chloe held her belly tight, smiling on the sideline. Once he settled into the thought of having a baby, he realized how blessed he was and now with a son he always wanted. Chloe didn't have a preference; she just wanted him to be healthy. Everyone was jumping up and down, hugging each other, getting paint all over the place. The cake is pretty… a two-tier all-white cake with brushes of blue marbled into the frosting, It's a boy cake topper, with moon and stars design. Someone put up an 'It's a boy banner.' Mrs. Alcott cleaned up while the guest enjoyed the cake and they changed. It was a small gathering of about 25 people. This was perfect timing, as they just moved into their new house a month ago, so it's kind of gender reveal and housewarming gathering. It was an adorable house about 2500 sq. ft, and in a great location. Reappearing, Chloe had on my old vow renewal dress; it shocked me.

"Oh, my gosh, look at my dress." Chloe moved in close to the camera with excitement.

"That's your dress when we got remarried. Well, I'll be sure is," Hosea said.

He sat down, smiling like someone painted a perfect smile on his face.

Looking hard into the computer screen, "twirl around again, let me see the back," He said.

"Nice. Girl, you look as good as your grandma did in that dress."

"What you think, grandma?"

"I can't speak," too chocked up.

Hands over my mouth, watching her strut around, "how on earth did you fit it?"

"I had it tailored; my seamstress did an amazing job."

Tears flooded my eyes. I saved that dress for her, but never thought it would happen.

"Girl, I just knew when you asked for that dress, you wouldn't ever do anything with it."

"See, you were wrong," smiling hard into the phone.

It was fabulous on her.

"But what if it was a girl… it is a blue dress?"

"The tailor-made a pink tulle insert that I would have pinned under the tulle portion."

Seeing her in that dress brought back so many memories when I remarried Hosea. I saw myself wearing it for a minute. I was so happy that day; I remarried my best friend! God made our second go-around even more significant than I ever thought it could have been, and now he has done it again. Seeing my grandbaby wear my old dress- just sent shivers down my spine. She wore blue and cream converse gym shoes with it.

Jeremai announced little man would be a Jr. We love the idea, "We had a blast sitting here with you all… enjoy the rest of your evening."

We blew kisses and air hugs; we were off. I hated to look over at Hosea because he was so busy pumping his fake muscles up and down, "I bet you glad you didn't place that bet."

"I sure am," walking away.

"Another boy, praying he's healthy."

"Oh, he will be healthy, he's one of us," banging on his chest.

"I can't believe she wore my dress," I was so brilliant red in the face I walked past the mirror thinking I was a rose, relishing at the moment.

The phone rang. It was my doctor telling me I had to come back in immediately because my breast exam showed a lump. Making the appointment things seemed different this time. I've had abnormal ones before, and they have me come in for another X-ray, and that's it. This time was strange. I had to come back for a consultation, X-ray, and an ultrasound. Never had to do that before. Then a letter came in the mail a few days later expressing the urgency of the matter, making sure I was taking this seriously. I had already made the appointment but concerned. Immediately after reading the letter, I got nervous. However, I finished going through the mail and a card from my good friend Julia came. The card was beautiful with flowers and ladybugs, and it read Jehovah-Rapha. There you have it just in time. I know my Lord is a healer; I was now ready to face my appointment. Look at God, running off to share with Hosea. As usual, he half listened to me. But I knew the message was for me not to worry, I went to my prayer room looking for ways to keep calm and not raise my blood pressure. Lying across the chaise, thoughts concerning last summer and how sick I felt.

❧

Driving to my appointment to check on the girl friends, saw a homeless man waving and smiling at cars swooshing by. I was prepared to do the same; he was happy, and I wanted to make sure I waved. Instead, the light changed and there I sat face to face with him. I heard a whisper, "give him twenty."

No problem digging in my purse, but only had twenty-one dollars. Man, I have to pay the fee to get out the parking lot and know for sure that they only took money and the walk we had trying to find a teller was awful the last time. So, I gave the one instead.

"Hi, what's your name?"

"Roman and yours?"

"Matea."

"Wow, I have a sister with that name and three other sisters, and a brother. I'm from Romana."

"That is great, keep smiling… it's a pleasure meeting you."

Driving off, I hated I didn't give him the twenty. Maybe I'll see him afterwards and give him my change from parking. Made it to my appointment and changed my clothes. They called a few other ladies before me and were getting anxious over my turn. They called me. The X-ray wasn't bad, just smashing of the buttercups was enormous. I survived. The tech was nice and chatted for a few before I returned to the waiting area. About ten minutes later, I was called for the ultrasound. Walking into the room, I saw my baby hanging with a bright light shining the vast mass about the size of a quarter. My eyes enlarged as she escorted me to the table, removed my breast and massaged the scanner until she found the target. Picking up the phone a few times to speak to the doctor, I could barely hear the muffled voices. I just prayed. Fifteen minutes later, she announced I was cancer free; it was a cyst that would be there permanently and didn't have to come back till next year. She held my shoulders tight and faced me, "Thank God," she said.

"Yes, he is so good."

Walking out of the office relieved, I noticed the nurses stood around smiling. It puzzled me as they were saying bye to me and other pleasant things. Weird. Got dressed and made it to my car. Leaving, I noticed the person who worked the booth was replaced by a machine that only took debit cards. Crazy. Dug in my purse, I paid with my debit card and drove off. The voice, "trust in me."

I stopped and thanked God for the reminder; I felt dismayed for a moment because I could have given him the twenty dollars and would be obedient the next time. Pulling into the local grocer, I parked next to a car that had a cancer survivor's license plate. Walking to the back of the car, I stared at it and felt like one. Called Hosea and shared the news and he was calm, but glad. Truly I felt like a survivor and wasn't sure why because it was negative but could relate to what others went through.

"Ouch."

"What's wrong, honey?"

"My tooth hurts," as I continued brushing.

Weeks passed as I continued feeling my one tooth bothered me. It wasn't a terrible pain, just nagging. My tongue floated to the spot, and it felt terrible. My jaw fell as it needed immediate attention. The dentist saw me right away.

"It's a severe infection. Going to have to extract it immediately."

"Today?"

"Yeah."

The extraction was horrible, thought I would die. He kept numbing me and nothing gave me relief except the force of the tooth breaking from my jawbone. Well, I hollered and screamed until it was out. My body appeared to float in midair, falling to the chair in relief. Tears rolled. The dentist claimed the infection made the extraction difficult and waved apologies around as I only wanted to run away. I got in the car and wept, "Lord, why did this happen to me?" Before I pulled off. My fibro pain was at level ten, as my entire being ached.

It was sabbath. Deciding to spend the evening on the couch watching Christian movies, I flicked to one that caught my attention. A young man who drowned in a frozen lake and was pronounced dead. His mother's prayers brought him back only for him to almost die again, and the community prayers brought him back. I cried, flicked off the TV and joined Hosea for lunch. I rambled about the movie, like I hadn't had my tooth extracted. He reminded me that maybe I shouldn't be so talkative. Sitting back focusing on my chewing, I heard a message, "would you rather lose a breast or a tooth, the cancer had to go somewhere."

My face fell to the table as I cried. Shouts of Halleluiah rang in air. Hosea ran over helping me pull myself together and I told him what I heard and hugged me. "Thank God baby, Thank God."

"Yes, thank God," holding my breast with the cyst and feeling my missing tooth as a reminder of how great He is.

❧

I have to get healthier and do better. After all the blessings He has given me, it's time to figure out why I have been having more flareups lately. Maybe it was just the matter of doing too much? I've started doing light exercises again; I'm sure that helps. One thing Chloe's visit encouraged both of us to do more things outside the house. Hosea and I got even closer, found a few new friends. I met the lady down the street who owns a local cafe. We started visiting her every morning, having coffee at the shop. She has a little storefront made up so cute and homely. I enjoy watching her create the most impressive floral arrangements for many types of events. She has even allowed me to make a few when I felt up to it. I started sending flowers to my close friends and family since we were there all the time. Hosea gets the local paper to do his Sudoku puzzles and gets so frizzled when he can't beat the tough challenges. He loves her homemade glazed donuts, and I love the coffee cake, not to mention her coffee makes your eyes spin. Instead of driving, we walk down there unless it's too hot or too cold. We hold hands on our walk. Never thought for one moment we would grow old together, heck I never thought I would grow old and blessed to still have my senses. I love sharing our relationship stories with others to encourage folks to stay together and love as if tomorrow will never come. We enjoy each other tremendously, never forgetting to tell each other how blessed we are to have found genuine love as Chloe says. This world is so twisted; no one follows God's word anymore. Keeping him at the head of our lives sure has made a difference in our household, instead of calling only when we needed Him. We've found peace in Him. Every day I see so much going on, that is just so against His word. People don't even want to hear nothing much about the Lord anymore. I see the world being just like the biblical days, rolling straight towards destruction. But you can only tell people so much.

❧

I hired a young man from the church to haul this stuff I got out of my closet. I finally got it done. The doorbell rang, it's him.

"Open the door, will ya?"

Hosea took sweet time getting to the door, walking all slow. Finally, he led the young man to the bags, grumping the directions to him. It didn't take him long to get all the stuff loaded in the truck.

"Outta stops having so much stuff."

"Shut up—with your evil self."

"At least I'm got rid of it… you ain't say nothing when it was in my closet."

"I ain't never go in your closet, or I would have."

"Get me the keys, will ya…?" glancing back at him, "uh, please."

"Where are you going?"

"Down to the donation store. I want to talk to the owner."

"Yeah, to buy some more junk," he mumbled.

Giving me the keys with a funky look on his face. Wonder what's all that about? I always wanted to check it out. I haven't been to one since I was young. Speaking about it brought back old memories of having everything I owned from the resale shop at one time, hardly ever getting anything from a regular store. Times were tough, but we made it and I had some good stuff too.

Taking a deep breath, I stepped in. Waiting for the clerk to finish working with her customer, I browsed around. The small crammed shop had many things that should have met with the dumpster. Odd smells lingered, filling my nose with a musty smell mixed with a scent I couldn't place. Maybe just old. Sliding by the clothing, I fingered through the items, showing most to be outdated or out of shape. Shoes were dusty and spider webbed, not a finger graced them since they were out there, so I wiped mines across and started hacking and sneezing. It didn't stop there the dust ran rampant through the entire store. Bugs scattered in circles, buzzing to see who disturbed things when I run into a hanging iron board, eyeing things and not watching my path ran me smack into it. They priced some items decent and some not so nice-looking things appeared expensive. Maybe they knew something I didn't, maybe they were artifacts from ancient times, or even mystical? Tools scattered in one area looked like someone emptied their old garage and threw them in the most unappealing arrangement. Everything was rusty or broken. Picking up a plastic garden stone, found to still have someone's key inside. Interesting, twirling it to see if their address was located anywhere. Making my next step, I felt a loose floorboard that gave off the most awful screech, feeling like I was about to meet with the basement. Forcing thoughts of what was down there? Quickly stepping over to the books, skipping the paperbacks to my favorite hard backs. Picking a few and fanning the pages, seeing many things stuck in them, one touched me—a yellow flower. Maybe a Marigold? Sniffing it like a crazy lady, wondering how the person who put it there felt? Running the pages back to the first page, I knew I would find a name. I did, but never expected to my findings. 'Forgive the unforgivable, C.R.' in a scribble type handwriting. I relinquished them back, but that one. The purse shelf was a disgrace, designer bags with high-end pricing because of a name, yet looked as someone wore the life out of them, sitting in worst shape than anybody's handbag I know. Even my grannies old crusty purse looked better, yet they had prices of insanity on them. Old stores like this force me to think who this stuff used to belong to? People like me getting rid of junk or those who passed? Picturing many items being used in households, now displaced in hopes for someone to bring them back to life, made the store appear like a graveyard. Rumbling over the shelves, I found an interesting piece that whole-heartedly caught my eye.

"Oh, my—I love this teapot."

"It is a delightful piece, but dirty," the customer next to me said.

Pulling it close to me as I saw how she eyed it, smudging the dirtiest areas off effortlessly with my sleeve. The dust turned greasy as the smears only cascaded into grimy swirls. It didn't stop me from smiling as I gazed over it, focusing my full attention on how different this teapot appeared. Blue that resembled the sky, on the darkest blue embracing the entire pot, with gold swirls that make your eyes follow the graceful lines. The spout has a Tape with sloppy handwritten words, ten dollars barely stuck to the bottom. Putting on my glasses, peeled the back the tape and found a name stamped on it, faintly visible along with porcelain stamp. Rubbing the bottom continuously until I made out the name 'John Barsad'. Wonder if it's authentic? Didn't mean much to me, I just had to have it. Hearing that name, I couldn't place where. I'll look him up later. The style was perfect for my collection. Digging in the box on the same shelf, I found a box of china cups. I went on a wild hunt for cups to match my teapot, with no luck. Combing the shelf, I knocked over a glass pitcher. Slowly it tumbled to the floor, shattered, and startled me. Instantly, the clerk chattering stop; I heard nothing until she appeared.

"What you do? You break?" she stated with broken English.

"I am sorry, how much is the pitcher?"

"You want?"

"No, but I want to pay for it, I broke it."

"No worry, but must buy something," she said.

"This blue teapot."

Taking it from my hands, she carefully studied it.

"Twenty dollars."

"It says ten on the bottom, are you charging me for the pitcher too?"

"No, the book under arm."

"Ten for the book?"

"Classic. Yes, no?"

"Yes, if you throw in..."

Quickly, I grabbed a silk scarf laying on the shelf behind me, "and this."

"Okay, deal."

"Deal."

"Here's twenty-five... no change, thank you."

"No, thank you. Here receipt for the donation and your purchase."

I love teapots and couldn't wait to clean it up. I saw one similar to it at the local tea store and they wanted $200 for it. I've paid this much for one or more. I never tell Hosea how much they cost because he would hit the ceiling. Well, he can't be crazy about this one; it was only ten, and it felt like a million in my heart. I came home, placing it on the kitchen counter.

Working the next day in my office, I remembered to look up the name I saw on the teapot... I couldn't think of his last name off-hand but looked up the name John and teapots. A few names came up... I noticed a teapot similar to mine, and the previous name was Bartlam. I didn't think he made this piece, but you never know. It was a dated piece. What if it was by him, oh wee, it would be worth a pretty penny? I was sure it was a replica, or else it wouldn't be in a resale shop, right? I called Hosea, asking if he would bring my teapot to me. He grumbled into my office... I noticed he had been cranky lately, wasn't for sure what was going on with him. Bringing it into the room, he flung it on the table.

"Thanks, babe, careful... it's breakable."

"What's the name on the bottom of it?"

"I don't know, I can't see it," grumpily displaying a significant attitude.

"Give it to me... dog on it."

"You're not even trying to see what I what I'm talking about."

"I don't care about no old teapot... you always buying some crap we don't need. You took some junk and brought more? Uh—for the life of me I don't understand women," abruptly turned to throw his hand up at me and rushed out.

Adjusting my glasses, focusing to see if I could make out the wording. I noticed the words 'porcelain' and 'John Barsad'. My eyes widened. This thing could be worth some money if it's real. I quickly got up, reaching for my phone, Face-timing Chloe to see her thoughts.

"Grandma, it's possible. Eh, let me see who can appraise it for you."

"Ok, it's a place downtown, let me call… hold on."

"Grandma, I have him on the phone… when you can bring it in for an appraisal?"

"Tomorrow at 1:00 PM?"

"Cool beans, I have to go. Let me know how it goes; I will text you the address and phone number."

❧

I ran and got Hosea; I was so excited. I rambled on, talking Hosea's ears off his head. He couldn't help but get excited.

"I hope its worth something."

"Shoot me too; I hear about stuff like this all the time on TV. Those antique shows always have people finding stuff at sales worth money."

"I know, never thought we would find anything worth something."

The next day we got there on time, waiting in the lobby for the young man to look over the teapot in the back room. Waiting, we scanned the shop, which appeared like a pawnshop. This place was much neater than the thrift store, much neater and smells way better. Pricey, too. I always loved electric guitars, and they had an assortment hanging high on the wall. Gazing at them, Mesmerized, but dare buy one. Wonder if I'm too old to learn? Hosea gave me the eye when I mentioned it, and I knew that look. They stayed in the back for a while. Moseying over to the jewelry case, the prices were outrageous. I went to the counter requesting a timeframe. The clerk said she was not sure and would let me know. Ten minutes later, she called us to the counter with the teapot.

"Can we call you in two hours?"

"Well, I don't want to leave my teapot."

"No problem," she handed over the teapot. I began examining the bottom to make sure it was the same one.

"Babe leave it so they can check it out. I'm sure we can trust them."

"Okay, but—."

"Leave it."

I gave her my number and left. We waited around for a few hours, no call. I figured it wasn't worth anything and went about my day. Winding down for the evening, it came to me they never called. Shoot, I'm not worried about it as I turned in for the night. Thinking about the teapot before I closed my eyes, a thought came, "Watch out! Be on your guard against all kinds of greed; life does not consist in an abundance of possessions, Luke 12:15 NIV."

I knew that thought well, made me think of what we wanted to do with my money when we got it. Ten percent to the church for sure off the top, give all the kids something, and Chloe. Charity would be next, not sure which one, maybe the Hope Center, and pay off some bills. Happy with the spreading of God's gift, I prayed things worked out and was excited.

❧

The next morning, they called.

"Hello, Mrs. Warren…"

"This is she."

"This is the Fair Time Appraisal Shop calling you concerning your teapot."

"Okay, shoot."

"We feel it was authentic, but we wanted to double-check before we called you back."

"Oh, okay, I understand."

"It is authentic, we called the local museum, and they say it's worth about $608,000. Ma'am it's dated over 100 years old."

"They are asking if you want to get it appraised by the museum to bring it by this afternoon, we can send it for you."

"Okay, thank you."

"You will hear from us as soon as we know."

Hanging up the phone, I couldn't wait to tell Hosea. What did I just hear? Now Hosea cares about my old teapot, talking about it like it meant something. A few days later, they called, letting us know that the Historical Tea Society wanted to purchase it and will pay the full price for it, and we had to go there to sign the papers. They asked for a fee for the work they did, and I agreed. Flicking through a stack of bible study booklets, a verse stuck out. "I will give you hidden treasures, riches stored in secret places, so you may know that I am the LORD, the God of Israel, who summons you by name (Isaiah 45:3)".

Pondering the verse, I felt grateful. "Thank you, Jesus, for this gift," with my arms outward to the sky.

Meeting the representative at the Historical Tea Society, she appeared snobby and stern. It made me nervous.

"$806,000, right?"

"Yes," Grabbing Hosea's hand, tightening my grip as I spoke. She sat stiffly in her chair as she cleared her throat.

"It's more than we're prepared to offer you," reaching for the teapot; she stopped me.

"We accept the offer."

We burst out laughing with excitement; she didn't move or blink an eye. Looking at her, she displayed no emotion. Unfazed by our enthusiasm, forcing us to act more thoughtfully. She cleared her throat and began speaking again.

"The society will take possession of the teapot today; within 6-8 weeks, we will cut the check."

"Do you agree with the terms?" Hosea looked at me as I sat quietly for a minute.

"We accept," and signed.

❧

Months passed; Chloe was due in two weeks; she's getting induced. We have the exact date of Lil' man's graces our world, and we're excited. Our flight to Michigan wasn't bad. Jeremai arrived just in time, stating Chloe didn't feel up to the long ride. We understood. Michigan weather is a beast—it's freezing. She wouldn't have us stay anywhere but with them. We were excited to see their new home, especially Jr's room.

"Oh, I love it! It's perfect for the three of you."

"Thank you."

"Girl, you got excellent taste."

"Yes, she does grandma, she decorated every room," Jeremai said.

"I just love her ideas," Jeremai said.

"Well, thank you, everyone. I get it from my grandma," as she blushed.

"She allowed me to help with the baby's room," Jeremai said.

"Thank you very much, honey," giving him a big kiss.

"Jeremai, we may have to put on sunglasses with that big smile of yours."

"This is so exciting. I'm about to be a daddy."

Looking over at Chloe, noticing she didn't seem quiet. She appeared to be—hm, kind of sad. I shook it off, figuring it was the pregnancy, getting close to the end. Our room is nicely decorated, with a welcome sign on the door and lovely flowers. She sure treated us well. What a welcome. Enormous windows and a private balcony overlooking a small lake outback was a beautiful addition to our room. We were excited to see our new great grandbaby Lil Jeremai come into the world. Jeremai glowed, his smile radiated throughout the entire house as he worked, making us comfortable. It was an invitation to his happiness... encouraging us to make ourselves at home.

That evening they invited the family over for a BBQ, nothing planned, sweet music playing, and lots of food. Sitting around the bonfire was very comforting. Jez and Sarah sat laughing, telling jokes. It was the most laid back I had ever seen Sarah since I knew her; it was nice to see. Even Chloe was happier at the moment with everyone being together again. Jeremai appeared with an announcement.

Clearing his throat, "I would like everyone to quiet down and enjoy this presentation," before stepping away.

Music started, The Family Reunion by the O'Jays filled the air. Bobbing our heads enjoying the rhythms- Jez slide across the deck singing like a lead singer with a mic in his hand, dancing with such enthusiasm. We laughed till tears rolled. Soon his back-up singers came out, squinting to see; it was Omar, Asher, Jez, and Elijah. My eyes grew enormous, filled with excitement. Hosea jumped up, grabbing me, hugging me with such happiness. Chloe started screaming, my uncles with her hands covering her mouth. This was the second time we've had all our sons together at one time. I cried. Hosea watched, joining in, feeling left out. They sounded so good, and their moves seemed rehearsed. My sons looked so good up there singing, dancing- nothing could have made this night any better.

Chloe hobbled around, visiting everyone, chatting away about becoming a mom. Every time you saw that girl, she was hugged around her uncle's necks. Even Sarah was chatting with everyone. Sitting back in my chair, I watched our family come together as once again, just like a family reunion. I realized how much we hurt each other and how much we love one another just the same. We needed to forgive ourselves and each other, work on becoming better. Chloe deserved a family who got along. Jeremai's dad enjoyed himself dancing with Lydia, stopped calling her Mrs. Alcott. We's family now. They both seem happier since the wedding, not to mention she and Chloe have been getting along very well. She has even been a great help to Chloe. The biggest blessing, we all had was Chloe and Jeremai bringing us all together, a huge reminder that we're blessed to have each other. I sat back thinking about all the tears I had shed over this young lady… none of them brought her back to us any sooner than God plans to do so. It was when I let God! That's when God worked his miracle in our lives. It is so essential for us to release control over situations that we cannot change. Learn to pray and wait over everything and worry over nothing. Not a thing in the world will change the fact that we missed her entire childhood and only God knows why, and only God made it right. He answered our prayers- that's all that mattered.

❧

Around midnight, Chloe knocked.

"Can I join you?"

"Sure."

"Granddaddy is downstairs with dad and thought was ok?"

"What's up?" "Nothing," still appearing down.

"Are you sure everything is ok, honey? You know grandma knows when her baby girl isn't happy."

"Yeah, I know. You're good at that, grandma."

Sitting in the corner chair, she began chattering away about all the things Jeremai's coworkers gave them at the shower. It sounds like it was the best shower ever, leaving them with most of the things they needed. Other items Jeremai bought.

"You know, grandma, I still feel some way with Jeremai not wanting the baby. I mean- I'm not mad, but I guess you can say hurt."

"Really..."

"Is that normal?"

"Yes, and no."

"What do you mean?"

"Yes, we will hold on to things that hurt us, we shouldn't, once we have truly forgiven someone it's done. In marriage, once you forgive, you let go, well, any relationship. You don't freely throw forgiveness, give it deep thought and prayer before you say it and when you mean it. It's difficult. Never said it wasn't. But to be free we must force it from our minds and repent when it enters."

"Your right."

"Holding on is not forgiveness. He has changed so much since then."

"Look how happy you both are."

"Yup."

"Things will be ok. Don't bring old feelings to a new phase of your lives."

"Pray for him to be the man you need and his strength to be the father Jeremai Jr. needs."

"Honey, enjoy the blessings." "Can we pray together?"

"Yes," we prayed.

"Thank you, grandma. I'm so happy you're here."

"Me too."

"No tears."

"Hey, can I read a section out of my journal?"

"Really? Sure can, this is a nice twist."

Chloe's Journal- When I met my grandparents, I was apprehensive, ready to tell them off. Not realizing what to expect, I let go of fear. Hurting deeply, I wanted to be positive that this was the right thing to do. Seeing a powerful woman in my grandma who had a zest for life that I had to know her. I also noticed I found my twin in her, wanting to be just like her. My grandfather was funny and a joy to be around. Within a few days, I wondered how my parents could not see them for 25 years? We all lost, but it wasn't too late to mend the broken pieces. Within a few weeks we all experienced true happiness, made fresh memories together, teaching each other the art of forgiving, marriage, and the importance of family. Not wanting to be like my grandma any longer. She is a unique person, but so am I. She taught me that. I'm whole with her in my life, becoming a much better person than I could ever imagine. She has shown me who I am, how to handle marriage, increased my faith, taught forgiveness, and, most of all, how to have a grandma. Her advice is always valuable and thank her for sharing her past with me, so I don't carry mines. I admire them both with all my heart, I now have my parents, grandma, and granddad. May we never part again. Chloe.

"That was so beautiful- shame on you making this old lady cry. You didn't have your par—."

My eyes caught Sarah standing at the door.

"Chloe, that was so sweet of you. What a beautiful array of words she has for you Matea."

"I agree, just touched my heart."

"Oh, before I forget. I have a surprise for you both."

"Grandma, you know I love gifts."

"Well, here is a card for you and one for you, Sarah."

"A card?" Chloe ripped it open.

"Her eyes got so wide, wow this is a lot of money."

"Sarah?"

She opened hers next, "Matea, this is a vast sum of money, we can't."

"Oh, my gosh grandma, you'll shouldn't have."

"We wanted to honey, you must take it, Sarah—for Jez too."

"Thank you, we sure can use it."

"Now don't spend it all in one day, ya hear me?"

Sarah agreed it was a gracious gift.

"I don't know what to say, thanks Matea."

"Nothing, thank you. We gave the others the same thing, had an unforeseen gift and wanted to share."

She couldn't get over to me fast enough, swaying over hugging me. She was huge, felt like I was hugging Lil' man too, seemed he leaped for joy.

"Whew, he is ready, over here beating poor grandma up."

Chloe glanced up at me and said, "he loves you already, grandma."

The Arrival

She will no longer remember sorrow but bask in joy. Her bag is packed and spent some time in the little man's room praying and perfecting every little detail. Chloe's appointment for her induced labor was in one day. Walking around with her back bent into a 'u' shape and uncomfortable to the point, sweating with each step. Leaning on everything, huffing and puffing, with Jeremai reminding her to inhale and relax. Dropping his coming home outfit on the floor, her eyes fell, preparing her body to accommodate the effort needed to pick it up. Knees bent with the sounds of crackles and moans filling the air, with Hosea running to aid her.

"Thank you, granddad," she smiled, "I'll be back to normal soon."

Gripping her tummy with small rubs made her eyes roll with small bouts of comfort. Laughter filled the air as she made light of the moment. Jeremai cracked jokes about the baby, saying he was going to be a pistol whipper like himself. Chloe hobbled around more on the serious note. Forcing him to get serious so they could prepare for the big day. The two together, was refreshing as kisses and small touches passed whenever they were close. Giggles and playfulness speckled in and out, as we enjoyed their love. Leaving them both deciding they had done everything. Jeremai rubbing her back, moving to her feet as she slide in the rocking chair.

"He's gonna be healthy and smart. I can feel it."

"The boy has no choice. Look at us," Jeremai stated.

"Well, well, the kid's personality won't be complete without hints of his granddad in him," Hosea said.

"Hosea, I must agree with you. Cause you are a cool guy; my son needs some of that coolness."

"Wait, grandma. His little stars are out of place," she hobbled to fix them.

"Girl, he won't even notice those little things you worry about… it's perfect, honey," cupping her face.

"I know, it seems like it happened so quick."

"In twenty-four hours, you will be a mommy."

"And I can't wait."

"Life will amaze you the second you lay eyes on him."

"As soon as skin touch skin, the passion. Awe, I remember those days."

"Sounds like to me, a daughter is happening soon."

"Oh, oh…" her eyes glistened, releasing a chuckle.

"I love you—lady, and proud of you."

"What if something happens to him? I've been a worried mess."

Jez stepped in with his camcorder, reminding her that everything was under control, and she would do great. Jeremai started taking a video of Chloe. She gave a small speech on how great she feels about becoming a mom while smiling into the camera. We thought it was a great idea. She went on telling us all the birthing details, added coverage of his room, and she even added a small secret she wouldn't tell us. Jeremai had the camera all in our faces, asking goofy questions. After a while, I pushed him along to his next camera victim.

"Pops, what do you want to say to your grandson?"

"You will read the Bible the first day you are born," Jez said, pulling out an engraved copy.

Jeremai zoomed in close to get a closeup, "your gramps got you the whole amour, preparing my boy for the world."

"I like that, thanks."

"Man, now that's a gift. Why didn't I think of that?" Hosea stood scratching his head.

"Dad, it's ok, I'll let you read it to him."

"I'm going to read it to you too. When was the last time I read you the Bible?"

"Never."

"Awe, I'll read to ya both."

"Dad!"

He stuck the camera right in Hosea's face, with Jez pointing fingers behind his head. Giving him something to film, they both made outrageous faces. Encouraging him to move to Sarah.

"Don't start with me."

"Say something nice for the boy child," Jeremai said.

She held her hand to the lens and shoved him away. He chucked, moving back to Chloe, who refused him too.

"You are so irritating."

"I'm ready for my boy to play sports."

"Hold up, first he has to grow up," I said.

"Chloe is so beautiful and handled the pregnancy well," Jeremai said.

"Your right, my baby, is glowing," Sarah said.

"Yes, that's the perfect word… glowing."

"Other than nausea, in the beginning, she had a healthy pregnancy," Sarah added.

"You're right. She worried about gaining too much weight, but she's mostly baby. Well, she also had a little anxiety, and that was mostly fearful of a premature delivery," I added.

"They did a lot during this pregnancy, a 7-day cruise, house hunting, prepping for Lil man, and dealing with me," Sarah said, "they were busy."

"Thanks, Sarah, for allowing your baby to come out for the summer. I was meaning to tell you that for the longest."

"Your welcome; I'm grateful she went, got us all together," Sarah's eyes welled up.

"I'm sorry," Sarah said, making her way to the door

"Awe, I am too… your forgiven. I love you. Thank Goodness for Chloe, were here today."

"I can't," Sarah said.

Jez stood silently in the corner, playing with the stars that hung next to him. Sarah glared at him, asking if he'll step out with her.

"Chloe, I need you to hon."

All of us left the room, disappearing. Hosea requested pictures but asked that they leave out the messy parts.

"I can't stand when folks do that," he grumbled as he fixed his pants.

"Dad!"

"I'm just saying, folks, do that junk all the time."

Jeremai stopped Hosea in the hall, I stood by adoring her maternity pictures laying on the table. Besides the pics, she had some nice wooden frames lying next to them.

"Pops, did you have any problems during the delivery?"

"Man, I was a mess, but you'll be fine."

He rattled on about their plans for the afternoon. "Eh, she has a few more things to pick up and wanted to find some rare stuff from the local thrift shop, like you Matea."

"I advised her not to go alone because she's close to her due date." He agreed, stating he was going with her.

"Hey, I wanted to tell you, I took a month off to spend time with the fam, your special gift made it possible, thanks."

"Your welcome."

Walking over to the window, looking out over the lake as the sunlight was shining immensely, clouds beautifully placed across the sky like a painter making a grand display. God is that incredible artist. Everything he creates is beautiful, never making a mistake. It delighted me to see another day of his wondrous works. Hosea came to the door, asking me to join them outback. Walking past the Chloe's bedroom, I heard an argument brewing. I slowed down being nosey.

"Have you told them yet?" Sarah said.

"No, and I'm not," Chloe yelled back.

Jeremai asked them to calm down, mumbling some things I couldn't make out.

"You said when you flew there you were telling them, and you didn't!"

"I know what I said. I couldn't… they we're gleaming with joy."

"Well, I'm going to tell them today, they must know."

I stepped into the room, "know what?"

Everyone stopped talking, looking like I was a burglar. Chloe started crying and stomped past me, I watched her leave. "What's happened?"

"Ma, Chloe—she is not your granddaughter."

"What—I don't understand. How could that be?"

"Matea, I'm sorry."

I just sat looking blank, "explain."

Tears ran down Sarah's face as she spoke. "We lost our baby months after we had that fall out."

"How?"

"Protective services. Homeless living out of our car, no food, and broke, she had some bruises, we didn't know how she got them. They didn't believe us. It proved us negligent, well that's what they said, but we were doing our best. They took her from us, and we couldn't get back on our feet. Fighting hard to get her back left us failing in our efforts and they adopted her and we never saw or heard from her again."

My mouth hit the ground, "Well—who is she?" pointing towards the door.

"Ma, we were too ashamed to face our family."

"A young lady we kind of adopted after her parents died in a boating accident about eight years ago. We took her in right after high school—uh, she rented a room and she adopted us. Her middle name was Chloe and her first name is Bernice, which she hates. So, everyone calls her Chloe, which is our baby's name," looking at his feet as he played with some paper on the floor.

Sarah looked towards the door, hiding her emotions and pain. While I looked at them both with disgust. "You lied to us."

"Mom, we just wanted to make you'll happy, but Chloe loved you guys so much—the grandparents she always wanted."

Tears rolled down my face as pain shot through my entire being. I was mad, angry, hurt, disgusted, and just plain ready to slap the taste out of both of their mouths all at once. Feeling nauseas, I didn't say a word, as my stomach was ready to release its contents on the floor if I moved a muscle. Hosea was walking the hallway when he spotted us and came in. He knew something was wrong as soon as he took one step inward. "What's—"

"Chloe's not our granddaughter," I stated.

"What?"

"Who is she then?"

Jez told him the same story they gave me, I looked away as I couldn't bear seeing Hosea's face. "Why?"

"Dad, I was going to—"

Chloe hobbled in and looked at Sarah and Jez, "I hate you both!" she screamed and stumbled away. Grabbing Jeremai's hand in her getaway efforts, with him mumbling down the hall, "what's going on?" They exited the house and sped away.

❧

Hours passed as we lounged around waiting for the two to return, requesting not to discuss the previous conversation until things we had a greater understanding. I wanted to leave hours ago as we decided to rent a room but wanted more information and speak to her. The longer I sat, the more irritated I became. They walked around like nothing happened. With anger growing in us each second. Glancing at the clock, *there goes that 3:33 PM again. What does it mean?* Pounding my fist on my knee. Lynda and Bill came in laughing. They sat down, sharing some jokes they had heard on the radio. We had no interest in laughing or hearing any jokes. Hosea turned on some jazz, which was nice soothing sounds taking our minds off things for a minute. Jez's phone rang. He took the call. Standing lifeless in the corner like the blood drained out of his face, similar to a plug up plucked from a sink. Concerned, we dared not interrupted him. He would respond loudly and go back to a soft tone as if he was trying to compose himself, which forced us to focus on him. Hosea asked if everything was ok? Holding up his hand for us to wait, he walked out of the room and returned. The doorbell rang before he could speak. Hosea got up to answer. It was a state trooper following him back into the sitting room. Looking astonished at the officers standing in front of us.

"Hey, what's going on Jez asked."

"Ah, it's been an accident on Orchard Lake Rd. and two folks are in route to the hospital. I'm looking for the parents of Bernice and Jeremai Alcott."

"Well, uh."

He pulled them into the living room to finish the conversation.

"Yea—I uh just got a call from an officer saying I was I.C.E. in Chloe's phone…" Jez said.

"What?" I yelled in a state of shock.

The room filled with faint sounds of everyone getting details at once. As the officer continued, he informed us they were alive, but in serious condition, ending with them escorting us to Detroit Memorial hospital.

Scrambling for our belongings, the race began as everyone made it to their cars, Hosea suggested we drive the SUV, which was big enough to accommodate everyone. Jez elaborated on the call, trying to make sense.

"Chloe has gone into labor and rushed in for tests. Jeremai is ok, but they are checking him out at the moment and that's all the info I have," Jez said.

The car was quiet, with occasional questions of what we figured could have happened. I prayed over the entire situation, knowing God could fix this. Entering the hospital, we mobbed our way to the front desk, speaking all at one time. Jez stopped us from talking, getting the information. Sarah was getting off work, meeting us there. The doctor and two nurses met us on the floor as soon as we got off the elevator and bent the corner. Everyone exploded with questions, with the loudest sound coming from Bill hushing everyone up.

"How are our children?" he bolstered.

"Quiet down… follow me."

The police joined us as the staff escorted us to a private room to discuss the event. They had given Jeremai a sedative. Hollering and scream for Chloe. As he shook the rails, he was all over the place, pulling at the bed rails and shaking them, demanding his release. They say he kept asking for the women who pulled them out of their car. The police elaborated on his findings.

"They'd pulled them out of the car and laid on the grass next to the accident. We do not understand by whom. The car is in terrible shape and it was no way they got out on their own," showing pictures of the car.

We all gasped. Lynda started screaming through her cries to see her son.

"Oh Lord, my babies," she hollered.

They had to sedate him, because they couldn't get him to calm down. He has grave concern about Chloe and the baby, and it's so they can do his exam. Chloe was doing fine but needed to further test to determine the health of the baby and was pretty banged up. As the airbags deployed, she got hit in multiple places, it's too early to tell was happening. The doctors insisted we wait in the waiting room until they had more information for us. Disappearing into the mysterious double doors, the state trooper continued giving us full details of the earlier events. We just sat listening. With waves of whimpers filling the air from Lynda, I consoled her, holding my feelings in like a prisoner trying to escape, I wanted to leave. Hosea sat with Jez as Bill paced the floor. The officer stood like he could collapse himself, as if he was a shell of a man. Clearing his throat, suppressing his emotions, he spoke, "I have a pregnant daughter myself about Chloe's age. Please bear with me," wiping his eye.

"A speeding car ran a red-light hitting Chloe and Jeremai's car at the speed of about 50 miles per hour, totally the car. The police and detectives are still there clearing the road and taking photos for evidence. The driver fled the scene. Arriving at the scene, we were prepared to use the jaws of life to get them out, but surprisingly, they were out of the car laying on the grassy side of the road. Neither was conscience at the time. We couldn't figure out how they could have gotten out. The front end as you can see is smashed; however, the car battery showed *3:33* PM on the clock."

The time struck me like lightning.

"Oh, my Lord," I yelled. "I've been noticing that time lately."

"The last time you saw it, ma?" Jez asked.

"Today after they left," everyone looked at me.

No longer controlling my stance, I broke down and began sobbing.

"What does it mean?" Jez asked.

"I don't know, wish I did."

Looking at Jez, face swollen with reddened eyes bulging with tears, I saw immense hurt in his eyes making me ball even more. The officer looked away from Jez, then cleared his throat—he continued talking, saying that Chloe mumbled that two women helped them before they sedated her. There's no evidence of women anywhere around the scene. Let us go over the records to see who placed the 911 call. We could not speak to Jeremai, he was too hysterical to tell us anything. Another officer with a gentleman appeared to contribute more information, as far as I know I was the only witness.

"I saw the accident and placed the 911 call, sir."

Cries fill the air in waves, having separate moments of outbreaks. Consoling each other through our own pain. The man appeared to be in his forties, slim in stature and pale as a ghost. He's shaken just as we were and struggled to speak.

"They stopped on a green light but sped off. A man in a black race type car ran the light hitting them dead on—he was on the phone. I don't know why they stopped at the green light, but if he would have stayed there, they would have been ok. However, he drove off rather fast, hitting the other car head on—yet he had the right a way. I sped up the road to see if I could see the car that hit him to get a plate number, but I couldn't. My truck can only go as fast as I had a trailer attached with my lawn equipment. When I returned, they were both laying lifeless in the grass; however, they had a pulse. I waited with them until the police and ambulance showed up. I don't know how they made it out of the car; felt like minutes passed before I returned. Feeling like I witnessed a miracle with the vehicle that crumbled. I believe sir, God had angels watching over them; had a calm sense of peace come over me."

"Excuse me sir," jogging over to the witness, Jez shook his hand.

"Few folks will help in these situations; I owe you, man—thanks."

The sheriff promised to work on the case, "we will do our best to bring justice to this case, if you learn anything new, keep us informed," flicking his card to Jez.

"We'll be in touch," the officer said.

"Thanks."

"Oh yeah, two more things… is her name Bernice or Chloe? Your relationship to her again?"

"Bernice, sir. Chloe is her middle name, and we are her landlord," moving his reddened eyes towards us.

Hosea whispered in my ear. "I think we should leave to sort things out. I mean—."

"Babe, I think so too."

Informing Sarah and Jez we were leaving, they talked much to get us to stay. Holding strong in our stance to get away from this crazy mess, we stopped negotiating. Hosea, firmly stated, "were leaving—keep us updated."

Jez stepped back, holding his hand out for Sarah to follow, "I'll call ya'll later. Love you."

We didn't reply, just nodded before walking off. Making our way to the exit, the guys rushed in. "Mom—dad, how are they?" Elisha asked.

"They are being checked out," Hosea said.

"Where are you all going?"

"Uh, em… some fresh air."

"Yeah, uh—well, see ya'll in a few."

Making our way to the car, noting the heaviness in the air. Bundling tight, as I kicked ice pieces off the path, feeling like I was kicking my thoughts around instead. Visions flooded my brain of the past summer, our travels, long talks, shared pains, watching her unravel because of our absence filled my mind, but they were lies. Blatant ones. What a traitor, imposter, and a thief. Where is our granddaughter? Hosea broke my thoughts by opening the car door. As my face graced his, he looked as saddened as I.

"Are you ok?"

"Yup…" as a tear ran down his cheek.

"It's going to be ok, babe," I wiped it and rubbed it on my jeans. I entered the car.

Sliding into his seat, he commenced to beating the steering wheel, shaking it as if he wanted to rip it out of the car. It didn't budge as his efforts became fiercer until he gave way to the tears, hitting it one last time. His head fell with comfort of the wheel, rolling it side to side with a continued grip.

"I tried so hard to protect us from their drama. I could not save you from this hurt and pain. I failed. Why didn't I see this coming? How does she look like you? Why did they think this was right?"

Everything he mentioned was the true. I hated it too, one moment feeling on top of the world the next like we were ripped into pieces and stepped on like pure dirt. I tried hard to ponder how they figured this would help us. Now this. What will everyone whom I spoke of say? I was downright angry the more I thought about it. "Ya know…" abruptly I stopped speaking.

Noting a sign straight ahead, with a man asking a question in prayer. "Lord, how many times shall I forgive my brother or sister who sins against me? Up to seven times? Jesus answered, I tell you, not seven times, but seventy-seven times. Matthew 18:21, NIV"

I pointed towards the sign for Hosea to read. The car was silent. "Uh—what do you want to do?" he said, scratching his head looking around.

"Can we?"

"What?"

"Forgive?"

"Man, it seems like we already past the seventy-seven times, what you think?"

"I agree, but babe we must see if she's at least ok, with the baby and Jeremai."

He cleared his throat. "Well, I have to pray about it, just like that man up there. It ain't gonna come to me this second. But, uh—we can go make sure the kids and that baby are ok."

"Okay. Trust me, I understand. Deep down I'm feeling the same," forcing a smile.

"Kind of really love the lads. But I need time."

"I know how you feel, I have the same emotions running through me. But we can't… if something happens to them and the baby, no matter what, we'll hate ourselves."

Silence filled the car as flakes of snow breezed the air. Sitting watching the flakes hit the window, noting the unique shapes as they crystalized into a speck of water. Nothing last forever ran across my mind, no matter how beautiful it is. "Can't deny how much we love her."

"I know," he said.

"Well, let's head on in. At least wait till we find out the details."

❧

"It's a miracle; he is so handsome; Sarah is with Chloe. They are cleaning him up and taking vitals. They will let you all back soon," Jez said.

The hospital staff kept everyone comfortable. We saw her. She looked pretty banged up and still sedated; I don't think she knew we were there. Seeing her with all those contraptions on her bothered us. I sat by her bed, holding her hand, saying the Lord's prayer. Anger poured through me, wanting to smack her, throw her across the room, or stomp her into the bed. I talked myself into wanting her to survive. Please save her, Lord, is all I could think of. We sat as the beeps cascaded through the air. She was groggy, mumbling words we couldn't make out. She delivered him via c-section, and laid there with her eyes strolling the room, until they fell shut. Sarah spoke to the doctor. Hosea and I went to the nursery laying eyes on his little round face with glossy eyes, hair slicked down with bubbles escaping the sides of his pink lips, bundled like a little peanut. The nurse came to change his diaper and fed him; it amazed us as his huge feet and hands dangling around, he kicked and cooed before his swaddling.

"Looks Jez when he was a baby," Hosea whispered.

I rolled my eyes at him, walking away. Many emotions ran through me, and the evil chatter that went on inside me was awful. I remained quiet, letting none of the messiness jumping around in mind grace my mouth. No matter how mad I am, I must speak life over this situation. "Let's get an update on Jeremai."

❧

They updated us on Jeremai conditions, seems like he was coming to, so we made our way to the 6th floor, bumping into his parents. Lyndia was balling, with a pile of tissue on the table. He was still out of it. The nurse informed us he should become more coherent as time goes on. All the machines, wires, and cords scared us even more than seeing Chloe. Our eyes widened in total fear. *He looks terrible* as the tears poured down my face like a waterfall. They didn't allow us to stay long, moving us back to the waiting room to lie around for more news. Not long after Jez called, missing both calls because we had dozed off to sleep, but he left a message to call him. Rubbing my eyes, I noted its 2:00 AM.

❧

Getting a cup of coffee, I noticed a nurse wheeling Jeremai towards Chloe's room. Holding my coffee warming both hands, I rolled the cup wondering how he would react to seeing his baby for the first time? It was hard to recognize him with his swollen face as the air bags hit him hard, slight cuts around his eyes, bruising over his ribs, back and thighs was bad, but the major concern was to assure he didn't have internal bleeding. Wearing double hospital gowns, it exposed his leg, revealing the covering a deep cut. Waiting for the secured door to open, his head was tilted with slight moans seeping from him. The porter comforted him by covering his lower body and adjusted his seating. He disappeared as the doors folded behind him. Jez informed the family that the doctors felt it was a miracle he was up and had improved. With their conditions, the nurse stated that the immediate family could come in for support. Stopping at the window to her room, noted Jeremai sitting next to her bed in silence with tears drizzling down his bloated face. He held Chloe's hand, whispering how sorry he was about the accident. Her hand tightened and released his fingers, falling to the side. His silent cry gave way to an immense out pour. Lynda ran out the room as Bill followed her. It broke Jeremai to see Chloe in such a shape, yet his prognosis was worse off than hers. Hearing a light tap at the door, a wide tooth smiling nurse came in embracing the baby. Swaddled, he looked around with his bright eyes, seeming like he was a big boy already. They handed him his son. He just sat looking at him, forcing a smile. "Look at my boy."

Sitting closest to him, he beckoned for me to take him as he was in pain. My mind raced with facts of this baby not being our great grandson, just like Chloe isn't our granddaughter. Yet not wanting to act ugly, I accepted Jr. Funny because somehow, I felt a connection and it was a beautiful feeling. Looking in his eyes, it reminded me of when I had Jez lingering on my thoughts to that special day, I held him for the first time. Smells of newness and babbles, as if he was trying to speak. Hosea invaded our time by rubbing his small cheeks with echoes of baby talk. His tiny self-whimpered into a loud yell. Been a long time since we've heard those sounds, making us nervous and happy to release him. Sarah rescued us and had troubles letting him go when the nurse came for his feeding. Hovering over him like a mother hen, couldn't help herself. Asking us to step out so they both could get some rest. Again, we returned to the waiting room. Waiting, I swear I couldn't shake the negative talks going through my mind. I loved her, yet the lies wouldn't let me fully be there for her. Hosea felt the same, releasing small whispers of the betrayal and wanting to leave. We'd decided it was best to head out for our own sanity, with Jez appearing. He looked exhausted. Stroking his hands through his hair, he nervously looked around.

"Hey, um—Chloe's blood pressure has risen and is experiencing some pain above her stomach, close to her sternum bone. She also had a severe case of acid reflux. They'd given her something for pain, with the reflux she couldn't hold it down."

"How bad is it?"

"So far we don't know."

"Ma—dad, you can sit with her while we take a break."

Standing in the window while the nurse took her vitals. They had Chloe lift her feet and move her hands. Looking concerned, she exited and returned with a pen light moving it side to side checking her eyes. Quickly this time she left and returned with a doctor. The nurse updated the doctor, telling him that Chloe could not move her right arm, nor her feet and could move her left arm but was weak. Performing his own test, he ordered a rush CAT scan for further evaluation. Removing us from the room. Looking at her laying there, *how could this be?*

Sitting in the waiting room thinking, how the mind is the killer or the builder of the soul. *Why am I thinking of the bad, sad, doom, and gloom and not of which are good, truths, and pure love? For what I think I am becoming. Lord let me capture my thoughts, make them peaceful and self-building and not slowly decaying and believing lies. When hurt succumb hope and drowns in pain, it's like landing in the clouded belief that one can't claim greatness in what is unseen? As powerful as love is it dies when hardened and the tired soul withers away. Please don't let this happen to me. Healing is mines for He that began his good work's in me wants things that are good. Let me take control and bound those thoughts he whispered to my heart ... will you claim the truths or believe the lies? Will join the wales of the fallen or believe the powers of your Master? For what you think you have become until the transformation is done and the battle of good and evil your mind is won. Things seem bad but find the joy in the moment.*

About an hour later, the doctor entered the waiting room. Their sad faces almost informed us before they said a word, almost paralyzing us. The doctors' reported her blood pressure had escalated with the possibility of a hemorrhagic stroke. If this happens, it may paralyze her for the rest of her life. With this insight, we brought in one of our best neurologists and have a talented team preparing to exam her. As the doctor walked away, Sarah got up singing what a mighty God we serve. We hummed along with her, holding hands with occasional outbreaks of prayer. Jez went into prayer, asking us all to join in a circle. We fell to our knees one by one.

"Let's speak life over our babies," I said.

"God, you have never failed us, and I know you won't fail us now. Let your will be done. God is a healer; he never makes mistakes, and today won't be different," Jez prayed as tears flooded his face.

We never saw our son pray before. He claimed to be a nonbeliever and was thanking God.

"Hallelujah," I shouted.

"How could this happen, Lord? She was just fine. So alive, so beautiful, so happy?" Sarah screamed and fell to her chair, sobbing.

Jez was updated via phone, "she has been vomiting and complaining of a horrible headache. They believe she might have a severe condition called um- HELLP syndrome. Her blood test reveals a reduced red blood cell count and elevated liver enzymes."

The guys walked into the waiting room, we updated them. Nobody was any good at this moment; nobody was fit to help anybody. A text came through. *'Jez said they are taking her up to surgery to prevent a stroke or blood clot.'*

"Is she going to be ok?" Elisha yelled.

"We don't know," Jez said.

Banging his fist into the end table until the pain stopped him. Asher sat with him to calm him down.

The doctor appeared, "Chloe is in great danger, and things are happening rapidly. We ran a few tests; she didn't respond well. None of the medications are working. We have given her a sedative and prepping her for surgery. She may pull out of this."

"May?" Omar exclaimed.

"Yes, don't want to get everyone's hope up; this is our last option to save her."

We all stood in front of the doctors, purely helpless, but full of hope. The questions we asked came back dejected, leading to more problems in the search for any chance of something positive. The doctor turned and looked sadly at us, dropping his head, and walked out. The family can have ten minutes with her. Escorted to her room, she looked peaceful. They brought the baby in, all wrapped up. The nurse laid him on Chloe's chest again, securing the sides of the bed.

"Wow, he looks just like Chloe," Asher stated.

"I thought he looked like Jez when he was a baby."

"Yeah, I can see that too."

As the tears flowed without my help. *My baby girl-the imposter*. The waiting room looked like a campsite. Her best friend Eve joined us. That poor girl cried ever since she walked in the door.

❧

"She's out of surgery," slowly the doc spoke. "We can only wait from to see how she does, at this point is questionable."

He stood there like he was losing his daughter too. Sarah lunged at the doctor with the look of fierceness. We scrambled to gain control of her while yelling for her to stop. "What did you do to my child? I'm going to sue all of you- this whole hospital is going down. Tell me your lies—this place is a nightmare," she held him tight, as the doctor stood lifeless, she whaled.

Seeming to understand her pain, I stood in shock and couldn't move much myself. We just met her. The doctors checked out Sarah, making sure she was ok. My heart was just too broken to move. I just sat there frozen, not a tear fell- I had none left, only prayers. *Jesus collects tears I heard; he had many jars today. He could have taken away all these older folks, but not this vibrant young woman. God, we don't understand.*

Sitting on a chair next to her bed with my head in my hands, propped against the wall. I was very uncomfortable in my tight space; I managed. I didn't want to leave her side, I couldn't. Hosea rubbed my back but left to see about Sarah and Jez. Jeremai sat on the other side, loosely embracing her fingers.

He yelled, "she moved!"

Chloe faintly smiled at Jeremai, "baby".

"Yes, he is ok… you're going to be ok sweetie," rubbing her face and looking into her eyes, "You can pull through this…," a single tear rolled down her face.

"Grandma," she weakly stated.

"Honey, I can't hear you," Jeremai replied.

She took a deep breath, forcing out, "grand—ma," turning her head towards the ceiling.

❧

Jeremai replied, "grandma?"

A week passed, and Chloe is still in a coma with doctors giving family little hope. We flew home and haven't gone to the hospital since, just lying in the bed riddled with pain and grief. I was mourning as if she had already gone to me as she had. Lying in misery, I struggled, wanting to blame everyone in my path, Jez, Sarah, and Chloe. In reality, I had no one to blame but myself. My insane desire to have my granddaughter in our lives was the root of the problem. Exhaustion riddled my body with streaks of pain to add to it, feet throbbing as I walked across the floor. Proving it difficult to walk to the restroom without tears being pushed from my eyes. My heart felt a horrible pressure, like it would stop beating any minute. The bed consoled me. Stiffness took over me, like I pushed past a tornado with full efforts and it was daunting. Stress caused it all. Why was I letting this mess steal my peace? When the hurt just seep from your swollen eyes, pain released through salted water's eyes pointed to the skies, when no amount of force can hold them in. I deplore crying. The fragility of a broken heart and its tenderness is an experience only those who love deeply will one day treasure. Please Lord, don't let my heart harden from the evilness of this world. For nothing last. Protect my ailing soul and keep it safe with you, for I know my father this too shall pass. *Think my child on the negative thinking we shared in the hospital.* Yes, I remember...why am I still struggling father?

It's been days since I've seen Hosea. He turned away once more, seeing me just lay here, knowing I would reject his efforts. No longer wanting to talk about the subject, he warned me in the beginning, which made me feel worst because I never listen to him and look at us now. Digging deeper into my pillow, I thought of things we did over the summer. Anger took me over as I tried to bring relief to my painful eyes.

The door creeped open.

"Go away."

"I'll be darn if I do, old woman," Candace said, ripping open the curtains.

"You are fired!"

"Get up."

Not a muscle moved as she snatched the covers from me and forced my spineless body from the bed to the chair. I stared at her tacky efforts of getting me up.

"Why are you here? I don't need your services anymore."

Pacing the floor, she kicked my shoes to the side and stopped in front of me with her hands on her hips.

"Your right, you fired me and then I quit. Not here to work, honey. You don't deserve me."

"Well, why are you here?"

"Because you need me, and you smell."

I chuckled, "Okay leave, I don't need you."

Watching her every move, she marched to the bathroom preparing the shower.

"That young lady needs you; she is dying, and you may be the one to help her."

"No, I'm not. Did they tell you she is an imposter, a fake, a liar, a con artist? She's not my granddaughter."

"Hosea told me everything, I had to get him straight, now it's your turn."

"Lady, go talk to them."

"Look, yes she, well—they lied. Not sure why? So settled in your ways it makes no sense you're not at the hospital seeing about her."

"No!"

"God sent."

"What?"

"Look at the blessings you two have. Got both of you up and living. You looked radiant over the summer and he did too. Your son and his wife were wrong, yet they thought about relieving you of your pain. Your marriage even improved, struck up your love for each other."

"Yeah, Yeah," as I threw my hand over at her. "Please leave me be, I just want to lie down."

"Today you are going to do better, show them what you're made of. Look at you—a mess."

"I'm broken. Now you have it. Broken. I give up. Do you hear me… give up!"

Another thought ran through my mind. "For the Spirit God gave us does not make us timid, but gives us power, love and self-discipline, 2 Timothy 1:7, NIV."

I dropped my head on the back of the clothes filled chair and wept. "I'm a failure."

"No, honey, you are a human. Look at me."

My withered eyes met hers. In them I saw hope. "What happened to all the spiritual growth you've gained? You have pulled yourself from the bottom to here and it was Jesus in you, I saw it. You are my friend and I love you with your big personality. The love, time, and effort you put into others, shows. Believe me, you made me a better person and in you I found my way. Your wisdom changed me."

"Really?"

"Yes."

"I never knew this."

"Now you do. What are you going to do?"

"I don't know."

"Well, I do. You are going to work your faith. Yes, they lied, they were wrong. My lady, you have faith that move mountains and you can forgive them. This is your family. Maybe they will see God in you and change their ways too.

She got up and started cleaning, moving things all over the place.

"I'm not paying you."

"Never asked you too. It's a gift."

"Hosea got you both a ticket to Detroit. You are going to go see Chloe and pray it's not too late."

Looking at the scribbled note laying on the table, "Be kind and compassionate to one another, forgiving each other, just as in Christ has forgiven you, Ephesians, 4:32, NIV."

"Oh, he has forgiven me many, many times and yet he still does."

"Excuse me?"

"Thinking out loud of the many times He has forgiven us and yet His love never fades."

"I agree, see why I am telling you about forgiveness. It's true."

Opening the window for fresh air; I missed it and the sun too. Candace was moving swift cleaning and packing my suitcase.

"My minds not made up, missy."

Hosea appeared, I grabbed him up before he could take a breath.

"Miss you."

"Thank you for loving me."

"I'll never stop, lady. Are you going?"

"Well—"

"She's packed, just have to shower."

☙

Jez and Sarah met us at the hospital. Jeremai stayed with the baby. Making it to her room, I couldn't go in. Pausing, I needed more time. Excusing myself and walked down to the chapel. Scanning the tiny area for the pastor to reappear, I found him changing the candles.

"Hello again."

"Hi, do you have time to pray for me?"

"Sure, what am I praying for?"

"The power to forgive the unforgivable and to mend the broken pieces."

"I don't think I—"

The dimmed lighting in the chapel was relaxing, with only a few candles flickering. Pastor sat a pew ahead of me and appeared comfortable. He listened, and it was comforting each time I broke from speaking to see his face. A look of concern without judgment, or at least it didn't show. Without hesitation, he stopped me.

"I understand your stance on the issue. Freedom comes from looking within yourself and seeing the good in your situation. There is some good inside the mess. Look for it. Trust me, anyone would be mad, but there is a reason for the betrayal."

"You perceive that?"

"Absolutely. Pray not for human strength, but for the supernatural support to not look at the problem itself, but the underlying issues. The entire family circle is hurting, Chloe fighting for her life is another one. Her son needs all of you, especially his mom. Losing both parents in one day, not long ago and finding out she's adopted, is heartbreaking. Your son and daughter-in-law making poor decisions added to this, there is tremendous amount of healing to go through."

"It's about the just of it."

"Lots of work ahead of you, but you already know the answer… forgiveness."

"Yea—I do."

"Pastor, thank you."

"It's my job, now you have one to do, I send you with blessings of healing."

ঌ

Meeting them back at Chloe's room, everyone gathered outside her door. Hosea moseyed over and forced a smile on his face. Jez glanced over and faintly smiled, dropping his head to the floor, studying his feet as he kicked a balled piece of paper on the floor. Sarah whispered if I would join her in a stroll? I accepted. The trail ended at the sitting room near the end of the hall. Neither of us said a word until we stopped.

"Shall we?"

"Sure."

"Matea, I can't say enough how sorry I am for this to happen. One thing landed to another. Chloe always wanted grandparents, plus she dealt with horrible depression and needed to take a class at the university in your area. Seemed like the perfect chance to make everyone happy."

"Where did she come from?"

"We've had her in our lives since the 12th grade, she is like a daughter to us, so—we thought it was a good idea— we were wrong. Can you please forgive us?"

Eyes wailed with tears and choking on words, "We needed her."

"Excuse me?" I said.

"The hurt I felt from all those years I overcame. But deep inside it was there. I've suffered long enough."

"I don't—"

"Fibromyalgia. Horrible condition, I've had for years. Becoming bed-ridden until I let go of many things that weighed my soul almost bringing me to dirt. Becoming a dead woman walking from carrying so much from my past in my heart and mind without healing."

"Because of us?"

"You were just a part of it, racism, sexism, family battles, failed marriages and current marital problems, issues with my parents and their death, horrible things from my childhood and adolescence, problems with my sons, bills, losing my job and friends… everything. It all weighed me down as I thought I was a warrior doing it all myself. None of this wasn't my fight."

"That could happen."

Wiping my running nose, "It can happen to anyone, it happened to me. I healed or so I thought, but Chloe… her and that key made me bring up those issues and I forgave each one and ridded myself from those things getting my life back."

"Oh ok," sipping her coffee.

"All those doctor visits, tears shed, riddled with pain. I was dying and had the answer the whole time. As bad as I want to slap the entire family, scream, and even want to choke everyone involved. He has a reason for everything, and I found comfort in that. So—I've asked for forgiveness for the role I've played in this… and—I forgive you."

"Thank you."

"Oh—Chloe threw the key at me before they left that day. I assume you want it back?"

I grabbed the envelope and opened it.

"The key… I am thankful because Chloe found my old coat, bringing her to us. Finding out she isn't our granddaughter is heart wrenching."

Sarah's head dropped, staring at the key embraced in my hand. Clearing her throat, "please don't look at us as your enemies, we made a horrible decision and am thankful for your forgiveness. Once you said you forgave me, it felt a like flood of relief wash over me freeing me to form a closer bond with you. I love you."

"Me too, I have sick over the issue and thought about the times God forgave me when I felt unforgivable. I lied to her too. She asked me why I stopped writing in my journal; I didn't tell her the complete truth."

"Like?"

"Everything in my life was in shambles, Jez's words were the final blow. I planned to die that very day. The key was to the journal I left for Hosea, detailing my life and how I'd been shattered to pieces. For once, I failed to understand how to put myself together."

"Hm, yeah— that day we were being evicted and looking for someplace to stay. A friend had Chloe and was hounding us to come get her. We tried to pack as much as we could before the eviction happened. Oh my, looks like it was a hard day for everyone."

"I didn't know."

"We were too ashamed to tell you."

"Sounds like shame seems to flow around here. Because that's how I felt about her reading my journal. Tore out the worst parts, couldn't stand for her to see me as a loser."

"Funny, she felt the same when she struggled with forgiving Jeremai and the baby issue. Her inability to forgive him made her feel you thought of her as a failure. She came a long way since we met her."

"Still wrapping my mind around the fact, she is not ours," shaking my head.

"Well—Jeremai stated that she struggled with finding out she'd been adopted and never told us. We knew of her birth parents… well, whom we thought died in an accident. She didn't get along with her father and adored her mother. Being the only child never sat well with her. She formed behavioral issues early on, they had great troubles bringing her up."

"How did she find out?"

"Going through some paperwork her parents had stashed away, right before they purchased their home. Jeremai says she took it hard."

"Never mentioned it."

"Jeremai's not a part of this, I wanted to let you know that. He met her in college."

"How did you meet her?"

"Riding her bike past the house, I was gardening. She stopped and started talking. Seemed lonely as her parents worked a lot and offered to help me. I was lonely too, missing my baby, and the pressure of another left our marriage in shambles."

"Life! it's something, our baby is somewhere out there—"

"Yes… somewhere," a tear rolled down her cheek without breaking the fall, looked away.

"This must be hard for the both of you."

"Crazy how much I miss her," struggling through her words. "It's amazing how much Chloe looks like Jez and you. I became her friend, seeing her once in a while, until they passed. It had been months since we saw her."

"So, we weren't the only one's she revived?"

"True."

"I've been praying like crazy she will be ok."

"Me too. What made her stay with you all?"

"She moved in with her aunt, who didn't want the responsibility. They got into it and she ran away. Walked an entire night to our home. We found her sleeping in the enclosed patio that morning. Begged me to let her stay and her aunt had no problem agreeing to it."

"So sad."

"Yeah, but not for us… we didn't know we could be so happy. We adopted her hearts, and that's the way it went. Became a family just like that."

"Did she know you had a baby in the system?"

"No, too ashamed with no reason too."

"I see."

"She wasn't adopted to her knowledge, and we never told her about our baby."

"Ya know, I am thankful the Lord spared and renewed me. He sure taught me to let go of things at the right time."

"Who, Chloe?"

"No… forgiveness. The old me would hold a grudge until it about killed me. I felt that way when I learned the truth, I didn't like feeling that way."

"It's hard sometimes, I've dealt with it too."

"Candace and Hosea showed me my ways. I didn't do it on my own, I failed at it again. I'm thankful God is a forgiver. If I want forgiveness, I must forgive others. I need to see Chloe."

Walking back to Chloe's room, chattering like young schoolgirls. We joined the rest of them. My eyes widened at the vast array of flowers and the silence of the room resonances throughout, giving into beeps of various monitors. Jeremai stepped inside, forcing a smile as his parents joined him. "Speaking to the doctors, I've asked them to remove the equipment and see what God says."

"Excuse me?" Sarah stepped over to Jeremai.

"Sarah, let me explain. I got a feeling that she's going to be ok. It came after I prayed with all my might. Calm down, from here it's not our will… but God's."

Her body fell to her seat like a rock. Looking at Chloe, "Ok. It's your decision and I support you."

Jez walked over hugging her as he fought tears but agreed and we did too.

"Let's see what God says," Hosea said.

We gathered around her bed, touching her speaking life over her, energies released, and tears fell. The monitor beeped as she laid, looking peaceful. A nurse walked in and two doctors followed. As they worked, taking off the support which held our babies' life. Not a sound lingered, nor a soul moved. We just watched and prayed. The heart monitored continued to beep without missing a beep; it slowed for a moment. Our eyes widened, and it picked back up and continued. And she remained the same—alive. One moment turned to two, which turned into hours, then days. Washing the dishes, I squinted my eyes… the sun seemed to give off a glare that seemed unusual. The phone rang, Jeremai jogged in answering it.

"Her eyes fluttered and opened. She is coherent and wants us to come down."

"Our baby is awake," I yelled.

Cheers filled the room with Sarah saying the last statement. "Thank you, almighty father."

❧

A week past and she was doing well, she came home. Excited to be home was an understatement. Candace arrived to help cook and do some light duties, which was a tremendous help. Hosea and I stayed longer to help with the baby, while the others worked. Chloe was almost back to her usual self and enjoyed spending time with JJ. His new nickname had set in and we loved it. Spending lots of time with family and making sure she didn't overdo it. We were enjoying ourselves and didn't see us wanting to leave soon. Jez and Sarah stopped by after work to check on things. Sitting around, we struck up a family conversation.

"Chloe, when were you going to talk to us about your parents?"

"Dad—why are you bringing that up?"

"Hon, it's things we are would like to share with you."

"Shoot."

"Jeremai shared with us you found some information about you being adopted?"

Looking at him, he nodded, "I did, but hear them out honey."

Rolling her eyes back to Jez, she smacked her back into the sofa getting comfortable. "Go ahead."

"Well?"

"I did and not happy about it, really—I don't think it's important."

"Okay, Jez and I never talked about it, but we have a daughter named Chloe about your age. Sadly, he was adopted.

"Wait—What?"

"She was about four months."

"Whoa, I don't believe you. Didn't you say you couldn't have kids?"

"True, we haven't been able too, but had her. Looking at your age, name, and features—could you be her?" Jez said.

Giving Jeremai the baby, she stood up and looked at Sarah and Jez. Dusting the hair from her face. She walked around the room without saying a word. Chloe darted with Jeremai handing JJ to Hosea, following her.

"I knew it was not a good idea," Sarah said.

"Give her space," I said.

"Your right, maybe we should go?"

"Let's wait, don't be too quick to run away."

"Well, I noticed she hasn't spending time with us as she has in the past," I said.

"Yea—eh I noticed too. Thinking she doesn't want to face any of the issues we dealt with before the accident," Jez said.

"I agree."

Hosea massaged my shoulders, I needed it too. Tense wasn't the best word to describe my bundled muscles. I hate to see her upset, but at least we'll know. Jez and Sarah snuggled into each other arms. He knew Sarah was about to go crazy to find out.

"Don't get your hopes up, she may not be," Hosea said.

"Dad. I eh—yeah, I know,"

JJ started crying, making Hosea nervous as he passed him to me. I walked the floor with him before leaving the room for more space. A few steps from the den, Chloe stopped me and relieved me from my baby duties.

"Grandma, can you join us, please?" Jeremai said.

"Sure."

Chloe walked in the room and we followed. Her nerves had her pacing the floor. She said nothing, focusing her attention on JJ. We sat, figuring it riled her nerves up worse than mines. Until she turned to Jez and Sarah, "why did they take your child away?"

"Honey, we were in big trouble with some folks, eh—financially? Became homeless with a certain amount of time to find a secure home and we couldn't," Sarah said.

"Meeting the lady who foster cared for our daughter, well—she was wonderful. Provided a life for her we couldn't… she adopted our baby and moved away, even after she promised she would allow us to see her."

Sitting emotionless, not even a blink.

"Do you care to share your adoption information with us, it may show us something that may help?"

Dropping her head, "I can't."

"Why not?"

"I destroyed them."

"A blood test can be a solution?" Hosea said.

"I can do that, but what if—"

"We'll love you like you are," Jez said.

I hadn't said a word, noting since she's been home has been avoiding quiet time with us like the plague. My thoughts are she is ashamed to face me, but I had forgiven her. I believe that talk will hurt us both, so I hadn't pushed the issue. Sitting on the loveseat playing with the lint on the pillows zoned out from the conversation. Until she had the melt down. Crying, trying to compose herself, she ran to Jeremai for comfort. Cupping his face with both hands, he held him and faced her.

"What should I do?"

"It's your decision, hun."

"Please answer me."

Clearing his throat. She released him and asked again. "I would take the blood test," he said.

He pulled it out of his pocket and handed it to her. With widened eyes, she stepped back in shock. "You already knew about this?"

"No, but after talking to Jez I figured this would be the only way we can get this all out in the open, no questions left."

Standing there with the test, she looked pale and riddled with anxiety. Walking over, rendering to a big hug as she cried. She snatched the test and handed it to Jez. "I'll do it."

"Do you mind if I help?" Hosea asked.

"No, dad it's fine with me—uh, if it's ok with Chloe?"

"Fine."

Hosea swabbed them and placed the test in the envelopes. Jeremai agreed to mail them off. Things went on like normal. No one spoke of the test or anything to do with the subject. However, Chloe seemed different, kind of withdrawn. Few times I approached her; she became busy heading off to a different direction. It bothered me to the point; I asked if she wanted us to stay or leave? Assuring us, she wanted us to stay, yet acted in a manner that made us question her answer. Days later, she approached me to sit with her, wanting to talk. Sitting in her office, she swirled in the huge office chair, laughing and joking about the days of meeting us and reminiscing on our adventures. Until I wanted more from the conversation.

"You could have told me the truth."

"I didn't want to."

"Really?"

"Why does it seem like a shock to you?"

"It was the right thing to do."

"As it was, it was the truth."

"Explain, please."

She smiled, "I always wanted grandparents, more than anything."

"Continue."

"Ya'll was everything I ever wanted. I had planned to stay only for a few days once I got there, I instantly fell in love with you both."

"The melt down… asking why we never looked for you? Uh, a few times."

"It was me being foolish, having a horrible life with my parents, not fitting in. I wished you would have been my real grandparents from the second I met you. If you were, I would have felt loved."

"You weren't the only one who lied, yet I felt more betrayed by you. I guess because you played to role... did you really fall in love with us or being an actress?"

"I'm sorry, please forgive me. I promise the lessons you taught me meant something—everything and in reality, I am so embarrassed and remorseful for my actions."

"I have forgiven you."

"You have?"

"Yes, weeks ago, it was one of the hardest ones I've had to do. I felt you were unforgiveable until I realized how much I loved you. How badly we needed each other and how nothing happens by mistake."

"Thank you, I love you so much. I swear I thought even though you were here, that I lost you both."

"Yeah, but you needed us and we tried to stay away, but it involved too much love. I will tell you this... I am thankful to the Master above for you being alive."

"Almost checked out, but God."

"Well, let's not do anymore lies."

"No more lies."

"Well, I'm getting JJ, he's cutting up."

Walking past, I grabbed her hand and rubbed it against my check.

"Let's take a selfie."

"Grandma, you don't like pics and my hair..."

"Wasting time."

❧

JJ turned six weeks today, Chloe scooped him up for his feeding. Lingering with much effort as she cascaded down the hall caught my attention, asking if she needed any help. Assuring me things were under control and just needed some rest. Smiling at the little man cooing and enjoying his mommy. Swiftly she whipped him on her other hip, looking run down with dark rings under her eyes. Taking a second glance, I told her I would join her after I did a few things. Sighing in return, bouncing JJ on her hip again relayed the message to take my time.

Heading out to collect the mail, a bright ray hit me with a blast of heat, rendering me to pause before proceeding to the mailbox. Making it half-way, their neighbor waved as he watered the grass, calling me over. Chit, chatting about the news and other events, realizing this man will never stop talking, having me inch away until my feet hit the sidewalk. Waving, I continued to the box, which appeared half opened with some handbills hanging out. Scanning the sales of the week, prime rib sure sounded good, running through a few more ads finding some pretty good deals. Grabbing the rest of the bundle, I noted the letter came with the results. Flicking the piece side to side. I tried to view any information without opening it, proved unworthy of anyone knowing until the right time. Making it back to the house, fumbling to the window with the brightest rays. Holding the piece up, allowing the light to penetrate the envelope, my last effort did nothing different. Giving in, I shoved it in my pocket, counting the hours till everyone got off work. Joining Hosea for a cup of coffee while he read the newspaper. Taking the first sip, savoring the aroma of pure creamy infused coffee beans, I sniffed in a heavy dose. Giving into telling him the letter came, patting my pocket.

"You better not look at it."

"I'm not."

"Oh boy, I know you."

"No, I wouldn't do that."

He dropped the newspaper, staring at me with the look of disbelief.

"What?"

"Don't ok?"

"Come on now, I wouldn't."

❧

Being eager the entire day about drove me crazy, finding small things to keep me busy did nothing. Calling Sarah informing her to stop by with Jez after work Like a kid in a candy store wondering if my treat would sweet or sour. Either way, I wanted to know. The anticipation was about to the cause of my next panic attack. Throughout the day, Hosea would bump into me or send me text messages reminding me of the consequences if I gave into looking at the results. This was when I regretted ever telling him, scurrying around I flew past the clock, the time was 2:50PM. Which reminded me to check on Chloe and JJ till my phone rang. My friend from college wanted to discuss some issues with her career. Cutting her short, promising I would be available late evening. Grabbed a granola bar and headed to her room. Taking the stairway, another call came through and this time it annoyed me. Answering it was a coworker from my department checking in to see if I wanted to teach a course next semester. Didn't want to make a hasty decision, telling her I'll get back with my answer this weekend. Approaching her room, I heard a muffled noise. I couldn't make it out. Listening, I tried to decipher which way it came from, then I heard nothing. Sarah jogged the stairs to meet with Chloe and stopped to check in with me.

"How did the day go?"

"Magnificent, so far."

"Good... the baby?"

"Chloe has him."

"I can't wait to see him."

"Guess what came today?"

"The results?"

"Yes, I am excited."

As we were talking Sarah's attitude changed. Dropping her smile like someone stomped on it and began shifting around like she was looking for something.

"Are you feeling ok?"

"Eh—yes, I am nervous."

"It's understandable, by this evening we will have answers and put your mind to ease."

"Matea, I can't get my hopes up. These weeks have been dreadful."

"Today it will be over. We will know the truth and move forward."

"Ok, let me run downstairs and get myself together. Are you checking on them?"

"Yes."

Standing outside the door, I massaged the letter again, shivering with extreme hope. Praying for her to be ours, I knocked with no answer. Did she leave? Glancing out the window, her car was still outside. I abruptly opened the door, seeing her under the covers appearing asleep. I tiptoed over swinging the curtains shut forcing out the strong sunlight from powering its way in disrupting her. Turning, I noted the odd fashion she was laying and figured it wasn't safe to leave JJ in the bed with her. Deciding to place him in his crib, thinking of how I would handle this without waking either. Approaching the bed, I smelled something putrid, maybe throw up or something similar. As I continued moving closer with a more defined feeling of unease flooded me. In a pace, pulled the covers back, she laid lifeless on her stomach, arms stretched outward and twisted at her waist. The white sheets infused with vomit surrounded her facial area, with her beautiful curls twisted within it and covering her face. Gasping I threw my fist over my mouth holding in emotions of all sorts. I couldn't think straight but forged my fingers to her neck to check for a pulse. Nothing. Placing my hand on her body, feeling of lukewarm heat was apparent, but was slowly drifting away. My face flushed with the deep feeling of faint taking over my body like a hostage. Wait, where is JJ? Working my way around the entire bed, finding nothing other than a corner of his blue plush blanket sticking from under her. My eyes widened as I yelled for help. Running to the other side rolling her over. She flumped. There he laid, smashed into her vomit covered chest, her breast shown. Trying to hold my finger steady, I checked his pulse, shaking as I wiggled my finger into his fattened neck feeling a slight thump, then nothing. Slight thump, then nothing this time it remained nothing. Picking him up, I felt life drain from my body, praying it transferred to him. CPR came to mind. Then it went blank. I'd never done it on an infant. But the thought came stronger this time, rapidly I grabbed his blanket off the bed, wiped his face and laid him on it. Again, I yelled for help. Too nervous to pull my thoughts together, drew in and released breaths in efforts of clarity. Working to expose his small chest my mind went blank.

"What to do, Oh Jesus, please tell me what to do," I cried out.

I positioned him with his head tilted back, forcing his mouth open. Then I heard a small voice. I started working as it told me what to do, between banging on the floor and yelling and moving back to his tiny chest thrusts. I stopped for a second, looking up at Chloe, praying she moved. Sarah barged in, scanning the room, and immediately called 911. Running to the bed, she checked Chloe's pulse and yelled, breaking into tears. JJ spat up and welled us a good one. Hair slicked with vomit and sweat; he was exercising his lungs for sure. I wrapped him in the blanket and gave him to Sarah and wiped her face with the sheet and began doing CPR on

Chloe. It wasn't long before paramedics showed up. Working as quick as possible, they threw in the towel and pronounced her dead at 3:33PM.

❧

Taking a much-needed nap, I laid in my room reminiscing on the first day I came to her home. She had things set up. Belly huge, excited, and mad as usual. I laughed to myself, holding back tears I no longer wanted to release. I've cried enough, yet I will never forget her bright personality. Before long I drifted. Laughing with her, seemed like hours. Before I realized...

"Chloe you died," I whispered.

"No, Grandma—please help Jeremai. I know he's hurting and will heal in due time. Sorry, I couldn't stay. I am so happy."

"Chloe, I'm going to miss you."

"Take care of JJ for me, help mom."

"I will."

"Hey, 333 is the Father, Son, and Holy Spirit. Don't forget it, they'll be watching over you."

She faded away. Awakened, I found it was a dream.

"That's my girl."

Days later, the funeral was in order with every detail in place. Except we weren't ready. The entire family gathered today to work on her obituary, bringing pictures and personal add-ins to make it nice. Sarah seemed to be in a good mood today, as she struggled since it happened. We all had, but it hit her worst. Things set well with me because I made peace with her, yet we all had enormous holes in our hearts. Strange, Chloe's auntie stopped by giving her condolences. Mentioning, she was the only family she had left. The rest of the family took to the kitchen, conversing and enjoying snacks during her visit. She sat quietly as folks scattered, continuing of how bad things ended between her and Chloe.

"The poor baby seemed to be a lost soul her entire life, especially after the death of her parents."

"She was fine to us—maybe depressed?"

"Our last argument before she ran off was dreadful, the days spent trying to find her."

"That had to be hard."

"I loved my niece, but something complicated our relationship."

"Complicated?" Sarah said.

"Yes, my husband and uh- Chloe's father were--"

Jez joined Sarah sitting on the armrest with his full attention directed at her.

"Go on," Jez said.

Glancing around the room, she swallowed.

"Never mind. I loved her and am very saddened by this news."

"May I place a few words in the obituary?"

"Sure—uh, would you like to see JJ?" Sarah said.

"JJ?"

"Yes, Chloe's son."

"Excuse me, I didn't know she had a child."

Jeremai collected him. He's happy, gurgling and bouncing around. She held him for a moment and returned him.

"He's beautiful and happy."

"Yeah, he is—uh, thank you," Jeremai said.

"Oh, I have something for you, almost forgot," she chuckled.

Mining in her bag, she pulled out a wooden box with carvings of flowers on it. She looked at it with tears in her eyes, sighed. Turning over the box to Sarah.

"It's hand carved, I believe Amo created it for her when they adopted her."

"Thank you."

"Amo and Robbie provided a good life for Chloe. Robbie loved her so much, well Amo couldn't shake his racism against other cultures and... Chloe struggled with his ways."

"Yes, she spoke of it."

"Robbie wanted her badly when she had her in foster care. Then she looked white, and he had no thoughts of it—well, until she grew and some of her Afro-American features became prominent. Chloe calls it bronzing but had no idea she was adopted from a mixed couple."

"Interesting," Jez said.

With a slight chuckle, "It's embarrassing, my husband is his brother— well that's the story. Chloe wouldn't have been happy in our home. She exalted you both, I knew she would want you to have this."

Standing up, looking around at everyone.

"I've stayed long enough, thank you for having me."

Jez walked her to the door, returning with eagerness of opening the box. Sarah couldn't figure it out. Hosea beckoned for a try, noting he knew the secret. He pushed a piece on the front panel and the top flung open as a ballerina with a white tutu popped up, stood still, then at a snail's pace twirled, playing a soothing Bach melody.

"Lovely, a tune I love," I said.

"What's inside," Sarah said.

First, it was the first picture of her parents. Second, her diary. Third, a charm with photos of Sarah and Jez inside. Sarah held the charm, dangling it in her hands rub as she ran her fingers over the pictures.

"I gave this to her the first night she spent at our home, didn't think she still had it."

Jeremai flipped the pages and two letters fell out, they read—

> Dear Auntie,
>
> Will you feel bad if I said I don't want to live with you? I love Jez and Sarah so much and they accept me the way I am. Feelings of not belonging here are overwhelming and there my heart feels at home. I fear that you will say no, but I have been praying God hears and you let me go. Think about it. Please let them know it's ok. Love you even more if you do.
>
> -Love Chloe.

"My precious niece, I miss her," dabbing her eyes.

Handing the letter to Jez, everyone eyes teared. Jez read the second letter.

> Hi Auntie,
>
> Living with Jez and Sarah is great. I know I haven't been writing as I promised, with school and meeting a

> wonderful guy, it has slipped my heart. Forgive me. You are all I have left in my family, so I thought until finding the adoption papers. Why did anyone tell me, maybe I could have found reason in daddy's anger? I could never forget mom or you. I'm engaged and have met Sarah and Jez's parents and I love them so much. Staying with them for the summer has been amazing. Somehow, I wish that they were my actual family and feel God has answered my prayers. Nothing has made me happier.
>
> -Love Chloe.

Handing the letter to Hosea, he nodded his head and walked into the kitchen with Matea following him. Returning with the letter which we all had forgotten about. Giving it to Jez, we sat to hear the results. His hands trembled opening it, he prayed. Sarah grabbed his arm and gave him a hard stare.

"Are we going to be ok?"

"Yes, hon."

He continued, "the results—she is 99% percent, yours."

About the Author

J. M. Harris, MBA, is an emerging author, overcomer, technologist, and entrepreneur whose perseverance, compassion, and work ethic have earned her the reputation as a service-driven leader. Above all else, she is a change maker on a mission to empower people to step into their best version and pave their way to the life of their dreams.

For as long as she can remember, writing has been J. M. Harris's go-to medium for self-expression. What started as a dream of becoming a novelist someday ultimately turned into the debut of her first novel titled "The Battle Was Not Hers". In addition to that initial novel, another book is currently underway, "Quenched From Within".

When she isn't inspiring others through the power of words, you can find this kid at heart gardening, singing, baking homemade cakes, exploring new dishes, or floral arranging. She is also an avid bookworm and lifelong learner. Most importantly, she loves spending quality time with her husband of nearly two decades, four grown sons, two grandchildren, and fur baby named Bluberri.

www.ingramcontent.com/pod-product-compliance
Lightning Source LLC
Chambersburg PA
CBHW030820310726
48980CB00006B/565/J

* 9 7 8 1 7 3 4 0 3 0 3 2 7 *